"Funny and Moving, a Pure Pleasure . . ."
—*The Cincinnati Enquirer*

"Weidman makes his people lovable and human . . . seeing the strengths and weaknesses in individuals, yet emphasizing the positive."
—*The Los Angeles Times*

"Readers raised in the Bronx will weep with pleasure. Anyone who has ever carried a hardboiled egg to night school will never be able to put this book down. It's a loving memoir to the time when happiness was keeping company, holding hands in the balcony, and taking a nighttime walk through the park."
—*The Cleveland Plain-Dealer*

"As Harry Golden would say, 'Enjoy! Enjoy!'"
—*The Winston-Salem Journal*

Also by Jerome Weidman

FOURTH STREET EAST

LAST RESPECTS

TIFFANY STREET

by JEROME WEIDMAN

PINNACLE BOOKS • NEW YORK CITY

TIFFANY STREET

Copyright © 1974 by Jerome Weidman

A Pinnacle Books edition, published by special arrangement with Random House.

ISBN: 0-523-00515-6

First printing, January 1975

Printed in the United States of America

PINNACLE BOOKS, INC.
275 Madison Avenue
New York, N.Y. 10016

For
My Sister Jean

When the sands were all dry,
He was gay as a lark,
And would speak in contemptuous
Tones of the shark.
But when the tide deepened,
And sharks were around,
His voice had a timid,
And tremulous sound.

Lewis Carroll

I

1

If you have to go to Philadelphia for a reason you don't want your wife to know about, the best way is to attend law school about thirty years before the time you have to be in the City of Brotherly Love. Being a lawyer is like being a bottle of ketchup in a restaurant that specializes in bad steaks. It covers a multitude of sins. This may not be a noteworthy comment to make on an ancient and occasionally honorable profession. But it is something I have come to value. I have been a lawyer for thirty years.

I have also been a husband for almost three decades, and a father for two. And I had to get to Philadelphia without allowing Elizabeth Ann or Jack to know why.

A grocer might have had some difficulty swinging it. Not Benny Kramer. I thanked you know who—God, of course —for my N.Y.U. law degree (evening session 1933–1937). I wrapped myself in the mantle of S. (for Shloymah) B. (for Berel) Schlisselberger, my most lucrative client. And I caught the 10:00 A.M. Metroliner for Philadelphia.

The verb "caught" plucks irritably at the mind. When I was a boy on East Fourth Street, we used to catch butterflies in Tompkins Square Park. Now I am a middle-aged man functioning on Madison Avenue (office) and Fifth Avenue (home), and I catch trains. Thorstein Veblen would, I am certain, know how to make the definitive comment. Benny Kamer did not have time to try. He had to get to Philadelphia.

I got there at noon, and I went directly to the office of S. B. Schlisselberger. I was not really interested in S. B. Schlisselberger. But he is, as I said, my client, and he was paying my fare, and he was providing what during my war was known as my cover story.

1

My war, by the way, was not The First Punic. My war was the affair supervised by Winston Spencer Churchill and Franklin Delano Roosevelt. Benny Kramer was young when he was caught up in it. And we beat the ears off a bastard named Hitler. When the days seem to be lacking in sunlight, Benny Kramer thinks about that. Even in Philadelphia. It helps. In Philadelphia anything helps. Especially a sinfully fattening lunch at the Bellevue-Stratford.

"Start with the pepper pot," said Shloymah Berel Schlisselberger. "After all, how often do you get to Philadelphia?"

Too often. Nobody goes to Philadelphia infrequently. Not even Benjamin Franklin. Even once is too often. So I started with the pepper pot.

I had to get Shloymah Berel Schlisselberger out of the way without letting him know I had come to Philadelphia to see somebody else. Even with the help of a bowl of pepper pot, Shloymah Berel Schlisselberger is a difficult object to get out of the way. By twelve-thirty the pepper pot had caused me to reach furtively for two tablets of the Gelusil I always carry the way James Fenimore Cooper always carried Natty Bumppo. Heartburn is a condition of middle-aged human existence.

"You understand the problem," said Shloymah Berel Schlisselberger.

I could go into detail, if you insist. Please don't. These details will not enlarge your emotional horizons. Or even provide you with a chuckle. The law is funny only to those who practice it. Also, my client is a nut. The preoccupations of nuts are not always amusing. They are, however, frequently expensive. This was the sort of case only a nut would get involved in. A wealthy nut, that is. At my age, fifty-eight, I have no other kind on my list of clients. In my tax bracket the thrilling old pennant-waving civil-rights cases are behind me. "Free Tom Mooney!" The stirring words no longer make my blood pressure rise. The sounds merely tell me the lamentable truth: no fee. I can no longer afford the luxury. I have three mouths to feed, one of them my own.

2

My client had made his money in real estate. Making money in real estate is childishly simple. Perhaps that is why so many people who have done it are simple-minded and childish.

All you have to do is come to America as a penniless immigrant in 1890. Go from door to door with a pack on your back, selling female undergarments and bottles of Lydia E. Pinkham's Vegetable Compound. Then use your tiny profits to buy worthless lumps of swampland within sight of Independence Hall.

My client bought the right lumps. On them, after he had nailed down the deeds, grew federal roads, apartment houses, and even a main street to which the Philadelphia fathers gave, as they then had a tendency to do, the name of a nut. On this street daring entrepreneurs had built several theaters. Good theaters they are, too. I have sat through plays in them. But the theater had done in recent years what the theater had been doing since Aeschylus with his stylus first scratched out "Act 1, Scene 1." The theater in Philadelphia has fallen on bad times.

I have often wondered why things, as well as people, fall on bad times. As I recall mine, and I have had what still seems more than my fair share of these unpleasant moments, I did not fall on them. *Au contraire*, as we used to say on East Fourth Street where I was born and raised. They fell on me. When they did, I proceeded to do what everybody around me did: I struggled to my feet and started again.

Not, however, my client. He didn't have to start again. Schlisselberger was loaded. He could afford to make other people start again.

In short, Schlisselberger brought an antitrust suit. Against a national chain of theater owners. He believed it was their monopoly that had caused the theaters he owned in Philadelphia to fall on bad times. He asked me to come to Philadelphia to help, not as a lawyer but as a witness. I logged the trip into my work diary, and went. With an eagerness I concealed. Even though I don't like to be treated as a liar, the unpleasant fact is that I am. So I repeat: My

3

reason for being in Philadelphia was not Mr. Schlisselberger's reason. As I have indicated, I had my own reason. Mr. Schlisselberger was my beard.

"The pot roast here is delicious," he said after the pepper pot.

Pot roast scares me. The gravy. The mashed potatoes. The green peas. Or, as we used to say on East Fourth Street, the petit pois. At least eight hundred calories. As my mother used to say: in tips alone.

"I think I'll settle for the pepper pot," I said. "It was delicious."

Shloymah Berel Schlisselberger stared at me across the menu as though I had suggested that we build in Central Park a monument to the memory of Gamal Abdel Nasser.

"You don't like pot roast?" he said.

"I love pot roast," I said. "But I have two problems. My doctor, Artie Steinberg, he says I should weigh one hundred and fifty-five pounds. This morning, before I left home, I checked in on the bathroom scale at one hundred and fifty-seven. Do I have to say more?"

"Sure you do," said Shloymah Berel Schlisselberger. "You said two problems. What's the second?"

"Before I meet you in court at two-thirty," I said, "I'd like to run over to Wanamaker's and pick up a wedding anniversary present for my wife."

Shloymah Berel Schlisselberger stared at me with what I can only describe as disbelief. And why not? Since I was lying.

"You live in New York," he said, "And you come here to Philadelphia to buy for your wife a wedding anniversary present in Wanamaker's?"

He made it sound as though I had come to Mecca to buy a set of phylacteries.

"When my wife and I met more than thirty years ago," I said, "she lived in Greenwich Village. Wanamaker's was the classy store in the neighborhood. On Astor Place. That's where I bought her wedding ring. For years, on our wedding anniversary, I used to get her a little something at Wanamaker's. But in New York Wanamaker's is out of

4

business now. So I thought, as long as I'm in Philadelphia . . ."

Shloymah Berel Schlisselberger dropped his menu. "Benny Kramer!" he said angrily. "What the hell are you doing here in the Bellevue-Stratford fooling around with pot roast? You get your *toochiss* over there to Wanamaker's and you buy that nice girl her wedding anniversary present, and you add to it a big fat one-pound box of Whitman's Sampler candy, which she gets compliments of Shloymah Berel Schlisselberger. No, make it a two-pound box. I will meet you in court at two-thirty. Hurry up!"

I did. It was not a long journey. Dr. McCarran's office was almost around the corner. In the Warwick Hotel. Checking my wrist watch as I came into the reception room, I saw that I was almost ME 7-1212 prompt: 1:15 on the nose.

"Mr. Kramer?" the receptionist said.

So I knew I was in good hands. The sensitive nature of my mission had been impressed on Dr. McCarran's staff: a pretty redhead in a starched white office smock that Dior would probably have considered too tight. Not Benny Kramer. The girl looked great. All the bulges were in the right places.

"Please come right in," she said. "Dr. McCarran is expecting you."

"Thanks," I said.

I followed her across the reception room, past the print of Rembrandt's "Anatomy Lesson" and the framed diploma from Cornell Med. She opened a door.

"Mr. Kramer," she said, dropping the four syllables into a room I could not quite see clearly.

"Ah, yes," a voice said. "Do come in."

I am susceptible to voices. I like human sounds. I had not yet seen Dr. McCarran, but I knew at once I had come to the right place. The softly spoken words did something Shloymah Berel Schlisselberger's bowl of pepper pot had not done. The tension with which Benny Kramer had been living for more than a month began to ease away. It was as though a ribbon, knotted tightly around my head, had been snipped with a scissors.

"It's very kind of you to allow me to come and see you," I said. I hesitated, then decided the hell with it. This was my last chance to tell the truth. "I've been more upset than I've been able to admit to anybody," I said. "Even to my wife."

Dr. McCarran waved his hand. The gesture seemed to break the light pattern in the room. As though a switch had been pulled. Suddenly I could see him. The sight was a shock. Dr. McCarran was a dead ringer for an actor I have admired ever since I was a member of Miss Merle S. Marine's Playgoers' Club in Thomas Jefferson High School. Osgood Perkins. Then playing in *The Front Page*. And—

I wonder if it is possible to convey the magic of that moment in time. Benny, I told myself sharply, stop wondering. It is not possible. Magic happens to you. When it does, be grateful and clutch it to your bosom. Don't try to do the impossible with it. Magic cannot be passed on. All right, then. It happened to me. And here I was. Forty years later. In a hotel suite doctor's office in Philadelphia. Remembering the magic. And feeling it again. A little bit, anyway. But it was enough. There had been only one Osgood Perkins.

"Please sit down," said Dr. McCarran. "And please try to relax. All men who come to see doctors in secret have things on their minds that they have not been able to tell their wives, and don't want to. Clap?"

The word hit me just as I sat down in front of Dr. McCarran's desk.

"What did you say?" I said.

"Clap," Dr. McCarran said.

I gave it a moment, then caught on. I was angry, but I knew I did not have the right to be.

"Nothing like that," I said. "It's about my son."

"Sons, I have found, are more likely to suffer from the ailment than their fathers."

"No, that's not what my son is suffering from," I said. "If he were, I would be troubled, naturally, but I would not

6

go to all this CIA subterfuge to arrange for his treatment. Our family doctor, Artie Steinberg, would know what to do."

"He would know better than most," Dr. McCarran said. "Artie Steinberg and I rode a Bellevue ambulance together for two years after we got out of Cornell Med."

I stared at him with delight. You think of life as something lived in compartments. Then you run head on into a surprise. There really are no compartments. Everything runs into everything else, like pancakes poured too close together on a griddle.

"Are you saying," I said nervously, "that you know Dr. Arthur Steinberg of 435 East Fifty-seventh Street?"

"New York, N.Y. 10022," said Dr. Osgood Perkins.

"Well," Benny Kramer said. And that's all he did say. Words—Miss Merle S. Marine probably would not believe this—words failed me. "He checked my blood pressure a week ago," I said. "On East Fifty-seventh Street."

"So he told me," Dr. McCarran said.

Astonished, I said, "He did?"

"Yes," Dr. McCarran said. "Artie called to say you'd been in, and among other things you'd talked about your son, and while he said you hadn't said anything, he suspected what you might do, and I'm the only man he knows who is capable of telling you what you want to know, so he called me here in Philadelphia and we talked about you. You're taking two Aldomet tablets every morning, one every afternoon, and one at bedtime. Correct?"

"Yes," I said. "And one Esidrix every morning."

"Yes, of course," Dr. McCarran said. "That's for getting rid of the water in your system. We must get rid of the water, mustn't we?"

"I don't know why," I said, "but I do everything Artie Steinberg tells me to do."

"Very sound," said Dr. McCarran. "Getting rid of the water is of the utmost importance."

"Well," I said, "I seem to be doing it."

The conversation seemed at this point to fall apart. I did not know what Artie Steinberg had told him, but Dr. Mc-

Carran apparently did not believe that I had come to see him solely about Jack. I wondered if Artie thought I did not trust him and was checking on his medication with another doctor. Anyway, I liked Dr. McCarran, but I did not know how to handle this. Until Dr. McCarran said in a most friendly way, "You've been a friend to Sebastian Roon for a long time?"

Light invaded the shaded room. Sebastian Roon is my oldest friend. That's the truth. I am a bald-headed boy from East Fourth Street, later Tiffany Street, and my oldest friend is named Sebastian Roon. Can you beat it? If you can, please don't tell me. We live by small bits of brightness. To me, for forty years, one of the brightest bits has been a man named, most improbably, Sebastian Roon. Don't take it away from me.

"Forty years," I said. "We met when we were both seventeen. That's forty years ago. He arranged this appointment, as you know."

"Indeed I do know," said Dr. McCarran. "If he hadn't, I'm afraid I would not have seen you. I met Seb during the war. He's a great actor, I think. Don't you?"

I was not sure. Acting is a troubling art. It seems to me it's largely an accident. If you have a face shaped in a certain way, if you bring out on the stage, or in front of a camera, an image that is *sui generis*, you are a great actor even if you are a dope. Sebastian Roon is no dope. And he is my friend. I knew what to say.

"He is the greatest actor I have ever known," I said.

Safe enough. I have known only two actors. The other one may be greater than Sebastian. But he is a bastard. Nuts to him.

"My wife will be pleased by your opinion," said Dr. McCarran. "She is very fond of Seb."

The last wife who had not been fond of Seb was Anne of Cleves, and we all know what happened to her.

"So is my wife," I said. "That's why I felt it was okay to come see you behind her back."

"It's perfectly okay," said Dr. McCarran. "I may not be the best doctor in the world, but I think I am about as

8

good a friend as most human beings. I have never violated the confidence of a friend. You can ask Seb."

"I have," I said. "He told me I can tell you anything."

"Then let me tell you what he told me," said Dr. Mc-Carran. "It may make things simpler, and probably speed them up. I understand you have to be in the Federal Courthouse on Walnut Street at two-thirty."

"Seb doesn't seem to have left anything out," I said.

"Good actors rarely do," said Dr. McCarran. "Here is what Seb told me. You have a son named Jack. He has just graduated from Harvard. He has gone to the University of Indiana to work for his masters in fine arts. His New York draft board has told him that they are forbidden to grant any more graduate school deferments. Your son Jack's draft board told him before he went to Indiana that, if he did go, he would be in the Mekong Delta in three weeks. Is that correct?"

"Pretty much," I said. "As Jack reported it to me, the draft board said two weeks."

"Close enough," said Dr. McCarran.

He lifted a pair of black horn-rimmed glasses that hung around his neck on one of those couturier braided ropes. He set the glasses on his nose, and looked at me exactly coldly but with a sort of clinical interest. As though up to now he had been going through a boring duty he had promised to go through for a friend, but now his own emotions had been engaged. My stomach reacted with a small tremor. He *was* Osgood Perkins!

"This is obviously difficult for you," Dr. McCarran said. "It's easier for me. May I continue?"

"Please," I said.

My mother did not learn English until I was almost eighteen. But she learned me my manners. In Yiddish. Thanks, Ma.

"Seb says you don't want that boy killed in the Mekong Delta," Dr. McCarran said. "Is that correct?"

I looked at him for a couple of moments. I decided that nothing would be gained by hitting him. Even though I knew just how to do it. Corporal Isherwood had taught me

9

the blow during a commando course I had to take in Kent a month before D-day.

"Strike for the bahstid's jug," Corporal Isherwood had barked at his dozen uneasy pupils. "It's where these bahstids are vulnerable. Get them while they're too confident to protect themselves. Make your choice. The nuts or the guts. The nuts is more decisive. But the guts is closer. Straighten you hand, palm flat, and swing like this, like you wuz cuttin' the bahstid's air flow. Which is what you'll be doon. Easy. Sharp. Hard. That will take care of the bahstid."

I never got a chance to put Corporal Isherwood's instructions into practice. By the time I got to Caen the bahstids were all runing like crazy from Patton's tanks. Just as well. I doubt that I could have done what Corporal Isherwood urged.

So I said, as calmly as I could, to Dr. McCarran: "No, I don't want that boy killed."

Dr. McCarran said, "Seb tells me he has told you in confidence about my service with the draft board during the last war."

"He has," I said.

"Please forgive the next question," Dr. McCarran said. "Are we both agreed on the phrase 'in confidence'?"

The bahstids. Even the best of them. They had to close the shutters.

"Completely," I said. "Except for my wife and my son. I will have to tell them, of course."

"Of course," said Dr. McCarran. "Okay, then. During the last war, I served as one of the chief medical advisers to General Hershey. The average citizen is quite savage about the draft. Understandably so. Since the days of Crassus nobody has looked with delight on a system that can take a son, a husband, a brother, a lover, perhaps even just a nice neighbor, from his normal routine and shove him into an enterprise where he may very probably get his head blown off, and often what gets blown off is worse than his head. Anyway, if you don't look with delight on something,

10

you begin inventing ways to circumvent it. The best way is to wet the bed."

"What?" I said. What would you have said?

"The army does not like to draft men who wet their beds," Dr. McCarran said.

The effects of human speech are, of course, as unpredictable as the effects of nuclear fission. I have no doubt that to Dr. McCarran his simple statement was no more startling than the dropping of The Bomb over Hiroshima had been to the pilot of the *Enola Gay*. We were fighting a war. When you fight a war you have to win. The methods are not your concern. You just follow orders.

"I don't understand," I said. "What's wrong with wetting the bed?"

Dr. McCarran gave me a look that had in it patience, because he was obviously a decent human being, but the look had in it also a number of not quite definable elements. They belonged to that area in which people with specialized knowledge, people like doctors, come to know so much about the human condition that they find it difficult to discuss the condition with even well-intentioned dumbbells.

"There is nothing wrong with wetting the bed in a private bedroom," Dr. McCarran said patiently. "In a barracks, however, a large chamber inhabited by dozens of men, wetting the bed is a disruptive act. It is a subject for ridicule. Ridicule destroys discipline. The army looks with disfavor upon the disruption of discipline. In fact, the army looks upon the destruction of discipline the way the priests of your race, Mr. Kramer, look upon the desecration of the Torah. The army wants men. But the army does not want men who wet their beds."

Another good thing about N.Y.U. Law School. It teaches you to put things together. It did in 1933–1937, anyway.

"So if you tell the army you wet your bed," I said, "the army will not draft you?"

Dr. McCarran nodded. But I noticed his face looked troubled.

"Not quite," he said. "If to stay out of the army all a

young man has to do is say he wets the bed, we would never have an army. It's an easy lie. So the army employs doctors."

The troubled look cut deeper furrows into Dr. McCarran's marvelous Osgood Perkins face.

"I was one of those doctors," he said. "The way I got to know Seb was that many actors, friends of his, wanted to stay out of the army, and they knew about the bed-wetting bit, but they didn't know how to, how shall I put it, yes, they didn't know how to activate it into plausibility."

I gave that a bit of thought. Dr. McCarran had obviously grown accustomed to visitors or patients who, at this point, needed a bit of thought. He pulled the fat silver stopper out of an expensive Abercrombie & Fitch thermos jug and poured himself a glass of ice water. He did not offer one to his visitor. I understood why he did not. At this point in a puzzling situation the visitor did not want ice water. Why waste time?

"The problem, then," I said, "would seem to be how to convince the army doctors, when a man says he wets his bed, how to convince the army doctors he is telling the truth. Is that correct?"

Dr. McCarran was so clearly pleased with me, that I was pleased with myself.

"Mr. Kramer," he said, "you have not only put your finger on it. You have poked a hole right through it. Bull's-eye!"

"So you worked out a system," I said. "How to check on men who say they wet their beds to find out if they are lying, or if they really do wet their beds."

"Precisely," said Dr. McCarran. "I am not proud about this. But I wanted my country to beat the pants off a son of a bitch named Hitler. I hated that louse. I still do. I would have done anything to help. What I was able to do was track down poor kids who said they peed in bed but actually didn't. Isn't that insane?"

I could see from his face that he intended it to be a serious question. I had come to him about a problem that had

12

been shaking the hell out of me. I saw that in his attempt to help me solve it, I was shaking the hell out of him.

"I don't know," I said. "If you saved some kids from dying, it can't be insane."

"Because you want me to save your son from dying," Dr. McCarran said.

He could have been behind the A&P counter asking me how many bunches of asparagus I wanted.

"Yes, I do," I said. "I don't want that kid to die. Any more than my parents wanted me to die in the war that was yours and mine. But my parents didn't try to stop me. My mother and father would have considered it a dirty thing to do what I'm doing here today. You see, my mother and father were immigrants. They had escaped from Europe on the run. With murderous bastards like Hitler breathing down their necks. My mother and father made it. Others didn't. My mother and father understood why it was necessary to fight savages like Hitler. They were proud to have their son in that fight. Their son is still proud that he was. But I'm not proud of this war. I'm ashamed of it. We're not wiping out an evil like Hitler. This time we're the evil. I don't want my son to be a part of it. He's going to die some day. Everybody dies, including you and me. But I'm damned if I'm going to let him die as a part of this plague. To save him from that I'll do anything, Dr. McCarran."

Dr. McCarran stared at me for a moment, or a minute, or an hour. I don't know. My heart was hammering so hard I couldn't count time.

"Okay," he said finally. "Sebastian Roon vouches for you."

"He is my son's godfather," I said.

"Your son couldn't have a better one," Dr. McCarran said.

He lifted the green blotter on his desk and pulled out a sheet of paper. It was not a letterhead. Just a sheet of white paper. And I could see it had about twenty or thirty typewritten lines on it.

"These are the questions I worked out during the crusade against Hitler," he said. Not without irony. "To check

13

the veracity of a boy who told his draft board doctor he peed in bed. And I've written down the answers. All your son has to do at his physical exam is rattle off these answers."

Osgood Perkins—no, sorry—Dr. McCarran bowed his head.

"Christ Almighty," he said to the green desk blotter. When he lifted his head, I was relieved to see he was not crying. "It's a pretty rotten way to live," he said. In a voice so low that I could only just barely hear him. But I did. "Teaching kids how to convince draft board doctors that they pee in bed. Wouldn't that have made Osler proud of us?"

I didn't answer. I just took the sheet of paper, stood up, and went to the door. I made it because he held my elbow all the way.

"Tell your son to memorize these simple questions and answers," Dr. McCarran said. "He won't be drafted."

"Thank you," I said.

I walked back to the Federal Courthouse. One of the most puzzling things about being alive, I have learned slowly, is that there are times when you don't know what the hell is going on inside your own head. Emotions are too complicated to sort out. They make you feel rudderless. I hate that. I like to feel I am in control. I like to feel I know where I am going. The infuriating truth is that I rarely do. For such moments I always carry the copy of *Bleak House* given to me by Miss Anna Bongiorno in J.H.S. 64 when I reached the semifinals in the New York *Times* oratorical contest on the Constitution in 1924. I did not make it into the finals, but I still have that copy of *Bleak House*. I never leave home without slipping it into my overnight bag. Even before I pack my razor and toothbrush.

You can always, I have found, buy a toothbrush. Or find a barber. But copies of *Bleak House,* I have discovered, are difficult to come by on short notice. So I carry my own, and in spare moments away from home I lean on it. The book gets you through. Art always does. Good art, anyway, and *Bleak House* is up there with the best.

14

It got me through a long wait in the Federal Courthouse on Walnut Street until I was called to the stand. After half an hour of foolish questions, Mr. Schlisselberger's Philadelphia lawyer asked if I, as an experienced and well-known New York real-estate lawyer, would or could—no lawyer ever uses one word when two can be squeezed in—tell the court if any new theaters had been built in the Times Square area.

"Not in my time," I said.

The defense attorney leaped to his feet. "And what, sir, if I may ask," he thundered (he was a basso, like Ezio Pinza), "what is your time, sir?"

Without thought, because it was simple fact, as much a part of my life as my home address, I said: "April fourth, nineteen thirteen, the day I was born, until today."

Pause. Defense attorney plops back into his seat, frowning furiously. I wonder why. The judge, a man who has hitherto been for me faceless, leans down from the bench. He proves to have a marvelous face. Plump, but not fat. Lined in a good way. The best way. Like a marbled steak. The lines underscoring the obvious fact that the face has been used. By thought. By worry. By preoccupation with the human condition, which is always troubling and never good. All these lines came together in a friendly smile, the whole head framed in a neatly tended mop of thick white hair.

"Mr. Kramer," the judge says to me gently, "that's the only time any of us can testify to."

So I'm doing it.

The decision was not made. It happened. I caught the four o'clock Metroliner back to New York. I had the afternoon papers. And I had *Bleak House*. But I did not read. I stared out the train window. As anybody who has been subjected to this ride can testify, there is not much to see. Yet the unattractive roadbed from Philadelphia to Penn Station held my attention. I was not, of course, seeing the dreary landscape. I was seeing that judge. His alive, concerned face. And hearing his totally unexpected words. Over and over again. Why?

15

I don't know. I had gone to Philadelphia to save the life of my son. To do so I had been forced to involve myself in a fragment of a stupid legal brawl. The only justification for its existence was the wealth of the plaintiff. He could afford to snarl the dockets of the nation's courts with a piece of idiotic vanity. He could afford to enlist my not inexpensive help in this shameful charade. As the train pulled into Penn Station, the core of what was troubling me surfaced in the form of a question. I wished it hadn't. The question was: Is this a way for a man to spend his life? The question was addressed to Benny Kramer.

Before I could answer it, things started to happen. There were, of course, no taxis. There have been no taxis at Penn Station since Commadore Perry opened up Japan, though most New Yorkers are either unaware of this fact or refuse to believe it. They emerge from the railroad station into the street, seem astonished to discover that there are no cabs waiting, and do something I feel I have a right to call stupid because I have done it so often myself: they ask a redcap to get one for them.

I did not. After all, I was carrying no luggage. Only *Bleak House*. And I knew more about the area around Penn Station than most redcaps. I had spent my early years in the garment center.

I surveyed the situation. This was a mistake. I should have walked away from it. But the days of my nonage were crowding back into my mind. When I was a boy on these streets the Hotel Pennsylvania had a 33rd Street entrance. And 33rd Street, even when Jimmy Walker was mayor, had always been westbound. Somebody was sure to be arriving at the hotel from the east side. Somebody in a taxi.

I made my move.

I leaped out into the stream of Seventh Avenue traffic. I dodged my way nimbly—every morning: twenty minutes of calisthenics, plus ten minutes of jogging—toward the southeast corner of 33rd Street. A man carrying a suitcase might have had trouble. Not a man carrying *Bleak House*. The prose is uplifting. Halfway across the moving current of savage traffic, I saw a cab do precisely what I had felt

16

some cab would do. It pulled up to the 33rd Street side of the hotel.

A passenger stepped out. The door slammed shut. The cab started moving toward me. At the 33rd Street corner it turned into Seventh Avenue, as I knew it would have to do; Seventh Avenue is now one-way, southbound. I waved *Bleak House*. The taxi pulled up and stopped at my feet. I seized the handle of the rear door and twisted.

Nothing happened. I twisted harder. Nothing. The door was locked. A voice came out of the late afternoon sunlight behind me.

"That's my cab, white boy."

I turned. In my youth I was a devotee of the work of Rex Beach. He would have written: "I spun around." I have a feeling Mr. Beach's account of my movement would have been more accurate. When I stopped spinning I found myself facing, in the middle of the Seventh Avenue traffic, a black young man in a zipper jacket who was eleven feet tall.

"Oh, no, it's not," I said mildly. My mother had taught me to be polite. "I got here first."

The black man replied by throwing a punch at my nose. I covered it with both hands and with *Bleak House* and I crouched away to the left. The black young man's fist missed my nose, as well as *Bleak House,* but it grazed the side of my head. My head slammed against the rim of the taxi's rear window. Time vanished from my consciousness.

When I again became aware of it, I grasped that it could not have been gone very long. The young man was still there, right smack in the middle of the insane traffic whoosing by on both sides of us, and he was throwing another punch at my head. It never landed. This black boy, clearly to his amazement as well as mine, had competition.

Behind him another black boy—no, a man: he could have been in his forties or his nineties but he was not in his teens—had taken an interest in me. He was taller and heavier than the boy, and he was carrying what looked like a stunted baseball bat. I learned later it was a long flashlight, but at the moment my capacity to learn was limited

17

to my popped eyes. They showed me the long, sweeping motion of one arm, with which the black man shoved the black boy out of his path, and the way both his hands came together at the bottom of the weapon, swung it up over his head and, like a headsman's ax, brought it down in the direction of my totally unprotected scalp.

I screamed. I crouched. And something came up out of the past to help me. The memory of that commando course I had been forced to take at a British staging area in Kent shortly before D-day in 1944.

"Kick," Corporal Isherwood had snapped at us over and over again. "Kick," he had barked. "As hard and as straight out at the bahstids as you can. The foot reaches further than the hand, and to do it you don't have to lean forward and expose the body's voytal parts. Kick, gentlemen, always kick."

A quarter of a century later, on a sunny afternoon in front of Penn Station, I did Corporal Isherwood's bidding. I kicked. And I added a touch of my own: I closed my eyes. The toe of my shoe caught the wielder of the headsman's ax right smack in the middle of the target that the Marquis of Queensbury spent his life telling Western Man no civilized pugilist must even approach.

I did better than approach it; I practically demolished it. Closing my eyes had obviously done the trick. The man screamed. He tumbled backward, clutching his voytal parts, and he flopped onto the black boy who had damaged my head. They went down together, amid a wild rasping of brakes and an insane honking of horns.

I heard a click behind me. The taxi driver had leaned over and snapped back the catch on the lock of his rear door. I twisted the handle and jumped in. Pulling the door shut with a bang, I fell back on the seat.

"Where to?" the driver said.

I looked at the card next to his meter. Ramon Fuentes. I looked at his Puerto Rican face. Twenty-five? Perhaps thirty. Certainly no more. He had not yet been born when Benny Kramer was being taught in Kent to "kick, always kick."

18

"Madison and Forty-ninth," I said. "Drive slow."

"They hurt you bad?" Ramon Fuentes said.

Not physically. Only in the place where I lived.

"I'll be all right in a few minutes," I said.

But I knew in my belly I would never be all right. Never again. A couple of hours ago, in Philadelphia, my life had turned a corner. A few minutes ago, in front of Penn Station, a road block had been dumped behind me. There was no way to go back.

The streets I had roamed at night, as a boy at N.Y.U. Law School, dreaming of Toby Wing and Judge Brandeis, those streets were no longer safe in the brilliant afternoon sunlight.

"Listen," I said to the taxi driver. "When you stopped the cab for me in the middle of the traffic back there, why didn't you open the door?"

"No taxi driver in this town goes to Penn Station to look for a fare," the driver said. "It's too tough. Even the cops are scared. It's all gangs. They tell a man or a woman, We'll get you a cab, mister. Then, when they get it, they surround him and his family and they say, That'll cost you ten bucks, mister. Or twenty. The poor guy, he's there with his wife, he's stuck. He doesn't pay? They get rough. Sometimes with the bags. Sometimes with the man. His wife and kids, too. He usually pays. Like those two guys who jumped you. They were probably promoting a cab for some poor sucker who just got off the train from some hick town out west and didn't know what was gonna happen to him. The only time a hackie goes to Penn Station these days is when he gets stuck, and then he gets the hell out of that neighborhood as fast as he can. Like this lady flagged me over on Fifty-seventh and Lex. She says take me to the Sheraton on Seventh. I'm stuck. I gotta take her. But I want to get out of there fast. So I take her to the Thirty-third Street entrance and then I lock the door. When I turn into Seventh, getting the hell out of there, I see you in the gutter. I'm heading south, down Seventh, so I figure okay, and I stop. But then I see these two guys be-

19

hind you. Boy, I tell you, mister, I want to get the hell out of there."

All at once so did I.

"You can go a little faster," I said. "I'm okay now."

I wasn't. But I knew as soon as I set eyes on Miss Bienstock, my secretary, I would be. She was what people mean when they say somebody is no longer a kid. And indeed Miss Bienstock was not.

When I had first met her in the offices of Maurice Saltzman & Company in 1930, she had been a pretty girl with dimples who had come to work in that office directly from her graduation at seventeen from Washington Irving High School. When I came to work in that same office, directly from my graduation from Thomas Jefferson High School, I had just passed my seventeenth birthday, and Miss Bienstock had been working there for five years. Any way you figured it, she was my senior by five years.

In 1930 it had seemed quite a gap. Especially since Miss Bienstock had been private secretary to our boss, and I had been the sort of office boy who was known in the slang of the day as a chief cook and bottle-washer. I did everything, including many things Miss Bienstock asked me to do.

It is the word asked that lingers. Even though Miss Bienstock had the authority, she never ordered. She always asked.

"Benny, I wonder if I could ask, some time today, no rush, any time at all, you're out on some errand, could you stop in at Pennsylvania Stationers and get me a box of these eight and a half by eleven manila file folders?"

I always did, and I was always pleased to do it. Years later, when I went into business for myself and needed a secretary, I happened to run into Miss Bienstock at the Riverside Chapel funeral service for another girl who had worked in our office. The sight of Miss Bienstock made me feel good. I had one of those inspirations that with more fortunate men lead to the White House or 10 Downing Street. But what's the White House? What's 10 Downing Street? Compared with a good secretary?

Nothing? Everything!

20

The relationship was never difficult. Even though she was then, and naturally still is, older by those five years. The key to our relationship is that, even though I am in my late fifties, a married man with a grown son, to Miss Bienstock I am still Benny Kramer, the Maurice Saltzman & Company office boy. And you know something? I like it.

"Something went wrong in Philadelphia," she said through a troubled frown when I came into the office. "I can tell."

I was on the verge of denying it, when my awareness of Miss Bienstock's concern for my welfare, to which I was accustomed, took an odd turn. I was suddenly jolted by curiosity. As though I had received a message that something important was about to be revealed to me.

"How can you tell?" I said.

Miss Bienstock continued to stare at me through her anxiously troubled frown. I stared back at her, with the same sort of anxiety. Perhaps an anxiety that cut even deeper. Her great talent, even as a young girl in the office of Maurice Saltzman & Company, had been a kind of innocent clairvoyance. I never knew how her mind worked. I doubt that she did. But she always seemed to cut through confusing irrelevancies.

Miss Bienstock always knew I had a head cold before I did. She sensed—there was no other way she could have known—when my shoes needed resoling, and would suggest that I stop in at the cobbler down the street. Before I had made up my mind, she would tell me she did not think a certain client would ever move beyond his big talk about buying a certain property with the hard fact of a contract and the hard cash of a down payment. I remembered all at once that she had felt I should not go to Philadelphia to testify in Mr. Schlisselberger's antitrust suit. She did not, of course, know the real reason why I went. Miss Bienstock was crazy about Jack. She always sends him Hallmark birthday cards. But I had never discussed with her Jack's draft problem.

"I don't know," Miss Bienstock said softly. "I don't

21

know ," she repeated worriedly. "All of a sudden, the few hours you've been gone, all of a sudden you look older."

"That's no surprise," I said. "Every hour that goes by, we all get older."

Miss Bienstock shook her head. It was a very attractive head. Her hair was going white, and even though she was almost sixty-four, she still had an enviable figure. And she had never lost that look of innocent, some might say mindless, girlish prettiness. The look I had found so attractive on West 34th Street in 1930. There was something indomitable about her.

"Sticks and stones can break my bones," we used to say on East Fourth Street, "but names can never harm me."

That, it seemed to me, was the word for Miss Bienstock. She was unharmed. It was as though the years, passing by, had taken their expected swipes at her, but she had parried them, fended them off, kept her basic self intact. I had always liked her. All at once I realized I admired her. She was what my father, who had spent his life making pockets in a pants shop, used to call good goods. I wondered how she had managed it.

"I don't mean getting older like in arithmetic," Miss Bienstock said. "I mean getting older like in . . ."

She paused. She seemed surprised by something that had apparently crossed her mind.

"When I was a little girl," she said, "I remember once my mother said about one of our neighbors—something terrible had happened, I think the woman's husband got killed by a truck on his way home from work, something like that—and I remember my mother saying about this woman, my mother said her hair turned white overnight."

"Well, I don't have any to turn," I said. "Anything important happen while I was away?"

"Nothing you have to worry about until tomorrow," Miss Bienstock said. She hesitated, then said, "Are you sure nothing happened?"

I went to the window and looked down on Madison Avenue at 5:30 in the afternoon. Once, when I was a boy on

Seventh Avenue, this street had seemed as unattainable as a seat in the House of Lords. Now that I had been a part of it for a quarter of a century it seemed pointless. The question that had hit me as the Metroliner pulled into Penn Station came back with a rising inflection: Is this a way for a man to spend his life?

Why not simply answer yes, and let it go at that? Nobody but Benny Kramer had heard the question. Nobody but Benny Kramer would know that he had turned away from an honest attempt at an answer.

The throb in the back of my head moved down into other parts of my body. The pain was settling into a steady pulsing ache. I turned back to face Miss Bienstock.

"No, nothing happened," I said.

I am not the noblest of citizens. I like to dilute my troubles by dumping at least part of them on others. Preferably friends. What else are friends for? But I couldn't do it to Miss Bienstock.

People who came in and out of the office were constantly reporting incidents of violence. Muggings. Thefts. Outrages on the subway. I had always accepted them as I accepted the news reports from Vietnam. I did not doubt they were true. I deplored them. But they were happening to somebody else. Miss Bienstock had always felt the same way.

"I live on Mosholu Parkway," she had said many times in my presence. "That's an hour on the IRT twice a day. And I live across the street from DeWitt Clinton High School, which is now ninety percent black during the school day, and the neighborhood is getting more blacks in it during the rest of the day, and I have never had a moment of discomfort personally on the subway or in the streets. I think people make up all this stuff."

I had agreed with her. Until a half-hour ago. Now my head throbbed.

"No, nothing happened," I said. "Mr. Schlisselberger proved once again what we've known for years. He's a horse's patoot. My testimony is not going to change that.

23

But having to give it proved more depressing than I thought it would be, and so maybe I do look as though my hair turned white overnight. Anyway, if there's nothing urgent, I think I'll carry these old bones home."

The phone rang. Miss Bienstock picked it up.

"Yes?" she said.

She listened, still scowling, obviously troubled about me. Anyway, that's what I wanted to believe. I was reminded of Miss Merle S. Marine in my English class. She used to quote Browning quite a lot.

You know we French stormed Ratisbon: a mile or so away, on a little mound. Napoleon stood on our storming day; with legs out-thrust, you fancy how, legs wide, arms locked behind, as if to balance the prone brow, oppressive with its mind.

Napoleon and Miss Bienstock. They knew their jobs. As long as she was around, even black boys on Seventh Avenue couldn't really damage Benny Kramer.

"Let me take a look," Miss Bienstock said into the phone. "I just heard the outer door open. Perhaps it's Mr. Kramer. He said if he got back from Philadelphia early enough he might stop in here at the office. Hold on, please." She put her hand over the mouthpiece and said to me, "It's Mr. Roon? He called earlier? He wants to have a drink with you at the club. He says you made a tentative date for after you got back from Philadelphia? Could you manage it? He seems quite anxious?"

I reached for the phone, then withdrew my hand. I didn't mind a drink. Indeed, I wanted one. But I did not want to talk on the phone. I had forgotten it was Seb who had fixed up my date with Dr. McCarran in Philadelphia. My head, which hurt, was full of Jack, and how was I going to break to him and to Elizabeth Ann what Dr. McCarran had told me? It is easy to be a liar. It is difficult to be a convincing one.

"Tell him I'm signing some letters, so I can't talk to him on the phone," I said to Miss Bienstock. "But I'll meet him at the club in ten minutes."

"I think you'd better tell him yourself," she said. "I think it would be better."

Her thoughts were not always clear to me. But they were always concerned with my welfare.

"All right," I said. "I'll talk to him."

2

Some books are written. Others happen. This book started to happen in 1930.

Curiously, I was not aware of this until today, when Sebastian Roon called me after I got back from Philadelphia. Sebastian and I have much in common. We discovered this on Tiffany Street in the Bronx in 1930.

It was a tough year for the country, but for the Kramer family—my mother, my father, and the author of these notes—it was actually a very good year. In fact, the best we had ever known. I had just graduated from Thomas Jefferson High School. With honors, I cannot refrain from adding with toe-shuffling embarrassment. No, I withdraw that. If you're going to show off, you might as well do it with at least a hint of nuts-to-tradition forthrightness.

So: I am proud of the fact that I graduated from Thomas Jefferson High School as valedictorian of my class. What makes me proud is the way it made my mother and father feel. I could see them doing something I had never encountered except in Jane Austen novels. They preened. And in the process, I discovered the pleasure of giving pleasure.

At seventeen I had never before been in a position to give my parents a present. In fact, it had never occurred to me to do so. Or even to feel it was necessary to take a crack at it. I was preoccupied with my own life, which I see now was almost doltishly simple, but in those early years seemed hopelessly complicated. Besides, my parents were a couple of illiterate peasants from Central Europe. Immigrants. My father had fled from the Austrian conscription machinery of Emperor Franz Joseph; my mother, from the serfdom of a dairy farm on the slopes of the Carpathian

26

Mountains in Hungary. They had met on East Fourth Street in the slums of New York, married, and spawned me. This was a reason for me to feel indebted to them?

Today, in 1971, recalling how Sebastian Roon in 1930 caused this book to start to happen, the answer to that question is yes. In 1930, no. Not because I am a bastard. Or was. At seventeen, as I recall, I was probably indistinguishable from most seventeen-year-olds: not much of anything. A bundle of what I suppose can be described as protoplasm, trying to stay afloat—God, how at fifty-eight the brilliant metaphors assault the tip of a ball-point!—in a turbulent sea of economics and sex.

Economics in 1930 was Maurice Saltzman & Company, where I worked. Sex was Hannah Halpern, where I—well.

Well?

Well, why not?

Boy! When I think back—but I'd better not.

Let's stick to the fact that I was the youngest employee of Maurice Saltzman & Company, Certified Public Accountants.

I don't know why. I mean I don't know why I was the firm's youngest employee. I was not hired because of my age. I was hired because I could do a number of things that in 1930 a firm of certified public accountants wanted or had to have done daily in their offices but did not want to pay more than one employee to do. As achievements, these things I could do were hardly noteworthy.

For example, I could arrive in the offices at 224 West 34th Street shortly before eight o'clock every morning. And I mean every. Including Sunday. M.S.&Co., as it was known to intimates, worked a seven-day week. I did it without difficulty.

Got out of my bed at 5:30 in the Kramer family flat on Tiffany Street in the Bronx. Ablutions. Not much shaving as yet. Dressed fast. Helped by my mother. She was fussy about my appearance. She was proud of my job with M.S.&Co. She wanted me to look spic and span. I did. Nobody exported from Asia to the Chinese laundries of the

27

Bronx ever washed and ironed a shirt the way my mother did. Or put on a kitchen table a breakfast so sensible for a young man who could not afford the cost of a downtown lunch.

My mother understood staying power. It was the rubric that had kept her afloat from the Carpathian Mountains to Tiffany Street.

Having been set afloat for the day, I trotted off to the 180th Street–Bronx Park South subway train at 6:30. Not too crowded at that hour. I usually managed to find a seat. I preferred one in the little cab at the rear. By the time the train cut across the Harlem River into upper Manhattan the train was jammed and to the surface of my mind came that uneasy problem: chivalry versus comfort. An awful lot of little old ladies were on their way between 6:30 and 7:00 from the Bronx to the sewing rooms of the garment center. They posed a problem for a nice Jewish boy, raised by a tough-minded lady like my mother.

She had started to teach me about life when I was just barely old enough to listen. Or hear. Three? Four? Five? Not much older than five, anyway. Her basic lesson applied to almost all aspects of daily existence. For going to work in the morning, it went as follows: "A boy must always stand up in the subway and give his seat to a lady. But only if he sees her."

In the little cab at the back of the subway car you didn't see her, or anybody else. Your nose was buried in Volume II—*Revocable Trusts, Amortization of Capital Expenditures, and Ancillary Depreciation*—of the La Salle Extension University Course in Higher Accountancy.

I had at that time about as much interest in Revocable Trusts, Amortization of Capital Expenditures, and Ancillary Depreciation as Rin-Tin-Tin had in the sunspot theory of economic cycles. Most of the country, however, was trying to keep its nose above the rising flood of Herbert Hoover's depression. I had been fortunate enough to land this job with a firm of certified public accountants, and I did not want to be fired.

To put it bluntly, my enrollment in the La Salle Extension University Course in Higher Accountancy was an activity that would have been described a decade later—after the Japs dumped the Sixth Avenue El back on us at Hickam Field and I began to rub elbows with the vocabulary of the U.S. Army—as brown-nosing.

I did not want my boss Ira Bern (the "Co." of M.S.&.Co.) to think I felt about accountancy the way my mother felt about suckling pig. I wanted him to feel I sat at his feet. It would not be straining accuracy to say I did.

One of my daily tasks as an employee of M.S.&Co. was to take Mr. Bern's shoes every morning at ten o'clock to the bootblack in the lobby of our office building. It sounds demeaning, of course, and there may be some who think it was. I did not. Mr. Bern was a generous and an expansive man. Every morning when he took off his shoes and handed them to me, he also handed me a dime.

"While you're waiting," he used to say, "get yourself a cuppa cawfee and a ruggle."

A cuppa cawfee was—well, I guess it still is—a cuppa cawfee. A ruggle, however. Now then.

A ruggle in 1930 was and may very well still be a piece of pastry called Danish, probably with good reason, although so far as I knew it was invented by Jews in places like Poland. It was steeped in cinnamon, studded with raisins, chewy as taffy, shaped like a crescent, and pleasurable beyond the erotic vocabulary in the Song of Solomon.

While Mr. Bern's shoes were being shined, I would sit at Mr. Rothman's brown marble counter in the section of the office building lobby then known as a coffee pot, and I would dunk.

A nickel ruggle in 1930 had in it eight dunks. Once in a while, as an experiment in the extension of delight, I did manage to stretch this to nine. I am certain others have made the same experiment, but my life has not provided me with opportunities to compare these experiments. Speaking for myself, from my own personal experience, I can say unequivocally the experiment did not pay off.

Shortly after the eighth dunk, Mr. Bern's shoes always looked like the mirrors in the penny peanut machines on

29

the IRT subway platforms. I do not exaggerate. You could see yourself, you actually could, in the gleaming mirror-like pieces of leather across the toes.

Mr. Bern had been a poor boy. A Fifth Streeter, actually. Born and raised one block up from my own native land: East Fourth Street. He had made it, as Fifth Streeters tended to do, and as a result he had certain peccadilloes. Shoes, for example. He couldn't stand brown. Black was Ira Bern's color, and a custom bootmaker on 48th made the shoes for him at $55 a pair—1930, remember—out of sheets of vici kid imported from Spain.

I did not then know what vici kid was. I still don't know. I am certain it would be easy enough to find out. A phone call to *The New York Times* would do it. Or could do it in the days when the paper sold for two cents, and on that they could afford to maintain a twenty-four-hour-a-day free information telephone service. Even if they still do, I would not make that call.

Vici kid to me is the black leather at which the Italian boy in the bootblack shop at 224 West 34th Street pummeled away every morning from 10:00 to 10:15 while I dunked a Rothman's ruggle into a cuppa Rothman's cawfee. I'll settle for that.

The good moments of life, I have learned, are always memories. I have never known better ones. I will stick with what I've got.

What I've got next adds up to a somewhat breathless period. Five minutes, perhaps. Somewhere between 10:15 and 10:30 every morning in the offices of M.S.&Co. at 224 West 34th Street in 1930. These were the minutes that started when I came back upstairs into the office with Mr. Bern's gleaming shoes, and the moment when I learned how Mr. Bern was going to dispose of my day. What made this period breathless was that Mr. Bern did not himself know what he was going to do with me. Until, that is, he faced the problem. Which was always minutes—moments, actually—before the problem had to be solved.

Mr. Bern was not a bad man. He was not even a stupid man. I see now his trouble was that he shared with the rest of the human race what Shakespeare grasped when he set himself the task of explaining the complexities of the heir to Elsinore. Most human beings are as indecisive as one of those tropical storms the National Hurricane Center makes such floundering efforts to track. For a man who was operating a firm of certified public accountants with twenty-two staff members who had to be paid every Saturday at noon, it was clearly hell on wheels.

Mr. Bern was a small, natty, nervous man with the sort of toothbrush mustache that Adolf Hitler was just about to spring on the world. Mr. Bern always seemed cold. I don't mean cold as in Heathcliff. I mean cold as in Admiral Richard Evelyn Byrd. Physical cold. Thinking back on it now I realize Mr. Bern spent a great deal of his time shivering.

In 1930 Mr. Bern was somewhere around forty. Now that I am fifty-eight I understand, or think I understand, things that did not even pluck at my attention in 1930. Now, today, if I were running a firm of certified public accountants with twenty-two staff members who had to be paid every Saturday at noon, I think I would do as much shivering as Mr. Bern did. Probably more. Friday night I could hear myself, sleepless, asking myself, sleepless: "Where is the damn money going to come from?"

Well, in theory, from clients. Maurice Saltzman & Company had quite a few. Dress manufacturers, hardware merchants, fabricators of leather goods, several cafeterias, shops on Grand Street that sold novelties and on Grand Concourse that sold wedding gowns, a locksmith, and many I remember not by what they sold to the public but by the faded and troubled faces of the men and women who owned them. In short, M.S.&Co. had enough clients to meet the payroll of their twenty-two man staff.

If they hadn't, the staff would never have grown to twenty-two. Or, having got there, the number would have been reduced as Mr. Bern and his partner lost clients. Ira Bern's problem was that he and his partner could never tell the precise moment when their firm had lost a client.

Most small businessmen in 1930 tended to think of their accountant's monthly fee the way Rawdon Crawley and

Becky Sharp thought of the bill from their wine merchants. They had every intention of paying it. Really, they had. But they had so many other unpaid bills that the wine merchant tended to be assigned a pretty low niche on their list. While most of Mr. Bern's clients were prompt in paying their rent and telephone bills, they tended to run behind in paying their monthly fees to Maurice Saltzman & Company.

What drove Mr. Bern crazy was the gap between cajolery and threat. Every morning when I brought his beautifully shined vici kids back into his office he was on the phone playing one or two highly dramatic roles.

First role:

"Lennie, for God's sake, you think I'm a bank? You haven't sent me a dime since May. Not a dime. Five months behind, Lennie. Five audits. You know what that means? Twenty weeks I've been paying out salaries to my staff. Twenty weeks, Lennie. Where do you think I get the cash to pay my men? You think I got a printing press in the cellar? I make my own ten-dollar bills? For God's sake, Lennie, you're one of my oldest and one of my most valued clients. I take care of your books like they were my own. My father should get such attention from me as you get. Be human, Lennie. Have a heart. You can't pay the whole bill? So all right. Send a check on account. But for God's sake, Lennie, send *something*!"

One of my most crucial duties as an employee of M.S.&Co. was helping, every morning between 10:15 and 10:30, to get Mr. Bern back into his freshly shined shoes. He had small feet, but Mr. Bern was a vain man and his shoes were smaller than they should have been.

Vanity of vanities, sayeth the Preacher, but the Preacher uttereth not a syllable about tight shoes. With the help of a shoehorn I managed to get Mr. Bern back into his, but I had to do it on my knees. The task was simple enough. A matter of mere leverage. But it was much simpler when Mr. Bern on the phone was playing the first of his two dramatic roles: cajoling.

For this performance he employed only the upper registers of his voice and the hand with which he was not holding the telephone receiver to his ear. When Mr. Bern was playing the second of his dramatic roles, I had trouble. For this performance he employed his feet for emphasis.

"Mr. Shimnitz? This is Ira Bern."

Stamp of right foot, narrowly missing Benney Kramer's left hand.

"Ira Bern, Maurice Saltzman & Company. Right. Now, Mr. Shimnitz, I think you should be informed that I am running a business, not an eleemosynary institution."

Stamp of left foot, not quite missing the knuckle of Benny's right hand. A small scrape. Not enough to worry about. Even in those days I did not infect easily.

"Do you realize what it means, Mr. Shimnitz, when you are callous enough not to pay one of my bills promptly? Let me tell you, Mr. Shimnitz, let me tell you what it means. It means you are striking a blow at the faith of the average citizen in the country's movers and shakers. We are in the depths of a depression, Mr. Shimnitz. Are you aware of that? The leaders in the White House don't know their ass from a hot rock how to get us out of it, Mr. Shimnitz. To be blunt about it, Mr. Hoover is a *putz,* Mr. Shimnitz. Do you know that? Well, Mr. Shimnitz?"

Stamp of right foot. Edge of vici kid toe scrapes Benny's thumb. Slow, hot, searing pain starts up hand and wrist.

"Well, Mr. Shimnitz, the country knows it. Oh, boy, do they know it, Mr. Shimnitz. The people who make up the country, the men selling apples on street corners, the poor bastards on the bread lines, do they believe in their leaders? Mr. Hoover? Mr. Curtis? The rest of those jerks down in Washington? Does the guy in the street believe them? You bet your ass, Mr. Shimnitz, they don't. And after you bet your ass, Mr. Shimnitz, you can bet your bottom dollar. What they believe in is the people who are still in a position to pay their salaries. People like me, Mr. Shimnitz. I'm no Herbert Hoover. I'm no Charlie Curtis. I'm just a common ordinary garden-variety American, Mr. Shimnitz. I'm just plain Ira Bern, a certified public accountant with a staff of twenty-two. Ira Bern, a simple Paul Revere type

33

patriot. And it's people like you, Mr. Shimnitz, who are cutting the ground from under the feet of the great patriots of this country. Yes, patriots. People like me, Mr. Ira Bern, who are fighting to prevent the revolution. I am fighting to prevent it for every decent American citizen, including deadbeats like you, Mr. Shimnitz. But you're acting like a man who doesn't deserve it. You're acting like a slob, Mr. Shimnitz, and for slobs a Paul Revere don't lay down his life. Unless you put a check in the mail at once, unless you clear up your bill but I mean pronto, Mr. Shimnitz, no member of the staff of Maurice Saltman & Company will ever again show up in your lousy office. As of this moment, Mr. Shimnitz, you can go get yourself a new accountant."

Slam of receiver. Stamp of left foot. Ouch!

This particular morning, as I was sucking my bruised thumb, Mr. Bern's secretary opened the door.

"Could you see Mr. Shimnitz?" she said.

Mr. Bern glared at her. "What do you mean, could I see him?" he demanded. "I just hung up on the son of a bitch."

Miss Bienstock looked the way she looked every morning when she handed me the sorted mail for distribution around the office. Or when I brought her a midafternoon container of coffee. Perplexed.

"Oh, no, Mr. Bern," said Miss Bienstock. No change of expression. No change, that is, from her normal perplexity. "That was Mr. Roon you just hung up on."

"Oh, my God," Mr. Bern said. "No!"

"Mr. Bern," Miss Bienstock said. "I don't understand. Mr. Shimnitz is out in the reception room. He came in a few minutes ago. You couldn't have been talking to him on the phone."

Consternation gave way to appalled astonishment. Not for the first time, incidentally. With Mr. Bern it was a common parlay.

"And it was Mr. Roon I was talking to?" he said in a choked voice.

"Yes, sir," Miss Bienstock said.

I suddenly couldn't stand the way Mr. Bern looked.

34

"Mr. Bern," I said, "I think all that happened, I think you got the names wrong, that's all, Mr. Bern."

He turned to stare at me. "What?"

I had a stab of revelation: Mr. Bern did not know who I was!

I had been crawling around his feet for seven months, shoehorning him into his vici kids, but to Ira Bern, it came to me in a moment of shock, I was not a human being. I was just a presence that did things. For the first time in my life I felt the compulsion to establish my identity.

"All you did, Mr. Bern," I said firmly, "you thought you were talking to Mr. Shimnitz, but you were actually talking to Mr. Roon. That's all."

In the realm of seminal revelations my statement hardly ranked with the "Eureka!" of Archimedes. Yet in the mind of Ira Bern, which I could not of course fathom, but in his eyes, which were as clearly visible as the sun at high noon, I could see that I had struck a hopeful note.

"That's right," Mr. Bern said slowly. Then, a bit more quickly. "Sure that's right." His expression shifted frantically from horror to nervously troubled scrambling for a rope ladder, so to speak, out of disaster. "It was just a mistake," Ira Bern said. "I would never talk that way to Mr. Roon."

I wouldn't have thought so. Mr. Roon was the president of I.G. Roon, Ltd. The most important client on the Maurice Saltzman & Company list. Most important in those days meant, as I suppose in these days it still does, most lucrative. Mr. Roon, or his Ltd., was in the rabbit business.

Mr. Roon had been born in Adelaide, Australia. Of how he spent his life between 1865, when all my research indicates he surfaced, and 1930, when he came into my life, I am totally ignorant. All I know is that in 1930, while I was just beginning my tour of duty with Maurice Saltzman & Company, Mr. Roon was sixty-five years old, he was the central figure in a British corporation with offices on West 21st Street in New York City, and he or his corporation owned rabbit farms in Australia. These farms supplied a good deal of the raw material for the hat factories of Danbury, Connecticut.

I had never as a boy thought much about hats. The kids I grew up with on East Fourth Street never wore hats except when we went to *cheder*, or Hebrew school, and to the synagogue on Saturdays. On these occasions we wore what were then known as caps. I think they still are. I see them regularly in newspaper photographs, looking not much different, on the heads of world-famous golfers playing at the Royal and Ancient in St. Andrews. Loose round affairs, somewhat like flat cabbages on top, with peaks in front presumably to shield the player's eyes from the sun. Nobody played golf on East Fourth Street, and there was very little sun, but that's what we wore to *cheder* and synagogue.

Hats were different. Hats were homburgs and fedoras and snap brims. Things I saw only rarely. Grooms wore them to their weddings. Or relatives to funerals. But in my youth on East Fourth Street I had attended very few weddings, and fewer funerals. Life, as I lumbered through my first two decades of it, had not yet struck an elegiac note. I was surprised, therefore, to discover when I came to work for M.S. & Co. that many men wore hats regularly, that the material from which hats were made was rabbit fur, and that one of the leading suppliers of rabbit fur to the hat manufacturers of Danbury, Connecticut, was I.G. Roon, Ltd. Our client.

Indeed, our best client. With Mr. Roon it was never necessary for Ira Bern to play either of his two highly dramatic roles on the telephone. Mr. Roon always paid his auditing bills promptly.

"Sure it was a mistake," Mr. Bern said desperately, as though he were pleading for forgiveness. "I would never talk like that to Mr. Roon. Would I, Miss Bienstock?"

"Of course not," she said.

"Then it's got to be a mistake," Ira Bern said. His expression changed. A look of accusation invaded his rubbery face. "Miss Bienstock," Ira Bern said sternly, "how could I make such a mistake?"

36

If you stand still long enough, life catches up with you. If your face is fixed permanently in the same expression, moments will inevitably arrive when you could not have worn a more perfectly appropriate expression. This was such a moment. Miss Bienstock's moment.

"I don't know," she said. Even her voice sounded perplexed. "The phone rang, and a man's voice said he wanted to talk to you, and it sounded like Mr. Shimnitz, so I put him through."

"You mean you didn't ask him what his name was?" Mr. Bern said. The stern expression vanished. Disbelief, like the tides of Fundy, came racing in. "You mean without knowing who you were putting on my wire you told me it was Mr. Shimnitz calling?"

"I thought it was Mr. Shimnitz," Miss Bienstock said. "I talk to him all the time. It certainly sounded like Mr. Shimnitz."

"It sounded like Mr. Shimnitz?"

A new expression on Mr. Bern's face. Not quite incredulity. Not quite astonishment. A shading of both.

"Miss Bienstock," he said. "To you Mr. Roon sounded like Mr. Shimnitz?" He strode to the door, hauled it open, and bellowed: "Mr. Shimnitz, come on in here!"

Mr. Bern's office door was perhaps four feet from the reception room. His roaring voice came bouncing back from the walls of that tiny chamber like a basketball snapped back into play. Mr. Shimnitz came hurtling with it. Mr. Bern stepped back. Mr. Shimnitz, looking somewhat confused, stood among us.

"Say a few words," Mr. Bern ordered.

Like all chronic debtors, Mr. Shimnitz had only two speeds on his gearbox: the bluff and the cringe. He swung his head to look at everybody in the room, as though reading our faces could help him decide which switch to throw. Since I was as confused as he was, Mr. Shimnitz could see at once that I was a total loss to him, and Miss Bienstock's expression of permanent perplexity was no road out of his dilemma. The only possible guide was Mr. Bern, and Mr. Bern was glaring. Mr. Shimnitz chose the cringe.

"A few words about what?" he said.

"What the hell do I care about what?" Mr. Bern thundered. "Just say a few words!"

Mr. Shimnitz scratched his head. It was bald. I could hear his fingernails rasping across the naked scalp.

"Good morning?" he said tentatively.

"Jesus Christ!" Mr. Bern shrieked. "Is that the best you can do?"

Mr. Shimnitz stepped back, as though he expected to be punished physically. I would not have been surprised if he had been.

"I don't understand what you want," he said.

"Who gives a damn what you understand or don't understand?" Mr. Bern said. "I'm not asking you to pay your lousy past due bills. I'm asking you to do something it won't cost you a nickel. Just say a few words."

Miss Bienstock leaned over and whispered in Mr. Bern's ear. He nodded and turned back to Mr. Shimnitz.

"Tell us why you came here today."

Having opted for the cringe, Mr. Shimnitz could not reverse himself. He looked around the room the way, in silent movies, the innocent country girl who has been kidnapped by a white slave ring looks around at the captors who have just ordered her to disrobe.

"I would like to tell you that in private, Mr. Bern, please."

"For a guy who is five months behind in his bills," Ira Bern said, "this is as much privacy as you're going to get. Speak up. Why did you come here today?"

"Well, uh, I'm afraid I won't be able to pay this month's bill either, Mr. Bern, but please don't cut me off because I got this letter from the Internal Revenue on my nineteen twenty-nine return, and I need your help to deal with them, and I promise, I honest to God promise, next month, honest, I'll clear up the whole bill, honest I will, if you'll just—"

Mr. Bern cut into the flow of words that weren't really words, but a sort of open faucet of tearless tears, with a sharp question directed at Miss Bienstock.

"This sounds to you like Mr. Roon?"

38

"I don't know," Miss Bienstock said. "I never heard Mr. Roon speak."

Ira Bern blinked at her. "You never heard Mr. Roon speak?" he said.

"No, sir," Miss Bienstock said. "He's never been here in the office, and I never had occasion to speak to him on the phone."

It was a prefectly sensible answer, I thought, but I felt there was something odd about it. If I had made it, the oddity would not have struck me. After all, I had been working for M.S.&Co. for only a few months. There were many of the firm's clients I had never seen, and almost none to whom I had talked on the phone. But Miss Bienstock had been Ira Bern's secretary for almost five years. In addition to her other duties, she took her turn at the switchboard when the regular operator went to lunch or to the washroom or was out sick. Was it really possible that she had never heard on the phone the voice of the firm's most lucrative client?

"Mr. Bern, please listen. I'll pay up next month, honest I will, but first will you handle this tax audit for me, my nineteen twenty-nine return, they say I owe them over—"

"Beat it!" Mr. Bern said. He shoved Mr. Shimnitz out the door. "And don't come back without a check!" Mr. Bern shouted into the corridor.

He pulled the door shut, went to his desk, and fell into the leather chair with a small, weary sigh of defeat. Miss Bienstock watched him with her usual expression, but I sensed she was frightened. Perhaps I felt this because I was frightened. It was a time when large issues were settled by small things. I didn't know how lucrative a client Mr. Roon was, but it was possible that if Maurice Saltzman & Company lost his monthly payment, the staff would have to be reduced. And who was more reducible than the newest and youngest employee?

I was reminded of the gas mantles we used for illumination down on East Fourth Street. They were small balls of white material more fragile than eggshells. If you touched them with nothing but flame they would ignite and glow

39

serviceably for months. sometimes longer. But if your hand shook when you applied the match, so that the ball of white was tapped or even brushed, it disintegrated at once into a puff of fine powder. The ambience in Mr. Bern's office at that moment was, I thought, not dissimilar.

"All right," he said in a low voice. "Get Mr. Roon back on the phone, and I'll see what I can do to apologize and maybe make him believe I thought I was talking to somebody else."

Miss Bienstock seemed to hesitate. Then she stepped around the desk, bent down, and whispered something in Mr. Bern's ear. My heart lurched. I thought I had heard my name. Mr. Bern's glance came up. His eyes told me I had indeed heard my name. Mr. Bern's eyes narrowed. He nodded.

"Good thinking," he said to Miss Bienstock.

She straightened up. Now they both were staring at me. I might have been a gobbler in a pen of turkeys into which a husband and wife were staring, trying to decide which one to choose for their Thanksgiving table.

"Benny," Mr. Bern said.

"Yes, sir?"

"I want you to do something."

"Yes, sir?"

Mr. Bern was writing in longhand on one of the firm's letterheads. I knew at once something ususual was in the wind. Mr. Bern enjoyed the process of dictating. I had the feeling he felt it was one of the appurtenances of success. There was, however, one office activity that Mr. Bern insisted on performing in longhand: sending out the monthly bills to the firm's clients. It seemed odd, because the fees were fixed and the list of clients was neatly indexed in a loose-leaf notebook on Miss Bienstock's desk. All she had to do was run the bills through her typewriter, and Mr. Bern would have been spared an onerous chore. Except that I don't think he found it onerous. I think he found in it what I imagine I would have found: a small, repeated ritual, in the very discomfort of performing which was contained the repeated reminder that for him the world had changed.

East Fifth Street boys, like Fourth Street boys, spent their early lives on the receiving end of bills. Or rather their parents did. From the landlord, from the gas company, from the coal merchant. What a secret thrill it must have been to Ira Bern to be reminded that now he was on the sending end!

I think it was the pleasure he took in this reminder that had dictated the choice of the instrument he used. It was a memorable tool.

By 1930 the fountain pen had already become a fairly sophisticated implement available to almost everybody. Even I owned a slender salmon-colored Parker, my father's barmitzvah present, with at the top a plunger for filling. Mr. Bern, however, used what even in 1930 must have been a museum piece. A very old Waterman, as long and as thick around as a banana. To fill it he needed help, which it was one of my duties to provide.

While I held the pen upright on his desk, writing end toward ceiling, Mr. Bern would unscrew the section that contained the gold penpoint. What remained was an enormous black tube or barrel. Into this he would empty an entire bottle of Waterman's blue-black, and screw the point back into place. When filled, this implement was not much lighter in weight than a sculptor's chisel. Yet on the first of every month Mr. Bern, happily hunched over his desk, would shove this writing tool back and forth for three or four hours at a time without pausing for rest.

To see him pushing this huge pen now, in the middle of the month, across one of his letterheads was an event so unusual that it jolted me.

"Now, Benny," Mr. Bern said. "Here's what I want you to do." He signed his name with a flourish, pulled an envelope from his drawer, and carefully lettered a name and address on the envelope. "I want you to take this over to Mr. Roon's office right away and give it to him personally. Personally, you hear?"

"Yes, sir," I said.

Mr. Bern lifted the envelope flap and licked it wet. Then he sealed it down with broad, totally unnecessary sweeps of both palms across his desk blotter. It was as though the more energy he poured into sealing his handwritten letter the more confidence he gained in what the contents could do for him.

"You know where Mr. Roon's office is?" Mr. Bern asked.

I didn't. I had never been there. But I knew how to read an address, and Mr. Bern had inscribed this one on the envelope in letters half an inch high.

"Yes, sir," I said.

Mr. Bern handed me the envelope. "Remember what I told you," he said. "To Mr. Roon in person. Anybody in the office, a bookkeeper or somebody, they say give it to me, I'll see he gets it, nothing doing. You want to deliver this to Mr. Roon personally. He's out? You'll wait. He's in a meeting? You'll wait until the meeting is over. To Mr. Roon in person only. Understand?"

"Yes, sir," I said.

Then Mr. Bern did a surprising thing. He pulled his wallet from his hip pocket, slid out a dollar bill, and placed it on top of the envelope in my hand.

"Take a taxi," he said.

A man who was capable of giving his office boy a dime every morning so the boy could enjoy a cuppa cawfee and a ruggle while he watched his boss's shoes being shined, obviously possessed at least some generous instincts. But I was fairly certain none of these instincts was involved in Mr. Bern's astonishing gesture on that morning of the Shimnitz-Roon confusion. In 1930 generosity to office boys stopped at a dime.

The address was on West 21st Street, between Seventh and Eighth avenues. A mere fifteen blocks. On nights when I could get out of the office early enough to save the nickel fare, I walked almost twice that distance to my classes in the 23rd Street branch of C.C.N.Y. I knew I could almost certainly walk from the offices of M.S.&Co. to the Roon office in a quarter of an hour. But I knew something else:

the contents of the letter Mr. Bern had entrusted to my care.

Though I had not read the words, I knew the emotion out of which they had come. It was evident from the whispering Miss Bienstock had done in Mr. Bern's ear immediately following his request that she get Mr. Roon on the phone. The letter was obviously a substitute for the spoken apology Mr. Bern had planned. Perhaps Miss Bienstock always looked perplexed because she was constantly struggling inside her head to invent improvements on Mr. Bern's moves.

They were, on the whole, good moves. Good enough, at any rate, to keep M.S.&Co. afloat in a time of many sinkings. But Mr. Bern was erratic. From a man like Mr. Bern a personal note was bound to be more effective than a phone call. Not only would it indicate an honest regret for a boorish mistake without the distraction of a boorish voice. It would also keep Mr. Bern off the phone, where he sometimes forgot whether he was cajoling or threatening.

Unlike Mr. Bern's morning dime, however, which represented an attempt to bring a few moments of pleasure into the bleak life of an underling, his dollar represented a dilemma of distressing dimensions for that same underling.

If I took a taxi and got to Mr. Roon with Mr. Bern's letter in the next few minutes, the Roon account might be saved for M.S.&Co. If I walked, and pocketed the dollar, the letter might come into Mr. Roon's hands too late. His anger might be building up right now to explosive proportions. Written apologies would be too late. Maurice Saltzman & Company would lose the Roon account. And I, of course, as the firm's newest and youngest employee, would be the first to be fired. My first lesson in irony.

At that time I don't remember getting many. Which is why I remember this one.

That dollar was killing me.

Before it did, I was saved. By something out of my past. At that time I didn't have much past. But for this moral dilemma I had just enough.

"Hey, Benny!"

43

I looked up. Struggling with my moral dilemma, I had not realized I had come down from the M.S.&Co. office into the street. I saw now that the flow of Seventh Avenue traffic had stopped for a red light at the 34th Street corner. Most of the traffic on Seventh Avenue, then as now, consisted of huge garment-center trucks. They were hearselike affairs, not unlike the vans in which horses are transported from race track to race track. On the front seat of the truck that had stopped practically at my feet sat Hot Cakes Rabinowitz. He had been in my scout troop down on East Fourth Street. Troop 244, of which I had been senior patrol leader. I had not seen him since the graduation exercises at Thomas Jefferson High.

"How you been?" he said.

"Pretty good," I said. "You?"

"Fine. How's your mother?"

The driver leaned across Hot Cakes. "You two mind stopping this class reunion? That light's gonna change."

"Where you going?" Hot Cakes said.

"Downtown," I said.

He opened the door of the truck and slid his rear end over toward the driver. "Hop in," he said.

I hopped in and pulled the door shut. The light changed. The driver put the truck into gear and we rolled off down Seventh Avenue.

"Whereabouts downtown?"

"Twenty-first and Seventh," I said.

"This is your lucky day, kid," the driver said. "We're taking this load to Ohrbach's on Fourteenth. Okay if we drop you at the corner of Twenty-first and Seventh?"

"That will be fine," I said. "Thank you very much."

Then Hot Cakes and I seemed to become aware of each other. He was wearing a pair of battered khaki pants, a torn and sweaty T-shirt, a pair of scuffed sneakers, and he smelled like the locker room in Thomas Jefferson High after a basketball game. I was wearing my graduation suit and shoes, my mother's beautifully laundered shirt, a tie that had been given to me for my bar mitzvah by my Aunt Sarah from New Haven, and I was certain I smelled better than Hot Cakes Rabinowitz. It would have been difficult to smell worse.

"You look like you're doing pretty good," Hot Cakes said.

"Not bad," I said. "It looks better than it is only because it's clean. A firm of certified public accountants. How about you?"

"I'm with Built-In Uplift Frocks, Inc.," Hot Cakes said. "It's actually not as bad as it looks because it looks so dirty. Right, Al?"

Al was dressed exactly as Hot Cakes was dressed, but Al was older, in his forties, I guessed, and he had not shaved for several days.

"It stinks," he said. "But these days what doesn't?"

"You still down on Fourth?" Hot Cakes said.

"No," I said. "We moved to the Bronx three months ago."

"Us, too," Hot Cakes said. "Just a coupla weeks ago. Where you?"

"Tiffany Street," I said.

"Jesus," Hot Cakes said with a grin. "We're just around the corner. Fox Street."

"Okay, Tiffany," the driver said as he pulled the truck up to the curb at 21st Street. "Here's your stop."

"Maybe we could get together?" Hot Cakes said.

We had never been close friends. In fact, I knew very little about him except that he had been very good at wig-wagging one-flag Morse code. But we had come from the same country, so to speak, and now we had rediscovered each other in an alien land. Previous friendship was unnecessary. From now on only death could us part.

"I'd like that," I said.

I opened the truck door and jumped down to the sidewalk. Hot Cakes moved over to the window and pulled the door shut. Al started the truck.

"Where can I reach you?" Hot Cakes called.

I replied with a phrase I'd learned from listening to Mr. Bern. It packed weight.

"I'm in the phone book," I called back.

45

The truck disappeared into the flow of downtown traffic. I turned west. Walking up 21st Street toward Mr. Roon's address, I was in the grip of two emotions. I felt virtuous, and I felt clever. I felt virtuous because I had arrived at Mr. Roon's address as rapidly as a taxi could have carried me. I felt clever because I had made a dollar on the deal. In the lobby I forgot my feelings.

It did not look much different from the lobbies of the other loft buildings in which Maurice Saltzman & Company clients functioned, and yet it seemed totally different. The difference puzzled me. I looked around the brown marble walls, but learned nothing. I walked over to the directory, found on the black felt the little white metal letters that spelled out I. G. ROON, LTD. 1201, and pushed the elevator button. As the car came rumbling down the shaft, I found myself sniffing. For what? The car arrived. As soon as I stepped in, and the operator slammed the door, I knew what was different about this building. It was the smell.

All the other loft buildings I knew, most of them on Seventh Avenue, had very distinctive odors. Not necessarily unpleasant. In fact, as you moved up the avenue from 34th Street (dresses) to 37th (frocks) toward Times Square (gowns), in the buildings around 39th Street, where the more expensive gowns were manufactured, the smell was not unlike that of the perfume shop in Macy's. The models were higher priced. The things with which they sprayed themselves came from distant countries. The Roon building was totally different. This building smelled clean.

"Twelve, please," I said.

The door marked I. G. ROON, LTD. 1201 was at the end of a long brown marble corridor. Except for being obviously very old, the door looked like any other office door. What I found behind it did not. The room into which I stepped could have served as the model for the Phiz drawing of the office in which the brothers Cheeryble functioned in *Nicholas Nickleby*.

The floor was covered with very old green carpeting. It was dotted here and there with small islands of brown where the green nap had worn away and the cording showed through. On the walls hung what looked like steel engravings of rolling farm country. I counted eight. Somehow they all looked alike, perhaps because they were all framed by the same kind of narrow bands of black wood.

One picture, over the door at the far end of the room, I did recognize. I had seen it many times in my high school history textbook. It was a picture of Queen Victoria, full-face, arms folded across her plump little middle, looking exactly the way a few years later Helen Hayes would look.

There was nothing unusual about most of the furnishings. Rows of very old dark green filing cabinets. I could tell they were old by the way the drawers sagged at the corners. A couple of long dark brown tables, stacked neatly with what looked like fat reference books, stood side by side against one wall. In one corner a wooden umbrella stand with a square brass pan in the bottom leaned over slightly because one of the knobbed legs was missing.

Two things, however, were so unusual that I felt, for a startled moment, they must have been purchased from the Cheeryble brothers when Dickens was shoehorned into the Poet's Corner in Westminster Abbey. Two things I had never seen before. A couple of stand-up desks. One on either side of the room.

Then I saw the two people in the room, and I forgot the desks.

At one of them, working busily over a fat ledger, stood a tall old lady. She wore a black alpaca dress buttoned up to her throat and held at the neck by a yellowing ivory cameo. At the other desk stood an old man working over two ledgers. He was bald, with tufts of white over the ears. He wore a gray alpaca jacket. What looked like a pair of black stockings without bottoms were pulled up on his arms from wrist to elbow, apparently to protect the sleeves of his coat. As he moved his head from side to side, glancing from one ledger to the other, I could see he had a pencil tucked over each ear.

Even more arresting than the appearance of these two people, and the desks at which they were working, was the

47

way they were working: facing opposite walls, their backs to each other.

I had time to take all this in for a somewhat disconcerting reason. Or rather, I realized after a while I was disconcerted because I'd had time to take all this in. There was a small, black bell over the door. An old-fashioned bell with a clapper. It was fixed in such a way that, when somebody entered, the corner of the door punched the bell and set it tinkling. It was not until the tinkling stopped that I realized neither the old man nor the old woman had looked up. They went right on working away at their ledgers.

It was the sort of situation I had never before experienced. I don't suppose my experience was unique, but it seems likely. How often would a young man have occasion to attract the attention of adults who are ignoring him? Clawing through my mind for examples of such occasions, I remembered a comic-strip character named Harold Teen who suffered endless misadventures every morning in the pages of the *Daily News*. Harold was constantly being ignored by his high school principal, to whose office Harold had been summoned for disciplinary action, or by the fathers of the girls on whom he called. After shifting uneasily from one foot to another for a long time, Harold Teen always broke the silence by saying, in a balloon over his head: "Ahem!"

I could not manage the balloon, but I had no trouble exploding a good, loud "Ahem!"

Without raising his head the old man said, "In a moment. In a moment."

He said it to one of the two ledgers on which he was working. Then he moved his head, made an entry in the second ledger, and looked up. Naturally, he was wearing thick glasses made of small fat halfmoons that were held to his head by thin gold strands. What else would a man working in the office of the Cheeryble brothers be wearing?

"What is it?" he said.

Staring at me over the halfmoon glasses he looked so severe that I was taken aback by the softness of his voice. He sounded kind.

48

"I'd like to see Mr. Roon, please," I said.

"About what?"

"I have a letter for him," I said. I held up the envelope. "From Mr. Bern."

"Maurice Saltzman & Company?"

"Yes, sir."

"I'll take it," the old man said.

He came across the room toward me. His gait was as surprising as his voice. He walked with long, crisp strides, as though he was trying to overtake someone without giving the appearance of hurrying.

"Are you Mr. Roon?" I said.

"No, but I'll take the letter to him." He held out his hand.

I put the envelope behind my back. "I'm sorry," I said. "My instructions were to give this to Mr. Roon personally."

"Don't be silly, boy, I'll take it in to him."

"No," I said. "I can't."

"What's the matter with you, boy?"

What was the matter with me was that my feeling of virtue and my feeling of cleverness about the way I had handled getting to Mr. Roon's office were going out the window in the face of a new threat.

"Mr. Bern told me if I did not deliver this letter to Mr. Roon in person he would fire me."

"That's ridiculous," the old man said. "I've known Ira Bern for years. Before Mr. Saltzman took him in as a partner. He used to come over here in person every month to do our audit. Ira Bern would never do such a thing."

There was a sound behind us. The old man and I both turned. The old lady was holding open the door at the far side of the room.

"Okay, kid," she said, and she jerked her thumb across her shoulder. "I told Mr. Roon you're here. Go on in."

Her voice was even more astonishing than the voice of the old man. She sounded like an enraged traffic cop with a bad bronchial ailment. I hurried across the room. Behind me the old man said petulantly, "Now, why did you want to do that?"

"Because I'm trying to get my work done," the old woman said. "How the hell can I do that with you braying away like a jackass?"

I walked through the door. She closed it behind me. A young man was standing behind a desk at the far side of the room, and when I say young I mean young. He could have graduated with me from Thomas Jefferson High School, until he opened his mouth.

"You have a letter for me?" he said.

Out of his mouth had come an English accent. Nobody with an English accent had graduated with me from Thomas Jefferson High School. If I didn't know every kid in the class any better than I knew Hot Cakes Rabinowitz, I had at one time or another during my four years at Thomas Jefferson heard every one of their voices. None of them had ever sounded like this kid behind the desk.

"Are you Mr. Roon?" I said.

I'm sure I sounded uneasy. I think I probably also sounded as though I didn't believe him.

He grinned. "I am," he said. "Truly I am." He held out his hand. I hesitated. He said, "Were you asked to get a receipt for the thing?"

"No," I said. "Mr. Bern just said I was to deliver it to Mr. Roon in person."

"Well," he said, "I'm Mr. Roon in person." He snapped his fingers. "Let's have it, shall we?"

I handed over the envelope. He tore it open, pulled out the M.S.&Co. letterhead, and read Mr. Bern's scrawled words, moving his lips as he did so. This gave me a chance to sneak a swift survey of the room. It was just about the same size as the outer room, and with a few exceptions much the same in atmosphere and furnishings. The same black-framed line drawings of rolling farmland. The same worn green carpet. The same brown furniture. Fewer but still the same kind of sagging green filing cabinets. There were no stand-up desks, however, and there was no picture of Queen Victoria. Oddly, I missed her. Where she should have been, behind the young man, there was a window that looked out on 21st Street, and his desk was an ordinary office flat top. I was paying so much attention to my surroundings because I sensed something was wrong with what was happening. This feeling was underscored when the young man started to laugh.

"Well," he said, "that explains it."

The fact that he was laughing did not sound as though he intended to fire Maurice Saltzman & Company as his auditors, which meant my job was safe. As safe, at any rate, as it had been half an hour ago, before Mr. Bern had started screaming on the telephone. This knowledge encouraged me to take a stab at erasing my feeling that something was wrong.

"Explains what?" I said.

I had almost added "sir." But I couldn't. Not to a kid who looked, even if he did not sound, as though he could have been in my graduating class at Thomas Jefferson High.

"Why, what happened on the phone just a bit ago," Mr. Roon said. Then he looked at me with suddenly aroused curiosity. "I take it you work for Mr. Bern?"

"That's right."

"Then it's possible you were there when it happened," Mr. Roon said. "Were you?"

"I don't know," I said. "I mean I don't know to what you're referring."

This was a lie, of course, but it was the only way I felt I could inch my way to the core of this puzzling experience. Besides, Mr. Roon seemed surprisingly amiable and chatty.

"Well, it was damned funny," Mr. Roon said. He plopped down into his chair behind his desk and pointed to another chair beside the desk. "Do sit," he said. "I want—"

The laughter overtook him again. While it had him tied up I noticed several things: his hair was blond; he needed a haircut; his teeth, at least the ones I was able to see, could have done with some attention from a dentist; and he was wearing a suit made of a material my father admired. My father, being in the pants business, although not very far in,

51

actually, after twenty-five years of making pockets had picked up some knowledge of fabrics. The shaggy herring-bone out of which Mr. Roon's suit had been cut, while identified by the rest of the world as tweed, was known to my father as tveet. This piece of tveet had been cut in an odd way. The lapels of Mr. Roon's single-breasted suit peaked upward, like the ears of a rabbit, and the three buttons down the front were set close together, like the keys of a cornet. He stopped laughing and waved Mr. Bern's letter in front of his face as though the laughter had made him feel warm and he was fanning himself.

"I rang up your office and asked for him," Mr. Roon said. "The girl who answered put me through at once, without asking my name, and before I had a chance to explain why I was calling, Mr. Bern—Mr. Bern—he—he—"

Mr. Roon dropped the letter on the desk and covered his face with both hands, as though he was ashamed of the new attack of laughter that was shaking him. When he came out of it his eyes were actually wet at the corners.

"I'm sorry," he said. He wiped away the tears with his knuckles, though he continued to heave gently up and down in his chair. "But it was the damndest bloody thing. As I said, I didn't even get a chance to say who I was, when he hurled himself at me."

Now a surprising thing happened. Mr. Roon drew himself up in his chair. He took the body of an imaginary telephone in his left hand. He lifted an imaginary receiver from its hook and placed it against his ear. Then, in spite of his unmistakable British accent, he launched into an unmistakable imitation of Mr. Bern.

"I am running a business, Mr. Shmootz, not an eleemo-synary institution. Do you realize what it means, Mr. Shmootz, when you are callous enough not to pay one of my bills promptly? Let me tell you, Mr. Shmootz, let me tell you what it means. You are striking a blow at the faith of the average citizen in the country's movers and shakers. We are in the depths of a depression, Mr. Shmootz. Are you aware of that? Are you—?"

This time it was my laughter that stopped him. Mr.

52

Roon was clearly pleased by my response. He cleared his throat, not unlike an actor acknowledging the applause of an audience.

"By the way," he said, "who is Mr. Shmootz?"

"No, not Shmootz," I said. "Shimnitz."

"Shimnitz?" Mr. Roon said.

"Yes," I said. "He's one of our clients. He's always way behind in his bills, and Mr. Bern is always yelling at him. I don't know what he wrote to you in that letter, but I guess he wanted to explain he didn't mean to talk to you like that. Mr. Bern thought he was talking to Mr. Shimnitz."

Mr. Roon scowled up at the ceiling.

"Shimnitz?" he said.

"Yes," I said.

"What does Shimnitz mean?"

It had never occurred to me that names had to mean something. Then it occurred to me that Shmootz meant something to Mr. Roon.

"I don't know what Shimnitz means," I said.

But I did know that *shmootz* in Yiddish meant dirt. How did Mr. Roon know what it meant? A boy with an accent like that? Named Roon?

"Well," I said, standing up, "I guess I'd better get back to the office."

Mr. Roon said, "Hahf a mo." He pulled a watch from his outer breast pocket. It hung from a thin gold chain that ended in a gold medallion stuck through the buttonhole of Mr. Roon's jacket. "Getting on for noon," he said, and dropped the watch back into his pocket. "Do you have a lunch date?"

He might just as well have asked where I housed my stable of polo ponies. In order to get through the week on my basic three dollars, lunch did not exist for me as a part of the day's program. This was no hardship. Between the staying-power breakfast my mother fed me before I left home, and the cuppa cawfee and ruggle to which Mr. Bern treated me while I was having his shoes shined, I had no trouble or discomfort in getting through to my Stewart's hot meal before classes at night. But it wasn't really a question of money. It was simply that lunch dates were outside my social experience.

In high school, to which I used to bring my lunch in a paper bag, I always ate the midday meal with a group of my friends on one of the benches in the yard. At night, in Stewart's, after my tray was loaded, I would look around the cafeteria and, if I saw a classmate, I would cross to his table and eat with him. But to make a date with someone in advance? A date to meet in a restaurant for the purpose of eating lunch? That happened only in novels.

"No," I said, "but Mr. Bern—"

"Why not come along with me?" Mr. Roon said, and then he seemed to grasp something. "I meant to say, come as my guest."

"But Mr. Bern—"

"Oh, I'll take care of that," Mr. Roon said. He reached across for his phone. "What's your office number?" I told him and Mr. Roon told it to the operator. A few moments later he was saying, "Maurice Saltzman & Company? This is Mr. Roon. I. G. Roon? May I talk with Mr. Bern? Thank you." Pause. "Oh, Mr. Bern. Sebastian Roon here."

Sebastian? What was that? It sounded like something out of Shakespeare. Miss Marine's English class took shape in my head. It *was* something out of Shakespeare Sebastian, a young gentleman of Messaline, brother of Viola. What was he doing here on 21st Street between Seventh and Eighth Avenues?

"Yes, he did give the letter to me," Mr. Roon was saying into the phone. "It was terribly decent of you to send it over, Mr. Bern, but really, you know, it was totally unnecessary. I knew at once that you had assumed you were talking to somebody else. It's quite all right, I assure you. No harm done, and no hard feelings. Quite. But I wonder if you would do me a favor? The young man who brought the letter? Oh, is that his name? Good. Could I borrow Mr. Kramer, do you think, for an hour or so? He's all fussed about getting back to the office on the double, but I do need him for a bit of business, and I wondered if you'd be good enough to allow him to—My word, no, I don't want

54

him for that long, but an hour or so of his time would be most helpful. Thank you so much, Mr. Bern, You are very kind." Mr. Roon hung up. He spread his hands wide and grinned at me. *"Voilà,"* he said. He came around the desk, put out his hand, and said, "Delighted to meet you, Mr. Benjamin Kramer."

We shook hands and I said, "Delighted to meet you, too, but I'm a little confused."

"About what?"

"You are Mr. Roon, aren't you?"

"Have been since birth," he said.

"But I just heard you tell Mr. Bern or the phone your name is Sebastian."

"Why shouldn't I? Since it is?"

"Then you're not. . . ?"

Mr. Roon laughed, "I see what's confusing you," he said. "No, I am not I. G. Roon. I. G. Roon is my uncle, who owns this bloody business. I'm his nephew Sebastian, and if I'm a good boy, and I don't blot my copybook, and if I play my cards correctly, someday *I* may own this bloody business. Now come along. I'm getting a bit peckish."

He led me into the other room. Neither the old man nor the old lady at the stand-up desks turned as we crossed to the front door. When he pulled it open, Sebastian Roon called to them across his shoulder, "Back at two."

In the elevator going down, I could see him examining me out of the corner of his eye. I didn't mind. I had been working downtown—when I first got the job with M.S.&Co., we were still living on East Fourth Street, and I thought of the area in which I worked as uptown—long enough to know that I was properly dressed. In fact, I had the feeling that my graduation suit was a bit more proper than Mr. Roon's oddly cut tveet. As for his blue pin-striped shirt, anybody could tell, anyway I could, that it was one of those two-collar jobs, and he was on his second day: the collar was crisp and fresh, but the cuffs were slightly soiled.

His tie. Well. Let's just say it wasn't even in the running

55

with my Aunt Sarah's bar mitzvah present. On the whole, in the muster-passing area of life, I felt I was passing this one without even panting. I was pleased, and I knew why.

In the move up from East Fourth Street to the Bronx, I had left behind something that had for so long been a part of my daily existence that it never occurred to me it would ever stop. But it had. On Tiffany Street I discovered I had left behind not only East Fourth Street, but all my friends. I missed them.

I had plenty of acquaintances. The members of Mr. Bern's staff. My fellow students in the evening classes at C.C.N.Y. Hannah Halpern. But the members of Mr. Bern's staff vanished after the workday was done. My fellow students materialized on 23rd Street at six in the evening and went home after classes. Occasionally I would see Hannah more than once a week, but it took a Jewish holiday to accomplish that. I no longer had what I'd had on East Fourth Street.

Natie Farkas. George Weitz. Chink Alberg. Kids I saw every day, all day. At school. At *cheder*. In the evening at boy scout troop meetings. Someone to walk to school with. Bat out a few fungoes. Play lievio. Swap dirty stories. Someone to discuss a piece of bad news with, or a rumor, or a plan, or make jokes with. Someone you could bring a piece of good news to, or a scrap of juicy gossip, or a troubling question, or with whom you could just share an idle hour sitting on the dock staring out at the river traffic. I no longer had any friends.

But I was keeping my eyes open. Which is why I was pleased when, in the elevator coming down from the I. G. Roon offices, I felt I had passed muster with Sebastian Roon. The thought that this might lead to our becoming friends was a startling mental leap, but pleasant to contemplate.

An Englishman and I? Friends? Like in the newsreels the Prince of Wales? Or in Dickens, David Copperfield and Steerforth? My friend? Jesus! On the other hand, he had invited me to lunch. Maybe . . . ?

I did not know it at the time, but this was my first experience with the heady temptations of snobbery.

"Do you mind if we go to Shane's?" Sebastian said when we were out in the street. Sebastian, eh? Not Sebastian Roon? Or Mr. Roon? Take it easy, Benny. You're not friends yet.

"On Twenty-third Street?" I said.

"Yes," he said. "I see you know it."

I knew it the way I knew the Metropolitan Opera House. Something I passed every day but had never been inside. Shane's was one of those restaurants that were mentioned regularly in the newspapers, usually in the Broadway columns, in connection with the activities of famous people: politicians, actors, sports figures, and radio personalities. The windows were curtained in heavy accordion-pleated brown rep, so it was impossible to see what went on inside. Whenever I walked by the restaurant on my way to C.C.N.Y., however, I would break step for a moment in the hope that someone would shove the door open and I might get a glimpse of the interior.

I never did. All I ever saw was the disemboweled deer that hung by its tied rear legs on a hook at one side of the door when venison was in season, and the cluster of grouse, tied together like a bouquet of feathers, heads down, that replaced the deer when the venison season was over. Or maybe it was the other way around. I never understood why Shane's did not serve venison and grouse at the same time, but I did understand that I had just had an unusual invitation.

"No," I said, "I don't know it. But I know about it. I mean I've never been there, but I read about Shane's in the papers all the time."

"Good," Sebastian Roon said. "Then you're in for a treat. At least I hope you'll find it a treat. The food's jolly good."

I didn't doubt it. Not only because it was a reasonable guess to draw the inference that a restaurant frequented by famous people would have to serve food that was jolly good, but also because coming to work on my first job uptown—now downtown—had caused me to experience a shock of disloyalty to my mother.

Like most kids on East Fourth Street, I had never eaten anything but my mother's cooking. I had always found it adequate. This may sound disparaging. Not at all. It seems to me the accurate word for describing a piece of daily existence without which you could not continue to exist and about which you have no complaints. Like breathing. Or sleeping. Some of the things my mother cooked pleased me more than others, of course, but none displeased me. Whether her best was better or worse than the cooking of somebody else, I did not know. The question never crossed my mind. How could it? I had never eaten anybody else's cooking.

Then I went to work on 34th Street, and my horizons, which I had been prepared to see widen, did more than that: they exploded. It happened one day while I was waiting for Mr. Bern's shoes to be shined.

I had got out of bed with a slightly upset stomach. So, instead of having my usual ruggle and cuppa cawfee, I kept the dime in my pocket. Later in the day, on my way to Lou G. Siegel's delicatessen on 39th Street for Mr. Bern's daily pastrami sandwich, I made the discovery that my morning queasiness had given way to midday hunger. Fortunately, I was on my way toward, not back from, Lou G. Siegel's. So I was not yet carrying the sandwich that would be considerably reduced in temperature if, before delivering the pastrami sandwich to Mr. Bern, I took time out to get something to ear for myself. Also, at that moment on my way uptown, I happened to be passing the Automat next to Macy's.

I had walked in and looked around the place several times. I was fascinated by the little windows out of which popped foods I had never heard of, but my fascination did not lead me to satisfy my curiosity. For a man working on a three-dollar-a-week base allowance, the prices were too high. On this day, however, I had a windfall: the dime I had not spent on my morning ruggle and cuppa cawfee. I did not wait to hear the arguments of caution surfacing in my head like bubbles of fat in a pot of boiling soup. I turned into the Automat.

The first thing you saw when you came in was the wall of sandwiches on the left. And the first thing I saw was in the top window of the first vertical row of windows: a big round roll, dark brown, covered with sesame seeds. It was sliced in half horizontally across the middle. The top half was separated from the bottom half by two thick slabs of pink meat. To the right of the window, in black letters on a white celluloid card set in a silver slot was printed: HAM SANDWICH 2 NICKLES.

It could not have been more terrifying to a boy from East Fourth Street and Tiffany Street if the words on the card had read: ABANDON HOPE, ALL YE WHO ENTER HERE.

My mother had always, of course, operated a strictly kosher kitchen. The concept of ham had never even crossed my consciousness, much less my lips. But I was not at the moment in my mother's kitchen. Nor was I, in actual fact, in my right mind. It was as though the notion of committing murder had crossed my consciousness as an idle fancy and then, to my horror, I found myself knife in hand, standing over a helpless victim.

I sent cautious glances around the crowded restaurant. Quickly, furtively, I dropped in my two nickles. I twisted the knob. The small glass door popped open. I pulled out the plate. Head bowed, I went to a table against the wall, sat down and picked up the sandwich. I took my first bite, and was lost. I have never been the same since.

Not only because until that moment I had never tasted anything so good. My life was changed irrevocably because with that initial pleasure came the knowledge that there were more delicious things in the world than the boiled chicken my mother had all my life set before me.

I carried the burden of disloyalty with a dismay and pain that were, of course, foolishly disproportionate. But I kept right on eating ham sandwiches, and soon the pain of my disloyalty vanished. Especially when I discovered bacon and eggs.

Nonetheless, any discussion of food in my presence

would jog the old tremors. By assuring me that I would find the food in Shane's jolly good, Sebastian Roon had hit me where I still, on occasion, lived. I forgot the address, so to speak, as soon as we entered the restaurant.

The only restaurants in which I had previously set foot were, as I have indicated, the Automat and Stewart's cafeteria. They were dissimilar, of course, but the dissimilarity was mechanical: the way the food was dispensed. In the Automat it came popping out of little holes in the wall. In Stewart's you picked it up from steam tables and long glass shelves arranged like showcases. The atmosphere in both restaurants, however, was the same.

Hurrying people. Bright lighting. A ceaseless assault of confusing noise: voices calling; the whir of revolving doors; dishes and silver being dropped into metal carts; knives and forks clattering onto trays; serving spoons being banged free of excess gravy against the aluminum pots on the steam tables; shouts from the kitchen across the ledges of the windows through which batches of freshly cooked food were passed to the servers; an occasional plate or coffee cup shattering to fragments on the marble floors.

I had always found the noise attractive. I had come to expect it as a natural accompaniment to the pleasant activity of consuming food in public. I did not think it through, but I see now how my thoughts must have been going.

If you got this much action when you stepped into comparatively modest-priced restaurants like the Automat for a ham sandwich or Stewart's for a plate of pot roast, the least you could expect when you entered a joint that hung gutted deer and clusters of grouse on the part of the front door where my father nailed our mezuzah, was the Edwin Franko Goldman band playing a Sousa march while Al Jolson bellowed "Mammy."

You could expect it, yes. But what you would get is what I got: a feeling that I had stepped into the place of worship dedicated to an obscure but well-to-do sect. The priests wore black mess jackets with red vests fastened by silver buttons. They moved about on their toes as, in hushed silence, they carried food and drink to votaries seated at tables covered with red and white checked tablecloths.

We were approached by a tall white-haired old man with a face he had obviously stolen from El Greco's portrait of St. Jerome. He bowed to Sebastian Roon. I couldn't believe I had actually seen it. But I had. The old man bowed!

"Mr Roon," he said.

"Hello, George," Sebastian Roon said. "This is a friend of mine, Mr. Kramer."

The old man bowed again. "Delighted to meet you, Mr. Kramer."

Then I realized the old man had bowed to me.

"We're famished," Seabstian Roon said. "Can you feed us?"

"With pleasure," George said. "This way, please."

It was only because he turned so promptly that he did not notice I had bowed back to him. But Sebastian Roon had noticed, and he grinned.

"Not necessary, old boy," he said, taking my arm. "He gets tipped quite liberally."

George stopped at a small round table to the left of the door and waited for us to catch up. He helped Sebastian Roon into his chair. By the time George turned to help me, I was already seated. I wondered if I should have waited for him. Nobody had ever helped me into a chair. Not since I was a little boy, anyway, when I could not get up to the seat on my own. I decided not to do anything on my own. I would watch Sabastin Roon and do whatever he did. The next thing he did was sneeze.

"Gesundheit," said George.

"Thank you," said Roon. He gave me a funny look, as though he wanted to say something but was not sure I would understand. Finally, he turned to George and said, "I think we might risk a couple of cups of coffee to start."

"Very good," said George.

He bowed and went away. I have never been in this sort of restaurant, so I assumed things were done not quite the way they were done in the Automat and in Stewart's. Start-

61

ing a meal with a cup of coffee seemed peculiar, but so did having El Greco's St. Jerome bow to a kid from Thomas Jefferson High School who fetched hot pastrami sandwiches from Lou G. Siegel's for Ira Bern.

"Do you know this city very well?" Sebastian Roon said.

It was like asking Ulysses if he knew the Aegean.

"Parts of it," I said. "I know downtown pretty well. I was born on East Fourth Street."

"What's that?" Roon said.

The question jolted me. I had never heard one like it. I didn't know how to put together the words of a sensible answer. What was East Fourth Street? It was my life, that's what it was. Up to six months ago, anyway.

"Well, it's sort of a poor section," I said, and because I didn't want him to think ill of me, I added: "We don't live there anymore."

"Who is we?" Roon said.

"My father and mother," I said.

"They're alive, then, are they?" Roon said, and then he laughed. "Sorry. That is a bit silly, isn't it? I mean if they weren't alive you wouldn't be living with them, would you? What I meant was it must be very pleasant to have a family. Where do you live now?"

"A place called the Bronx," I said.

"Oh, yes, I've heard of it," Sebastian Roon said. "Do you like it?"

Again his question jolted me. Did I like the Bronx? I must have. We'd fought so hard to get there.

"Sure," I said. "It's okay."

What I meant was do you like it better than East Fourth Street?" Roon said.

How could I not like it better? East Fourth Street was a slum. The Bronx was uptown.

"It's a much nicer neighborhood," I said.

George arrived with two coffee cups. He set down one in front of me and the other in front of Sebastian Roon.

"Thank you," Roon said.

George bowed and went away. I stared into my cup. It contained two lumps of ice. No coffee. Just two lumps of ice. Since it is not necessary to say I was surprised, I will not say it. But I will say that I had a sudden glimpse of the fact that education is a long and endless process. In my six months as an employee of Maurice Saltzman & Company, I thought I had learned a good deal about the customs and practices of the businessmen in the midtown area. At least during the business day. I had no idea what they did at night or where they did it. Perhaps I thought I had learned it all. Now, staring at the two lumps of ice in what was supposed to be a cup of coffee, I realized I had a long way to go.

The obvious move was to stick to my resolve of a few minutes ago. I would do nothing until Sebastian Roon did it first. What he did now was pull from his breast pocket a silver flask. It was flat, about the size and shape of the *Othello* we had used in English class at Thomas Jefferson. I had never seen such a thing before except in movies about Flappers with John Held, Jr., faces and college boys in raccoon coats.

"This stuff is perfectly reliable," Roon said. "My uncle gets it from one of the best merchants in town."

He twisted off the silver cap, leaned across the table and poured a couple of inches of amber fluid into my cup. Then he did the same for his own cup. He recapped the flask, slid it back into his breast pocket, and from the cluster of salt cellars, pepper mills, and mustard pots in the center of the table he picked up a small pitcher of water.

"Or would you prefer soda?" Sebastian Roon said.

"Er," I said.

I may not be spelling that correctly. But I didn't really say "Uh." I simply heard myself utter a sound that was popped out of me by my confusion. Not stupidity. Confusion. I knew about Prohibition and bootleggers and speakeasies and the fact that there were people who drank various forms of alcohol every day as regularly as they consumed food. I did not know this from personal experience. I knew it from reading newspapers and seeing Emil Jannings movies in which he played the boss bootlegger who is unaware until the second reel that his own syndicate has supplied the hooch for the wild party at which his son, a clean-cut college boy, drinks his father's product and goes blind for the remaining three reels.

My personal experience with alcohol was not unlike that of pretty nearly every kid who was raised on East Fourth Street, and probably similar to that of most seventeen-year-olds who in 1930 lived in the Bronx.

The only alcoholic beverage even a practiced revenooer could ever have found in our house was sacramental wine. My father made it himself from blue Concord grapes that were peddled from pushcarts in our neighborhood every summer. Once a year, at the Passover Seder, I was given a timbleful of this aromatic sweet brew. The timbleful was part of the ceremony. It was also part of a rather primitive but effective method of child control. The ceremonies at a Passover Seder are lengthy; once the excitment of the first stages wears off, children at the table tend to become restless. With a small dose of sacramental wine coursing through their very young veins, however, they are inclined to become sleepy. At this point they are carried off to bed and the adults continue the complicated ceremony without the sort of interruptions that are more appropriate to a park playground.

My only other contact with alcohol occurred once a year in the synagogue during Rosh Hashanah. Boys were called up at regular intervals to chant a short section from the Torah. When my turn came I never knew what I was chanting, but I knew how to chant it. Rabbi Goldfarb had seen to that. When I had satisfactorily uttered the appropriate decibels of sound, the cantor tweaked my cheek—the gesture was known as a *knip*—to display his approval, and the *gobbe*, or sexton, led me to a table in a corner of the synagogue for my reward: a sliver of golden yellow sponge cake dipped into a small glass of booze known as *brohmfin*.

Half a century of more complicated living has placed me, and my palate, in contact with many beverages, but I've never encountered anything quite like the *brohmfin* doled out by the *gobbe* of my father's synagogue. I have a feeling it was some form of whiskey, homemade of course,

64

but I seem to recall my father on one occasion saying disapprovingly that they—whoever "they" were—had made this batch, of which he disapproved, with an inferior type of prune. So perhaps it was not whiskey.

Whatever it was, it tasted like what I suppose Victorian novelists had in mind when they wrote of a character who had suffered the tragedy of pride-shattering humiliation that he had been forced to drink a draught of bitter aloes. Those characters should have had a crack at the *brohmfin* that was the house drink in my father's synagogue. They would have run back to bitter aloes as though they were heading for a chocolate malted. I never complained, however, about the taste of what I was offered in my father's synagogue. Gulping that piece of alcohol-soaked sponge cake was a sign of manhood.

(Footnote for Arab statesmen: in the virility sweepstakes Jewish boys win their spurs early.)

I certainly felt I had won mine long before that day in Shane's when I found myself staring at the two ice cubes in my coffee cup. The problem was, however, the place in which I was doing my staring: a restarurant on West 23rd Street, dimly lighted, hushed, with red and white checked tablecloths, waiters in red mess jackets held together by silver buttons, and gutted deer—or bouquets of head-down grouse—hung at the door.

There was nothing about this place even remotely reminiscent of the other places in which I had previously consumed alcohol. I did not know what to do. What Sebastian Roon did was not helpful. He lifted his cup.

"Skoal," he said.

I wondered why. The only ones I knew were P.S. 188, J.H.S. 64, Thomas Jefferson High, and the 23rd Street branch of C.C.N.Y. None of these seemed at this moment the proper subject for a toast. However, I did not want young Mr. Roon to think I was as backward as I felt. I lifted my cup.

"School," I said.

He drank. I drank. And I had the immediate feeling that death had come to carry me away.

The moment the amber fluid slid past my epiglottis I was seized by the sort of coughing fit out of which Fatty Arbuckle used to squeeze a six-minute sequence.

Whatever I had swallowed came right back up in a fine spray. My forehead went down like the cutting section of a guillotine and banged against the red and white checks. My eyes blurred with a sudden cloudburst of tears. And my knees, hurtling upward to ease the sudden stiffening of my esophagus, hit some sort of metal fastenings on the underside of the table. With two results: the table rocked, and I screamed.

When I had smeared away the tears, the pain in my knees was receding, my coughing fit was simmering down to a series of rasping, unpleasant gasps, and I saw that a third person was sitting at our table.

"You must sip," Sebastian Roon said, "not gulp. This is my uncle." He waved toward the man who had joined us during my seizure.

"Pleased to meet you," I said, still bubbling with gasps and tears as I put out my hand. "I'm sorry."

Sebastian Roon's uncle took my hand. He shook it, laughed, and said to his nephew, "He's pleased to meet me, but he's also sorry."

So I knew the head of I. G. Roon, Ltd., was a wise guy.

"I didn't mean it that way," I said through a nervous giggle. "I meant I'm sorry about, you know, all the, well, the coughing and the noise. I guess I swallowed the wrong way."

I. G. Roon laughed again and said, "Or the wrong stuff."

So I knew something else. I hated this man.

"Yeah, I guess," I said.

I found myself embarking on another nervous giggle, and shifted to a stab at a laugh. It came out all right, I think, but it also made me hate myself. Brown-nosing is never a pleasant activity. There are times, however, when it has to be done. The year 1930 was one of those times, and I did my share. But I was able to put a poultice on my

66

pride by choosing the areas where I could tell myself this detestable activity was necessary.

Ira Bern, for example. Getting his shoes shined. Fetching his hot pastrami sandwiches. Damn it, I had been valedictorian of my class at Thomas Jefferson. I had won a bronze medal from *The New York Times* in an oratorical contest about the Constitution of the United States. Dean Foote had said I could have a scholarship to Long Island University, to N. Y. U., or to Harvard if I was able to pony up the living expenses.

Well, I couldn't. I couldn't even accept the scholarships on condition that I would take one of those waiting-on-table jobs with which the flower of American manhood, from Frank Merriwell to Justice Brandeis, seems to have worked its way through college. What the Kramer family needed in 1930 was not a scholarship to Harvard but a nice steady flow of Yankee bean soup coming in over the window sill every week, and so I had to get a job.

Fair enough. When my father had needed a job to support his family, he had gone out and got one. So I went out and got mine. It was a good enough job to have enabled the Kramer family to move from East Fourth Street to the Bronx, and I was not complaining.

I really wasn't. I enjoyed the sense of achievement it gave me. Besides, I was moving ahead scholastically at C.C.N.Y., and I had the satisfaction of detesting the rich kids in my Thomas Jefferson graduating class who had gone on to college. They gave me something I had never had when we were all young: a goal. I knew what I was going to do. I was going to show the bastards.

I had no doubt I could. And if the process of showing them meant brown-nosing a man like Ira Bern, okay, I could do that, too. But I. G. Roon? Where did he fit into the contract?

I never really got a chance to find out. By the time my jumping gut, and my carefully concealed fury, were under control, I noticed that Sebastian Roon and his uncle had apparently forgotten completely that I was sitting at the same table with them.

They were leaning forward, foreheads almost touching, talking in a way that reminded me of one of those Conrad Veidt spy movies. They seemed to be exchanging information of a confidential nature in a manner they felt or hoped would not arouse attention from people nearby. They were talking. They were uttering sounds. But it was as though they were studying to be ventriloquists. Their lips did not move. Not much, anyway.

"No, Danbury Hat is out," Sebastian said. "I talked with Maltz twice. They can't meet the eight-fifty price."

"Can't or won't?" I. G. Roon said sharply.

"I think they can't," Sebastian said. He seemed to be talking to his own cuticle. "I told them we wouldn't come down, and they had until this morning to come up. I told them if they didn't accept before I met you for lunch, we'd go to York."

"Did they?" I. G. Roon said.

"No," Sebastian Roon said. "Not a word."

"So?" I. G. Roon said.

"Bugger it, I thought," Sebastian Roon said. "Why wait for lunch? At ten-thirty I called York."

"Which one?" I. G. Roon said.

"Irving, I think," Sebastian said. "Yes, Irving. He's the one with the lisp, isn't he?"

"Actually, it's a cleft palate," I. G. Roon said. "But go on. What happened?"

"He'd take the whole New South Wales shipment, he said."

I. G. Roon's voice rose slightly. "The whole shipment?" Small scream on first syllable: *ship*.

"Yes," Sebastian said. "On condition that we let them have all of North Adelaide in the spring at the same rate."

I. G. Roon scowled. I. G. Roon's scowl was not pleasant.

"The son of a bitch," he said.

"Yes, quite," Sebastian said. "That's how I reacted. But I suppose being a son of a bitch is part of his game."

"It sure is," I.G. Roon said. I wondered how he came to have a nephew with a British accent.

68

He scowled down at the red and white checked table-cloth. I was surprised to see he, too, had a coffee cup in front of him. When had it been placed there? My explosive reaction to the dose of amber fluid Sebastian Roon had fed me, it suddenly appeared, must have consumed more time than I thought. It had also, it seemed obvious, either dulled or for a few moments at least blacked out my powers of observation.

"What do you want me to do?" Sebastian Roon said.

I. G. Roon lifted his coffee cup and took a long, slow sip, scowling as he did so at the small pitcher of water in the middle of the table. The way he did it I found interesting. The only executive I'd had an opportunity thus far to observe at close range was Ira Bern. I. G. Roon was the second. That is, if you didn't count the man who with brilliant dexterity put together the pastrami sandwiches at the take-out counter in Lou G. Siegel's, and it seemed to me reasonable in this context not to count him.

Ira Bern, a Fifth Street boy I admired and envied, never seemed to think. Or rather he never seemed to pause for thought. He reacted. Usually explosively. I. G. Roon, on the other hand, did not seem to react at all. When he said about Irving York with the lisp or the cleft palate, whoever Irving York was, "The son of a bitch," Mr. Roon had sounded not unlike the counterman at Lou G. Siegel's when he said, "Mustard or mayo?"

But it wasn't the sounds I. G. Roon made that plucked at my nervous and at the moment somewhat disheveled attention. It was his physical appearance. The way he looked. I. G. Roon could have been mistaken for Arthur Rackham's painting of the Mole in the copy of *The Wind in the Willows* from which Miss Kitchell used to read aloud every Friday afternoon to her classes in P.S. 188.

There was that same overall impression of black hair, much too much of it. The sharp snout. The leaning-forward stance. Even the curiously old-fashioned gold-rimmed eye-glasses that had to be called spectacles. What else? And the odd, ambivalent feeling that you were in the presence of either a delightful little creature from the animal kingdom, or Jack the Ripper in not very skillful disguise.

"If we're over a barrel," I. G. Roon said, "we're over a barrel. It's not a comfortable situation to be in, but it's a hell of a lot more comfortable than having every goddamn rabbit's hair from our New South Wales ranches go rotten because the people of this lousy country are quitting wearing hats, the dumb bastards, I hope they all die of double pneumonia."

I tried to bring him into sharper focus by squinting through my still tear-blurred eyes. Had he meant what he said? Or was it just the flamboyant rhetoric of an irritated man? Before I could do much toward arriving at an answer to this question, I became aware that the light had changed. Not too noticeably, of course. There wasn't much to begin with. But I sensed that something had come between me and Sebastian Roon's uncle in the illumination provided by Shane's restaurant for its clientele. I looked up and saw Edmund Lowe.

Long lean jaw. Slicked back India-ink black hair parted in the middle. Impeccably knotted tie. Man of the world skirt-chaser. Dandy. Fop. I don't mean that he was really Edmund Lowe. But he sure as hell looked like Edmund Lowe. Especially in the scene from *What Price Glory?* where he was fighting with Victor McLaglen over what I had been taught by Miss Kitchell, a remarkable person but a modest lady, to think of as Dolores Del Rio's favors. I thought of them often.

"Gentlemen," said Edmund Lowe.

And a curious thing happened. I. G. Roon stopped looking like Moley in *The Wind in the Willows*. He became a dead ringer for my old *melamed,* Rabbi Goldfarb on Columbia Street. An absolute dead ringer, including the obsequious smile reserved for parents in the throes of negotiating the price of a bar mitzvah.

"Mr. O'Casey," said I. G. Roon. "This is a pleasure."

Even in my damaged state I sensed something wrong in Mr. Roon's words. No. Not in his words. His words, on checking back, seemed okay. What was wrong was the look on his face. And the strange tone of his voice. He could have been Jesus, unexpectedly a sudden stickler for the amenities, telling Pontius Pilate what a pleasure it was to be brought before the Procurator of Judea, and apologizing for the imposition of getting him out of bed in the middle of the night.

"If it's a pleasure, like you say," said Edmund Lowe or Mr. O'Casey, "you'd invite a guy to sit down."

His voice disappointed me. Edmund Lowe never sounded like that. Not even in the early talkies. Edmund Lowe was a gentleman.

"So sit down," said I. G. Roon, and he pulled out a chair between himself and me. Until this moment I had not even noticed it was there. "Take a load off," I. G. Roon said. "And have a snort. Seb?"

Sebastian reached into his breast pocket and pulled out his silver flask. To my surprise, before he had unscrewed the cap George had materialized with another coffee cup. He set it down in front of Mr. O'Casey. For some reason, not very clearly thought out, I felt it would help in my confused condition if I counted the ice cubes in Mr. O'Casey's cup. I made the attempt. I failed. The amber fluid splashed down out of Sebastian Roon's silver flask on probably two, perhaps more, ice cubes. Mr. O'Casey raised his cup.

"Here's to business," he said.

I. G. Roon's eyebrows ascended toward his widow's peak, and almost made it. "Business?" he said. "What business?"

"I thought I heard you and your nephew here discussing the rabbit's fur business," Mr. O'Casey said.

I. G. Roon shook his head. His face looked sad. He might have been responding to a toast by George V in honor of the Kaiser's skill as a woodcutter at Doorn.

"You and your thinking," he said. "If you did less of it, Mr. O'Casey, you wouldn't have to spend so much of your life chasing after me in restaurants where I'm having a pleasant little lunch with my nephew and his friend."

"Oh," Mr. O'Casey said. "So this is just another one of your pleasant little lunches with your nephew?"

71

"And with my nephew's friend," I. G. Roon said.

"What is your nephew's friend's name, may I ask?" said Mr. O'Casey. In a tone of voice, *I* may add, that Edmund Lowe, who was a gentleman, would never have employed.

"Seb," Mr. Roon said. "What's your friend's name?"

"Franklin Kramer," said Sebastian Roon.

"No, not Franklin," I said. "Benjamin."

And that was the last thing I did say. Or the last thing I remember. About Shane's restaurant, anyway. The next thing I actually knew, I was lying on the couch in the file room of the Maurice Saltzman & Company offices on 34th Street. My head ached. All my insides bubbled. The taste in my mouth seemed to have been scraped from the rusted plates of the *Leviathan* in dry dock. I wanted to die. Mainly because, among the three people standing over me, was Sebastian Roon.

"He'll be all right," Roon was saying to Mr. Bern and Miss Bienstock. "I'm afraid I miscalculated his capacity for spirits."

Miss Bienstock's expression of perplexity deepened to pandemonium proportions. "Spirits?" she said. "What spirits?"

"That chap from the insurance company," Sebastian Roon said. "O'Casey. He stalked us to this restaurant. Shane's on Twenty-third Street."

Ira Bern looked troubled. "Anything?" he said tensely.

Sebastian Roon laughed. "Nothing at all," he said. "My uncle and I had finished the York transaction before O'Casey arrived." He laughed again. "Poor Mr. Kramer."

"Mr. Who?" Mr. Bern said.

Sebastian Roon nodded toward me. "He *is* your Mr. Kramer, is he not?"

Miss Bienstock, without losing the grip on her look of perplexity, said, "You mean Benny."

"I suppose I do," said Sebastian Roon. "Yes, he did say his name is Benjamin. Well, he did nobly. He was most helpful to me and my uncle, and we're both grateful, we really are, Mr. Bern."

"You are?" Mr. Bern said.

72

"Indeed yes," said Sebastian Roon.

"But what should I do with him?" said Ira Bern, staring down at me.

Sebastian Roon looked thoughtful. "Why don't you simply let him sleep it off?" he said.

3

Take a fool's advice, my mother used to say. And then she would casually drop into your lap a ladleful of wisdom for which Benjamin Franklin would have fought to obtain the rights. For inclusion, that is, in *Poor Richard's Almanack*.

"If there's two people in the house," I remember my mother saying one day, "always let the other person answer the telephone."

She said this at a time when Alexander Graham Bell's invention was to her life not unlike what the Beagle was to Darwin. Every day was a revelation. I don't think my mother had ever used a telephone until I paid to have one installed in the Bronx apartment on Tiffany Street.

I thought my mother would be pleased by this electronic addition to our life. Not only because it provided a rather spectacularly new contact with the outside world, but also because it was a visible symbol to relatives and friends that the Kramer family had moved up the economic and social ladder. Visible symbols were important to my mother. I have felt for years that she practically invented conspicuous consumption single-handed. My mother had always been a snob. William Makepeace Thackeray, take note. My mother had been a snob even when we were very poor down on East Fourth Street.

I see now that living with a telephone, while it may have pleased my mother, confused her. Perhaps it even frightened her. Yes, I think it probably did. I remember coming home late at night, after my long day in the offices of Maurice Saltzman & Company, after my classes at C.C.N.Y., and asking if anybody had called. My question was silly. I didn't really expect anybody to call me. As I have indicated earlier, I had left all my friends behind on

East Fourth Street. Without telephones, of course. And I had made no new friends during my months on Tiffany Street. There had been no time. I was always downtown. Just the same, the Kramers now had a telephone, and I had seen enough movies to know that when you came home you asked whoever was around if anybody had called you while you were out. Usually, it was a butler. But the Kramer family had not yet made it up to butlers. I had to lean on my mother.

This was easy to do. She always waited up for me with "something to go in your stomach," as she put it. And it was always something good. Food does not always depend on the shop it came from. The best depends on the feeling with which it is prepared.

My mother prepared mine for me the way legendary French chefs, according to their memoirs, prepared his for Louis Napoleon: with love. That's why my mother was always around. It took me some time to grasp that there was something wrong in this. On East Fourth Street she had rarely left our tenement flat. Aside from her daily shopping expedition to the Avenue C pushcart market for the ingredients of our evening meal, I don't remember that she ever went out into the street except for an unusual reason. A visit to Dr. Gropple, for example. Yet there had seemed nothing wrong in this. I don't really know why. My guess is that my mother was doing what most women on East Fourth Streed did.

It was a place where a good deal of life was lived outdoors. By children, who went to school. By men, who went to their jobs. But not by women. They stuck close to what it seems foolish to call the family hearth. Some hearth. A black cast-iron coal-burning stove in the kitchen. Nontheless, I feel the image is accurate. Women stayed home because that was where women belonged. Up in the Bronx, on Tiffany Street, my mother stayed home for what struck me long after we moved there as a different reason. My mother on Tiffany Street in the Bronx was not unlike Pocahontas on Ebury Street in London.

In the social sense she had moved upward. But in the

emotional sense she had moved into *terra incognita*. On East Fourth Street my mother had known the boundaries of what she was afraid of. On Tiffany Street there were no boundaries. A large, sprawling, shapeless world poured itself away in all directions from the tight little block of yellow apartment houses to which we had moved from East Fourth Street. So she stayed home. And when I came home Saturday night after my lunch at Shane's and asked my foolish question about whether anybody had called, there she was, with plates full of food, trying to pretend I had not asked a foolish question.

"Yes," she said casually. Her notion of casually was to look up at the ceiling as she spoke. "This afternoon, when I put this honey cake in the stove—eat the piece on this side first, it has a nice *rindle*—a man named Reibeisen called."

"Reibeisen?" I said.

What else could I say? In 1930 a reibeisen in Yiddish was a grater. I'm sure it still is. On it you could then, and probably still can now, reduce raw potatoes to the batter-like material from which *latkes* are made.

"Yes, Reibeisen," my mother said. "What's the matter? You don't know anybody named Reibeisen?"

"I don't think so," I said.

"So a telephone it's a thing you pay for only to receive calls from people you know?"

I thought about that for a moment. The answer was, of course, yes. Or so I had always believed. Why would strangers call you on the phone?

"Not necessarily," I said. In Yiddish. My mother did not speak English. When I feel that my light is not shining as brightly as I could wish in the auditorium of the world, I remind myself that I know how to say "not necessarily" in Yiddish.

"Did this Mr. Reibeisen leave his number?" I said to my mother.

"Would I let a man call here and not ask him to leave his number?" my mother said. "Of course he left his number."

"Okay," I said, "let's have it, and I'll call him back."

"Not so fast," my mother said. "Give a person a minute to think. I have it in my head." She closed her eyes. "It begins with like a Susskind?"

"Susskind?" I said. "Ma, I doubt it."

"I'm the one who answered the telephone," my mother said. "So he doubts it."

"All I mean," I said, "I don't think there's a New York telephone exchange named Susskind."

"What's like it, then?" my mother said.

I considered what did not seem a very large problem until you tackled it. What, indeed, is like a Susskind?

"Susquehanna, maybe?" I said finally.

My mother nodded with approval. Her brilliant son, valedictorian of his class in Thomas Jefferson High School, had come through again.

"That's it," she said. "Susquehanna."

Susquehanna is not an easy word to say in Yiddish. But my mother managed. Even though the way she managed it would probably have been confusing to the New York Telephone Company.

"Susquehanna what?" I said.

"What what?" my mother said.

"The numbers," I said. "After the word Susquehanna there have to be numbers."

My mother's examination of the ceiling became more intense. When my mother examined a ceiling she brought to my mind, which was even then earnest but untidy, an image: Marie Antoinette studying the jewel case on a top shelf, trying to decide whether diamonds or rubies were more appropriate for a ride in a tumbril.

"Well, then, all right, Susquehanna," my mother said. "At least we have that settled."

"Yes, but the numbers," I said. "I can't call Mr. Reibeisen back unless I have the numbers that go with the Susquehanna."

"Don't I know that?" my mother said. "What do you think I am? A stupid greenhorn?"

Stupid? My God, no. Given the proper education—or

even any education—my mother could have guided Einstein to the only correct method for splitting the atom long before General Groves was appointed to the Manhattan Project. But my mother had been given no education. And pride had prevented her from seeking it at a time when she could have had it for the asking.

If you went to school at night, as most immigrants on East Fourth Street did, you were making a public confession that you were ignorant. My mother was not a confessor. My mother was a battler. She did not go to night school. She made it all up out of her head as she went along. And when I say all I mean all. Everything.

What God had in store for you. Why the price of potatoes on the Avenue C pushcarts was the result of a conspiracy among the "bosses." How many ounces there should be in a pound. The longest distance between two points. Why you should add lemon to soap when you wash your hair. How to answer a telephone. Everything.

"Of course you're not stupid," I said. "And it's a little late to discuss whether you're a greenhorn. You've been in this country for twenty-five years."

"Thirty," my mother said. "The president was Tiddy Roosevelt."

"Teddy," I said.

"What's the difference?" my mother said.

I didn't bother to answer that. Many of my mother's questions defied the polite q. and a. of simple logic.

"Never mind the difference," I said. "Just give me the numbers after the Susquehanna."

My mother resumed her contemplation of the ceiling. She was not, of course, seeking answers in the unevenly painted plaster. Hungarian girls, when they are no longer girls, tilt their eyes toward heaven quite frequently. It smooths the jowls.

"It begins with a two," my mother said. "A two to begin."

"Susquehanna two," I said. "Okay. Susquehanna two. And then?"

"A seven," my mother said. "Could it be this Mr. Reibeisen he has a Susquehanna, and a two, and then a seven?"

"Possibly," I said. "Seven happens to a lot of people."

"But after a two?" my mother said. "And first a Susquehanna?"

"No," I said. "I must admit that's more rare."

"What's with the rare?" my mother said.

"It's like, say, unusual," I said.

Getting a phone number out of my mother was not unlike reeling in a tarpon. If you wanted the fish it was foolish to make waspish remarks to the rod and reel. If you wanted the fish you played the game. Patience was not always rewarded, but it was the only highway to possible success.

"If we have the Susquehanna and the two and the seven," I said, "okay. But we still have to get two more numbers."

"Four numbers?" my mother said.

"As a rule," I said, "yes."

This was 1930. Even zip codes had not yet surfaced. The flow of life was simpler.

"With a Susquehanna?" my mother said. "Four numbers also in addition on top of the Susquehanna?"

"It's the system," I said. "The telephone company. They have to work out something that will take care of the thousands of people who have telephones. Millions. The only way is numbers."

"We didn't have numbers in Hungary," my mother said.

"We didn't have them on East Fourth Street," I said. "But here uptown in the Bronx it's different. What comes after the seven, Ma?"

My mother's chin went up to the ceiling. I saw the wisdom of the gesture. It took years off her profile.

"A nine, maybe?" she said.

"I don't know, Ma," I said. "You were the one took the message."

"Message?" my mother said. "What message? The bell rings. I answer it. A man says this is Nachman Reibeisen. This is a message?"

79

"Nachman Reibeisen?" I said.

"What difference?" my mother said. "It's a Reibeisen. He says could I talk to Mr. Benjamin Kramer, the accountant. That's you, no?"

"Yes, and of course he couldn't talk to me because I was not home," I said. With rather ostentatious patience, I must add. The biblical character I have learned to dig the most is Job. So would you, if you had been my mother's son. "So you asked for his number and said I would call him back. Right?"

"What else could I say?" my mother said. "Go ahead, tell me, what would you have said?"

I knew this ploy. Pickett had used it at the post-mortem after Gettysburg. Where would you have hurled your cavalry? Hmm?

"I would have said my son Benjamin is not at home now," I said. "I would have said my son Benjamin Kramer usually comes home on Saturday about six o'clock. Because on Saturdays he has no classes at C.C.N.Y. Saturday is one of his two free nights every week. When he does come home, I will ask my son to call you back. May I have your number, please? That's what I would have said."

"So what did I say to him?" my mother said.

"I don't know, Ma," I said. "I wasn't here when Mr. Reibeisen called. What did you say?"

"I said my son Benjamin Kramer is not at home," my mother said. "My son Benjamin Kramer, I said, he comes home Saturday nights about six o'clock. Maybe a little later. When he comes home tonight I'll tell him to call you back. You'll give me please your number?"

"Which he did," I said. "And it starts with a Susquehanna, goes on to a two, proceeds to a seven, and then seems to stop dead."

"From a Susquehanna and a two and a seven," my mother said, "you can't call back a Nachman Reibeisen?"

"Not any kind of a Reibeisen," I said.

"This is some country," my mother said. "In Hungary we didn't have telephones, but believe me, in Hungary, if you had a Susquehanna, and a two, and a seven, you could

80

find not only Nachman Reibeisen, but Sam also, and his father and mother, too."

"No doubt," I said. "But this is not Hungary. This is Tiffany Street in the Bronx."

Her eyes came down from the ceiling. They were blue. Or rather, they had been blue. In Hungary, which was a guess on my part, of course, and on East Fourth Street, which was no guess but a vivid recollection of my youth. Blue as the grapes from which my father used to make our Passover wine.

"There's times here on Tiffany Street," she said, "I wish it was Hungary."

I don't think my mother meant that. I did not learn about her life in Hungary until almost half a century later, when my Aunt Sarah from New Haven told me. My mother's life in Hungary had not been pleasant.

The phone rang. My mother stared at it with distrust. She did not move. "If there's two people in the house, always let the other person answer the telephone." I picked it up.

"Hello?" I said.

"Is this Intervale one-six-two-three?"

The voice brought back with an almost physical thrust the sidewalk at Seventh Avenue and 34th Street the day before.

"Hot Cakes?" I said.

"I beg your pardon?"

"Isn't this Hot Cakes Rabinowitz?" I said.

"No, of course not."

But it had to be. Hot Cakes was the only person who had ever asked how he could get in touch with me. Only yesterday, when I had jumped down from the Built-In Uplift Frocks truck at 21st and Seventh, I had yelled after him: "I'm in the phone book!" Who else would know such a thing?

"I say, are you there?"

Then I caught the British accent.

"Oh," I said. "It's Mr. Roon."

"No," he said. "Sebastian."

"Yes, sir," I said.

He laughed. "Wrong again. Mister Roon and sir are hardly what one calls a chap with whom one's been sozzled at high noon. Try Seb."

"Seb?"

"Why not?" he said. "All my friends call me Seb."

How many did he have? And if I called him Seb, would he now have one more?

"Go ahead," he said. "Try it."

"Seb," I said.

It sounded wrong. I had spent my life in a world where people were called Benny and Hot Cakes and Ira. Seb? It sounded like one of those games that came in cardboard boxes with decks of cards and small celluloid counters of various colors which you pushed around on a marked board.

Sebastian Roon laughed again. "There, you see? Not difficult, really, is it?"

Up through my confusion came a distressing thought. Was I dealing with a type that would almost certainly have been identified at Thomas Jefferson High School as a wise guy? I hoped not. I had liked young Mr. Roon. Roon? That, too, sounded odd.

"What can I do for you?" I said.

It didn't sound very friendly, but I had noticed it was the way Mr. Bern started a great many of his telephone conversations.

"Nothing, really," Mr. Roon said. "I just happened to be in the neighborhood, so I thought I'd give you a tinkle."

The statement made just about as much sense as if he had said he was heading toward 1600 Pennsylvania Avenue and it had occurred to him to check the directions with someone he knew who lived along the way. Happened to be in the neighborhood meant happening to be in the Bronx, and nobody "happened" to be in the Bronx. You got there the way Lewis and Clark got to Oregon. By setting out deliberately, as you would set out on an expedition, with a specific destination in mind. I couldn't believe a young Englishman who was in a position to invite guests

82

to lunch at Shane's on West 23rd Street "just happened" to be in the neighborhood of our apartment house in the Bronx.

"Well, uh, hello," I said.

"Are you all right?" Roon said.

"Sure," I said. "I'm fine."

"Good," he said. "Delighted to hear it. One couldn't help wondering, you know. And feeling guilty. I mean to say, when I left you in Mr. Bern's office yesterday, you did look a bit on the bleak side."

He laughed. My face grew hot.

"Oh, yeah," I said. "I'm sorry about that. But I'm okay now. I really am."

There was a pause. I had the feeling I had missed something.

"Look here," Roon said. "I'm not interrupting anything, am I?"

I looked across the narrow hall into the kitchen. Our telephone sat on a small table near the front half of the hall. It was tiny. A sort of cupboard just inside the front door. My mother was laying out her "turning" on the table near the stove. On Saturdays and Sundays I came home directly from my chores in the Maurice Saltzman & Company offices. On Saturdays I did not even expect a meal from my mother. I came home about six or six-thirty, gave my mother the salary envelope Mr. Bern had given me, and started cleaning up for my weekly meeting with Hannah Halpern.

This started at her home, which I reached by walking north across to 180th Street for perhaps half a mile, and then east for four blocks to Vyse Avenue. It was not much of a journey and, with the visions of sugarplums that danced in my head as I walked, it was scarcely noticeable.

In subsequent years, indeed even today, I have on occasion wondered if my mother had any notion of those sugarplums.

In 1930 the age of sexual permissiveness had not yet really surfaced. True, there was D. H. Lawrence. Every literate kid at Thomas Jefferson had waited his turn at

George Weitz's copy of *Lady Chatterley's Lover*. And Chink Alberg had charged a nickel a shot at his older brother's copy of Krafft-Ebing. But these were literary experiences. The real stuff was hearsay. For Benny Kramer, anyway. Until we moved up to the Bronx. Then my mother introduced me to the Halperns.

It was an eye-opener. They were an eye-opener? Well, one member of the family was. Hannah.

I have wondered many times since it happened if my mother had done something casually innocent, or sensibly and calculatedly sophisticated. On East Fourth Street she had never introduced me to anybody. The people I knew were the people I met on my own. In school. On the docks. At the Hannah H. Lichtenstein Settlement House. Here on Tiffany Street, one day my mother told me she thought I ought to meet the Halperns. Who were the Halperns? They were a nice family. Used to live around the corner from us on Lewis Street, a little to the right of the Fourth Street corner, between Mr. Raffti's barbershop and Mr. Slutsky the glazier. Mr. Halpern was a pocket maker in the shop upstairs over Papa's factory on Allen Street. They had moved to the Bronx shortly before we did.

On one of my mother's Saturday night trips to Mr. Lebenbaum's store for her weekly allotment of "turning," she accompanied me as far as Vyse Avenue. She introduced me to the Halpern family, and then went off on her errand. Mrs. Halpern offered me an apple, which I politely refused, then a piece of honey cake, which I have never been able to refuse, and then she suggested that maybe Hannah and I might like to go out to Bronx Park for a walk. We did.

Wow!

It had been wow every Saturday night now for months, and it was wow to which I had been looking forward on this particular Saturday night, when I found myself at the other end of the phone from this character named Sebastian Roon.

"No, no, you're not interrupting," I said. "By the way, I never thanked you for lunch yesterday."

"Why should you?" said Roon. "Since you never really had it."

"Well, it was nice of you to invite me," I said. Then, because Hannah's sugarplums were beginning to move from a dance in my head to a rather uncontrolled mazurka, I said: "Well, it was nice talking to you."

"Look here, old chap," Roon said, "as long as I'm in the neighborhood I wondered if I might pop in for a moment?"

Leaving aside Hannah and her sugar plums, the vocabulary was all wrong. On East Fourth Street people had never popped in. Nor had they done so during our few brief months on Tiffany Street.

"Sure, but—"

I got no further. The phone went dead. I hung up slowly.

"Who was that?" my mother said.

I stared at her for a long moment, then realized why. "Mr. Reibeisen," I said.

"Nachman?" my mother said.

"No," I said. "Sebastian."

"What?"

It was a "What?" from the heart, and who could blame her? Not someone who heard her pronouncing the two dissimilar names in Yiddish. It is a language in which Latin verbs can be made to rhyme with the names of Tel Aviv taxi drivers.

"The man whose number started with a Susquehanna, went on to a two, proceeded to a seven, and then seemed to stop dead."

"See?" my mother said. "I told you. Nachman Reibeisen."

"No," I said. "Sebastian Roon."

"That's a name?" my mother said.

"He says it is," I said.

"Who is he?" my mother said.

I explained the relationship of I. G. Roon, Ltd., to Maurice Saltzman & Company.

"And he's coming here?" my mother said.

"He said he's in the neighborhood," I said. "Mr. Roon just said on the phone—"

There was a knock on the door. My mother and I stared at each other.

"Well," she said, "it's a small neighborhood."

She was not joking. Geographically Tiffany Street was larger than East Fourth Street. But emotionally, well—I had not figured it out yet. I went to the door and opened it.

"Hello, there," Sebastian Roon said.

"Hello," I said. "Come in." He did, and I said, "This is my mother."

"How very nice to meet you," Roon said, bowing over her hand. I stared. Not because he looked like Lewis Stone bowing over the hand of Barbara LaMarr in *The Prisoner of Zenda,* but because my mother accepted the gesture with as much casual grace as it was offered.

"Likewise," my mother said.

It was one of her few English words.

"That was rather quick, wasn't it?" Roon said. He must have seen the look on my face. He laughed. "I actually rang you from a booth in the chemist's round the corner."

The chemist's? All at once I could see the biology and chemistry lab in Thomas Jefferson High, complete with high stone-topped tables and bunsen burners.

"Ask him should sit down," my mother said.

I wondered where. A visitor was an unusual experience. My mother and father and I spent most of our time at home in the kitchen. The kitchen table, however, was covered with my mother's "turning." My father, who lived in a wheelchair, was in the bedroom. Since the accident that had made him an invalid he did not like to be seen by strangers. He spent most of his time in the bedroom, reading "A Bintel Brief" and "Yenta Telabenda" by B. Kovner in the *Jewish Daily Forward.* He enjoyed the former because it made him ponder, and the latter because it made him laugh.

"I do seem to be interrupting," Roon said. "I'm awfully sorry. I think I'd better be going. It was very nice to meet you, Mrs. Kramer."

86

"What did he say?" my mother said.

"He said it was very nice to meet you," I said.

"Twice he said it," my mother said. "Bring him in the front room. I'll get some honey cake."

"No, no, Mrs. Kramer," Roon said. "Please don't bother."

I gave him a quick look. My mother, as usual, had spoken in Yiddish.

"Bother?" my mother said. "Since when is honey cake a bother?"

And she left the hall. I nudged Roon's elbow and we followed her into the kitchen. My mother went to the large blue plate covered with a damp dishtowel under which she kept her honey cake. I went with Sebastian Roon toward the door that led to the front room. He was, after all, a guest.

I realized, in a moment of revelation, that since we had moved up to the Bronx we had not had any. The moment was unexpected, yes, and then unexpectedly unwelcome. I felt a stab of panic for what we had left behind. We had moved up in the world. Yes. But we had also moved out of it. Out of the part we had known. I was flooded by a sudden sense of loss. Then I heard Sebastian Roon's voice.

"I think you'll do better, Mrs. Kramer, if you snip the squares apart with a pair of scissors. It prevents the thread from clotting."

My mother stopped lifting the damp dishcloth from the honey cake and waited. The way she always waited when anything but the simplest statements in English—Yes. No. Go. Why? Who? Where? How much?—were made in her presence. She waited for a translation.

I was usually equal to the occasion. The English spoken in my mother's presence on Tiffany Street was not, as it had not been on East Fourth Street, very complicated. So far as I was concerned, however, Sebastian Roon might have just uttered a quotation from the Koran in the original Arabic.

He laughed at what I assumed was the expression on my face. Who could blame him? Not I. Slack-jawed, pop-eyed, open-mouthed confusion is not really an expression. It is a look. The look of a dim-witted fool, and that's precisely how I felt at the moment. Roon laughed again.

"Here, note if you will," he said. He stepped to the kitchen table. He picked up a strip of my mother's "turning" and pulled a small pair of scissors from his jacket pocket. He made a few deft snips at the skein of thread. "You see?"

I did, and I'm sure my mother did, too, but I think an explanatory pause would not at this point be what Jane Austen identifies as amiss.

Our family had always been poor. Not desperately so, but the lack of desperation was due to my mother. She was a no-nonsense girl. Early in her marriage she had accepted without complaint the fact that my father was never going to earn enough to support us. She accepted it, and she did something about it. What she had done down on East Fourth Street was become a bootlegger. In a very small way, of course. Al Capone and Dutch Schultz were unknown to her. What my mother knew was a minor source of supply. She learned how to find an occasional bottle for a wedding or a bar mitzvah. Her share of the transaction now seems ludicrously small: twenty-five cents, or half a dollar. But it was a time when, and East Fourth Street was a place where, twenty-five cents or half a dollar was important.

On Tiffany Street things were different. Not because I was earning more than I had earned when we lived on East Fourth Street, although I was. Things were different on Tiffany Street because Tiffany Street was different. It was a quiet place. Too quiet. I missed the noises of East Fourth Street. The river traffic. The horse-drawn wagons carrying coal and lumber from the docks. Mothers yelling from their windows to their children in the street. I did not miss the noises as much as my mother did because I was almost never at home during the day.

On East Fourth Street my mother had been on intimate terms with all our neighbors. On Tiffany Street she did not know the names of our neighbors. Neither did I. The

Tiffany Street tenements were smaller than the monstrous gray stone buildings in which I had been raised on East Fourth Street. The toilets were indoors. We even had a bathtub. The sidewalks were cleaner. But they were deserted. People did not sit out on the stoops in the evening eating Indian nuts and gossiping. In fact, there did not seem to be any people. It was my first experience with a neighborhood that was essentially a bedroom for people who worked in other parts of the city.

It was my mother's first experience, too, but she felt it more intensely. After all, I was downtown all day. I came home late at night, as apparently almost everybody on Tiffany Street did, to go to bed. But my mother was there every hour of the day, every day of the week. I see now what I did not see then: my mother was not only frightened, she was also puzzled. Fear is tough to handle. But not as tough as puzzlement. What you don't know can kill you.

All of her years in America my mother had dreamed of "improving" herself. Escaping from the slums. Moving her life uptown. Now she had done it. And what did she have? In her own Yiddish words: "A great big fat empty day with nothing to do except cook for Papa and stare out at the trees."

But it was the trees that eased her fears and enabled her to turn her back on what I see now was a disappointment. A street with trees on it was what America was all about, and she had finally made it to a street with trees. They were pretty terrible trees. Once, when I discovered that I was worrying about my mother and our new home, I made it a point to find out what these scruffy trees were called.

Ailanthus.

Can you imagine? I can't. Not even now. But my mother could. I don't think she saw them as they were. She saw those miserable trees the way Moses saw Canaan. And to make sure we were not swept back from them to treeless East Fourth Street she went to work for Mr. Lebenbaum.

Philip Lebenbaum was an entrepreneur who operated what my economics textbook in Thomas Jefferson High School called a cottage industry. Mr. Lebenbaum was a manufacturer of men's neckwear. Not the sort of neckwear that requires knotting. Mr. Lebenbaum manufactured what we used to call on East Fourth Street "jazz bows." Permantly knotted bow ties with elastic neckbands that snapped into place. He operated out of a store on Intervale Avenue, around the corner from our home on Tiffany Street. In this store Mr. and Mrs. Lebenbaum performed the groundwork functions, so to speak, that enabled the women of the neighborhood, my mother included, to produce the completed jazz bows.

Mr. Lebenbaum worked feverishly over a huge table. He sliced up endless bolts of gaudy silk into rectangles twelve inches long and three inches wide. These Mrs. Lebenbaum, bent over her sewing machine like a jockey flogging his mount into the stretch, stitched into endless belts of folded-over cloth that looked like tiny purses. These belts were bundled and tied with lengths of clothesline, then piled up on the floor, like sacks of laundry, for the women of the neighborhood who performed the next step in the manufacture of the Lebenbaum jazz bow. This step was known as "turning." My mother did a great deal of it.

Every day she would go over to Intervale Avenue. She would pick up a bundle of sewed silk belts and a stack of canvas rectangles that were to be stuffed into them. At home, working at our kitchen table, my mother would rip the silk belts into individual pieces. She would stuff each piece with a rectangle of canvas. And with a deft and curiously graceful movement flip the rectangle inside out. This process was known as "turning."

When my mother finished her task, what had been a long ribbon of stitched-together rectangles of silk, and a bundle of canvas scraps, had become a neat pile of colorful rectangles about the size of bathroom tiles. These she fastened with fat rubber bands provided by Mr. Lebenbaum. The next day she carried them to his store, where his wife crimped and sewed the rectangles into finished jazz bows. While she did that, Mr. Lebenbaum counted the results of my mother's labors and made an entry in her small notebook. At the end of the week he totted up the entries and paid my mother in the most ragged and crumpled dollar bills I have ever seen. They felt like lettuce leaves that should have been eaten a week ago.

My mother did not mind what those dollar bills looked or felt like. She enjoyed her capacity to earn money. It is a trait her son has inherited, but I don't think Benny Kramer has ever quite approached the sheer physical relish my mother took in those decayed dollar bills she earned by working for Mr. Lebenbaum on Intervale Avenue. She was up to twelve a week on the night that Sebastian Roon came to visit us without warning on Tiffany Street.

"If you tear the bits apart, look," he said, and he tore a couple of bits apart. "You see?"

My mother and I looked. The threads at the ends of the two bits had balled up. The word Sebastian Roon had used was "clotting." I was surprised by the accuracy. The two tiny balls of sprung thread did look like bits of clotted blood at the ends of a shaving cut.

"One thinks one is saving time by tearing them apart," Roon said. "But one isn't, actually, because then one has to smooth away the clotted bits." He smoothed away with his thumbnail the two bits of balled-up thread. "Whereas if you snip with a pair of scissors to start with."

He pulled out a chair at the kitchen table, sat down, and snipped away at the chain of my mother's turning. With a dexterity that impressed me and clearly surprised my mother, Sebastian Roon flicked two scraps of canvas out from under the fastenings of one of Mr. Lebenbaum's neatly prepared bundles and poked them into the two rectangles of silk. Then he pulled a fountain pen from his pocket and, with the blunt end, stabbed swiftly into the four corners of each rectangle. This smoothed the canvas inserts absolutely flat. And finally, with obvious delight in his own skill, he slapped the rectangles of silk flat on the table with an almost musical punctuation: tum-ta-ra-ra-ra, tum-tum!

He laughed, threw his hands up and out, and said, *"Voilà!"*

It was the gesture, the mood, the very word he had used the day before. In his office on 21st Street. When he had

91

invited me to lunch and, seeing I was uneasy about taking the time, had called Mr. Bern to fix it. It was the same gesture, the same mood, and the same word, but this time it annoyed me.

This was Saturday night, remember. And Hannah Halpern was waiting for me under Goldkorn's clock on 180th Street and Vyse Avenue. The visions of those sugarplums dancing in my head were interfering with my capacity to appreciate the dimensions of an encounter that, I see now, was at the very least a startling confrontation: the meeting of Georgian England with Herbert Hooverian Bronx in a tenement kitchen on a thoroughfare named Tiffany Street. By comparison, "Mr. Livingstone, I presume?" was not even in the running.

Until the day before I had never met an Englishman. Like most Jewish boys from the Lower East Side, I was from my very early years an Anglophile without knowing what the word meant or how the condition came about. Now I know.

The New York City public school curriculum, in my youth, at any rate, was built solidly around Chaucer, Shakespeare, Milton, Dickens, Burke, Swift, Coleridge, Thackeray, Addison, Steele, Lamb, and other prominent members of the Atheneum. I don't know how they managed to pay their dues. There were no movie sales for Charles Lamb's *Essays of Elia* or *Paradise Lost*.

"Excuse me," I said. "It's very nice to see you again, Mr. Roon, but it's sort of, well, sort of unexpected."

"You mean you have an appointment?" he said.

"Frankly, yes," I said. "But if there's anything important, anything I can do for you, I'll be glad to—"

"No, no," he said. "It's not that important. I merely thought I'd pop in and explain that strange lunch we had yesterday."

He laughed. It occurred to me he did an awful lot of laughing. I had drawn the inference from my reading that, aside from some wine-bibbing types in *The Pickwick Papers,* most Englishmen were dour.

92

"By the time I was in a position to explain it," he said, "you were in no condition to hear it."

"Thanks to you," I said.

I was careful to add a laugh. An apologetic little titter, anyway. This was 1930, you must remember. Benny Kramer never allowed himself to forget.

"Believe me," Roon said, "it was unintentional. The situation is a bit ridiculous. I'm surprised Mr. Bern didn't explain it to you. He helped arrange it, you see. My uncle, the I. G. Roon who *is* I. G. Roon, Ltd., as it were, is a very shrewed man, as I think you will probably have suspected from your brief meeting. A number of years ago he contracted for an insurance policy that says if he is physically incapacitated, and can no longer go to his office, he is to receive a monthly indemnity from the insurance company. Well, a few months ago my uncle did in fact suffer a heart attack. I don't know how severe it was, but he decided it was severe enough to keep him from going to the office, and he filed his claim. The insurance company was understandably annoyed because the monthly indemnity payments they had contracted to pay are rather large. My uncle sent for me to come over from England. My father is his brother. He installed me in his office in which he no longer sets foot, but I do meet him for lunch every day in some restaurant like Shane's. The insurance company suspects that my uncle and I do more than consume a few potables and some comestibles at these lunches. In fact, they strongly suspect my uncle is continuing to conduct his business affairs through me."

He laughed again.

"I shouldn't be at all surprised, you know, but the insurance company has to prove it, and so they've got my uncle under constant surveillance. We had a near thing the day before you accompanied me to Shane's. I made the mistake of pulling a bill of lading from my pocket at the lunch table, and the detective saw it. So the next day, yesterday, I thought I'd ask you along as a sort of cover, you might say. I hope you didn't mind too much?"

I thought of the gutted venison hanging outside the restaurant door. Well, perhaps some other time. I was still working on ham sandwiches and bacon and eggs.

"That man who came over to the table?" I said. "Mr. O'Casey? He was a detective?"

"One of several my uncle and I have come to know."

"Well," I said.

It did not seem an adequate reply, but I could think of nothing else.

"If you have a date," Roon said, "why don't you just buzz along?"

"But what about you?" I said.

He pulled over the bundle of "turning" and started snipping at the rectangles of silk with his scissors.

"Oh, you mustn't mind me," he said cheerfully. "If you'll just explain to your mother that I'd enjoy staying here for a bit and helping her, I'll be very happy."

"You sure?" I said.

"Oh yes, quite," Sebastian Roon said.

While I explained this odd development to my mother, I noticed the way she was looking at Roon. With suspicion, of course. She never really trusted anybody. But also with something I had noticed on other occasions: interest. My mother had always had an eye for a good-looking man. I looked back at Roon. Ramon Novarro? No. But not Louis Wolheim, either. He was attractive.

"My mother says fine, if you want to stay," I said. "I'm sorry that I can't. I've got this date, see?"

"Of course I see," Sebastian Roon said. "And of course I want to stay." He smiled at my mother, then looked around the small room. "It's very much like our scullery in Blackpool," he said.

4

To this day, when I hear smart alecks make cracks about fat girls, I have to restrain a tendency toward uncharacteristic violence. When I hear this sort of talk, I think back to that night in 1930 when I was walking Hannah home from Loew's 180th Street and we reached the corner of Vyse Avenue and 180th Street, a hundred feet from the stoop of Hannah's house down the block. I think about it, and everything inside me begins to swell.

"Hannah," I said, "how about we go back and pick up a couple more Gabilla's knishes? We can make the midnight show, easy."

We did make it, and the second knish was even better than the first. As a result, I did not get home until three in the morning.

This was unusual. After all, Maurice Saltzman & Company worked a seven-day week. Even though the next day was Sunday, I was due in the office down on West 34th at 7:45 A.M. This meant I had to leave Tiffany Street no later than 6:30 in the morning. I had done this every Sunday morning since we had moved up to the Bronx.

Difficult? Not at all. I usually left Hannah on Saturday nights at her house on Vyse Avenue around 1:00 A.M. The walk back to Tiffany Street took about twenty minutes. I was in the sack, snoring away, at 1:30 A.M. Who needed more than five hours of sleep? Not Benny Kramer. Not in 1930.

On this particular night, however, it turned out that Benny needed something more. Not sleep. Something more important. Something my mother would have identified as *koyach*.

I don't believe Noah Webster was ever put to this particular test, but I do believe he would have brought to the word *koyach* some of his more penetrating talents for definition. Thus: *koyach,* n. *koy,* as in coy. *yach,* as in Bach. (Bach, as in composer.) So we have the word *koyach.* A common Yiddish expression meaning strength. Ex.: *Samson, before Delilah gave him his world-famous haircut, had koyach.* But the word has a much broader meaning. Of a person who is said to possess *koyach* the word usually means that he or she is imbued with intestinal fortitude (see *Bertha Broygiss, The Brass-Bottomed Barmaid* by Damon Runyon). Or guts (see *Bull in the Afternoon* by E. Hemingway).

Ex.: Let us take a boy named Benjamin Kramer (1075 Tiffany Street, the Bronx, N.Y., U.S.A., North America). He is walking home in the wee (early) hours of a Sunday morning in May. Benny is tired but his step is light. He has had an exhilarating evening. The streets are deserted. Once you turn off 180th and head south, there are no restaurants or delicatessens or movie theaters. No neon signs. Not even an occasional taxi. And very few streetlamps. Benny has entered one of the more modest residential sections of the Bronx. He is aware that socially it is a cut above East Fourth Street. So he disregards the fact that he wishes he is smelling the sharp, oil-rich odor of the East River, and hearing the creak of the barges as they tug at their moorings. That's kid stuff, and nobody knows it better than Benny, who is no longer a kid. Ask Hannah Halpern.

As he approaches the small tenement in which he lives, Benny glances at his watch. It is a pocket watch. A Waltham. A bar mitzvah present from his Aunt Sarah in New Haven. Benny wishes she had given him a wrist watch. Wrist watches are the new thing. Mr. Bern, Benny's boss, wears a wrist watch. But the wish is a passing fancy (idle thought). Benny is startled to learn from his Waltham that it is three o'clock in the morning. Where have the hours fled?

Benny comes into the Kramer kitchen. The ceiling light is on. It is electric light. Much better than the Welsbach mantles fed by gas down on East Fourth Street. Electric

96

light. What a marvelous thing. It slides into every corner of a room. Like batter into every corner of a honey cake pan. It shows you things you never saw before. Like Benny's mother sitting at the kitchen table. At three o'clock in the morning. She looks up at her son.

"Where were you?" she says.

This is where Benny realizes he needs *koyach*.

"Hannah and I decided to take in the midnight show," I said.

"The midnight show?" my mother said. "One movie a night it's not enough for you?"

"We didn't plan to see the midnight show," I said. "But when the picture was over, around eleven-thirty, the lights went up and a man came out on stage and he said there was going to be a sneak preview."

"A what?" my mother said.

"A sneak preview," I said. "A movie it has not been shown yet."

"Then why do they show it in the middle of the night?" my mother said.

Because the people who make them wouldn't dare show them in the broad light of day.

"I don't know," I said. "They sort of want to get a reaction from people. The people have come in to see an entirely different movie. Like me and Hannah. A movie that's advertised outside. They then put on this other one. It's not advertised yet. They want to know how people like it. So if you stay in your seat, you can see this new new movie. You can see it free. For the price of admission to one picture they surprise you and you get a double feature. Ma, why are you whispering?"

"Because there's people asleep," my mother said. "On East Fourth Street when people were sleeping, other people screamed. Like animals in a farmyard. Here, on Tiffany Street, it's not animals. It's people."

I assumed she meant the other people in the building. In our apartment the only people who could be asleep were my father and my mother. My father would have slept through the fall of the Bastille. Down on East Fourth Street he had slept through the celebrations of the False Armistice and then the real one. When he lay down on his bed my father was a toppled statue.

"I'm sorry," I said in in a whisper. "I didn't realize I was hollering."

"I said you were hollering?" my mother said. "I said people are sleeping."

"Okay," I said. "I'd better get some sleep myself."

"Do it in the front room," my mother said.

It was as though my mother had told me to take my bath in the font of St. Peter's. Our front room was our showplace. The Kramer family's royal enclosure at Ascot. It contained our dining room "set." It was the place we entered once a week, on Friday night, to eat the Sabbath meal.

"In the front room?" I said.

"Now you're hollering," my mother said.

"Why can't I sleep in my own room?"

It was one of the marvels of moving up to the Bronx. I could no longer smell the river, but I had a room of my own.

"Because that boy is sleeping in your room," my mother said.

For a few moments I didn't know what she was talking about, but I knew she always did. My mother used words the way she used money. With care. Her supply of both was limited. I looked around the kitchen. On the table I saw the neatly stacked piles of "turning." Like bricks of colored cloth. Held together by rubber bands. Ready for delivery to Mr. Lebenbaum's jazz bow factory on Intervale Avenue. It was the first time since I had left the house at eight o'clock that our unexpected visitor had crossed my mind.

"That boy?" I said. "You mean Sebastian Roon?"

"A mistake," my mother said. "His name is Rubin."

Astonished, I said, "Who? Roon?"

"No, Rubin," my mother said.

My mind darted back to the day before, in the office of I. G. Roon, Ltd., on West 21st Street. I remembered Sebastian Roon's assumption that Mr. Shimnitz was actually Mr. Shmootz.

"You mean he's a Jewish boy?" I said.

"Why not?" my mother said. "Everybody is Jewish." It was her most firmly held conviction.

"I'm talking about our visitor," I said.

"He's a Jewish boy like you," my mother said. "He doesn't sound like you, because he doesn't scream in the middle of the night when people are sleeping, and he doesn't go to double features, and he comes from a different place."

"Who's screaming?" I said. Like jesting Pilate, I did not stay for an answer. "Blackpool?" I said.

"That's the place," my mother said. "He explained to me. His uncle Isaac—"

"Wait a minute," I said. Things were falling into place in my head with thuds that left aching reverberations. The I. in I. G. Roon, Ltd., practically dropped through my brainpan into my peritoneal membrane. I said, "You mean I. G. Roon, Ltd., is Isaac G. Roon, Ltd.?"

"No," my mother said. "I. G. Roon is Isaac Gustave Rubin, and then those extra things you said. The I, or the L, and the t, and the d."

I took a stab at pulling myself together. It was like clawing together the contents of a suitcase that has burst in a railway station.

"How do you know all this?" I said.

"We talked," my mother said. "Me and Seymour."

Boing!

"Seymour," I said. "You mean Sebastian?"

"No, Seymour," my mother said. "He told me his name is Seymour Rubin, but when his uncle brought him over here from this Blackpool, he needed him in the business, the uncle said from now on you're not Seymour Rubin. From now on you're like me, a Roon, and also the first name, I don't know how to say it."

I could scarcely manage it myself.

"Sebastian," I said.

99

"All right," my mother said. "You call it what you want. His real name, it's Seymour Rubin. He told me."

Hannah and the Gabilla's knishes we had consumed in the balcony of Loew's 180th Street fled from my consciousness like Dick Turpin putting the spurs to Black Bess on his way to York. The cold wind of reason swept through my mind.

"Ma?" I said. "How did he tell you?"

Her eyes narrowed. They looked like the penny slots in a child's coin bank. My mother stared at me as though in the midst of an intimate conversation with a friend or relative it had suddenly occurred to her that she was talking to an impostor.

"How did he tell me?" she said.

"Sebastian," I said.

"You mean Seymour?" she said.

"Yes," I said, "I suppose I do. How did Seymour tell you all this?"

My mother repeated the words slowly. As though she were dictating a telegram.

"How—did—Seymour—tell—me—all—this."

She shifted her glance. My mother had an impressive glance. When she narrowed it she could split the electric beam guarding the main vault at Fort Knox. I felt nailed to the wall.

"You mean how did we talk?" she said.

"Yes," I said. "What language?"

"Yiddish," my mother said. "How else could we talk?"

How else indeed? And why not? Being a Jew is an endlessly rewarding thing to be. You start from way back, especially if you are a ghetto or East Fourth Street Jew. No lessons needed in crining. Or crouching away from blows. Or pretending you have not heard insults. They all come with the package. Including the necessity to learn slowly how to straighten up and close your hands into fists and give as good and better than you are forced to take. This is the exhilarating period of the awakening. Then reason takes over. Reason leads to pride. Pride leads to incredulity. What in God's name was I afraid of? These pigheaded

100

fools? These savage idiots? The questions answer themselves, and then the fun begins. The dividends of emancipation start rolling in. Tearing away curtains. You meet someone you like. Someone you are drawn to. But you are afraid to be drawn. Or you were, and you can't forget it. Not yet. You are a Jew from East Fourth Street, functioning uptown, being circumspect. In blunt words, pretending not to be a Jew. There are so many ways to act out the pretense without having to speak the lie, that what you are doing does not seem reprehensible. After all, you've made it to Tiffany Street. Let's not rock any boats at this intermediate stage. You're not going to remain on Tiffany Street forever, are you? You've got to keep your nose clean for the next move. Which will naturally be in the general direction of up. And this guy is an Englishman named Sebastian Roon. Sebastian Roon? Even Dickens wouldn't dare. Chuzzlewit? Okay. Nicholas Nickleby? Well, all right. Barnaby Rudge? Let it pass. But Sebastian Roon? Jesus Christ on a raft! What's going on here? Answer: a Jew discovering the pleasure of discovering another Jew.

"And he's sleeping in my bed," I said.

I was aware that I sounded like the dopey member of the Three Little Bears who pulled it all together, but I was also aware of something else: my mother was pleased. She was not a woman whose life had been dotted with many good moments. I could see this night had given her pleasure. So I reaped the dividend. It gave me pleasure. And for the moment I stopped worrying about my relationship to her. For the moment I liked her.

"What else could I do?" my mother said. "When we finished the 'turning' it was already after eleven."

"The 'turning,' " I said. "Did he tell you how he knows about jazz bows?"

"Sure he told me," my mother said. "In this place where he was born. What's the name?"

"Blackpool," I said.

"That's the place," my mother said. "It's a terrible name to give a place."

"Why?" I said.

101

"It sounds so dark," my mother said.

I hadn't thought of that.

"It's like Coney Island," I said. "There's sun and sand and fresh air."

"Maybe," my mother said. "But Seymour told me about this Blackpool, and to me it sounds like East Fourth Street. His father was a butcher, but he died. So his mother had to do something to put the bread on the table. What she did, she did like the other women did. She started to take in 'turning' for a man he manufactured jazz bows. Look." My mother touched the neatly stacked rectangles of colored silk. "You ever saw such beautiful work?"

Not on Tiffany Street.

"He's good," I said.

It was not really what I wanted to say, but I didn't know how to say what I did want to say. I was jealous.

"He's a wonderful boy," my mother said.

Oh, come on, now, I thought. You've just met him. But I didn't say it. I couldn't spoil her pleasure.

"He's not bad," I said. Holding down the grudging tone.

"So when he finished with the 'turning,' " my mother said, "I looked at the clock. It's late. Why don't you sleep over here by us?"

"And he said yes," I said.

I couldn't think of any dialogue for myself. So I filled in with his.

My mother nodded. "I put him in your room," she said. "And for you I made a bed on the floor in the front room."

It was not exactly a bed. My mother had pushed the round fake mahogany dining room table to one side and, on the floor, had spread one of the *perrinas,* or feather beds, she had brought from Hungary when she came to America as a girl. It may well be the perfect sleeping accommodation. If you are young, that is. And have just taken in the midnight show with Hannah Halpern at Loew's 180th Street. The next thing I knew it was six o'clock and my mother was shaking me awake.

"I'm cooking for you an egg," she said.

I couldn't have been more surprised if she had said she

102

was hatching it. My staying-power breakfast was heavy on things like oatmeal, farina, and chunks of rye bread. I had never in my life had an egg for breakfast.

"An egg?" I said.

My mother's voice was sharp. "What's wrong with an egg?"

Six o'clock in the morning. After two and a half hours' sleep. The offices of Maurice Saltzman & Company on West 34th Street waiting for my ministrations. And your mother asks you what's wrong with an egg.

"Nothing," I said. "It's just I'm not hungry."

"Since when are you in the morning not hungry?" she said.

Since I ate two Gabilla's knishes the night before. They had more than staying power. They had a tendency to take up permanent residence. I could still taste them.

"Just a piece of bread and a glass of milk," I said. "That's all I want, Ma."

"So what should I do with the egg?" she said.

I refrained from the traditional reply. She was, after all, my mother.

"Save it for Sebastian," I said.

"Who?" my mother said.

So I knew I had a right to be jealous. He had won her heart.

"Seymour," I said.

My mother smiled. She was then, as I work out the arithmetic, in her mid-thirties. She was then also, as she had always been, a Hungarian. Need I say more? My mother did not smile often. Her life had not been anything Lehár would have chosen as the libretto for an operetta. But when my mother did smile you believed all those movies in which Jeanette MacDonald sang her heart out to Nelson Eddy as they leaped from *Schloss* to *Schloss*. My mother was a Gabor sister before the Gabors were invented.

"All right," she said. "I'll save it for him."

While she was saving it, I was on the subway. I arrived in the offices of Maurice Saltzman & Company on time.

103

Mr. Bern had told me, when I was hired, that he expected me to have the office "ready" at eight sharp. He had made it sound as though he expected me to have a regiment fed, equipped with ammunition, and checked out for possible weapon failure by the time he was ready to step in and give the order to go over the top. This was pretty much the basic situation every morning in the M.S.&Co. office, so I made it a point to arrive on 34th Street, and let myself into the office with my key, at 7:45. The moment I pulled that key out of the lock, and the door slammed shut behind me, I went into action.

Reception room: remove inverted five-gallon empty jug of Western Spring Water from cooler near Mr. Saltzman's green stagskin. I grab the fat paper sack of cracked ice from the brown marble floor outside the reception room where it was dumped by the Seventh Avenue Ice Delivery Corporation while I was on the subway. I pour the cracked ice into the circular trough on top of the water cooler. I pack the ice into place. Packing ice in 1930 meant whacking the stuff down with hard sharp slaps of the open palm. I have the scars to prove it.

I dump the empty ice bag and the empty Western Spring Water jug outside in the hall. From the file room I drag a fresh jug of Western Spring Water. Water in bulk is heavy. I jockey the jug into the reception room, hoist it up onto the cooler, neck down, and pant as I watch the big greenish-white bubbles come exploding up. Glug, glug, glug. There is something satisfying about a five-gallon jug of Western Spring Water settling into place in a cooler. What can it be? A sense of accomplishment, probably. Well, that's done. Now the cigarette butts.

I do not smoke. So I don't really feel I have the right to comment on this addiciton. But I think it is a matter of simple honesty to record that in 1930, on West 34th Street, I hated every son of a bitch who touched flame to tobacco in the offices of Maurice Saltzman & Company.

I dump the contents of all the ashtrays into a brown tin wastebasket. Phew! I run the wastebasket into one of the pots and flush it. Then I run the wastebasket back into the office, collect the empty ashtrays, and take them out to the file room.

The file room has a basin with running water. I rinse the ashtrays. Phew again. I give each ashtray a fast swipe with a wad of damp toilet paper, distribute the trays around the office, and tackle Mr. Saltzman's green stagskin. He brought it back from the premises of a bankrupt leather goods firm on Leonard Street where we were doing an audit for the Irving Trust Company, and he had spread it on the table in our reception room. Mr. Saltzman was crazy about that green stagskin. I had to polish it every morning.

I was buffing away at the stag's rump when he came out into the reception room. This was a surprise. Mr. Saltzman was the senior member of the firm. He rarely arrived in the office before nine-thirty, after Ira Bern had assigned the members of the staff and sent them off on their tasks for the day. Yet here it was not quite eight-thirty, and here was Mr. Saltzman.

"Benny," he said.

"Yes, sir?"

"Come in a minute in Mr. Bern's office, Benny."

Mr. Saltzman turned. His eye caught the rump of his beloved green stagskin. He stopped moving. His eyes spread wide. He went to the table. He stroked the green leather. He turned to me. Mr. Saltzman was beaming.

"Benny!" he said. "You did it!"

"What?" I said.

"You brought up the lights!"

I turned to take a look of my own. By God, I had! I smiled shyly and scuffed the toe of my shoe across the carpet.

"Oh, well, Mr. Saltzman," I said. "They were always there, I guess. It was just a matter of giving it the old elbow grease."

Mr. Saltzman put his arm across my shoulders. "You're a good boy, Benny," he said. "Come into Mr. Bern's office."

I followed him. Seated beside Mr. Bern's desk was Mr. I. G. Roon.

"You look better than you did Friday," he said.

His voice was not friendly. But it had not been friendly on Friday at the lunch table in Shane's on 23rd Street. I remembered that I had not liked him on Friday. Then I remembered a number of other things. They did not help me like him on Sunday.

"I wasn't feeling good on Friday," I said.

"You can say that again," said I. G. Roon.

Like most people, I don't like to be disliked. When I learn that I am, my first reaction is dismay. Here I am, a first-class charmer, stepping forward at my most charming, and what happens? I walk into a wall of wet cement.

"I'm sorry," I said.

It was no moment for repartee.

"So you know Benny?" Mr. Saltzman said.

"Maurice, yes, Isaac knows Benny," Ira Bern said. "I told you about the lunch Friday at Shane's."

"Oh, yes," Maurice Saltzman said, and he must have had a vision of his green stagskin out in the reception room, because again he put his arm across my shoulders. "Benny is a good boy," Maurice Saltzman said.

"He's a lousy drinker," I. G. Roon said.

"At his age," Maurice Saltzman said, "who is a good one?"

Mr. Roon grunted. It occurred to me that he looked terrible. In Shane's on Friday he had been no prize package but he had looked trim. He did not look trim now. In fact, he looked seedy. I noticed he was wearing the same suit in which he had walked into Shane's on Friday.

"Let's get going," he said. He looked at his watch. "We don't have too much time to waste."

"You're right," Mr. Bern said. He pulled out his wallet and set it on top of some papers on the desk. "Benny, here's a ten." He drew a ten-dollar bill from the wallet. "Go over to Lou G. Siegel's and bring back three hot pastrami sandwiches."

"Corned beef for me," I. G. Roon said.

"Two hot pastrami, Benny," Mr. Bern said. "And one corned beef."

106

"You mind, Ira, I have tongue?" Mr. Saltzman said.

"Mind?" Ira Bern said. "Why should I mind?" He held the ten-dollar bill out to me. I took it. "Benny, make it one hot pastrami, one corned beef, and one tongue."

I took the ten-dollar bill and hesitated. "Mr. Bern," I said. "It's half past eight in the morning."

Mr. Bern tapped the tiny mustache under his nose. My remark seemed to have confused him. I knew the next step. I had lived through it many times. He was about to get sore at me.

"What difference does the time make?" he said.

Not sore. Not yet, anyway. But not friendly.

"The kid's right," I. G. Roon said. "Lou G. Siegel, this hour of the morning, they're probably still closed."

"You mean not yet open, Isaac," Maurice Saltzman said. He gave my shoulder a squeeze. "What we want, Benny, we want three sandwiches, and we want them fast. Lou G. Siegel's is closed, or not yet open? Go in any place and get three sandwiches, but get them fast, Benny."

"Yes, sir," I said. I started for the door.

"Coffee, too," Ira Bern called.

"No, tea," I. G. Roon said.

"Mine with lemon," Maurice Saltzman called.

"For me cream," I. G. Roon called.

"Yes, sir," I said. And I got out of there.

I did not get very far out before I realized it was foolish to go all the way up to Lou G. Siegel's delicatessen on 39th Street. At eight-thirty in the morning, on a Sunday, the only place that can possibly be less dead than Seventh Avenue in the heart of the garment center is the north bank of the river Styx.

Out on the street, trying to think what course of action to take, I saw the sign over the Automat, winking on and off briskly next to Macy's. I couldn't help wondering. Electricity costs money. To whom were the owners of that sign winking? There was not a living movement visible as far north as Times Square and as far south as the eyes of Benny Kramer could see. But that sign kept banging away. I decided to take the hint. I ran across the street and

107

slapped down my ten-dollar bill on the marble counter in front of the cashier's booth.

"Nickels, please," I said.

"A dollar?" the cashier said. "Two?"

I took a chance. There was something about those three men up in Mr. Bern's office at eight-thirty in the morning that sounded a note I was to catch years later, over and over again, as my work caused me to examine the expense accounts of other men, and the tax structure forced me to compose my own: if it's a deduction, always choose the higher figure.

"Two dollars, please," I said.

The girl spilled out the nickels. I swept the coins across the marble into my left hand, shoved into my pants pocket the paper money she had given in change, and realized I was in trouble. At Lou G. Siegel's, when you bellied up to the "to go" counter, whatever you bought was wrapped in wax paper and placed in brown bags so you could go with it. In the Automat the food that came popping out of the small boxes in the wall sat on plates, ready to be eaten on the spot. The "Take-out" Automat had not yet been invented.

I stood there, in that huge white, white, blindingly white chamber, weighing my future. As avoirdupois, I must confess it didn't seem to come to much. The tension when I was hustled out of Mr. Bern's office had been unmistakable. What the tension was about I did not know. But the sight of those three men, Mr. Bern, Mr. Saltzman, and I. G. Roon, crowded around a desk in an office at eight-thirty on a Sunday morning was not something a boy from East Fourth Street could accept as normal. I felt like a seismograph recording the distant tremors of a disaster, the nature of which was still unclear. The food I had been ordered to bring, and bring fast, was obviously part of an attempt to keep the disaster from reaching the door of Maurice Saltzman & Company. My fate depended on doing my part. Whatever my part was.

"Benny."

I turned. Miss Bienstock had appeared beside me. She was carrying a tray.

"Good morning," I said.

She received this greeting in the Automat as she received it every morning in the Maurice Saltzman & Company office: with that perplexed scowl which somehow added rather than detracted from her basic comeliness.

"Benny," she said. "What are you doing here? Why aren't you downstairs in the building lobby getting Mr. Bern's shoes shined?"

"Because he sent me to get three sandwiches," I said.

"Three?" Miss Bienstock said. "Eight-thirty in the morning?"

"Plus coffee for one," I said. "And two teas, one with lemon and one with cream."

"Oh, my God," Miss Bienstock said.

"What's the matter?" I said.

"You're sure one of those teas is with cream?" Miss Bienstock said.

"Absolutely," I said.

"That means Mr. I. G. Roon is in the office," she said.

"He is," I said. "With Mr. Bern and Mr. Saltzman."

"Mr. Saltzman, too?" Miss Bienstock said. "At eight-thirty in the morning?"

"Yes," I said. "They were all sitting around Mr. Bern's desk. He wants with lemon. Mr. Saltzman."

"Oh, my God," Miss Bienstock said again.

There was in her voice the feel of lights burning late in embassy offices, the smell of midnight fires hurriedly burning secret papers in chancellery compounds.

"Are you okay?" I said.

"Me?" Miss Bienstock said. "It's not me."

She turned and set down her tray on the nearest table. It rocked back and forth because of the bumps in the aluminum. The coffee splashed out of her cup. So did the orange juice out of the glass beside the cup. Both slopped onto the plate of toast. Miss Bienstock had obviously been about to have breakfast.

"You get the sandwiches," she said. "I'll get the coffee and tea."

She raced away toward the wall of beverage spigots.

"The other tea is with lemon!" I called after her. "One with cream! One with lemon!"

She came back as I was working my stack of sandwiches onto an empty tray.

"You carry," Miss Bienstock said.

I picked up the tray. The top sandwich, unsupported, fell off the stack.

"Never mind," Miss Bienstock said. She grabbed the sandwich. "Follow me."

Holding the ham sandwich aloft—a banner with a device strange indeed—as though under it she was leading her troops into battle, Miss Bienstock charged the revolving door. Before I could follow, a busboy grabbed my arm.

"Where you going with that tray?"

Fortunately, the hard shove with which Miss Bienstock had entered the revolving door kept it spinning. A fast backward glance gave her the picture. She did not allow the door to spill her out into Seventh Avenue. Miss Bienstock remained in transit. Completing the circle, she erupted back into the Automat with considerable thrust. It taught me an important lesson. Always trust centrifugal force. It carried Miss Bienstock up to the busboy and, without pause, she shoved the ham sandwich into his face.

"We're going across the street," she said. "He'll bring the tray right back." To me: "You first." She shoved me into the revolving door. "This time," Miss Bienstock said, "I'll follow."

She did. So rapidly that, when we popped into Seventh Avenue, the sandwich she was carrying crunched damply against the back of my neck.

"Ooh!" I said.

"Never mind," Miss Bienstock said. "I'll clean it off later. Come on. We've got the light."

We also had luck with the elevator at 224 West 34th. When we came racing in from the street, the elevator was sitting in the lobby. They were not very good elevators. It was a very old building. So were the operators. And on Sunday only one was on duty.

"Lennie," Miss Bienstock said. "Take us up. Quick!"

Her voice had the ring of Paul Revere clattering through the Middlesex night.

"Yes, Miss Bienstock," Lennie said.

Up we went. Out into the fifth-floor corridor. Around the brown marble bend to the double doors on which was lettered MAURICE SALTZMAN & COMPANY. Miss Bienstock clattered the doors open. I followed. And stopped so suddenly that I hit her in the left buttock with the Automat tray.

"Oh," she said.

"I'm sorry," I said.

She didn't answer. Who could blame her? She was doing what I was doing. Staring. At Mr. Bern, at Mr. Saltzman, at Mr. Roon, and at a fourth man. I had no trouble recognizing him. This was the man who on Friday had interrupted the lunch I was having in Shane's restaurant on 23rd Street with Sebastian Roon and his uncle.

"Hi, kid," Mr. O'Casey said. I didn't realize he was addressing me until, through a sour grin that was really not a grin, he said, "How's your head?"

The answer was: confused. I did not make it, however, because odd things began to happen.

One: Mr. Bern raced across the reception room, grabbed the Automat tray from me, raced back to the table near the water cooler, and slapped the tray down on the haunches of Mr. Saltzman's green stagskin.

Two: Mr. O'Casey sauntered over to the tray, looked down at the sandwiches and cardboard containers, and said, "This is a Sunday morning breakfast?"

Three: I noticed that the face of Sebastian Roon's uncle looked not unlike Mr. Saltzman's stagskin—green.

Four: Mr. Saltzman came closer to the table and said, "Sure. We have breakfast here every Sunday morning. My partner here, Mr. Bern, and me, and our former client, Mr. Roon."

Five: "Your former client?" Mr. O'Casey said.

111

Six: "What else," Mr. Bern said. "A man he's had a heart attack, he can't work anymore, we like to remember the old days, so we invite him in every Sunday morning, because it's not a business day, we invite him in for a little friendly breakfast. No business, of course. Mr. Roon, he's not allowed to conduct any business, as you know."

Seven: "We sure do," Mr. O'Casey said. "That's why my company is paying him that big fat monthly check every single goddamn month in the year."

Eight: Sebastian Roon's uncle, his coloration changing slightly until he resembled the shamrock in the ads for the Irish Tourist Bureau, said: "I bought that policy fair and square. You bastards were glad enough to collect the premium all these goddamn years. Now, now I'm a sick man, now I can't work, you bastards you're trying to get out of paying me what you insured me for. Well, you bastards, you're not getting out of it. I'll fight you bastards in the courts if it takes my last penny, you bastard." He moved toward the table, pulled up a chair, sat down, and said, "Come on, Ira. Come on, Maurice. Let's eat."

I will not omit the numbers. At this point things became too confused for numbers. I'm not sure I can sort out the confusion into separate acts. They all seemed to bleed into one another, like the paints in the watercolors Miss Kahn used to try to teach us how to do in P.S. 188 kindergarten class. The last sharply etched single act I remember is Mr. Roon picking up one of the sandwiches. Mr. O'Casey lunged forward and snatched the sandwich from Sebastian Roon's uncle.

"Give me back my sandwich!" I. G. Roon shouted.

"And let you get kicked out of heaven?" Mr. O'Casey said. "My company gives its customers not only financial protection, but also spiritual. This is ham, Isaac. Ham. You want to go to hell?"

"Listen," Mr. Saltzman said. "It's Sunday. On Sunday we always have ham sandwiches."

"Mr. Saltzman," Mr. O'Casey said, his hard, angular face twisted in a spiky look of terrifying reproach. "What would your mother say if she heard you speak like that?"

112

Mr. Bern stepped in and picked up the second sandwich. "I knew Mr. Saltzman's mother," he said. "She was a wonderful woman. She's now gone, God bless her, she should rest in peace, but I think I can speak for her without fear of contradiction or erroneous statement."

"You trying to tell me," Mr. O'Casey said, "Mr. Saltzman's mother would approve of him eating ham?"

"Only on Sundays," Mr. Bern said.

"What the hell has Sunday got to do with it?" Mr. O'Casey said.

"On Sundays," Mr. Bern said, "it doesn't count. How about joining us, Mr. O'Casey?"

The detective for the insurance company glanced at the Automat tray sitting on the green stagskin. "Looks to me like you've run out of sandwiches," he said.

After forty years I am still not certain that I now saw what it seems to me I must have seen. Miss Bienstock, looking as perplexed as ever, stepped forward.

"Here, Mr. O'Casey," she said. "Have this one."

What she was holding out, of course, was "Excelsior!" The banner with a strange device under which she had led me out of the Automat: the last of the three ham sandwiches. It had lost much of the sheen it had possessed when I drew it out of the small metal box on the Automat wall. After all, Miss Bienstock had dented it when she shoved it into the face of the busboy, and she had damaged it further when she splashed it against the back of my neck on the Seventh Avenue sidewalk. It looked a bit lopsided. Perhaps that is what caused Miss Bienstock to stumble.

She lost her grip on the battered sandwich. It flew up and out, missing Mr. O'Casey completely, and landed with a plop on the other end of Mr. Saltzman's green stagskin. Just in time for Sebastian Roon's uncle to fall face down into the sandwich.

I did not understand what was happening until I heard the hoarse, choking noises that came out of his mouth. They sounded like great rusted spikes being drawn with tremendous effort out of a waterlogged plank. Then I saw Mr. Roon's shoulders heaving. When I realized what he

113

was doing, I turned away. The sight of a man vomiting is not entrancing. On that Sunday morning it was more than a sight. It was a bell tolling.

I learned later that Mr. Roon was having his last heart attack.

5

Forty years after it happened, sitting at the desk in my office on Madison Avenue, I could suddenly feel again the sense of dismay that had overwhelmed me on that strange Sunday morning in 1930. I stared at Miss Bienstock. She was holding the telephone out to me. For a moment I couldn't remember why.

"It's Mr. Roon," she said patiently. "He wants to talk to you."

I took the phone. "Seb?" I said.

"Benjamin, my boy."

One of the nice things about our relationship is that for forty years I have called him Seb but he has never called me Ben.

"How are you, Seb?"

"I don't really know," he said.

The clipped British phrases made, as always, a pleasant noise in my ear. They gave me the feeling I was a citizen not only of Tiffany Street or even Madison Avenue, but of the world.

"I'm anxious to know how you made out with Dr. McCarran in Philadelphia," Seb said.

It occurred to me that the charming voice had changed since those early days on Tiffany Street and in the Maurice Saltzman & Company office. There was in Seb's voice now four decades of Scotch and sodas and Chesterfield cigarettes. They had converted the boyish, slightly Cockney piping of 1930 to what my wife calls the sexiest baritone on the English-speaking stage.

"I don't think I should discuss it on the phone," I said.

"Then come have a drink with me at the club," Seb said. "I can't wait to hear, even though you must be absolutely

115

flat out after a full day in Philadelphia testifying for the squid Shtinkenpopfer."

"Schlisselberger," I said. "And how did you know that? All I told you was that I was going to see Dr. McCarran."

"My dear chap, how did Walter Winchell know when Agamemnon set out for Troy to retrieve Helen from the arms of Priam? By the bye, have you seen him lately?"

"Who?" I said.

"Winchell," Seb said.

"Lately?" I said. "Seb, I have never seen him."

"Very much into the sere and yellow he is these days," Seb said. "Pity. He was always nice to me."

"Everybody has always been nice to you," I said.

True enough. There are charmers, and there are charmers. Seb was both.

"Including you," Sebastian Roon said. "I hope it hasn't been a matter of regret to you?"

There are questions that stop you cold. Even in a kidding conversation. Where nobody means anything more with his words than the pitcher in the bull pen means with those fancy warm-up throws. They look good, but will they do any good when he gets out on the mound?

Longevity, however, does more than please the life insurance statisticians. It adds shadows. Things you never before thought about suddenly stand out in clear outline. Sebastian Roon had asked a kidding question. But all at once it didn't sound kidding. Maybe it was because my head still ached from what the black boy had done to it at Penn Station. But I don't think so.

I think it suddenly seemed more than a dart of innocent fun, even though Seb may have intended it to be no more than that, because it came out of experience. Or rather, I'd had the experience with which to check it out. Forty years of it. I hope, Seb had said, being nice to me hasn't been a matter of regret to you?

"No, it hasn't," I said. "There are times when you are irritating, and maybe there have been more of those times than I would have liked, but on the whole, no. You have not been a matter of regret to me."

116

"Good," Seb said. "Will's in ten minutes?"

"I'll be there," I said.

It had been Will's in ten minutes for many years. Seb had put me up for membership soon after I was admitted to the bar. I walked around to 48th Street and climbed the linoleum-covered stairs that sagged. Those stairs always brought to mind that moment during the war when, in a practice exercise at that staging area in Kent before D-day, I had been forced for the first time in my life to climb a rope ladder.

Seb was sitting at the large round table up near the windows that look out on 48th. His forefinger and thumb twirled the stem of his martini glass as he smiled at Dr. Claude Pfeiffer. The N.Y.U. professor, who had lost most of his hair since I had first joined Will's, was telling the group around the table the story about Willie Maugham and the Internal Revenue Service. Coming down the long room toward the performance, I suddenly had a revelation about the core of Sebastian Roon's charm.

Seb must have heard that story, over the years, dozens of times. Even I, who came to the club far less often than he, had heard it more times than I could with any sense of accuracy count. And yet Seb was listening with a smile of eager anticipation.

He had the true actor's gift. Making it seem, night after night, performance after performance, that this was the first time he had ever uttered the lines. Or heard the other actor utter his.

Seb saw me, changed the smile, and waved me toward one of the smaller tables at the back of the room, under the Howard Chandler Christy painting of Robert Benchley. Walking toward it, I saw Seb rise. On his way to join me, he paused at the bar and said something in a low voice to the stern-face, white-haired old lady in black bombazine. She nodded severely and started to mix my drink. I knew it would be a martini even though I disliked martinis. The first day I came to Will's I ordered Cutty Sark on the rocks and the Madame Defarge at the bar had made me a martini. After all these years I still did not want a martini, but if

117

I wanted a drink at Will's that was what I was going to get.

"I say," Sebastian Roon said as he plopped down into the chair facing me. "What sort of horrors have you been involved in?"

The remark annoyed me. He sounded exactly like Miss Bienstock saying she could always tell when something troublesome was going through my mind.

"I've just been mugged," I said.

Sebastian Roon's glass, on its way to his mouth, did not falter. He took his sip. He is a Stanislavsky man.

"You mean mugged as in all those stories on page two of the New York *Daily News?*" he said.

"Page three," I said. "Page two is fading Hollywood stars who take overdoses of sleeping pills."

I gave him the details.

"Bad show, Benjamin," Sebastian Roon said. "Bad show indeed. Have you been to see a man?"

"It's too late in the day," I said. "I'll call Artie Steinberg in the morning."

"Any pain now?" Seb said.

"Nothing a drink won't fix." How I wished it was not a martini.

"Well, here it is, old boy."

The grim-faced old lady in bombazine set the drink in front of me.

"Take a good long pull," Seb said. I did. "Better?"

"Much," I said.

It wasn't. But I didn't mind that. If you can't lie to a friend, what's friendship all about?

"Now tell me about Dr. McCarran," Seb said.

I did.

"Do you think it will work?" Seb said.

"You ought to know," I said. "McCarran said you got him to do it for several of your actor friends during the war."

"Quite," Seb said. "And it did work for them, but this is a different war."

"I know," I said. "But the chemistry of the human body that leads to bed-wetting can't have changed much since

118

the Persian wars and earlier. I'm not too worried about that. McCarran struck me as a man who knows his stuff."

"But you're worried about something," Seb said. "I can tell."

"How would you like to have facing you the job of breaking this to Elizabeth Ann?" I said.

Seb twirled the stem of his glass for a few moments. "Yes," he said finally. "I see your point."

I thought he would. He had known Elizabeth Ann before I met her. In fact, Seb had introduced us.

"Anyway," I said, "don't you worry about it."

"It's not Jack and the draft board I'm worrying about," Seb said. "I'm sure McCarran has wrapped that up okay. And it's not your breaking it to Elizabeth Ann that worries me, either. You've been breaking things to her for thirty years. You'll pull this one off, too."

"So it must be something involving you," I said.

Sebastian Roon did quite a bit of worrying about things involving himself.

"Yes," he said, "and even raising the subject with you at a time like this makes me feel a bit of a stinker."

Sebastian Roon had been deploring for forty years that he felt a bit of a stinker. But the feeling had never even slowed him down in the process of asking his friends to immerse themselves up to their navels in his affairs. My experience with them was that Seb's affairs were never silly. Preposterous? Possibly. Outlandish? On occasion. But silly? Never. Was it silly for Columbus to tell Isabella he could reach India by sailing west?

The average citizen, when he comes to see a lawyer, wants a will written. Or a real-estate deal closed. Or a divorce arranged.

Not Seb. He had at war within him the instincts of a high spirited but thoroughly inept adventurer and the innocence of an enthusiastic schoolboy. He could drive you crazy, but he could never bore you. Not Benny Kramer, anyway. I felt about him the way my mother had felt about him. I loved the irritating son of a gun.

"Let's skip the clipped 'Oh, dear' malarkey," I said.

119

"You're not at the Lyceum in a revival of *The Last of Mrs. Cheney*. You're at Will's with your dopey old friend Benny Kramer from Tiffany Street. And actually, now that Benny is here, he's glad he is here. My head hurts, but you soothe me. Tell me slowly all about your current problem."

Seb stared down into his glass. He seemed troubled. As with all actors pushing sixty, especially good actors, when Sebastian Roon seems troubled your heart leaps. Being troubled seems right. It makes you both bigger men. Seb looked like Abraham Lincoln staring down from that marble armchair in the memorial on the Potomac.

"My problem," Seb said quietly. "My problem," he repeated. He sighed. "My problem, Benjamin, is that I'm suffering from an incurable disease."

My gut jumped. During the past eight months two friends had gone. My barber, and the man who had sat beside me in Bills & Notes at N.Y.U. Law School. The big C. I knew people who hated this euphemism for cancer. I just hated cancer.

"That's rough," I said as calmly as I could manage to enunciate the words. "Are you sure it's incurable?"

Seb's glance came slowly away from his glass. What was he doing in Will's? That profile belonged on Mt. Rushmore.

"Absolutely certain," Seb said.

The place where my head had hit the cab door was suddenly throbbing.

"What have you got?" I said. "Or don't you want to talk about it?"

"Of course I want to talk about it," Seb said. "If I didn't, would I have raised the subject?"

Probably not, I thought. But not very clearly. My head was going like a metronome.

"All right," I said. "Once on Tiffany Street we were small boys. Comparatively speaking. Now we're big boys. Undeniably. If you can face telling me, I can face hearing it. Seb, for God's sake, what damned incurable disease have you got?"

"It has a curious name," he said. Pause. "It's called Being Fifty-nine Years Old."

I wanted to laugh. But I didn't. My experience with wits is that it is a mistake to encourage them in setting up jokes. They think they've done it all themselves. And they continue.

"You're not fifty-nine," I said. "The fact that we are exactly the same age was established in 1930 on Tiffany Street in the Bronx, and I am fifty-eight."

"Four months past sunset and evening star," Sebastian Roon said. "You're on your way to fifty-nine, old boy, as surely as Leander was on his way to Hero when he dove into the Hellespont. Fifty-nine, Benjamin. Fifty-nine."

"No," I said firmly. "Fifty-eight."

"You like looking backward more than you like looking forward," Seb said.

I gave that a moment of thought. It was not easy, with my head going like Man O' War breaking away from the barrier, but it was rewarding. Things suddenly came clear.

"Yes," I said, "I do. Looking forward is for young people. Mariners. Olympic shot-putters. Pot smokers. Wampus baby stars. Black welterweights. Groupies. Professional football players. Vasco da Gama. Battling Siki. Charlie Paddock. Toby Wing. Mick Jagger. Jerry Rubin. Kids with years to waste. That's what those years are for. To be wasted. That's what being young is all about. You know that. We were young together. On Tiffany Street. At fifty-nine —no, damnit—at fifty-eight the view changes. It's a matter of simple arithmetic. You don't know my barber. A rare human being. Truly rare. Came to this country from Salerno about the time my father came from Austria. He had finally earned, after forty years of saving, he had in the bank the dough to nail down the title to his shop in the basement of the Crawford Hotel. I handled the closing for him. You would have thought he had been knighted. God, what a performance. Nothing beats pure joy. I wanted to sit there and watch him for the rest of the day. But Miss Bienstock would have disapproved. I wouldn't take a fee, so he gave

121

me a free haircut. Three weeks later the poor bastard was dead."

I closed my eyes and counted four throbs inside my head. They came steadily, at carefully spaced intervals. I thought of the day Jack had been born. Elizabeth Ann had waited until the pains were steady, coming at regularly spaced intervals, before she would let me call a taxi and she rang up Artie Steinberg. What a wife. Sorry, I mean what a life. But I'm going to let it stand. I've been lucky. I've had both. I opened my eyes.

"Looking forward is great when you're twenty," I said. "It's pointless when you're sixty. You know what's going to happen. Like everybody else, you know you're trapped by the numbers. You know people are going to die. Including you. Meaning me. So why not look back? To the time when we were all going to live forever."

"That's what Jim Mennen said at lunch today," Seb said.

"Jim who?" I said.

He gave it the eye spread he had used as Captain Hook in the Ina Claire revival of *Peter Pan* when he brought down the house with his malevolent pronunciation of the words: "Rrrrrich—dampppp—cake!"

"Do you mean to sit there, one of the most successful barristers in the Mecca of the Western World, and tell me you don't know James V. Mennen?"

"What's the V for?" I said.

I learned how to parry from Professor Simeon Tompkins who taught Evidence at N.Y.U. Law School. He also taught me his one joke: "Parry in haste, repeal at leisure."

"Victor," Sebastian Roon said. "James Victor Mennen is the president of the Anglo-British TV network."

"Oh, him," I said.

"What does that remark mean?" Seb said.

"I don't know," I said. I didn't. So I concentrated. It helped. "Yes, I do know," I said. "He's always in those Broadway columns that Elizabeth Ann reads and quotes from every morning while we're having coffee."

"That's right," Seb said. "But he's more famous for having boosted the ABTV common stock from forty-two, when he took over the presidency of the network three years ago, to one hundred and eight today when he took your chum Sebastian Roon to lunch."

"Where?" I said.

"What?" Seb said.

"Where did Mr. Mennen take you to lunch?"

"Now what the hell difference does that make?"

"None," I said. "Unless he took you to Shane's on West Twenty-third Street."

Seb laughed. "You are a silly ass," he said. "Shane's burned down the day Franklin Roosevelt closed the banks."

"I know," I said. "I just thought it would be nice if Mr. Mennen had not been aware of that, and wanted to take you to the place formerly frequented by Graham McNamee and Julius Tannen."

"Jim Mennen probably doesn't even know who Julius Tannen was," Seb said. "He took me to lunch at The Huffing Hickey."

"What's that?" I said.

"A restaurant without lights on East Forty-sixth," Seb said. "Where people go to discuss business deals if they don't want to be seen doing it."

"If they don't want to be seen doing it, why do they go to restaurants?" I said.

"Where do *you* go?" Seb said.

"I don't," I said. "I ask the party of the second party to come to my office."

"Ah, yes, you would," Seb said. "Thus taking all the fun and games out of it. The idea is to go to a place that is known as a rendezvous for people who don't want to be seen rendezvousing. Then you can issue indignant denials or demand retractions from gossip columnists who print that they saw you there."

"Have you demanded any retractions?" I said.

"Not yet," Seb said. "But I may."

I could almost see inside his head. I could chart the course of his mind. He liked to talk about his affairs, or

123

rather he liked to talk around them, but he hated to come to the point about them. Decisions frightened him. He had started to tell me whatever it was he had started to tell me, but now he was beginning to shy away. He wanted more time. Well, today he was not going to get it. Not from me. Not with my head throbbing.

"I've got to leave in a few minutes," I said. "Tell me about this Jim Mennen thing, or call me tomorrow." I waved to Madame Defarge. She came over, moving majestically, like the vessel that carried Charles Dana for two years before the mast. I handed her the martini. "Please take this damn thing away," I said, "and bring me some Cutty Sark on the rocks."

"But sir—" she said.

"Please don't argue," I said. "Just take this away and bring me some Cutty Sark on the rocks."

She sniffed. Yes, she did. Will's is that kind of club. Down at heel, but up on sniffs. She sniffed again and carried the martini away.

"My, but we're getting touchy with the advancing years," Seb said. "Aren't we?"

I gave that a moment of thought, too. The result surprised me.

"I think I am," I said. "Yes."

"You mustn't be," Seb said. "It's bad for the liver."

"It's not my liver," I said. "It's a touch of your malady. Time's running out, and I keep wondering what I've done with the time I've had."

"That's what Jim Mennen said."

"But I always thought he was a fairly young man?"

"He is," Seb said. "Fortyish, I would say. But he was talking to a fairly oldish man. Me."

"About what?" I said.

"He's got an idea for a TV series," Seb said.

All at once I remembered that Dr. McCarran had asked me to tell Seb that Mrs. McCarran wanted Seb to do some sort of TV series about which the McCarrans had heard from an ABTV executive in Philadelphia who was one of Dr. McCarran's patients.

124

"Involving you?" I said.

"Jim Mennen was not buying my lunch at The Huffing Hickey to tell me about his idea for a TV series involving Johnny Carson," Seb said. "Of course involving me."

"In what way?"

"As master of ceremonies," Seb said. "Or host."

I closed my eyes. It did not help. I could see the damn thing. My dear old friend. This tall, lean, handsome Englishman with the prematurely white hair and the sexiest voice on the English-speaking stage. Prancing out in a fanfare of foolishly noisy music, holding a clipboard and screaming in an adenoidally Cockney twang: "Hellew everybody! We have an absolutely marvelous, wonderful, extraordinary, delightful and truly formidably super shew for yew tonight! Truly super! The absolutely marvelous and super Jukes Kallikak and his world-famous ocarina! The utterly delectable and absolutely marvelously super Chesty Uplift and her Four Things! Buzz Saw Sapling and her incredibly super collection of wildly super woodpecker holes! Plus many many more! Many many more indeed! All wildly and frighteningly and enchantingly super! So now, on with the shew! Okye, Billye!" I opened my eyes.

"Is that all Jim Mennen told you about the show?" I said.

"No, no," Seb said. "He's got it all very clear in his head."

"Well," I said, "at least that's concrete."

"Don't be cynical," Seb said. "Mennen is quite bright. He's been thinking about the Bicentennial."

"The what?" I said.

"My dear chap," Sebastian Roon said. "Does it take an Englishman to remind you that in nineteen seventy-six this nation, one and indivisible, will be two hundred years old?"

It certainly did not. In restless moments on trains and planes, when *Bleak House* did not work, I closed my eyes and thrust myself back to Miss Bongiorno's Elocution Class in J.H.S. 64. At once, across the years, came the booming, resonant, lovely voice of the beautiful, white-haired old lady. Standing up in front of the class, head

125

thrown back, eyes shining. Bellowing—well. Well, yes. Bellowing. Miss Bongiorno liked volume. Bellowing: *"When —in—the—course—of—human—events—"*

"It slipped my mind," I said.

"According to Jim Mennen it seems to have slipped the minds of most Americans," Seb said. "Which caused him to do some thinking, and he came up with the idea for this series. He wants to call it *One Nation Indivisible*. And he wants me to be the star because I'm a rather well-known Englishman who has lived here for forty years."

"What's an Englishman got to do with America?" I said.

"Why, you bloody chauvinistic ass," Sebastian Roon said. "We lost the damn place to you. Remember?"

There she was again. Miss Bongiorno. Inside my head. Reciting—no, bellowing—Burke's "Conciliation with the Colonies."

"It was before my time," I said.

"It was before the time of all contemporary addicts of the boob tube," Seb said. "That's what Jim Mennen feels will make it go. I mean to say, most Americans have heard of Bunker Hill. But they don't really know the details of what happened. The way most Englishmen know about Guy Fawkes, but what do they really know? A schoolboy jingle. *Remember, remember the ninth of November.* Anyway, Mennen feels I'd be very good for this, and I think, if you don't mind my saying so, I think Mennen is right."

"So does Mrs. McCarran and Dr. McCarran," I said.

"What's McCarran got to do with it?" Seb said.

"After we finished talking about Jack and the draft board, Dr. McCarran said he hoped you would do this TV show."

"Well, I'll be damned," Seb said.

"Why?" I said.

"He's a man I met during the war," Seb said. "The same sort of thing you met with him today about Jack. I never realized he was interested in my career."

"Maybe he's not," I said. "Maybe it's Mrs. McCarran."

Pause. Seb's scowling absorption in the stem of his martini glass had become total.

126

"Good Lord," he said finally, in a very soft voice.

"I think she's very sick," I said. "Anyway, Dr. Mc-Carran hinted she was. She may be dying. There was something in his voice when he talked about her. He added that she would be eased if you did this TV series."

"Good Lord," Seb said.

"You've said that," I said.

"And I'll say it again," Seb said. "Good Lord."

"You mean you don't remember her?" I said.

"Not very clearly," Seb said.

"The way you don't remember Hannah Halpern?" I said.

"Benjamin," Seb said. "I don't expect a lawyer to be charitable, but neither do I expect him to hit below the belt."

"I am merely bringing you a message from Dr. Mc-Carran in Philadelphia," I said. "He told me his wife would be pleased if you agree to do this Jim Mennen TV series. If you don't mind my making a guess, I would say that, because of her illness, it's the only way she feels she will ever see you again, but that's only a guess, as I said."

"Good Lord," Seb said.

"You've got to stop saying that," I said.

"I don't see why," Seb said. "I don't think I even remember the girl."

"She remembers you," I said. "She and McCarran seem to have heard about the series from one of his patients. A man who is some sort of executive with the ABTV affiliate in Philadelphia. And she seems to feel you'd be absolutely right for this TV series."

"She *is* absolutely right," Seb said. "Just as Mennen is."

When Seb wanted to do something, he always felt the person who wanted him to do it was right, and Seb always wanted to do it for the same reason.

"Seb," I said. "Are you broke?"

Again he became absorbed in the stem of his glass.

"No," he said at last. "I'm getting sixteen hundred a week for this silly piece of bumf I'm prancing about in now, and it's silly enough to look as though it will go through the year. We're not selling out, but we're doing

127

quite well, and should be for another four or five months. Then twofers will carry us for another four or five. My TV residuals on the assorted rubbish I've done in the last dozen years come to a nice bit of featherbed to fall back on. So all in all I'm probably as unbroke as I've been since my uncle had his heart attack in the offices of Maurice Saltzman & Company on that horrendous Sunday morning in nineteen thirty."

"Then it's not because of money that you want to do this TV series?"

"I didn't say I want to do it," he said.

"Seb," I said. "I've just had my head hammered in front of Penn Station. It's throbbing. But it's still working. I don't know, however, for how long. While it is, tell me whether you want to do this series or not, and we can go on from there."

Through the scowl that cut deep into his cheeks the dimples that had won him his place in the hearts of the American housewife, Sebastian Roon continued to inspect the contents of his glass.

"Yes," he said finally, "I do."

"Why?" I said.

"I'm getting on," he said. "I've been here in America for forty years. I think—" Pause. "No," he said. "I know. I'd like to go home."

It's one of those words. To me it meant the apartment where Elizabeth Ann was at the moment trying to decide what I would like for dinner. To Robert Frost it was the place where, when you came back, they had to take you in. To lesser poets, who strive for the colorful image, it was where you hung your childhood. To Sebastian Roon—

My God, I thought. He means Blackpool!

"To England?" I said. He nodded. The fact that he didn't speak, just nodded, told me something. "Seb," I said. "You mean for good?"

"Why not?" he said. "I'm getting on for sixty. Retirement age, you know."

The words jolted me. If Seb was getting on for retirement age, how about Benny Kramer? We had been the

128

same age on Tiffany Street. Forty years later the arithmetic had to be the same here in Will's on 48th Street.

"What has that got to do with this Jim Mennen TV series?" I said.

"I've had a good life here in this country," Seb said. "I've always loved you Americans, and you've always been good to me. I have no complaints. But . . ."

Pause. If you're going to pause on a word, you can't do better than the word but. One syllable. With all the impact of a called strike whacking into a catcher's mitt. It gives you more than a pause. It gives you an audience. I leaned forward.

"But what?" I said.

"Declining years, failing powers, fear of losing favor with the public, all that sort of thing," Seb said. "I haven't given much thought to England since I arrived here in nineteen thirty. But now, the last few months, I don't know. England's been increasingly much on my mind."

"I still don't understand what that has to do with Jim Mennen's TV series."

"I'm not broke," Seb said. "As I've explained, at the moment I'm almost detestably solvent. But I don't have any capital to retire on."

It came home to me. Suddenly and chillingly and with the rancid flavor of selfishness. He was my friend. I loved him. And behind my back he had been planning in secret to go away from me. The unpleasant day suddenly became more unpleasant. I realized the depth of the hurt, and why it hurt. At my age, I did not want to lose people.

"You plan to retire to England?" I said. I forced myself to repeat his words: "For your declining years?"

Sebastian Roon nodded. "I'd like to," he said. "I haven't realized for years that it would come to that, but I suppose, underneath, it's been crouching in my mind for some time, waiting to pounce." He hesitated, took a sip from his glass, then said quietly: "Benjamin, I want to go home to die."

He was not a man who spoke in riddles. Seb didn't always say what he meant. When he meant what he said, however, I had never had any trouble understanding the words. Now, for the first time, I did have trouble. I believed him. I accepted the fact that he believed he wanted to go home to die. What I could not grasp was why? Dying was no picnic. Why go to the trouble and expense of arranging to have it happen to you in a place like Blackpool?

"Any special place in Blackpool?" I said.

"Islington Crescent," Seb said.

"Why?" I said.

"It's the street on which I was born," Seb said.

"I was born on East Fourth Street," I said. "I'd rather die on Fifth Avenue and Eighty-third."

"Why?" Seb said.

"I don't have to climb down five flights of tenement stairs to the backyard to get to the toilet."

"There's more to life than ready accessibility to a bathroom," Seb said.

"But not to death," I said. "And to die is why you say you want to go back to Islington Crescent."

"Don't you want to go back to East Fourth Street?" Seb said.

"It's gone," I said. "Buried under the cement of the East River Drive."

"Islington Crescent is still there," Seb said. "I want to go home to die."

I thought of suggesting that he read Thomas Wolfe. But he was a friend. I couldn't do that to a friend.

"How will this Jim Mennen series help you do that?" I said.

"Mennen said he wants the series desperately."

"Desperately?" I said.

"Yes," Seb said. "That's the word he used."

So I saw the point. "And he's willing to pay to get it?"

Seb nodded again. "He said he would work out any deal I wanted. All I had to do was get my lawyer together with his."

"You're sure about that word desperately?" I said.

"Absolutely," Seb said.

"Okay," I said. "Give me the name of his lawyer. I'll get you enough to retire on."

130

6

It was not an arrogant statement. Basically, every business deal is a fire sale. The man who wants to sell, will. At the buyer's price. I learned that early. From Ira Bern. On that Sunday morning in 1930 when Seb's uncle I. G. Roon died of a heart attack on Maurice Saltzman's green stagskin.

It was Miss Bienstock who phoned for the ambulance. While we were waiting, Mr. Saltzman removed from the table the three ham sandwiches Miss Bienstock and I had brought up from the Automat. He gave one to Ira Bern, took another for himself, and handed the third to me.

"You might as well eat it, Benny," Mr. Saltzman said. "In times like these a ham sandwich is not to be sneezed at."

"Thanks, Mr. Saltzman," I said. I turned to his partner. "Mr. Bern," I said, "while we're waiting, would you like me to take your shoes down to be shined?"

"It's Sunday," Mr. Bern said. "They're not open."

I had forgotten that. But I have never forgotten what happened next. After the ambulance arrived and the body of I. G. Roon was carried off to Bellevue, Mr. Saltzman pointed to the green stagskin.

"Benny," he said. "Take this away."

"Yes, sir," I said. "I'll take it out to the men's room and wash it."

"No," Mr. Saltzman said. "Get rid of it."

"You mean throw it away?"

"Yes," Mr. Saltzman said. He sounded sad but firm. "Get rid of it."

"Yes, sir," I said.

I rolled up the green stagskin on which I had so recently brought up the lights. I carried it out to the men's room,

131

and did a stupid thing. I stuffed it down one of the toilets, and flushed. What happened was not unlike what happened at Johnstown in Pennsylvania when the dam broke.

I retreated slowly, then ran for the door and slammed it shut. Outside I waited. Soon the roaring of the mechanism stopped and the seepage from under the door diminished. I went back down the corridor into the Maurice Saltzman & Company offices.

Ira Bern and Maurice Saltzman and Miss Bienstock were standing in a group around the desk in Mr. Bern's office. Miss Bienstock looked normal. That is to say, she looked perplexed. Mr. Saltzman and Mr. Bern looked as though they had just come out into the street from a subway wreck. Miss Bienstock, as usual, cut through to reality.

"Maybe Benny knows," she said.

Mr. Bern and Mr. Saltzman turned to look at me as though Miss Bienstock had suggested that maybe I knew the whereabouts of Justice Joseph Force Crater.

"Why should Benny know?" Mr. Bern said.

"He had lunch with him on Friday," Miss Bienstock said. "Only two days ago. You remember what happened, Mr. Bern."

"Oh, yes," Mr. Bern said. "That's right. But what has that got to do with—?"

"He in-*vi*-ted Benny," Miss Bienstock said, giving to her pronunciation of the verb a significance that she obviously wanted Mr. Bern to grasp. "Mr. Roon invited Benny to lunch, didn't he, Benny? Mr. Sebastian Roon?"

"My mother says his name is Seymour," I said.

"Your mother?" Mr. Bern said. "She knows Mr. Roon?"

"She knows him about the way I know him," I said.

"How come?" Mr. Bern said.

I hesitated.

"Benny is a good boy," Mr. Saltzman said. "He'll tell us. Won't you, Benny?"

I did. I left Hannah Halpern out of it, of course, but on the whole I related the events of the previous night with ac-

132

curacy. The information was received in troubled silence. Miss Bienstock broke it.

"You mean, then, Benny," she said, "that the young Mr. Roon is right this minute up there on Tiffany Street? Sleeping in your bedroom?"

"I don't know if Mr. Roon is still sleeping," I said nervously. "But he's probably still up there. He didn't seem to be in a hurry last night to go any place else. By now, my mother is probably making something for him to eat."

"Benny," Mr. Bern said. "Could you call him for us?" I must have looked undecided, because Mr. Bern said, "You have a telephone, no?"

"Oh, yes," I said proudly.

"Would you give him a buzz then?" Mr. Bern said.

"Sure," I said.

"Here," Mr. Bern said. "Use my phone."

Since it was the only phone in the room, I assumed he was paying me a compliment by allowing me a rare privilege. So I used his phone. My mother answered.

"Hello?" she screamed.

She did not, of course, understand electronics. She thought it made her sound more clear at the other end if she hurled her voice as loudly as she could into the mouthpiece at her end.

"Ma," I said. "Please bring Seymour to the phone. It's very important."

"What's very important?" my mother said.

"Seymour's uncle just died," I said.

My mother was very good about death. To my mother it did not mean fainting spells and screams of despair. To my mother death meant rolling up your sleeves. Funerals were as important as marriages. Perhaps more so. Who had time to weep? There was work to be done.

"He's coming!" my mother yelled. "He's finishing a potato *latke*."

That settled it. Nobody and nothing could provide greater proof of something I already knew or at least suspected. She had fallen in love with him. The potato *latke* is not a breakfast dish.

133

It is one of the great inventions of Western Civilization, but it is not a breakfast dish. It is a pancake made from ground raw potato to which are added a half a dozen ingredients. Or perhaps a dozen. Who knows except Brillat-Savarin and my mother, and they are now both gone. These ingredients zing the ground potato up to the point where people fight for the end product. Your genuine potato *latke* never gets served at a table. It is snatched out of the pan when ready, and gulped standing up at the stove, and it is not, repeat not, a breakfast dish.

"Hello, Benjamin?"

"Yes," I said. "It's me, Seb."

"What's the sweat, old boy?"

I told him. In that hushed tone I was beginning to learn was the uptown way of conveying the news of death. On East Fourth Street, except in the case of my no-nonsense mother, the melancholy event was always heralded with a long, loud scream.

"The silly ass," the voice of Sebastian Roon crackled in my ear. "He always chose the most inconvenient times to do the damnedest things."

"What?" I said.

"Where are you calling from?" Sebastian Roon asked. I told him. Pause. "Look," Seb said, and I wondered why people say that. Look at what? "Benjamin," Seb said. "Do you think you can keep them there? Mr. Bern and Mr. Saltzman? Until I get down? There are some things I must talk to them about at once."

"Hold it a second," I said. I turned to the three people in Mr. Bern's office. "He wants to know would you wait here for him? He'll come right down."

"Of course we will, Benny," Miss Bienstock said. "We're not going anywhere."

I told this to Sebastian Roon, and he said he would see us in about an hour.

"He's coming downtown right away," I said.

"Benny," Mr. Bern said. "The water cooler."

"Yes, sir," I said.

I had forgotten about the water cooler. Mr. Bern and

Mr. Saltzman retreated behind the closed door of Mr. Bern's office. Miss Bienstock went out into the stenographers' typing room. And I tackled the water cooler. My preoccupation was not total: the water cooler, the ashtrays, the wastebaskets all helped, but people don't die of heart attacks in front of you on green stagskins every day in the week. I was still somewhat dazed by the performance. I was still somewhat dazed when Sebastian Roon came into the reception room.

"Where is the silly ass?" he said.

I had a startled moment or two before I realized he was referring to his dead uncle.

"At Bellevue," I said. "The ambulance came and carried it, him, I mean the body, they took it away."

"Good riddance," Sebastian Roon said.

The remark upset me. On East Fourth Street there had been firm conventions of conduct about such things. None were more firm than the conventions about death. It was an event about which you were expected to be sad. I had not thought it would be different on Tiffany Street. Or, more accurately, on West 34th Street. A man had died. You were expected to look sad, appear distraught, and sound as though you were about to hurl yourself on the bier.

"It was terrible," I said in a confused voice.

"I don't doubt it," Sebastian Roon said. "Most events to which my uncle lent his talents were at least that, frequently worse than terrible. Where is Mr. Bern?"

"In his office," I said. "Over this way."

I led him to Mr. Bern's office door, knocked on it, and shoved it open. Sebastian Roon went in. I pulled the door shut and walked out to the stenographers' typing room.

"Miss Bienstock," I said, "does this mean we're in trouble?"

"Yes, Benny," she said, "I think we are in trouble, but I don't know how much trouble."

"I don't get it," I said. "I know Mr. Roon was a client, but after all he was only one client. We have dozens of clients. I know it's bad for us to lose any client, but why

135

does losing just one make so much difference to Mr. Saltz-man and Mr. Bern?"

"Well, you see, Benny, Mr. Roon was not just one client."

"He wasn't?"

"No," Miss Bienstock said. "You know Grantham Estates?"

Of course I knew Grantham Estates. I knew it the way a Fifth Avenue bus driver knows Saks Fifth Avenue. Something he passes regularly on his way downtown to Washington Square. One of my duties in the M.S.&Co. Offices was to keep the files tidy. Twice a day I collected the file folders from the various "out" boxes on different desks, and replaced them in the green metal cabinets that lined the walls of the file room. "Grantham Estates" was a thick folder just behind "Gogen-Heimowitz High Styled Kitchen Smocks, Inc."

"What about Grantham Estates?" I said.

"It's one of Mr. Roon's companies," Miss Bienstock said. "He's got about twenty."

I got the message. It took the form of a hot. terrifying wind of revelation: interlocking directorates; holding companies; conglomerates; cartels; write-offs; amortization; tax shelters; the whole complex, slippery apparatus that leads from tenement flats on East Fourth Street with toilets in the hall to huge villas at Montreux with doxies in every eiderdown.

"You mean Mr. Roonwas more than just one client?" I said to Miss Bienstock.

"Like I said, he was about twenty," she said. "From each one we drew about a hundred and a quarter a month. So you see, Benny . . . "

Benny saw. The Kramer family had just barely made it to Tiffany Street. We had been living there for what? Six months? Seven? And already we were being threatened with the Bronx equivalent of a *moof tzettle,* an order from the court to vacate for nonpayment of rent. At that particular moment, valiant was not the word for Benny. Then Sebastian Roon came into the file room.

136

"I've got to go over to our office and sort things out," he said. "Why don't you come along and help?"

I hesitated.

"Don't worry about Messrs. Bern and Saltzman," Sebastian Roon said. "I've asked them to release you in my custody, and they've agreed. Shall we go?"

We went out to the elevator and then out into the street. It was like coming out onto one of those moors to which Shakespeare always brings his main characters for their big soliloquies. I winced away from the sunlight.

"Are you equal to a brisk stroll?" Sebastian Roon said. "Thirty-fourth to Twenty-first. Thirteen squares. Not insurmountable, really. After all, Benjamin, we are young, aren't we?"

To my astonishment, I found myself laughing. There was something funny about this British kid from Blackpool, in his funny three-button tveet suit, and needing a shave, making jokes about our both being young. It doesn't sound like the raw material from which great comic masterpieces like "Casey at the Bat" are fashioned, but it did sort of part the clouds.

"We are," I said. "Let's go."

We went down Seventh Avenue at a good clip. I noticed the way he walked. As though it was not just a form of locomotion but an activity to which one devoted the sort of attention that a golf nut devotes to his follow-through. Sebastian Roon walked as though he were entered in a competition in which points were awarded for the form you displayed while doing it. He rocked back and forth from heel to toe. I just panted.

When we reached 21st Street I though of Hot Cakes Rabinowitz and the lift he had given me on Friday in the Built-In Uplift Frocks, Inc., truck. Could it really have happened on Friday? Only two days ago?

"Did they know you were coming?" I said to Seb when we came into the offices of I. G. Roon, Ltd.

I referred to the tall old lady in the alpaca dress buttoned up to her throat, and the old man with the tufts of white hair over his ears who wore long black stockings on

137

his arms from wrists to elbows. They were working away at their stand-up desks, their backs turned to each other, exactly as they had been on Friday. I wondered when they slept. Or went to the bathroom. They did not look up when Sebastian and I came into the outer office.

"Do they know what's happened?" I whispered.

"Without any doubt," Seb said, his voice low. "They've been with my uncle for donkey's years. They know everything that's been going on, and they've been expecting what's happened to happen for longer than you and I have lived. That's why they're here on Sunday. They haven't taken a day off in years. When things toppled, they wanted to be in at the death, you might say. And from the fact that I've come into the office on Sunday, accompanied by you, you can be sure they know things have finally toppled. Come in here, Benjamin, if you will, please."

We went into the private office with the windows that looked out on 21st Street.

"Now, Benjamin."

"Yes?" I said.

"I want you to be a witness to this," Sebastian Roon said.

He had pulled out a drawer in one of the wooden filing cabinets that lined the wall to the right of his desk. From the drawer he brought a green metal cashbox and set it on his desk. It was the sort of box in which Miss Bienstock kept the petty cash that paid for shining Mr. Bern's shoes every morning and underwrote his Lou G. Siegel hot pastrami sandwiches. Sebastian pulled from his pocket a key ring, selected from it a small key, and opened the green box. There were no coins in the small compartments up front, but the long rectangular compartment at the back was stuffed with paper money. Sebastian pulled out the bills and slowly counted them out onto the desk, muttering as he did so.

"Nine twenty," he said finally. "Nine hundred and twenty dollars. Correct?"

A moment went by before I realized he had asked me for corroboration.

"Is that correct?" Seb said sharply. "Nine hundred and twenty dollars?"

"Yes," I said hastily. "I guess so."

"You guess so?" Seb said. "You saw me count it, didn't you?"

I had, and I hadn't. Yes, I had seen the physical act of counting. And yes, I had heard Seb muttering as the total mounted. But I had not been aware of what I was seeing. I was not quite sure of what I now saw. Nine hundred dollars in real, live American money had about as much reality for me as the headwaters of the Amazon. I was still pleasantly dazed by the fact that every Saturday afternoon Mr. Bern handed me an envelope containing two fives and three singles.

"Yes, " I said. "I saw you count it."

"Good," Seb said. "Now come with me, please."

Carrying the batch of bills, he walked into the outer office. I followed. Seb went to the old lady. In front of her, on the stand-up desk, he counted out some bills.

"Twenty, twenty-five, thirty, thirty-one, thirty-two," he said.

So now I knew how much an old employee of I. G. Roon, Ltd., had earned each week.

"Thanks," the old lady said.

She picked up the bills, rolled them into a tight sausage, and did something my mother always did with paper money. She lifted her skirt and stuck the roll of bills into the top of her stocking. Seb moved across to the old man and repeated the performance.

"Thirty-six," he said at the end.

So I knew which of the two old people had seniority.

"This is the last?" the old man said.

"I'm afraid so," Seb said.

"Then he's gone, is he?" the old man said.

"This morning," Seb said. "Heart attack."

The old man nodded as he gathered the money and jogged the bills into a neat packet.

"Your uncle was not a bad man," he said. "He was near with the dollar, but he was not a bad man." He looked up at one of the framed pictures of rolling countryside. "Those rabbit ranches in Australia," the old man said. "Solid gold, once. Solid gold, now. It wasn't your uncle's fault men stopped wearing hats." He put the money in his pocket. "Any last things you want done here?"

"You're very kind to offer," Sebastian Roon said, "but it won't be necessary. Mr. Bern tells me all the last things will be done by the Receiver in Bankruptcy." Seb put out his hand. "Goodbye."

The old man took Seb's hand and shook it. Seb walked over to the old lady and put out his hand.

"Goodbye," he said.

The old lady looked down on Seb's hand as though he were showing her a rare geological specimen. She stared at it for a couple of moments. The specimen obviously held no interest for her. She turned back to the desk and picked up her pen.

"Let's go, Benjamin," Sebastian Roon said quietly.

On the way across the outer office he picked up a rubber band from a bowl on the table near the door. Out in the hall, while we waited for the elevator, Seb snapped the rubber band around the remainder of money he had removed from the cashbox in the inner office. He tossed the small bundle in the air and caught it as we stepped into the elevator.

"Well, there's the lot," Seb said. "One hundred and seventy-six quid, give or take a few bob. Odd, how life works out. I've been a good boy, and I've played my cards correctly, and I haven't blotted my copybook, and this bloody business, which I came to this country in the hope of some day owning, the whole damn things has gone up the spout. I'd probably have been better off if I'd remained in Blackpool."

I felt the way I used to feel in school when I read a question on an examination paper. Uneasy. Not because of the death of Mr. I. G. Roon. I had learned on East Fourth Street that death was a fact of life. Kids were born. People died. Next! What made me feel uneasy was the way Sebastian Roon was wrapping it up. From the moment he had

140

arrived in the Maurice Saltzman & Company office, up to this moment in the elevator going down to West 21st Street, it was as though he had been conducting a privately worked out funeral. The old lady in black, the old man wearing the black stocking sleeves, had they been rehearsed? And what kind of talk was that about how life works out? From a young kid? I, too, was young. How life works out? Christ almighty, I was only too acutely aware that my life had not even started working.

The elevator stopped. We walked out into the street. Sebastian Roon looked down toward Seventh Avenue, then up toward Eighth. He spoke without looking at me.

"Don't you believe a bloody damn word I've just said," he said quietly. "Nobody is better off in Blackpool."

"What are you going to do?" I said.

"Probably go back to where nobody is better off," he said. "Blackpool. I haven't sorted it out yet. You see, my uncle was spread pretty thin, as you probably know. Your firm regularly audited twenty of his companies, but they didn't seem to have any substance. No offices, no employees, no bank accounts. So far as I was able to figure out, they existed in the files of Maurice Saltzman & Company and nowhere else. Even the fees for auditing their records, the money came from the I. G. Roon, Ltd., bank account. I used to sign the checks every month. Only last month I made it a point to go over all the balance sheets. Not a farthing. So it's probably back to Blackpool, but I'll start the journey by going over to Shane's. They're open seven days a week, you know. But their intelligence service may nod a bit on Sundays, so they can't possibly yet know that my bloody uncle has turned up his toes. I intend to order up the most expensive funeral meats in the larder, and put it all on tick. The old sod is dead, but his credit at Shane's is still alive and kicking. Benjamin, won't you join me?"

I did some thinking. What had happened to Sebastian Roon was bad, and I felt sorry for him. But I felt sorrier for myself. The death of his uncle, Miss Bienstock had implied, might mean the death of all I. G. Roon's mysterious companies such as Grantham Estates, and Seb had just

141

pretty much confirmed that. If that was all true, then the death of I. G. Roon may have killed Maurice Saltzman & Compnay. If it had, Benny Kramer was also dead. Rent on Tiffany Street came higher than rent on East Fourth Street. In 1930, Tiffany Street was no place on which to be unemployed.

"Over at Maurice Saltzman & Company," I said, "we also work a seven-day week. I think I'd better get back to the office."

"I could call Mr. Bern and tell him I need your services for another hour or two," Seb said. "The way I did on Friday."

"That was on Friday," I said. "I don't think it will work today."

Sebastian Roon gave me a sharp look. As though he had been moving along and talking to someone familiar, a person he had known for a long time, and it suddenly occurred to him that he had been talking to a stranger. He exploded with one of those wonderfully infectious laughs that, years later, would lay the ladies in the aisles. Among other places.

"How right you are," he said. "Nothing is going to work from now on. Except Shane's, and I rather imagine that will work only for a few more hours." Sebastian Roon put out his hand. "It was a pleasure knowing you," he said.

I took his hand. It was bony and muscular. He squeezed hard. It hurt, but I didn't mind.

"Damned decent of you to let me use your bed last night," he said. "First good night I've had on American soil. Do give my very best to your mother. She's quite a person. I'll be seeing you."

It was one of those phrases. Come to think of it, it still is. Like: "Good night, sleep tight, don't let the bedbugs bite." I haven't heard that one for years. In 1930, however, it was big stuff on East Fourth Street, and there were still a few wits who used it on Tiffany Street. So, when Sebastian Roon said I'll be seeing you, the words made no impression. A discharge of polite syllables under cover of which people parted and went their separate ways.

I went back to Maurice Saltzman & Company. Mr. Saltzman was gone. Mr. Bern was on the phone screaming at Mr. Shimnitz. Miss Bienstock said a bankruptcy audit had come in through the Irving Trust just a few minutes after I left the office with Sebastian Roon. Would I go over to 498 Seventh Avenue? Feld-Korn Frocks, Inc. Mr. Karp, our top senior, and Bill Breiner, our top semi-senior, could use an extra hand with the audit. The Irving Trust wanted a report by tomorrow. We would probably have to work through the night.

We did, and the Irving Trust got its report, and promptly rewarded Maurice Saltzman & Company with another audit. I began to breathe more easily. I sensed no feeling of disaster in the office as a result of the death of Mr. I. G. Roon. Perhaps Mr. Bern had screamed his back payments out of Mr. Shimnitz. Perhaps the fees for the two Irving Trust audits of that week were larger than usual. Perhaps Grantham Estates and the other I. G. Roon companies were in better shape than Sebastian Roon had thought. I don't know. I know only that there was for the staff a curious sense of unreasonable but hysterical prosperity.

All in all, it was quite a week. I could hardly wait for Saturday night to roll around so Hannah Halpern and I could dig into those Gabilla's knishes. As it happened, I did have to wait.

When I came into our Tiffany Street kitchen at six-thirty on Saturday night, I almost fell into a scene as improbable as the meeting in which Aunt Betsey Trotwood, with the terrified David Copperfield crouched behind her chair, faces up to Mr. Murdstone. Except that this scene took place not in Dover but in the Bronx. The language being exchanged by the participants was, therefore, Yiddish.

"Show me your book, Mrs. Groshartig," my mother was saying.

She was saying it to a plump, middle-aged woman in a blue and white checked housedress. I had never seen her before. I wondered where she had come from. Not from very far, was my guess. Not in that dress, shielded by a grease-spattered apron. Mrs. Groshartig could have been a

143

neighbor who had dropped in for a cup of chicken fat. But here on Tiffany Street I had never seen a neighbor.

"My book?" she said.

Mrs. Groshartig sounded as though my mother had asked to see her appendectomy scar.

"Yes, the book," my mother said.

They sat facing each other across the kitchen table. On the north side of the table, between them, sat Sebastian Roon. He was the only one of the three who was smiling. It was the same smile he had used when on the telephone from his uncle's office he had arranged with Mr. Bern for me to be freed for the lunch at Shane's and, again, the previous Saturday night, here in our kitchen, when he had demonstrated to my mother a better way to do Mr. Lebenbaum's jazz bow "turning." It was the smile that had accompanied Seb's *"Voilà!"*

"The book?" Mrs. Groshartig said again.

She sounded the way she looked. Uneasy. Or stupid. Perhaps both.

"The book you take to Mr. Lebenbaum when you bring back the 'turning,' " my mother said.

It was obvious that she was making an effort to be patient and friendly. I knew her well enough to understand what that meant. My mother was engaged in the process of cajolery. She did not suffer fools easily.

"May I, Mrs. Kramer?" Seb said.

My mother nodded. Seb turned the smile on Mrs. Groshartig. It might have been a tranquilizer. The plump woman seemed to stop quivering.

"What Mrs. Kramer is referring to, Mrs. Groshartig," Sebastian Roon said in impeccable Yiddish, if there is such a thing, "is the book in which is recorded your relationship with Mr. Lebenbaum, if I make myself clear. Do I?"

It was obvious from Mrs. Groshartig's face that no bells had been rung. The smile on Seb's face did not change. Even then, he had stage presence. But he did hike himself forward an inch or two in his chair.

"Let's take it one step at a time," he said. "Mrs. Groshartig, you do work for Mr. Lebenbaum, do you not?"

144

"I go every day to his store on Intervale Avenue," the plump woman said. "He gives me a bundle 'turning.' "

"You bring the bundle home to your flat, do you not?" Seb said.

"Downstairs," Mrs. Groshartig said. "Here on the first floor."

So she *was* a neighbor! They did exist on Tiffany Street as they had existed on East Fourth Street! It was merely that here on Tiffany Street, instead of screaming through their open windows, they cowered behind locked doors.

"And in your flat," Seb said, "downstairs on the first floor of this building, you work on the bundle until all the 'turning' is completed. Is that correct, Mrs. Groshartig?"

The tranquilized look of confusion on her face seemed to break up. Mrs. Groshartig giggled at this charmer from a land across the sea.

"*Avodde,*" she said. Esperanto, or Yiddish, for "of course." "Otherwise why would a person walk all the way over to Intervale Avenue and schlepp home a bundle it takes the *koyach* out of a person just to lift it."

"Why indeed?" said Seb. "Now, then, having completed the bundle of 'turning,' Mrs. Groshartig, the next morning you carry it back in its finished state to Mr. Lebenbaum on Intervale Avenue. Is *that* correct, Mrs. Groshartig?"

The giggle swung toward my mother. "This is some *vitzler* you got here, Mrs. Kramer," the plump woman said.

"Wait, wait," my mother said. "When this *boychik* really gets started with the jokes, you'll *plotz.*"

"Don't, Mrs. Groshartig," Seb said. "Not quite yet. There is one further point. Thus: when you bring the completed 'turning' into Mr. Lebenbaum's store, he counts your work. Again correct, Mrs. Groshartig?"

"He has to count it," the plump woman said. "Another person he wouldn't trust if it was his own father."

"We musn't criticize," Seb said. "Sound business practice is something that must be admired. Having counted your work, he multiplies the number of pieces you have brought in by the price he pays you per piece. That, too, is correct, Mrs. Groshartig, is it not?"

145

The plump woman nodded. "A nickel a *shtikl*," she said.

Even to me, who had been hearing this phrase all my life, it sounded funny in connection with the piecework rates for making jazz bows. The phrase was usually encountered in delicatessen stores, lettered as a sign on a small wooden spatula stuck into a bowl of two-inch lengths of knubbleworst sitting on top of the counter. These were what is known as a *nosh*. Something to nibble at while you watched the proprietor put together your hot pastrami sandwich.

"Good-good," Seb said. "And after Mr. Lebenbaum has done his multiplication, and he reaches the figure you have earned, what does he do with this figure, Mrs. Groshartig?"

The plump woman dug into the pocket of her apron and came up with a small notebook from Woolworth's.

"What should he do with it?" Mrs. Groshartig said. "He writes it down here in my little book."

Seb swung the smile toward my mother. *"Voilà!"* he said.

"What?" my mother said.

"Your witness, Mrs. Kramer," Seb said.

My mother took the notebook from Mrs. Groshartig and thumbed the pages.

"So all right," she said. "A nickel a *shtikl* is correct. Right?"

"Mrs. Kramer." the plump woman said. "You know it's correct. You also work for Mr. Lebenbaum. We all get paid the same."

"But we all don't get paid enough," my mother said. "Why should it be for you and me, Mrs. Groshartig, always a nickel a *shtikl?* Why shouldn't it be, let's say, six cents a *shtikl?"*

The plump woman shrugged. "I don't know," she said. "That's what Mr. Lebenbaum always pays."

"There's maybe a law?" my mother said. "It says Mr. Lebenbaum he's not allowed to pay more than a nickel a *shtikl?"*

This question was obviously beyond Mrs. Groshartig's

146

mental capacities, but the sardonic tone in which my mother delivered it made an impression.

"Mrs. Groshartig," my mother said. "If somebody came to you and they said let Mr. Lebenbaum grow with his head in the earth like an onion, you come do 'turning' for me, and I'll pay you not a nickel a *shtikl* but six cents a *shtikl*, what would you say, Mrs. Groshartig?"

The plump woman scowled at the table. "If it wasn't far to go," she said, "sure I'd say yes. I'd be a real big dope to say no. But Mr. Lebenbaum he's just three blocks away, on Intervale Avenue."

"Suppose to make six cents a *shtikl*," my mother said, "you didn't even have to go to Intervale Avenue. Suppose all you had to do was climb up three floors, from your place downstairs on the first floor up to this kitchen on the fourth floor? What would you say then, Mrs. Groshartig?"

While Mrs. Groshartig was considering this question, Seb saw me standing in the kitchen door.

"Ah, good evening, Benjamin," he said.

My mother said nothing. She was staring at the plump woman from downstairs.

"What goes on here?" I said.

"None of your business," my mother said without removing her eyes from Mrs. Groshartig's face. "Hurry up and wash, and then just hurry up. Hannah is waiting."

"Hannah?" Seb said.

"It's a girl," my mother said. "Every Saturday night she and Benny go to double features."

"Not every Saturday night," I said. "It just happens once in a while."

"See if you can make it happen tonight," my mother said. "Seymour and I have a lot of work to do. *Nu,* Mrs. Groshartig?"

Mrs. Groshartig scowled in silence at her nickel notebook.

"Seb," I said. "When I saw you last Sunday, didn't you say you were on your way back to England?"

"I thought I was," he said. "But it seemed such a dismal

147

prospect that I dragged my feet for a few days, and then I had a much better idea."

"What sort of idea?" I said.

"Benny," my mother said. There was no impatience in her voice. She always talked as she walked. With deliberation. Only someone who had known her all his life would have sensed the steel runners on which she had slid out the two syllables of my name. "Benny," she said again. "Hannah is waiting."

Indeed she was.

"You're late," Hannah said.

I looked up at the big clock over Goldkorn's jewelry store at the corner of 180th Street and Vyse Avenue. It showed five minutes after seven. The first time Hannah and I had made a date we'd set it for seven-fifteen. I arrived under Goldkorn's clock at seven. Hannah was waiting. Every Saturday night since then, for almost a year, our Saturday night dates were set for seven-fifteen. Every Saturday night for almost a year I had been arriving at Goldkorn's clock at seven o'clock sharp. And every Saturday night Hannah had been waiting at seven o'clock sharp. Tonight was the first time I had arrived a few minutes after seven. Technically, I was still ten minutes early.

"It's only five minutes after seven," I said.

"You're late," Hannah said again.

She was right, of course. Custom had replaced contractual arrangements.

"I'm sorry," I said.

"Something is wrong," Hannah said. "I can always tell."

I was fated, apparently, to go through life surrounded by women who could always tell.

"Nothing is wrong," I said, although I knew that something was. "It's just when I got home from work the house was a mess, and I had trouble getting out."

"What kind of mess?" Hannah said.

She knew my mother did not allow her house to get into a mess. My mother's neatness compared favorably with the surgical cleanliness of the Bellevue operating room.

"That Englishman," I said. "He showed up again."

148

Hannah laughed. "I guess you're going to sleep on the floor of the front room again," she said.

The same guess had crossed my mind.

"Not before we see Ruth Chatterton in *Madame X*," I said, "and we put away a couple of Gabilla's knishes."

We put away four. It proved to be another double feature night, so I didn't turn my key in the lock of our front door until almost two-thirty. There was a light in the kitchen. I could hear voices. I tiptoed across the foyer and looked in. My mother and Sebastian Roon were bent over a pad of ruled paper. The sight shocked me. My mother was doing something I had never seen her do before. She was holding a pencil.

"No," Seb was saying. "An eight is like this. Two small circles. One on top of the other. Watch."

I had not noticed that he, too, was holding a pencil. After a puzzled moment, I saw why. Sebastian Roon was holding his pencil the way I did, the way most people hold a pencil. Nothing to strike the eye as unusual. My mother was holding her pencil as though it were a sculptor's chisel poised against the marble, waiting for the hammer blow. In the slanting light from the electric bulb that dangled on a black cord over the kitchen table, I could see beads of sweat on her upper lip. She dug the pencil across the pad awkwardly but with determination, then with a sigh of relief leaned back in her chair. Seb leaned forward. He examined what she had done.

"Jolly good," he said. "Now let's try something a bit more sophisticated. Instead of making two separate circles, and setting one on top of the other, let's do both in one easy sweeping motion." Slowly but smoothly Seb guided his pencil across the pad. "We give it half the top circle on the left," he said. "Then we cut across and do half the lower circle on the right. Then we go back to the left, moving the pencil upward to complete the lower circle. And finally we cut across to the right, still moving the pencil, until we complete the top circle. Let's try that, shall we?"

With the back of her hand my mother wiped the sweat from her upper lip. She looked worried.

149

"That's hard." she said.

"Nonsense," Sebastian Roon said. "Remember the five and the six? How they frightened you when we first tackled them?"

My mother looked at him the way I remember seeing her look at Mr. Velvelschmidt, our landlord on East Fourth Street, when the son of a bitch used to try to wheedle the rent out of her by making the sort of primitive jokes he obviously used and found effective with other tenants. My mother had never equated herself with other tenants. She hated Mr. Velvelschmidt because he obviously did.

"I was not frightened of the five and the six," my mother said in that voice that rolled out quietly, on concealed steel tracks. "I am not frightened of anything."

This was not true. But Sebastian Roon didn't know that.

"Then let's have a go at the eight," he said.

My mother took a tighter grip on the pencil, leaned forward, and started shoving. She made it.

"*Nu?*" she said with a gasp.

Seb leaned forward to examine her handiwork. "Jolly good," he said. "Absolutely super."

I cleared my throat. "Before you get started on the nine," I said, "will somebody please tell me where I'm sleeping tonight?"

My mother didn't answer. She was leaning forward again, scowling down at her eight, wiping away the sweat on her upper lip.

"On the floor in the living room," Seb said without looking up. Under my mother's eight he was slowly fashioning a nine. "I hope you don't mind, old boy."

I did mind. I minded so much that it hurt. What I minded was not the discomfort of the hard floor. I'd just gone through four knishes and a double feature with Hannah Halpern. I could have slept on gravel. I didn't even mind that neither Seb nor my mother looked up or answered my good night when I left the kitchen. What I minded was his easy triumph after my long failure. I had never been able to teach my mother anything.

Down on East Fourth Street, when I first became aware

150

of her as an individual. I became aware also that she was different from the other immigrant mothers on the block. Those other mothers all went to night classes at P.S. 188. They learned to read and write and speak English. For a long time it did not seem to me to be much of an accomplishment. About the time I turned twelve however, it occurred to me that I was ashamed of my mother for not being able to do at all what the mothers of Hot Cakes Rabinowitz and George Weitz and Chink Alberg did with ease. One night at supper, driven by curiosity, totally unaware of the necessity for prudence, I asked my mother why she did not join the other mothers of the block in going to night classes at P.S. 188.

"Eat with bread " my mother said sharply.

To take a forkful of meat, or a spoonful of soup, without accompanying it with a liberal bite of rye bread was, in my mother's private penal code, at least a misdemeanor and in all probability a felony.

I took a bite of bread and, around it, said: "Chink's mother goes. George's mother goes. Hot Cakes' mother goes. Why don't you go, Ma?"

My father, at the other side of the table, had a mouthful of bread. It did not prevent him from making a remark that I see now required great courage on his part. He was afraid of my mother.

"If she goes to school at night," my father said, "it'll show everybody on Fourth Street she doesn't know something."

"You use the mouth to eat," my mother said. "Not to talk."

She said it to my father, but I knew she also meant me. I never said another word. Not for several years, anyway.

When I became a freshman at Thomas Jefferson High, however, I came to know boys from all over the city. Many of them had parents who were not immigrants. I suffered a new attack of embarrassment for my mother's illiteracy. I was the darling of Miss Merle S. Marine, my English teacher. The more she praised me for my work, the more terrified I became that some day she would meet my illiter-

151

ate mother and realize the crudity of the bolt of cloth from which I had been cut. I decided to teach my mother to read and write and speak English. In secret, of course.

"Nobody will know," I said to her late one night when I made my proposal. "We'll do it here in the kitchen, late at night, after Papa goes to bed."

She looked at me for several long moments. Even today I have the distinct impression that her eyes did not blink. I might have been a heifer whose weight she was trying to guess before making an offer for me in a stockyard.

"Why do you want to do this?" my mother said finally.

I could not, of course, tell her the truth.

"English is fun," I said. "You'll enjoy it, Ma."

"You want me to have fun," she said.

It was not a question. It was a statement. Laid out on the table like a bet in a crap game. It was up to me to fade it.

"Yes," I said.

"All right," she said. "Let's start."

I thought it would be best to start with numbers. Two things had left with me the impression that she had a good head for arithmetic. Listening to her talk about the price of vegetables in the Avenue C pushcarts, and watching her make computations of profits during her bootlegging days on East Fourth Street. After a week of late night sessions, I came to the uncomfortable conclusion that I must have been wrong. I managed to get her to pronounce the digits in English, but when I tried to teach her to write them down I failed miserably.

So I decided to abandon writing, for the time being, anyway, and concentrate on speech. She did well with nouns. She learned soon enough that a *leffel* was a spoon, a *tishtoch* a tablecloth, a *ferd* a horse. But connecting these nouns with the simplest verbs resisted her.

I don't remember how long the struggle went on. But I remember the night I surrendered.

"Let's stop it," my mother said in Yiddish. "All I'm doing is make you lose sleep."

Two reactions lived with me for a long time.

One, the tone of her voice when she threw in the towel. I could not escape the feeling that she had thrown it in my face. She did not sound defeated. She sounded triumphant. As though, in some way I did not grasp, she had beaten me at my own game.

And two, I remember my very real sense of having lost out in a struggle I had wanted desperately to win.

Four years later, lying awake on the floor of our front room in Tiffany Street, listening to the murmur of her voice out in the kitchen with Sebastian Roon, it all came clear in a wave of jealousy so unbearable that it made my mouth feel sour, as though I had been vomiting.

What I had wanted to win was what it had not occurred to me as a boy I had never had. And, until it was too late, had not missed: her love.

When I finally got around to the realization that I did miss it, and I made the attempt to win it, that inner core of metal around which she existed had given her the strength to resist the ease and comfort of speaking the language of the country in which she had come to live, and take for herself instead the pleasure of revenge.

She had led me on, as though I were a fisherman who felt he had hooked his game. And then, just as I was about to bring her to the gaff, she had with her own hand cut herself loose.

What she had denied me, she was now giving to Sebastian Roon. I was sure she would be speaking English in a matter of weeks.

My estimate was not too far off the mark.

Two nights later, when I came home from my classes in the evening session at C.C.N.Y., my mother and Seb were seated at the kitchen table with a woman named Mrs. Klockner. She looked not unlike Mrs. Groshartig. I suppose all plump Jewish housewives, wearing flowered gingham housedresses shielded by grease-spattered aprons, look, like all bald-headed men, somewhat alike. Nobody paid any attention to me. I disposed of my briefcase, hung up my coat in the hall, and came back to tackle the glass of

153

milk and the slab of honey cake my mother had set out for me on the drainboard beside the sink.

As I munched and sipped, my mother and Sebastian Roon went through with Mrs. Klockner almost exactly the same performance I had seen them go through two nights earlier with Mrs. Groshartig.

Almost, but not quite. There were a few differences. While Mrs. Klockner, I soon gathered, also worked at "turning" for Mr. Lebenbaum, she did not live in our building. She lived around the corner, on Fox Street.

Either she was somewhat brighter than Mrs. Groshartig, or my mother had with practice grown more skillful. She and Seb had clearly been interviewing many, perhaps all, of Mr. Lebenbaum's employees for several days. While I had been downtown on my job with Maurice Saltzman & Company.

In any case, this time Seb did not interfere with helpful suggestions when the going got rough, the way he had done during the interview with Mrs. Groshartig. Seb stayed out of it. Except for his encouraging smile, of course. Short of encasing his handsome head in a pillowcase, it would have been difficult to keep that smile out of even the execution chamber at Sing Sing.

The most interesting difference—for me, at any rate— was the end of the interview. Up to that point, my mother and Mrs. Klockner had talked Yiddish. When my mother reached the penultimate argument about what was wrong with a hard-working woman receiving not a nickel *shtikl* but six cents a *shtikl,* she went on to utter the final words in English: "So what do you say, Mrs. Klockner?"

It was not the sort of English spoken at Jesus College, Cambridge. But it was recognizable on Tiffany Street. Considering that my mother had obviously learned this scrap of English during the past forty-eight hours, hers was a creditable performance. Sebastian Roon was either a superlative teacher, or he was dealing with a brilliant and eager student. I did not doubt which of the two it was.

"Excuse me," I said while Mrs. Klockner scowled down at her small nickel notebook and tried to think of an an-

154

swer to my mother's question. "Would one of you two entrepreneurs mind telling me where I sleep tonight?"

My mother did not take her eyes from Mrs. Klockner's face. Seb, however, looked up.

"Oh, it's you," he said.

"Yes," I said, "and it has been for some time."

"Don't be testy," Seb said. "We're getting a large project under way here. Try the spot on which you dossed down last night."

I went out into the living room. The spot on which I had dossed down last night was now occupied by my mother's old foot-treadle Singer. On East Fourth Street the sewing machine had stood in a corner of our only bedroom. Here on Tiffany Street, where we had two bedrooms, my mother had stored the Singer in a corner of my bedroom. The fact that it had now been moved into the living room was an event not unlike that of a manager ordering a pitcher into the bull pen. Things were about to happen.

The first thing that happened was negative. When I came out of the front room in the morning, my mother was not at her usual post in front of the gas range, preparing my breakfast. I tiptoed down the hall and put my ear to her bedroom door. I could hear two sounds. One was, of course, my father's snore. I had been hearing it for years. I had always been impressed by my father's snore. He did not just rip off the traditional dreary buzz. My father added music.

A moment or two of the low strong buzz. Pause. Slight gasp. Then a tinkly skipping note, as though a small bell had been tapped. Another moment or two of the low strong buzz. Pause. Then a series of rapidly varied tinkles, as though a cat was dancing across a xylophone. The sequence usually continued, with fluty little variations on the basic theme, until my mother's voice said, "Joe! Turn over!"

She did not say it this morning. She was snoring away herself. Most unmusically, I might add. I could hardly blame her. It had been almost three in the morning when I left my mother and Seb with Mrs. Klockner in the kitchen

155

and I went out into the living room to doss down on the floor beside my mother's Singer.

I tiptoed back down the hall and put my ear to my bedroom door. I had never before heard a snore with an English accent. At another time I might have found things in it to admire. The clipped terminal point of each sequence, for example. Or the broad university drawl that gave a touch of elegance to the part that with my father was merely a low strong buzz. But this was not my morning for exploring a new art form.

I took a *toochiss* roll from the paper bag on top of the refrigerator. I cut it open and smeared both halves with butter. I slapped the halves together and left the house, munching my roll all the way to the subway.

Figuratively speaking, I kept munching it all day. At the office. In my C.C.N.Y. classes. On the subway going home. I was thinking, and my thoughts did not please me.

I didn't really mind what my mother and Seb were doing. What I minded was being excluded. They acted as though I were a piece of furniture. Worse. A piece of furniture about the existence of which they were unaware until they stumbled into it, and then they merely shoved it aside.

It was one thing to have your mother give your bed to a visitor for a single night. But I had now been sleeping on the living room floor for almost a week, while Mr. Roon was corking off his Oxford-accented snore in my bed. It was undignified. I felt I should complain. I felt I should assert myself.

Climbing the stairs to our apartment, the pretense of indignation, on which I had been working all day, fell apart. I didn't feel I should assert myself. I knew what I felt. An intensification of the old jealousy. For the fact that he was teaching her English. No, for the fact that from him she was willing to learn. I was almost afraid to open the door on another lesson.

When I did open it, what was going on could hardly be described as a lesson.

"You listen to me," my mother was saying.

My spirits soared. She had said it in Yiddish. Then I saw

to whom she had said it, and my spirits changed direction. My mother was speaking to my father.

"Chanah, please," my father said.

His snoring may have been heavy, but his voice had always been light. Even before the accident that had put him into a wheelchair, he had always sounded like a polite and friendly usher directing you to your seat in the darkness after a performance has begun. Since the accident, my father's voice had become something that was not quite human. A tiny animal bleat. I tried to remember how he had once sounded, but it was difficult because for years I had rarely heard him speak. Certainly not in my presence. Not anymore, anyway. Because my presence removed itself every morning while he was still in the bedroom, and he was back in his bedroom when I came home at night.

I stared at him as though I had never seen him before. This skinny little man wrapped in the thick khaki Austrian army greatcoat he had brought with him to this country in 1905 and had worn as a bathrobe ever since. This wreck of a human being huddled in a wheelchair. Was this my father?

I had not seen him for weeks. He did not like people to come into his bedroom. Not even his son. I realized with a sense of shame that this was a matter of relief to me. I did not like to go into his bedroom. It was shocking to see him out here in the kitchen.

"You've been hiding in that bedroom long enough," my mother said. "The time it's now the right time for you to come out and be a human being again like everybody else. Come on."

She grabbed the bar at the back of his wheelchair and swung it toward the living room. I came further into the kitchen.

"Ma," I said. "Can I help?"

"Everybody can help," my mother said, not to me but to the place from which my voice had come. Then she seemed to become aware of my presence. "Oh, hello, Benny," she said. "There's milk and *lekach* on the sink. Go eat."

She started to push the wheelchair toward the front room.

"Chanah, please," my father said again.

"Wait till you see," my mother said. "You'll enjoy."

She shoved the wheelchair into the living room. Munching my honey cake and sipping my milk, I followed. In the doorway I stopped and stared. If I had to doss down tonight on the living room floor, it would take a bit of doing to find an available spot. Something had been added to the Singer.

The round table in the middle of the room, on which we ate our Sabbath meals, had vanished. It was concealed under four long planks that converted the small round mahogany into a large rectangular cutting table. On it, layers of colored silk had been stretched to form a pad that seemed to be about an inch thick.

"I chalked it out for you," my mother said. "I've watched Mr. Lebenbaum do it for over a year. Anything that Litvak can do, Joe Kramer can do. You were the best pocket maker on Allen Street."

"Making pockets, Chanah," my father said, "it's not the same like cutting jazz bows."

"How do you know till you give it a try?" my mother said. "Pockets is with tveet. Jazz bows is with silk. It's both cloth. All you have to do is with the cutting knife, you follow the chalk marks. Here."

My mother picked up one of those ugly knives I had seen on the cutting tables of bankrupt Seventh Avenue dress firms to which the staff of Maurice Saltzman & Company was sent almost daily to audit the records for the receiver. My mother thrust the knife at my father. He winced back in the wheelchair, shoved out both hands as though to ward off an assassination attack, and managed to seize the black bone centerpiece with both hands.

"Then like this," my mother said. "Watch."

She leaned over the cutting table. I noticed there was a row of nails set in the wood all along the top edge of the plank and another set in along the bottom edge. The nails stood about two inches up from the wood. Stretched tight between the nails at the top and the nails at the bottom was a series of strings dividing the thick pad of silk into a sort of miniature football gridiron.

"These things here, these cords," my mother said. "I rubbed them with chalk. Watch." Delicately, with thumb and forefinger, she lifted one of the tightly drawn pieces of string. When it had come up from the silk about two inches, she allowed the string to snap back to the silk. A small puff of chalk dust rose in the air. My mother lifted the string again and held it in the air so my father could see what had happened. The silk was now marked by a neat white line running from the nail at the top of the cutting board to the nail at the bottom.

"What you do," my mother said, "you snap all these cords, one by one, until the whole silk it's marked with straight lines. Then with the knife you start cutting, one line at a time. When you finish with the cutting, I take the cut pieces over here." She went to the Singer and tapped the small nickel-plated hand wheel. "I sew them into the long belts, the little pockets, for the women when they come to pick them up to take them home for 'turning.' It's easy," my mother said. "You cut. I sew."

My father looked around the room.

"Yesterday it was a place to eat on Friday night," he said. "Today it's a factory."

"From eating on Friday night," my mother said, "you don't get rich."

My father looked down at the ugly knife in his lap. When his head came up, his cheeks looked a little more shrunken. When he spoke, he sounded a little weaker.

"On Friday night," he said. "The candles. Where will you *bentsh licht?*"

"It doesn't say in the Torah God will throw you out of heaven if you light the *Shabbes* candles in the kitchen," my mother said. An edge came into her voice. "On East Fourth Street I once had a chance for a life, and I lost it. Now here on Tiffany Street I have something I thought I'd never have again. I have a second chance. I'm not going to lose it. You hear me? I'm not going to lose it. Not a second time. You'll cut silk. or you won't eat. You hear?"

My father reached out and touched the pad of silk.

"On East Fourth Street," he said. "I used to walk two miles to the Hebrew Immigrant Aid Society on Lafayette Street to write out the papers to bring people over from Europe. Here, on Tiffany Street, I sit in a wheelchair and I cut jazz bows."

"That's America," my mother said.

Down on East Fourth Street I had slept in the tiny back storage room, tucked snugly into a small bed next to the wooden keg in which my father fermented the Blue Concord grapes for the Passover wine. Here on Tiffany Street I slept on the floor of a jazz bow factory. My father and I finally had something in common.

"Ma," I said, "can I go back into my room tonight?"

"Certainly not!" Sebastian Roon called in from the kitchen. I had not heard him come into the apartment. He now came into the front room, peeling off his coat. "Selfishness is most unbecoming to you, Benjamin," he said. "I've had a frightfully exhausting day, lining up our outlets."

"They'll take?" my mother said.

I was only mildly surprised to hear her utter the two words in English. I didn't doubt that before long she would know as many as Mr. Lebenbaum, Henry Ford, or Harvey Firestone, and in her spare time would be quoting Shelley.

"Every bloody jazz bow we can produce, and more if we can produce them," Sebastian Roon said. "They're so eager, they said if our first delivery is up to standard we won't have to advance our own money to buy the silk. They'll provide the silk for us."

"What means standard?" my mother said.

"It means as good as the work they've been getting from their other suppliers," Seb said.

I thought my mother looked puzzled. Then I saw what had invaded her face was not puzzlement but anger. I knew her well enough to understand what was going through her mind. Having learned a few English words, her confidence

160

in her intelligence had led her to believe she knew them all. Seb seemed to grasp this, too.

"It means," he said in Yiddish, "that if what we give them is as good as what they've been getting from other manufactures, they'll give us for free the silk to work with. Which will be our salvation, I assure you, because my nine hundred dollars won't last forever."

"It won't have to last forever," my mother said, "and you'll get it back every penny. They want, you say, they want we should make as good as?"

"Very much so," Seb said.

"Don't worry," my mother said. "We'll make better." It was soon obvious that they would.

I did not know just when every morning my father started cutting and my mother started sewing, because they were both asleep when I left for the office. But they were still at it when I came home at night. My father said nothing. He just worked, and he worked well. His years of experience in the pants shops on Allen Street had made his fingers nimble. His old dedication to doing a job well, his sense of craftsmanship, which had atrophied with inactivity in the wheelchair, started to come back. I may have been reading things into his new look of well-being, but it seemed to me a bit of color had come back into his cheeks.

Even though my mother said nothing either, there was no mistaking her elation. The sense of fear about her new surroundings, the sadness of having "improved" herself out of the pulsing life of East Fourth Street into the sterility of Tiffany Street, the puzzle of having finally achieved a street with trees only to find that staring out at them from her front-room window brought her a sense of despair, the months of floundering around inside her head for an answer, all that was gone. She had found the answer.

Sebastian Roon had brought it to her.

He had brought her much more, of course: the English language. What I could not figure out was when he found time to give her lessons.

He, too, was always asleep when I went to work in the morning. It was my understanding that he spent the day delivering the finished jazz bows to the various outlets downtown with which he had established business relationships, and bringing up to Tiffany Street the bolts of silk for my father to cut. Sometimes when I came home at night Seb was in the living room, helping my father stretch the strings from nail to nail across the silk on the cutting board. From his wheelchair my father could reach only those nails in front of him. For the nails at the top of the board he had to wheel himself around to the other side. He could do this, but it was an inconvenience because the room, which had always been small, was now too cluttered, and wheeling around among the clutter took a great deal of time. Seb's help saved time. And time, as Seb had taught my mother to say, was money.

The money, of course, was the point. Just as it had been the point of her small bootlegging activities down on East Fourth Street. For a long time I did not know how much of it she was making. I did know two things, however. I knew that Seb had started a savings account for her at the National City around the corner on Intervale Avenue, and had taught her how to use it. And I knew the early evening spectacle in our kitchen every Saturday.

It was the day when Mrs. Groshartig, and Mrs. Klockner, and all the other women who had formerly worked for Mr. Lebenbaum and now worked for my mother, came to our Tiffany Street kitchen to be paid.

They came after sundown, when the Sabbath was over. It was forbidden by Holy Writ to handle money during the Sabbath. Thus it was possible for me to witness the scene because I came home at the same time from the Maurice Saltzman & Company offices to wash up before going off to my weekly date with Hannah Halpern.

Three points impressed me very soon about the way the scene was performed.

First, my father never attended. Long before the women started to arrive, he would wheel himself out to his bedroom.

Second, Sebastian Roon always attended but never participated. He sat at the kitchen table with my mother,

162

watching in silence, playing that salubrious searchlight, his smile, over the scene.

Third, it was my mother's show. She played it to the hilt. The women always arrived in groups. Sometimes in a single group. I don't mean that they gathered at central meeting places and walked together to our house. I mean that as soon as the Sabbath sun started to go down they all set out from their different homes in the neighborhood. Who could blame them? They worked hard for their money. They wanted it promptly. They didn't run. But they did hurry. As a result several of them would arrive from different directions at our apartment at the same time.

My mother made them wait in a line that always stretched from the kitchen door out across the foyer, and frequently out of the foyer into the hall. Even though there were four places at our kitchen table, and during this weekly ceremony only two chairs were occupied, by my mother and by Seb, she never asked her employees to sit down. I don't think it would have occurred to any of my mother's employees to sit down unvited.

Not because during this ceremony there was anything forbidding about my mother's manner. On the contrary. She was always pleasant. And even though she never smiled, because handling money was an intensely serious business, she always managed to convey a jovial heartiness that perhaps only I, washing up at the kitchen sink a few feet from the table. knew was spurious. I'm sure it would never have occurred to any of my mother's employees to sit down because they must surely have received the impression that there was no time. My mother was a crisp performer.

"Good evening, Mrs. Jakow," she would say.

In English, of course.

"Good evening, Mrs. Kramer."

Sometimes in English. More often in Yiddish.

"The book, please," my mother would say.

Mrs. Jakow would hand over the book. My mother would flip the pages, making notes as she did so on a pad of paper. She made the notes with a pencil. She no longer

163

held it the way a sculptor holds his chisel. My mother now held her pencil the way I held mine. With it she drew a line under her figures and, scowling and moving her lips, she did a swift bit of adding.

"Twelve dollars and ninety cents. Correct?"

"Correct," said Mrs. Jakow.

It was always correct. My mother's employees always knew to the penny what they were owed. Just as, when my mother had worked for Mr. Lebenbaum, she had known.

"Okay," my mother said.

She pulled open the drawer in the kitchen table that, during the rest of the week, contained the Kramer family's knives and forks. From the drawer she counted out the money she had withdrawn the day before from the National City.

"Five, ten, eleven, twelve, a half-dollar, a quarter, a dime, a nickel." She looked up. "Twelve ninety, Mrs. Jakow."

"Thanks, Mrs. Kramer."

Mrs. Jakow scooped up the money and left.

"Next," my mother said.

Another woman stepped into the kitchen. The line out in the foyer inched forward.

"Good evening, Mrs. Groshartig," my mother said.

"Good evening, Mrs. Kramer."

"The book, please," my mother said.

She had said it in my presence for perhaps the fourth or fifth Saturday night when, instead of a woman, a man came into the kitchen. Or rather, he exploded into the kitchen. He was not wearing a coat. His unbuttoned vest flopped around his skinny body like shutters on an abandoned house during a storm. He looked wild. I knew who he was. On several occasions, when my mother's shopping bag full of completed "turning" had been too heavy, I had carried it for her to Mr. Lebenbaum's store on Intervale Avenue.

"Mr. Lebenbaum," my mother said. "Since when do you work for me?"

Even though I had noticed the change in her during the

past few weeks, her imperturbability on this occasion surprised me.

"The day I work for you," Mr. Lebenbaum snarled, "I should find in my belly growing a trolley car."

"A trolley car in your belly, then, you'll never find," my mother said. "Because I wouldn't let a bloodsucker like you work for me if you did it for nothing. Good night, Mr. Lebenbaum. I'm busy."

"I'm not!" he shouted. "Because you've taken away all my workers! If I don't get them back, I'll have to close my store!"

"These ladies," my mother said, "they're now workers for me, not yours. I didn't take them away from you. I just told them I'll treat them like human beings, not like animals. Here by me it's no more a nickel a *shtikl*. You want them back? Pay them more."

Mr. Lebenbaum sent a fearful glance across his shoulder. As though he were a murderer or an embezzler who, after years of successful concealment, was suddenly in danger of exposure.

"I can't!" he cried. "I have rent to pay on a store! You don't!"

He was a small man, totally bald, who had made the mistake many bald men make. To compensate for what he did not have on top, he had allowed his hair to grow long at the sides and then combed the strings across the top of his head. It made him look like a Lindy's waiter.

"I'm forcing you to have a store?" my mother said.

"Not you!" Mr. Lebenbaum shouted. "My wife! She won't let me cut silk in the house!"

"My husband cuts my silk here in the house," my mother said. "Maybe what you need, Mr. Lebenbaum, is not a wife but a husband."

"You're killing me!" Mr. Lebenbaum screamed. "You're throwing me out of business!"

My mother shrugged, "That's America," she said.

"You dirty rotten—!"

"Here, now," Sebastian Roon said. He stood up and grabbed Mr. Lebenbaum in two places: the small man's

165

collar and the seat of his pants. "That will be enough of that, my good man."

He hustled Mr. Lebenbaum out of the kitchen.

"Next!" my mother said.

7

My mother's affluence did not affect her fiscal relationship with me.

The following Saturday night, when I came home, my mother was paying off her last employee. When the woman left, Sebastian Roon stood up, stretched, and yarned.

"My word," he said. "It's been quite a week. Benjamin, my boy, congratulations are in order. We've earned back the nine hundred dollars I invested, and as of Monday your mother goes into the black."

"But tonight it's still Saturday," my mother said.

She held out her hand. I took the Maurice Saltzman & Company pay envelope from my pocket and handed it over. My mother opened the envelope and counted the two fives and three singles. She handed me the three singles, rolled the two fives into a tight little tube, and shoved the tube into the top of her stocking.

"I asked Seymour to stay and eat," my mother said. To Sebastian she said, "On Saturday nights to get Benny to eat at home it would take wild horses."

Seb laughed and said, "Off somewhere painting the town, is he?"

"Painting?" my mother said. "No, on Saturday nights he goes to eat with Hannah Halpern."

"Oh, yes, you did tell me," Seb said. "A dazzler?"

"No, a girl," my mother said. "I told you she and Benny they go to double features together."

She made it sound as though we spent the evening cooking up vials of communicable flu virus.

"So you did," Seb said. "So you did." He looked at me thoughtfully. Finally he said, "I haven't tucked into a good

167

double feature for some time. Miss Halpern wouldn't have a friend, would she?"

"I don't know," I said.

I did not like the turn this conversation was taking.

"You could be a good chap and give her a ring and ask," Seb said. "Couldn't you?"

I could have said Hannah had no telephone. But my mother was in the room and she knew the Halperns had a telephone. Or I could have said I didn't want to be a good chap. I wanted to get up into that balcony of Loew's 180th Street with Hannah Halpern and her knishes. What was this damned Englishman doing in our kitchen on Tiffany Street all these weeks, anyway? Why the hell wasn't he back in Blackpool where he belonged?

"But, Seymour," my mother said. "I told you I'm making for you potato *latkes*. The potatoes, they're already all ground up."

"I know, Mrs. Kramer," Sebastian Roon said. "And jolly good your potato *latkes* are, too. But a truly smashing double feature, you know. I mean to say, smashing ones are rare, aren't they? Perhaps I could have the potato *latkes* tomorrow morning for breakfast? As I did that first Sunday when my uncle died? Eating them on Sunday morning, Mrs. Kramer, adds a dimension to your potato *latkes*, truly it does."

"Wait a minute," I said. "You mean tonight I'm still going to have to sleep on the floor in the front room?"

"Not at all," Sebastian said. "I will happily take the floor if you will call Miss Halpern and get me in on a good double feature."

Thank God our telephone was out in the hall. I went to it feeling not only furious, but weak and defeated and ashamed. A sucker. That's what I was. A spineless patsy. When would I learn not to let people walk all over me?

Hannah's mother came on the phone. "Mrs. Halpern?" I said. "This is Benny Kramer. Could I talk to Hannah?"

"Why not?" Mrs. Halpern said. "She's got something wrong with her tongue? But why aren't you already here, Benny? It's almost like nearly seven o'clock?"

168

"That's what I want to talk to Hannah about," I said.

"Benny, you're sick, God forbid!"

I had the feeling that at any moment I might be.

"No, no, I'm just a little late. Could I talk to Hannah?"

"I'm holding her back from the telephone? Of course you can talk to Hannah. This is a free country, Benny. Hannah, here, it's Benny. He's sick, but he says no. Find out, Hannah."

"Benny," Hannah said. "Where are you?"

"I'm here at home."

"On Tiffany Street?"

"Hannah, for God's sake, how many homes do I have?"

"But how can you be home, Benny? It's almost seven o'clock. In four minutes you're supposed to be under Goldkorn's clock?"

"I've got sort of a problem."

"Then it's true?"

"What's true?"

"You're sick, Benny?"

"Don't sound so eager," I said. "No, I'm not sick. But I've got this friend."

"What friend?"

"The Englishman."

"Oh, him."

"Yeah," I said. "Him. I'm sorry about this, Hannah. I'm not responsible. He's been sort of living with us. I mean, I came home from work just a few minutes ago, and there he was, as usual."

"Where?"

I began to regret that the Kramer family's fortunes had risen to the point where we could afford a telephone.

"Here, in our kitchen," I said. "That's where."

"What's he doing in your kitchen?"

I closed my eyes, prayed for help, and got it. I was certainly entitled to it. If you live a clean life, Mr. O'Hare, my old scoutmaster, used to say, you can always count on God to be in your corner.

"He's been helping my mother with her jazz bow business," I said.

169

Hannah's voice, a seductive knish-larded murmur in the balcony of Loew's 180th Street, could on the phone split an eardrum.

"You mean he's an Englishman and he knows how to make jazz bows?"

"Don't scream at me," I said. "I've had a rough week. Yes, he does know how to make jazz bows. Apparently it's a very popular way to spend an evening in Blackpool."

"Boy," Hannah said, "I would certainly like to meet this guy."

"It could be arranged," I said. "In fact, that's why I'm calling you. Hannah, do you have a friend who might want to go out with him tonight?"

"A *girl*?"

No, a musk ox.

"Yeah," I said. "He's sort of lonely, I guess. He'd like to take in a double feature."

"We-ell." Pause. "Benny?"

"I'm here."

"I could call my friend Grace Krieger?"

"Who is she?"

"She works with me in the office at Gold-Mark-Zweig, Inc. Grace is very nice. Really, she is. She's in charge of apartment rentals. All the files and everything. She's very efficient."

"Is she pretty?"

"Well, Alice Faye she's not, but she's really very nice. You'll like her, Benny."

"Who cares if I like her?" I said irritably. "I'm trying to get a date for Sebastian Roon."

"That's some name, Benny."

"It's not much different from Kramer or Halpern," I said. "It's just a name. Could you call her and find out if she's free tonight?"

"Sure," Hannah said, and then: "Benny?"

"What?"

"There's just one thing."

"What's that?"

"Grace Krieger is a very nice girl."

170

"Good," I said. "I do not like un-nice girls."

You should live so, Benjamin Kramer.

"No, now wait, Benny." Hannah paused, then: *"Grace—Krieger—is—a—very—nice—girl."*

"Okay, fine," I said. "You told me."

"But I want it clearly understood, Benny."

"What understood?"

"Grace—Krieger—is—a—very—nice—girl."

Bong!

"Oh," I said.

"Yes, oh," Hannah said.

"Well, for Christ's sake, I didn't say—"

"No, you didn't. Because you are a gentleman, Benny."

"Me?"

"Now look who's screaming."

"Sorry," I said. "It's just that all I asked is—"

"I know what you asked," Hannah said. "But this Englishman, he could be expecting more."

"Oh," I said again. Then: "I don't see what it has to do with me and you. You're my date. She's his date. Let them work it out for themselves."

"One of the reasons I know Grace will be home tonight," Hannah said, "is she doesn't like boys who want to work things out for themselves. *Grace—Krieger—is—a—very—nice—girl.*"

That, I figured, was Sebastian Roon's tough luck.

"Good," I said. "All this Englishman wants is a double feature."

"Okay," Hannah said. "As long as that's understood, you two meet me and Grace under Goldkorn's clock in half an hour."

"Don't you want to call her first and find out if she's free?" I said.

"Grace is free," Hannah said. "Don't you guys be late."

We weren't, and as soon as I clapped eyes on Grace Krieger I knew why she was free. It isn't that she was homely. Having said that, need I say more? Yes. As some of our more hectoring playwrights keep telling us: attention

171

must be paid. Sebastian Roon, I noticed, was paying attention.

"Now," I said after the introductions were over. "This is what Hannah and I usually do. We get a couple of knishes in the Hebrew National and we go up into the balcony. You two, you can do anything you like."

"Why, that sounds like an ideal program," Sebastian Roon said, smiling with obvious delight at Grace Krieger. "Is the purchase of knishes, I think you called them, is that a difficult operation?"

Hannah nudged me. "Benny, you get them," she hissed.

"Oh, yes, well," I said. "Why don't we do it this way? We'll get the tickets, then you three go up to the balcony, and I'll go next door and get the knishes and bring them up."

"Jolly good," Sebastian Roon said. "Are you sure you're up to it, old boy?"

"Ask Hannah," I said.

Benny Kramer, the rooster.

"Benny is the best knish-getter in the East Bronx," Hannah said.

Everybody laughed except Grace Krieger.

"Very well, then," Sebastian Roon said. "On with the show."

In the lobby of Loew's 180th Street he bought two tickets and I bought two. I gave one of mine to Hannah and whispered in her ear.

"Get rid of these two clucks," I said.

"How?" she said.

"Take them all the way over to the right," I said. "By the exit sign. Then you go where you and I always sit, all the way on the left. I'll bring up the knishes, give them two, and then they're on their own."

Hannah giggled. "Benny Kramer," she whispered. "You are a terrible person."

I went off to the Hebrew National feeling like a Jewish Errol Flynn. What a girl! My feelings dampened somewhat in the delicatessen store. In those days a knish was served on a small square of glazed paper. It was perfectly

172

adequate for one knish. Even two had never been a serious inconvenience. But four were a new experience. It means two in each hand, and the knish of 1930 on 180th Street in the Bronx was not a gumdrop. Each one was about the size of a catcher's mitt. The girl behind the counter saw my problem.

"Here, wait." She came up with an empty hot dog roll carton and set the four knishes into it. "How's that?"

"Great," I said. "except for one thing. Would you put this between my teeth?"

I indicated the theater ticket tucked into my breast pocket. She laughed, pulled it out, and set it between my teeth.

"Don't say thanks," the girl said. "You'll spit out the ticket."

I almost did, in the theater lobby, but the ticket-chopper caught it in time. I climbed the stairs to the balcony and stood in the back until my eyes grew accustomed to the darkness. When I felt safe, I moved over to the far left, where Hannah and I always sat. No Hannah. This confused me. I felt my confusion would clear up if I unloaded my two excess knishes. I worked my way across to the far right. Grace Krieger was sitting on the aisle. The seat beside her was empty.

"Where's Seb?" I said.

"Why don't you ask Hannah?"

Even at that early age I disliked people who answer a question by asking another one.

"Where is Hannah?" I said.

"Why don't you ask your British friend," Grace Krieger said icily.

Her voice had an odd effect on what I was carrying. The knishes in the hot dog roll box seemed to get hotter in my hands.

"Where is he?" I said.

"How should I know?" Grace Krieger said. "They left together."

The theater's sound system exploded into action.

"*Out of the shadow of the silent screen,*" the sound track

bellowed, *"strides John Barrymore in, and as, GENERAL CRACK!"*

I stood there in the dark theater, holding my four knishes, and watched stupidly as John Barrymore came striding out of the shadow of the silent screen.

8

I am not clear about what John Barrymore did after he stopped striding. I am very clear about what Benny Kramer did.

I sat down beside Grace Krieger and, in silence. offered her one of the four hot knishes. With an angry shake of her head, she refused. I had to get rid of them somehow. So I ate them. All four.

When John Barrymore won the last battle, and wrapped up the last countess, the screaming sound track went silent. The screen flashed a familiar, flickering announcement:

REMAIN IN YOUR SEATS!
DOUBLE FEATURE TONIGHT!

I turned to Grace Krieger. "Do you want to see the second picture?"

From the sound of my voice the answer I hoped to get was apparent even to me. Nevertheless, I don't think the way I asked the question dictated Grace Krieger's reply. It was obvious that she'd had that worked out before John Barrymore stopped striding. She stood up before she made the reply.

"No," Grace Krieger said curtly.

And she embarked on some striding of her own. Up the aisle, across the back of the balcony, down the stairs, and out into 180th Street. Keeping up with her was not easy. Four Gabilla's knishes were, and I suspect still are, quite a load to carry. I caught up with her under the marquee. Grace Krieger stared up at me as though she were posing for a Salem woodcarver hacking out with an adz the figurehead of Medusa for a whaling ship.

"Where do you live?" I said, and belched. "Sorry."

"Why do you ask?" Grace Krieger said.

She snapped the words at me as though I were a masher who had accosted her in the park. In those days in the pages of the *Daily News* the masher was the equivalent of today's mugger.

"I thought I'd take you home," I said. Another burp. A new experience. With Hannah I had never eaten more than two knishes at one balcony sitting.

"Why?"

I stared at this coiled spring of a girl. Chin up. Lips pursed in a tight little circle. Eyes hurling almost visible darts of savage light, like tracer bullets in a movie about the Lafayette Escadrille.

"I don't know why," I said, ducking my head to one side to avoid getting hit by a spent shell. "I always take Hannah home after the movies." The remark struck me as being somewhat deficient in chivalry content, so I added hastily, "I mean, it's late at night."

"What's that got to do with it?"

I had to restrain an impulse to smash my fist into her face. In spite of what the four knishes were doing to my gut, however, my brain told me it was not Grace Krieger I was sore at.

"Look," I said irritably, "I'm just trying to be polite."

"I'm well aware of that," she said, shaving the words from an invisible block of ice.

I blinked at her. It had never occurred to me that she had expected more. After all, who the hell did she think she was? Hannah Halpern?

"For Christ's sake," I said, "everybody knows when a guy takes out a girl, especially it's late at night, he escorts her home."

"I don't know about the intelligence of the girls you are accustomed to taking out," Grace Krieger said as though she were spitting out grape seeds. "But I am quite capable of finding my own home. I suggest when you find yours, you take a teaspoon of bicarbonate of soda in a glass of warm water. Good night, Mr. Kramer."

And she was gone. I saluted her departure with a belch of relief and turned toward my own home. When I reached it my mother was at the kitchen table, working with her pencil at the large notebook in which Sebastian Roon had taught her to record, every Saturday night, all the wages she had paid earlier in the evening to her turners. I had not realized, until I saw the alarm clock on the refrigerator, that, for a Saturday night, it was still early in the evening.

"No double feature?" my mother said.

"Not tonight," I said. "Hannah had a headache."

Even as I uttered the unimaginative, spineless little lie, I was aware of a small, pulsing, hopeless flicker of hope that it might be true.

"Where's Seymour?" my mother said.

I was afraid to imagine. Once you left Loew's 180th Street, there were not many places in that neighborhood of the Bronx where you could take a girl late at night. I had taken Hannah to all of them.

"His girl didn't have a headache," I said. "So they stayed for the double feature. Good night, Ma."

I started down the hall.

"Where are you going?" my mother said.

"To sleep," I said.

"Where?"

"In my room," I said.

"So where will Seymour sleep?" my mother said.

I stared at my mother without seeing her. It came to me at this moment that at the back of my mind there had been a small frightening hint about the meaning of the disappearance of Hannah with Sebastian Roon that I did not want to face.

"Sorry, Ma," I said, coming back into the kitchen.

"I put two extra blankets for you under the mattress on the floor," she said. "Now it's nice and soft."

It was one of those rare moments when it occurred to me that perhaps she liked me. The moments came, of course, when she was free from her preoccupations with other things, when she remembered me. But that didn't

177

bother me. I was grateful for those moments, even if they were afterthoughts. They always made me feel good. This one helped now.

"Thanks, Ma." I said. "Listen, do we have any bicarbonate in the house?"

"What did you eat?" she demanded, pushing herself away from the table.

"Just a knish," I said, and belched.

"From one knish," my mother said. disappearing into the bathroom, "you don't get a thunderstorm like that."

I emitted a few more thunderstorms before she came back with a glass of water in which she was rattling a teaspoon.

"Here," she said. "Drink."

I drank. "Thanks, Ma," I said, handing back the glass. "I'll go to sleep now."

I went into the front room, got out of my clothes, and slipped into my makeshift bed on the floor between the cutting table and the Singer. The extra blankets under the mattress helped. My bed was much softer tonight than it had been since Sebastian Roon had come to live with us. But the extra blankets did not help enough. I could not sleep.

I lay awake all night, thinking myself into and out of a maze of feverish guesses about what had happened, and frantic plans for what to do. None of these made much sense. In fact, I couldn't retain any of them in my head for more than a moment or two before my mind went galloping off after a new possibility or a new plan.

It is customary, in an account of such a sleepless night, to put an end to the nightmare by stating that at long last, with the dawn, came blessed sleep. Not for Benny Kramer. With the dawn came the conviction that, before I went crazy, it would be a good idea to get out of the house.

All night, through the whirling fragments that had been chasing each other in my head, I had been listening for the sound of the front door opening and closing. I heard nothing.

I dressed quietly, went out into the kitchen, and stood

178

motionless, listening. From behind the closed door of my parent's bedroom down the hall came the sound of my father's musical snore. Around it, as though his sounds were a sapling to which a vine had taken a fancy, wound the less decorative noises made by my sleeping mother. I tiptoed to my room and put my ear to the closed door. Not a sound. I worked the knob slowly and eased the door open. The bed was empty. I closed the door and tiptoed out of the house.

My mind was still circling in and out and around the puzzling but ominous blow of the night before. My movements, however, were automatic. Seven days a week, at this hour of the morning, I walked to the subway. I did so now.

Without knowing I was doing them, I did all the other things I did every morning. It was only after I had distributed the emptied and rinsed ashtrays around the office, and realized all my morning chores in the Maurice Saltzman & Company office were completed, that I looked at my watch. Ten minutes short of eight o'clock. The staff never started drifting into the office before nine. The realization that I had over an hour of absolute privacy, seventy minutes of guaranteed freedom from eavesdropping, seemed a gift that had to be used. I forced myself not to think or hesitate. I went out to the switchboard, sank one of the brass-tipped red rubber plugs into an outside wire, pulled the corresponding black key, and gave the operator the number I never had to look up.

"Hello?" It was Mrs. Halpern's voice.

"Hello, Mrs. Halpern."

"Who is this?"

"Benny."

"Benny *Kra*mer?"

"Yes," I said. "Mrs. Halpern, I wondered if——"

"Benny, you're sick!" Mrs. Halpern said with satisfaction. "I knew it last night when you called a few minutes before seven. I knew it, Benny! I knew it in my bones! Benny, what have you got?"

I wondered if there was a word for it. "I haven't got anything, Mrs. Halpern."

179

The irony of my own remark snapped back at me like the flick of a knotted handkerchief. The bruise inside my head winced away from the blow.

"You mean you're not sick?" Mrs. Halpern said.

The fact that she sounded disappointed did not surprise me. She had made her diagnosis the night before on the phone. She would stick to it until she was proved right. Guiltily, I wondered if it would not be only fair to Mrs. Halpern for me to get sick at once.

"No, I'm fine, Mrs. Halpern. I really am."

Fine for what? I would not earn my salary for Mr. Bern on this day. That much was certain.

"Then why are you calling so early in the morning?" Mrs. Halpern said. "It's not even yet eight o'clock, Benny."

"I wondered if I could talk to Hannah?"

"I'm afraid not now, Benny." Mrs. Halpern's voice, always as hearty as that of an umpire, had sunk to a whisper. "She's sleeping like she was hit on the head."

In a flash of savagery, I found myself wishing she had been. But it was only a flash.

"Is she sick?" I said hopefully.

After all, maybe that was the simple explanation. She'd had an attack of something or other in the balcony, while I was buying the knishes, and Sebastian Roon had hurried her home.

"No," Mrs. Halpern said. "She's just a little crazy."

Hannah? That quiet, calm, smiling, soothing, acquiescent girl? With whom I had been eating Gabilla's knishes for almost a year?

"Mrs. Halpern," I said. "How do you mean crazy?"

"What do you call a person, Benny, she comes home it's almost six o'clock in the morning?"

The answer that surfaced on my surge of rage seemed better left unuttered.

"Six o'clock in the morning?"

It seemed safer to retreat behind a repetition of Mrs. Halpern's words. She seemed to like my response. So she repeated the words.

180

"Six—o'clock—in—the—morning," Mrs. Halpern said. "Can you imagine, Benny?"

Only too well.

"Where was she?" I said.

"I thought she was with you in Loew's 180th Street," Mrs. Halpern said.

"Not till six o'clock in the morning," I said.

"Of course not," Mrs. Halpern said. "I knew Benny Kramer would not keep my Hannah out until six o'clock in the morning."

Perhaps Benny should have tried.

"Did she say where she was?" I said.

"What she said, she said don't bother me with questions, Ma, I'm a wreck, I have to get some sleep, and she's getting it," Mrs. Halpern said. "God knows where she was."

It was a cinch I would not get the answer from Him.

"Mrs. Halpern, when she wakes up, would you tell Hannah I called?"

"What else?" Mrs. Halpern said. "A call from you, Benny, I'm going to keep it a secret? You want she should call you back?"

"Yes, please," I said. Then: "No, wait. I'm at the office, so I—"

"Now?" Mrs. Halpern said. "Sunday? Eight o'clock in the morning?"

"Well, we're pretty busy these days," I said. "So I don't know where my boss will assign me today. I mean on what audit he'll send me. So maybe it would be better if I called back?"

"If you want," Mrs. Halpern said. "Sure, Benny."

"What would be a good time?" I said. "I mean when do you think she'll wake up?"

"I don't have to think," Mrs. Halpern said. "In this house nobody sleeps after twelve o'clock. Even on Sundays. I'll wake her up twelve sharp."

"Okay," I said. "Then suppose I call, say, a quarter after?"

"Perfect, Benny," Mrs. Halpern said. "That will be fine."

181

It proved to be somewhat less than that. Mr. Bern did not send me out on an audit. After he had given the members of the staff their assignments for the day, and they were gone, Mr. Bern told me he wanted me to spend the day with Miss Bienstock, straightening out the file room. These fits of tidiness seized Mr. Bern two or three times a year. It annoyed me that he should have chosen this day to have one of these fits.

There were no unexposed phones in the Maurice Saltzman & Company offices except in the private rooms of Mr. Bern and Mr. Saltzman. All the rest were out in the open: in the room where Miss Bienstock and Lillian Waldbaum worked. I did not see how I could possibly call Hannah in their presence. As Miss Bienstock and I worked away, I kept an eye on the Seth Thomas that hung over the switchboard. When the hands touched noon, and the minute hand started creeping to the right, I started to sweat.

"Miss Bienstock," I said. "Maybe if we don't go out to lunch we could finish this job today? I could go down for sandwiches?"

For a few moments Miss Bienstock gave the matter her perplexed attention.

"Let's just get through G," she said finally. "We're near the end of it, and after we have a bite we can tackle H. Okay, Benny?"

"Sure," I said.

I poured myself into the letter G as though I were chained to an oar in a trireme. We finished, and stood on the brink of H, at seven minutes after twelve.

"I know what I want," I said. "Ham on a roll and coffee. Okay for you too, Miss Bienstock?"

"Well," Miss Bienstock said through her troubled frown, "I was thinking maybe an egg salad on white toast?"

"Whatever you say," I said, heading for the door. "Egg salad on white toast. With coffee?"

"No, milk!" Miss Bienstock shouted, snatching up her purse and running after me. "Here's the money, Benny!"

"Pay me later!" I shouted across my shoulder, and pulled the door shut behind me.

182

The elevator was my first piece of luck that day. It must have been on the way down, and just above our floor, when I jabbed the button. The door opened promptly, the car swayed a bit as I jumped in, but the operator brought it smoothly without a stop to the lobby. I was in the Liggett's phone booth at twelve minutes after twelve, and it was thirteen after when Mrs. Halpern answered the phone.

"It's me," I said.

"Benny?"

"Yeah," I said. "Could I talk to Hannah, please?"

"Benny, I'm sorry, no," Mrs. Halpern said. "She woke up half-past eleven and when I told her you called, and you were calling again a quarter after twelve, she said she couldn't wait. She had a date for twelve o'clock."

My heart, dropping swiftly in the general direction of my rubber heels, gave me the courage to say, "With who?"

"That girl who works in Hannah's office?" Mrs. Halpern said. "Grace Krieger? You know her, maybe?"

"Well," I said, "I've met her. Mrs. Halpern, you wouldn't happen to have her telephone number? Miss Krieger?"

"No, but wait," Mrs. Halpern said slowly. "I think it's a Walton? No, wait. The Walton, that's my brother Aaron in Brooklyn. Honest to God, me and my head for numbers. Wait, Benny, wait, I think maybe—"

"That's okay, Mrs. Halpern," I said. This was no time for one of those performances at which my mother excelled. I didn't want to wait, and I didn't want Mrs. Halpern to think. I said, "I'll look it up in the phone book, Mrs. Halpern. Thanks, anyway."

There were no Kriegers in the Bronx phone book. Bitterly, I thought this was just as well. I recalled the ambience of the encounter during which the night before I had fallen from Grace.

I stared out of the phone booth and watched the soda jerk behind the fountain as he lovingly built a banana split. Inspiration struck. I invested another nickel and called my home. My mother answered the phone.

"Ma," I said. "It's me. Benny."

183

"Something is wrong?" she said. "It's the middle of the day. Why should you call me in the middle of the day, Benny?"

"I'm worried about Seymour," I said. "He didn't come home all night, and before I went to the office this morning I looked into my room. His bed had not been slept in, Ma."

"When did you go to the office Benny?"

I had not looked at my watch when I left the house or when I reached the office. But I made a swift backward calculation. I had completed my chores by ten to eight. That meant I had started them ten minutes earlier, at twenty to eight. On Sunday the trip down from the Bronx on the IRT took almost exactly one hour. So I had been in the subway at twenty to seven. Five minutes for the walk to the train, and I must have left the house at twenty-five minutes to seven.

"Ma?"

"Don't scream," she said. "I'm here, Benny."

"I left the house at around six-thirty, twenty-five minutes to seven this morning, the latest," I said. "At twenty-five minutes to seven this morning, Ma, Seymour had not slept in that bed."

"He started sleeping in it ten minutes after you left," my mother said. "I woke up when he came in. It was a quarter to seven. I went out and asked him if he wanted a glass of milk, maybe, but he said no. He just wanted to go to sleep, he said. So he went to sleep. You don't have to worry, Benny. Seymour is one hundred percent all right."

"Did he say where he was all night?" I said.

"In Brooklyn," my mother said. "There's two men they want to buy finished jazz bows for their store, it's on Bushwick Avenue, but they couldn't see Seymour until after the store closed, and on Saturday night it closes, the store, it closes one o'clock in the morning or later. They talked, they went out to eat something, and then the long trip back to Tiffany Street, the poor boy, he didn't get into bed before a quarter to seven, like I said. But don't worry, Benny.

184

Like I also said, Seymour he's one hundred percent all right."

A bit of vitriol came boiling up inside me, but I did not let it pass my lips. My mother loved that double-crossing, two-timing Cockney bastard. Loved him enough to believe his silly story about Bushwick Avenue in Brooklyn.

"I'm glad to hear it," I said. "Could I talk to him, Ma?"

"If you know where he is," my mother said, "sure you can talk to him. I'm stopping you?"

"Isn't he in the house?"

"Not anymore," my mother said. "He woke up half past eleven. I said I'd make him a few *latkes* for breakfast, but he said no, he didn't have time. He had an appointment for twelve o'clock."

Social life in the Bronx, I thought sourly, had suddenly started to center around high noon.

"Did he say when he'd be back, Ma?"

"Do you tell me when you'll be back?" she said. "And you're my son yet."

"Well, Ma, in case he should get back, please tell Seymour I'll call him at six o'clock."

Even though at six o'clock Miss Bienstock and I were still only halfway through T, I was able to make the call without going down to Liggett's. Mr. Bern had gone home at five. He and his wife were going to a wedding. At six o'clock I went to his office and used his phone.

"No," my mother said. "Seymour didn't come back yet."

I hung up, tried not to think, and called that goddamn number which I never had to look up.

"No, Benny, I'm sorry," Mrs. Halpern said, "Hannah didn't come home yet. When she comes home, is there anything you want I should tell her?"

The temptation to make the classic reply was almost overwhelming, but I resisted it. As long as I didn't slam any doors shut, there was still hope. Anyway, I could believe there was still hope. That, in itself, was an achievement.

"I'll try her later tonight," I said. "Tell Hannah I'll call her later tonight."

185

When I did, at nine o'clock, Hannah had not yet come home. I did not have to call about Seymour. I had made the call to Hannah's house from my own home. Seymour was not in it.

He was not in it when I went to the office the next morning. Again, his bed had not been slept in. And again, when I called Hannah from the office, Mrs. Halpern answered.

"The girl must be going but real crazy, I mean it," she said. "Like yesterday morning six o'clock? Again this morning she came in six o'clock. And this morning it's not like yesterday morning. This morning is a Monday. She has to go to work."

"Is she?" I said.

"She's got to," Mrs. Halpern said. "If Hannah gets fired, how are we going to pay the rent?"

It was a problem with which I did not feel at the moment I wanted to cope.

"So she *is* going to work?" I said.

"How much work she'll be able to do today, God alone knows," Mrs. Halpern said. "But she said I should wake her up at eight o'clock so she can get to the office. Two hours sleep. After yet yesterday only five hours. Benny, can you believe it?"

I was beginning to. Nevertheless, when I took Mr. Bern's vici kids down to the lobby, I skipped the ruggle and cuppa cawfee. Instead, I went across the street to the phone booth in Liggett's, looked up the number in the phone book, and called the office of Gold-Mark-Zweig, Inc., on Mosholu Parkway.

"Gold-Mark-Zweig, good morning."

I recognized the voice of Grace Krieger. So I disguised my own. "Miss Halpern, please," I said.

"Who is calling, please?"

Through the phone booth door and the plate-glass window beyond, I could see the huge sign on the gray building on the Seventh Avenue corner: NOBODY IS IN DEBT TO MACY'S.

"This is the Macy's shoe department," I said. "Miss Halpern ordered a pair of shoes from us two weeks ago,

186

and she said I should call her at her office when they came in. They've just come in, but I'm afraid they're not exactly the color she wanted, so I thought I'd better talk to her before I send them back. May I talk with her, please?"

"Not today," Grace Krieger said. "Miss Halpern won't be in today."

"How about tomorrow?" I said. "May I call her tomorrow?"

"If you don't mind wasting a nickel," Grace Krieger said. "Miss Halpern doesn't work here anymore."

I hung up and called the Halpern house. Mrs. Halpern said I could reach Hannah at her office. She had gone to work an hour ago. So I knew that either Mrs. Halpern or Hannah was lying about whatever it was that was happening. By now I had no difficulty with deciding in my own mind which of the two I could believe. I settled for Mrs. Halpern, and wasted no more nickels on Hannah.

I concentrated on trying to arrange a face-to-face meeting with Sebastian Roon. I got nowhere, except with working on and building up to rather large proportions the suspicion that my mother was covering for him. There could not, it seemed to me, be any other explanation for what was happening.

Every night, when I came home from C.C.N.Y., Sebastian Roon was out. Every morning. when I left for the office, his—or rather, my—bed was empty and had not been slept in. Every noon, when I called my mother. she said he had come in soon after I left. slept for a few hours, and left the house just before I called. The third day I called at eleven. My mother said Sebastian had just gone out. The fourth day I called at ten. He had just gone out. The fifth day I called at nine. He had just gone out.

"After less than two hours' sleep?" I said.

"He's a big boy," my mother said. "I should go counting how many hours he sleeps?"

"How about the jazz bow business?" I said. "Without sleep. he can't be giving you very much help."

"Who needs help?" my mother said. "I know how to run my own business."

187

That night, when I came home from C.C.N.Y., I took one more stab at it.

"Ma," I said as I munched my slab of honey cake and sipped my glass of milk, "I just thought of something."

"What?" my mother said.

"Maybe Seymour has found another place to sleep?"

She looked up from her account book and gave me a long, cool stare. I had the feeling that she was trying to decide whether or not to let me in on something she knew. The decision went against me. My mother shrugged.

"Who knows?" she said, and went back to her account book.

Saturday morning I decided there was only one way to settle the confusion with which I had been living. I called the Halpern house. Hannah was out, of course. Mrs. Halpern was friendly, as always.

"I may not get a chance to call again today," I said. "So would you mind giving Hannah a message for me, Mrs. Halpern?"

"Mind?" she said. "For you, Benny, anything."

"Tell Hannah I'll meet her under Goldkorn's clock tonight," I said. "Regular time."

Regular time was not, of course, seven-fifteen, the time Hannah and I had agreed upon when we arranged our first date almost a year ago. Regular time was seven sharp, the time I always arrived at Goldkorn's clock and always found Hannah waiting under it. On this Saturday I arrived at Goldkorn's clock at a quarter to seven. Hannah was not under the clock. I settled myself against the tall iron pillar on top of which the clock sat. Waiting was all that was left for me.

Goldkorn's clock was enormous. Four feet across from the nine to the three. Sitting twenty feet in the air, on the pillar against which I leaned, Goldkorn's clock could be seen and read clearly all the way up to Bronx Park and all the way down to Grand Concourse. The digits were as big as the identification numbers on the chests of long-distance runners, and the hands could have been used as baseball bats.

These hands, which were moved by some sort of electrical mechanism, did not move smoothly and imperceptibly, like the hands of a watch. On Goldkorn's clock it was never, say, ten and a half minutes after the hour. On Goldkorn's clock it was always either ten minutes after or eleven minutes after. The electrical mechanism sent the minute hand forward in jumps, a full minute at a time. If you were anywhere within ten feet of the clock, you could hear the heavy muffled thump as the hand moved.

When I took up my position under the clock that Saturday, the minute hand was on nine. A quarter to seven. When I heard the thump overhead, I did not bother to look up. I knew it was fourteen minutes to seven. Fourteen thumps later I did not look up. Seven o'clock on the button. Then I looked up to Bronx Park, and down toward Southern Boulevard. No sign of Hannah.

Fifteen bumps later there was still no sign of her. So I knew for certain what I had suspected from the beginning: she was not coming. I remember that night, only a month ago, the night Sebastian Roon showed up on Tiffany Street for the first time. I had arrived under the clock five minutes after seven. Hannah had bawled me out for being late.

The clock overhead bumped again. Sixteen minutes after seven. Time to go home. Nobody was going to bawl out anybody under Goldkorn's clock tonight. Still I lingered.

Another bump. Another. And another. Nineteen minutes. Just one more bump, I decided, and then—

And then a curious thing happened.

A taxi came out of Vyse Avenue, turned into 180th Street, eased up to the curb at my feet, and stopped in front of Goldkorn's clock. I couldn't make out who was inside, but I could see hands moving forward, across the back of the front seat, and the driver turning toward them, and I realized the fare was being paid. A moment later the door opened and a fat woman, in a series of panting jerks, as though she were saddled with a heavy knapsack, started to heave her way out. There was something familiar about the movements, but I did not recognize Mrs. Halpern until she stood up on the sidewalk and the cab pulled away.

189

Then I realized why I had not recognized her. Mrs. Halpern, like my mother, was not a taxi rider, and I had never seen her except in her own kitchen where, like my mother in our kitchen, she always wore a housedress covered by an apron. Here, on the sidewalk under Goldkorn's clock, Mrs. Halpern was wearing a blue silk dress with white flowers embroidered at the neckline, and an Empress Eugénie hat.

"Benny!" she cried. "Thank God you waited! Hannah said you're always here by seven o'clock, so she gave me money to take a taxi from the ship, but it was traffic from downtown there by the dock, Benny, such traffic I never saw, and I got scared you wouldn't be here, and even though I knew I could call you up at home and tell you what Hannah said, I knew it would be nicer if I told you straight from the ship, like Hannah wanted."

"The ship?" I said.

Mrs. Halpern nodded and smiled happily and poured out a stream of hopelessly disorganized facts that clearly were not disorganized to her. So I thought I'd better listen and place them in some sort of order that would make them comprehensible. It took a bit of doing, but I managed it. I was so pleased with my achievement that I did not immediately grasp the extraordinary nature of the story.

More or less coherently, it went like this:

Seven days ago, the night John Barrymore came striding out of the shadow of the silent screen in, and as, General Crack, Hannah had been offered a job in England. The story, which Mrs. Halpern had heard only late this afternoon, when Hannah asked her mother to come to the ship to say farewell, was that my firm, Maurice Saltzman & Company, had a client over there who manufactured hats made from rabbit hairs raised in Australia by another client of Maurice Saltzman & Company. The English firm was in trouble, and had appealed to Maurice Saltzman & Company for an American bookkeeper to come over and straighten out its records. Only an hour ago, on board the ship that was taking her to England, Hannah had told her mother that I had recommended her for the job, and the reason her movements had been so erratic in recent days

190

was that all week she had been busy with passports, steamship tickets, buying clothes, and packing. Indeed, Hannah had been so busy, she told her mother, that she had forgotten to tell me the hour her ship was sailing. She was kissing her mother goodbye out on deck when Hannah remembered.

"She felt so terrible," Mrs. Halpern said, "honest, Benny, she started to cry, and she gave me money for a taxi because she said she wanted me to say goodbye for her, not on the telephone, but real people talking face to face, and Hannah said I should hurry, because she knew you'd be waiting under Goldkorn's clock. So I hurried, and Benny, look, here I am."

She threw her arms around me and gave me a fierce kiss.

"That's from Hannah," Mrs. Halpern said. "She said I should do it, and I should tell you why I was doing it, and you would understand."

"Thanks, Mrs. Halpern," I managed to say. "I understand."

Mrs. Halpern kissed me again, not so fiercely this time.

"That one is from me alone," she said. "Because you did such a wonderful thing for my Hannah."

"It was nothing," I said.

Through the rolling mass of my emotions, which reminded me of angleworms squirming in a bottle, came a brightly lighted sliver of cynicism: perhaps I had spoken the truth; perhaps it *was* nothing.

"Nothing he says," Mrs. Halpern said to Goldkorn's clock. "Benny," she said, "you should have seen Hannah's face on that ship. Like she was born again. It would have done your heart good, Benny."

I didn't know what to say to that, so I said nothing. I walked Mrs. Halpern down Vyse Avenue to the stoop of her house, where she kissed me again.

"Oh, Benny, Benny," she said with a joyous smile. "What a wonderful boy you are!"

It was not much, but it was something, to know that at least one member of the Halpern family thought so.

191

"Good night," I said, and walked slowly in the dusk to Tiffany Street.

My mother was sitting at the kitchen table working on her account book.

"I saved you soup and *kiggle* and a nice piece chicken," she said, getting up. "I'll warm it good so you'll enjoy."

So I knew she knew. My mother never fed me on Saturday nights.

"Thanks, Ma," I said.

"Take off the jacket and the tie," she said. "A good piece chicken you must eat it in comfort."

She made no attempt to stop me when I went into my room. I took off my jacket and tie and came back out into the kitchen. My mother had set out enough food to carry my old East Fourth Street boy scout troop through a Labor Day weekend camping trip to the Palisades. I suddenly felt famished. I cleaned the plates.

My mother never mentioned Sebastian Roon. It was as though the young Englishman had never been with us. Or had never existed. But he had left his mark. He had given my mother her basic grounding in English, and she moved ahead steadily. Occasionally she would ask me to explain a difficult word. There was no deference in her request. It was not Benny Kramer asking Miss Bongiorno a question in class. My mother asked as an equal. That pleased me.

Also, my mother's jazz bow business prospered. Soon she allowed me to keep not three but five dollars a week out of my Maurice Saltzman & Company pay envelope. And, of course, I owed that to Sebastian Roon. But I managed to restrain my gratitude. I kept it to myself.

One day, as she was cooking my breakfast, my mother asked how much time Mr. Bern allowed me for lunch every day.

"I don't have a regular lunch hour," I said. "If I'm working away from the office, I usually do what the other men on the staff do. I go out, have a sandwich, walk around for a while, and then come back to work. A half-hour. An hour. Like that. If Mr. Bern keeps me in the office for the day, I grab a bite when I'm out on an errand for him or Miss Bienstock. Why do you ask?"

"I'd like to buy a spring coat," my mother said. "I'd like you to come with me."

She had long ago lost the capacity to surprise me. Now it came hurtling back. My mother had never owned a spring coat. Her few clothes were functional, almost primitive. She made most of them herself. They had no style. She was not a good seamstress. But she was good enough for her purpose, which was protection from the elements. In the winter heavy, she used to say, in the summer light.

"Why do you want to buy a spring coat?" I said.

"It's coming soon spring," my mother said. "In America, it comes spring, you buy a spring coat."

It had taken an Englishman to lead her, after a quarter of a century of immigrant darkness, onto the bright road of Americanization.

"Why do you ask about my lunch hour?" I said.

"I want you to come help me," she said.

"On my lunch hour," I said, "I don't think I could get up to the Bronx and then back to work. It's an hour on the subway each way."

"Who said the Bronx?" my mother said.

I got it. "You mean downtown?" I said.

"What else?" she said. "You want something good, you have to go downtown. Everybody goes to buy downtown."

It was clear that she meant everybody who was in America.

"Is there any particular store you have in mind?" I said.

I was absolutely certain she had. Until she knew, my mother would never have asked me to accompany her. She did not mind unanswered questions, so long as it was somebody else who did not know the answer. My mother did not like to be tagged off base.

"This place Klein's," she said. "On Fourteenth Street. You know it?"

Did Martin Chuzzlewit know the Monument to the Great Fire in Pudding Lane?

"Sure," I said.

193

"You could meet me there today?" my mother said. "Say like maybe half past twelve?"

"Sure," I said again. "But there's still that problem. An hour up here by subway to get you, an hour back downtown, maybe a half-hour for buying the coat, then I'd have to bring you back up here, and I'd have to go back downtown again. Five hours, Ma, at least. Maybe six."

"Not if all you have to do is come from your office and meet me at Klein's," my mother said. "You help me buy the coat, then you go back to your office."

"What about you?" I said. "How will you get to Klein's?"

"Don't worry about me." my mother said. "Just tell me where it is. I'll get there."

I knew there was no point in protest or argument. She had made up her mind. So I told her and, as I told her, I drew a crude map on the back of a grocery bag. My mother studied it for a few moments.

"I'll meet you here," she said, pointing to the Union Square entrance. "Twelve-thirty."

I had a bad morning. My mother had never before set foot in the subway. She was bound to get lost or worse. Fortunately, that day I was helping Mr. Breiner and two other members of the Maurice Saltzman & Company staff with a bankruptcy audit of a passementerie manufacturer on 23rd Street. When I got to Klein's at twenty minutes past twelve, my mother was waiting in front of the Union Square entrance.

"Did you have any trouble?" I said.

"What kind of trouble?" she said. "There's signs. All you need to know is how to read them." Pause. "And also you must have a nickel."

The ability to read signs was for her of course a tremendous achievement. So she wanted the credit, and she got it. In her own way. By making little of it. And giving the weight of her remark to something anybody could achieve. A nickel.

It was the touch that set her apart. It was what made her

194

not just anybody's mother. It was what for Benny Kramer made her his mother.

The next Sunday morning, when I came out of my bedroom for breakfast, she set before me a plate of piping hot potato *latkes*. My heart thumped. I knew what she was telling me. The wedge that her feelings for Sebastian Roon had driven between us, that was gone. From now on she had only one son.

She demonstrated this in many ways. For me the most significant was that she never mentioned Hannah Halpern. I don't know how much my mother knew, but she always knew a lot that you did not suspect she knew. What she didn't know, she knew how to find out. She and Mrs. Halpern were friends. My mother, by introducing me to the Halperns, had introduced me to Hannah.

I was fairly certain that my mother had talked to Mrs. Halpern on the phone during the day, when I was downtown. And I was equally certain that Mrs. Halpern had given my mother her joyous version of the good luck that had befallen Hannah. What Mrs. Halpern had no way of knowing was what my mother knew: a boy named Sebastian Roon, of whose existence Mrs. Halpern was unware, had disappeared from Tiffany Street at the same time Hannah had sailed for England.

When I started coming home for supper on Saturday nights, and she set out my meal, I knew she knew that there was no longer any Hannah around for me to go to double features with.

Eight or nine months after she sailed, I had a letter from Hannah. It was friendly, but short. She invited me to come to her wedding in Blackpool. The fact that she knew I couldn't possibly accept seemed to contain a concealed message. For a while I tried to figure it out, but I couldn't. Then I became interested in another girl.

I forgot Hannah.

9

One day, without warning, Lillian Waldbaum came out into the file room where I was working.

"What are you doing Tuesday night?" she said. This was about a year after Seb and Hannah had disappeared from the balcony of Loew's 180th Street.

"Nothing much," I said uneasily, feeling my face grow hot. In those days when girls came at me out of the blue, I went into the red. "I mean aside from my classes at C.C.N.Y."

"What time are they?" Lillian said. "These classes?"

"Eco Two is six-thirty," I said. "French One is seven-thirty. And Debentures Three is eight-thirty."

"You crazy about Debentures?" Lillian said.

The answer was: of course not. I detested Debentures. I did not understand them. But I felt it was a proper course to take for a young man who worked for a firm of certified public accountants. I was trying to impress Mr. Bern. He felt about debentures the way Tom Mix felt about his horse Tony.

"Well," I said nervously, "not about Three."

"I hear One and Two also stink," Lillian said.

She was not a subtle girl. All you had to do was see her lean across the wash basin in the file room.

"Anyway," I said, "I got through them."

"You got Debentures Three on Tuesday night?" Lillian said.

The way she said it made me look at her more closely. God knows, when Lillian Waldbaum leaned over the wash basin in the file room, I looked at her closely enough. But that's all the attention I had thus far paid to her. Now I realized I had probably overlooked something.

196

I was a one-woman man. As long as Hannah Halpern had been up there on Vyse Avenue, waiting for me every Saturday night, I'd had eyes for no other girl. But now Benny was older. And Hannah had vanished.

Looking at Lillian Waldbaum, I was suddenly wondering about the problems of fidelity. It seemed to me I was making a very big and very important discovery. It was a time in my life when I was more excited about making discoveries than I was about—

Steady, Benny.

"Yes," I said. "I've got Debentures Three on Tuesday night, but I've got Debentures Three five nights a week, and it gets to be sort of, you know, a pain. I could use a little relief, and I've got a few cuts coming to me. What did you have in mind?"

"Here," Lillian Waldbaum said. "Take a look at this. This ad for The New Theatre."

She held out a copy of *The Nation*. Or it could have been *The New Republic*. Or maybe it was some other magazine. I don't really remember.

In 1931 there were a lot of publications around that were very thin and printed on what Westbrook Pegler used to call butcher's paper. They were full of calmly ferocious articles by people named George Soule that made shattering attacks in good, clean prose on Big Business, the merchants of death, cartels, primogeniture, Washington lobbies, child labor, the judges in the Sacco-Vanzetti case, amphictyonies, and allodial tenure. These articles were printed in between small ads for the Martha Graham Dance Studio, manuscript typing services, and something called The New Theatre.

All these publications cost fifteen cents. Each, that is. I never bought any of them. Fifteen cents was half a dinner in Stewart's cafeteria.

I took the magazine from Lillian. The ad for The New Theatre pleaded with the reader to come to one of eight previews of a new play by a new playwright in a new theater on a new part of Fourteenth Street. I remember an inward creasing of the brow. Fourteenth Street was a very

197

crowded thoroughfare. How had they managed to slip in a new part?

"What about it?" I said.

"I've got a friend playing in this thing," Lillian said. "She tells me it's very good. She gave me a couple of passes, and I'd like to go, but I don't want to go alone."

"Gee whiz," I said.

I wince now when I think of the gee-whizzing I did at that time of my life. I wince, but I also shrug. Gee-whizzing is a part of the time of innocence. The young David, entering for the first time the tent of King Saul, was a gee-whizzer. Why not Benny Kramer?

"You mean," I said to Lillian Waldbaum, "if I cut Debentures Three we could go to this thing next Tuesday?"

"Yop," Lillian said. She was a very pretty girl. And she had something Benny Kramer was just beginning to appreciate: style. But she talked most of the time like a truck driver. "How about it?"

"Thanks very much," I said. "I'd like that."

I am not sure now what I was actually saying then. I didn't, to be truthful, care very much about The New Theatre. I had not yet sunk my teeth into the Old. But I missed Hannah Halpern. And stirring in the back of my mind was the thought that maybe, by just sort of tagging along, I might find a substitute in this tough little beauty, Miss Lillian Waldbaum. She reminded me of a movie actress named Evelyn Brent. Tense. Pulled in. On the verge of exploding. Like a drawn bow before the twang when the arrow is released. She opened vistas. Memories of Gabilla's knishes had been disturbing my sleep.

"And listen," Lillian said. "You don't have to worry about buying my evening groceries."

"I wasn't thinking of a meal," I said. "What I had in mind, all I was thinking, I thought maybe we could have a couple of knishes, that's all I had in mind."

"Yop," Lillian Waldbaum said coolly, "I know what you had in mind."

She certainly did. Which proved to be a big surprise to Benny Kramer.

198

Until Benny encountered Lillian Waldbaum, I had always assumed girls didn't know what you were after. Every Saturday night, when I went into the Hebrew National for the hot Gabilla's knishes that I was about to carry up into the balcony of Loew's 180th Street, I always felt like the first kid on the block who had latched onto Casanova in the Hamilton Fish Park branch of the New York Public Library.

My God, the stuff that goes on in books. I suppose that's why they are the plinth on which all education stands. When I think of the things I first learned about what really goes on in life, just by using my library card, my mind responds as it did in the days of innocence: it boggles.

It was from books that Benny Kramer learned how to feel when he was up in the balcony of Loew's 180th Street with his hot Gabilla's knishes. Shrewd. Clever. A canny conspirator. Setting the trap in which I would catch that lovely, seductive, sexy butterball waiting for me so innocently in the balcony seat near the red exit sign. And why shouldn't Benny Kramer have thought so? After all, I always did catch her. But there are women and women. And Lillian Waldbaum taught me the difference.

They both know the score. But the sweet ones, the Hannah Halperns, allow you to think they never even suspected there was a scoreboard, and so what happens is a delicious surprise. You think so, anyway. The others, the non-sweet ones, they let you know right away that while they know the score they are not particularly impressed with the knowledge. Okay, buster, they say, I know what you want, let's see if you can get it. You usually do, and it is not bad, but there is no sweetness in it. As the oddballs who climb mountains are reputed to say, you do it because it is there.

Benny Kramer, on his first date with Lillian Waldbaum, knew it was there. And precisely where it was located. Staking out the terrain, it was in the fourth row, on the left, of the Preshinivetz Playhouse on West Fourteenth Street. The Preshinivetz Playhouse was a fascinating place for Benny Kramer.

West Fourteenth Street is a shallow thoroughfare. It was anyway, in 1931. It had the feel of a neighborhood that knew it was being exploited. And it gave you the sense of being watched that is common to all ghettos. You felt that people were peering out at you. Not necessarily with hostility. But not with open-hearted warmth, either.

The Preshinivetz Playhouse was located in the Hoboe Kioboe Catholic Church of St. Francis the True. The church had been started by a small, passionate sect of—the confused owner of the building believed—Poles from Woloshonowa. They never got very far beyond starting. They faded away, leaving behind them a small mountain of unpaid bills, and a large room that looked like a grocery store without shelves into which had been dragged three aisles of primitively constructed benches. These had been intended to serve as pews.

I liked the place at once. This was the sort of dump in which Benny Kramer had spent the recreational hours of his youth. I was very young, but already I thought of part of my life as my youth. It seems odd to me now. But not in 1931. The young tend to confuse themselves with the world, which is old.

When Lillian Waldbaum and I came into the Preshinivetz Playhouse it was almost full. But the passes provided by Lillian's friend had effectively held our seats in the fourth row on the left. Lillian and I settled down and looked around. Now that I was off my feet, I liked the place even better. All the people who were jamming the benches looked like me and Lillian.

I don't mean that all the girls were as pretty as Lillian and all the men were as interesting looking as Benny Kramer who, as we all know, never claimed to be the model for the Arrow Collar ad.

I mean they all looked and smelled like young people who had dashed, without time out for showers, naturally, from their jobs on 34th Street or their courses in the evening session at C.C.N.Y. Hurtling themselves across the city to reach this redolent theater on West Fourteenth Street because they believed it was important to see a group of amateur actors perform a play called *Walda Wexler Wait for Willie Wishingrad: Urgent!* In 1931 they knew how to put together titles.

Yet, even for 1931, *Walda Wexler Wait for Willie Wishingrad: Urgent!* was unique. I did not realize it at the time. At the time it seemed perfectly normal. Especially if you went to see such a thing with an intense girl like Lillian Waldbaum. She had deep, dark, tragic, erotic circles under her eyes.

Two or three years ago, however, in 1969 I think it was, *Walda Wexler Wait for Willie Wishingrad: Urgent!* resurfaced in the life of Benny Kramer in a rather odd way.

I have a client named Kermit Klinger. His family is loaded. Kermit's father, Gershon Klinger, invented the underarm dress shield at a time when my father was bending over a sewing machine in an Allen Street sweatshop. Gershon Klinger is almost ninety and, as we say in the trade, I do his work. I like the old man because he reminds me of my father. If my father had been solvent, that is. Gershon Klinger has worked out and keeps enunciating a rule of life with which I do not know how to quarrel.

"Take it away from the old bastards," he says, "and give it to the kids."

He has given an awful lot of it to his son Kermit. I know. I drew the papers.

Young Kermit, in addition to the money, has all sorts of weird, not very well thought out but extremely intense ideas for proving to the world he is more than a rich man's son. He is. Kermit Klinger is a rich man's son who is also a Broadway press agent. I am told by other clients that Kermit is the best Broadway press agent in the business. Which is why he is constantly scheming to get out of the business. In 1969 he came to see me in my office.

"Benny," he said, "I got it made."

Kermit Klinger is thirty years my junior. But I like the way he calls me Benny. Nothing patronizing about it. Kermit calls me Benny the way he calls his shoeshine boy Tony. He's paying for a service. Part of the service includes the right to enjoy the pleasure of being on a relaxed first-name basis with the servitor.

"What is it this time?" I said.

With Kermit Klinger there have been many times.

"No, this time I've got it," Kermit said. "No kidding, Benny, I've got it. I've found a play. Brenda found it for me."

Brenda is Kermit's wife. Her father invented the disposable diaper. Ours is the century in which the big fortunes are made not in heavy metals, but in simplifying matters at almost any human orifice.

"Everybody thinks Brenda is a dum-dum," Kermit Klinger said of his wife. "Because she's not always in there pitching with the bing-bing talk, and her father made it with the disposable diaper, and she went to Sarah Lawrence."

"My wife went to Sarah Lawrence," I said.

Kermit Klinger looked at me with annoyance. "Are you comparing your Elizabeth Ann to my Brenda?"

If I were, my Elizabeth Ann would have been justified in sending me to Coventry until the ground hog sees his own shadow.

"No," I said. "Of course I'm not. I merely want to make the point that just because a girl went to Sarah Lawrence—"

"Listen, Benny," Kermit said. "At the rates you log me in on your billing diary for these visits, don't make points I can get for free from the kid who takes my shoes down to be shined in the barbershop in the lobby of my office building."

"Are they vici kid?" I said.

"What?" Kermit Klinger said.

"Your shoes," I said. "Are they made of vici kid?"

"What the hell is vici kid?" Kermit said.

"Let me have a look," I said.

Kermit put his right foot up on my desk. Lovely. Ira Bern would have approved.

"It's vici kid all right," I said.

"So what?" Kermit said.

I took a dime from my pocket and tossed it across the

202

desk. "Give that to the kid who takes your shoes down to be shined," I said.

Kermit picked up the dime. He looked puzzled. Who could blame him? "What for?" he said.

"Tell the kid to buy himself a ruggle."

Kermit laughed. "Benny," he said. "How long since you had your last ruggle?"

My mind darted back to Maurice Saltzman & Company. "Nineteen thirty-one, I think."

Kermit shook his head. "Boy, oh boy, oh boy," he said. "You pay lawyers a fortune to give you advice, and they don't even know about ruggles. Benny, boy, I have a ruggle and coffee for breakfast every morning at the Stage Deli before I go up to the office. At the Stage Deli, Benny, a ruggle today goes for sixty cents. You add the twenty-five cents for the cup of coffee you need to dunk it in, and you've shot the ass out of a buck before you even get to the tip."

"Well," I said, "in nineteen thirty-one—"

"Benny, I was not around in nineteen thirty-one," Kermit Klinger said. "When I first encountered the ruggle, the Japs had just dropped the old Sixth Avenue El on us at Schofield Barracks, and I was getting my brains knocked out by Mr. Frohnknecht, my intermediate algebra teacher at James Monroe High School. So stop already with the price of ruggles and let's get back to this wonderful play Brenda found for me in the public domain."

"You mean it was copyrighted more than fifty-six years ago?" I said.

"No," Kermit said. "It was written during the Depression, and they did it in one of those dumps on West Fourteenth Street. A mimeograph job. They never bothered to copyright the damn thing."

"What's so wonderful about it?" I said.

"It gives the period," Kermit said. "I mean—boy, does it give the period! Get with it, Benny. Everybody these days is nuts about nostalgia. Picture books at twenty bucks a throw on how to make clabber down in Williamsburg at the time Cornwallis was surrendering to Washington at

203

Yorktown. Old photograph albums with that cockamamy *Police Gazette* type face showing women in bustles eating turtle soup with Diamond Jim Brady at the old Waldorf on Thirty-fourth and Fifth. People breaking down the doors of the Imperial and the Majestic at ice prices to see revivals of these cruddy musicals from the days when chorus girls were as flat-chested as Buster Keaton, and DeSylva, Brown, and Henderson were writing those songs for diabetics called 'When I Take My Sugar to Pee.' You know, Benny. Everything was simpler in nineteen thirty-one. Simpler and better. Remember? There were breadlines, sure. But people helped each other. They shared what they had. And what they had was guess what? Bubkes. Natch. Al Capone was beating out the brains of rival gangsters with a baseball bat at public banquets, but he did it in a nice way. Norman Rockwell was painting those covers on *The Saturday Evening Post* that showed The Old Country Doctor putting his stethoscope to a little girl's doll. There was no drug scene. The only thing high school kids shot was baskets in the gym. No campus riots. College kids were too busy swallowing goldfish and seeing how many freshmen could fit into a phone booth. No acid rock. It was 'Sweet Adeline' and 'The Whiffenpoof Song' all the way. Kids just hustled out of high school to compete for that job in the bank, and if they got it, and they kept their noses clean, they ended up Judge Brandeis or Howard Hughes. That crap."

"It is not crap," I said. "I mean it wasn't. It was a time when—"

"I know," Kermit said. "I've heard about it. It's coming out of my ears."

"Then why," I said, "why do you want to produce a play written about it?"

"Because this play is not *about* it," Kermit said. "This play *is* it. The damn thing jumps at you off the page. It's not Norman Rockwell. It's real. So real it hurts. This play wasn't written. No pens, no typewriters, no pencils. This play was walloped out with a sledge hammer. It takes place in one of those cheap dumps they used to call meeting halls. On West Fourteenth. A strike meeting is about to take place. Taxi drivers. They're sick and tired of starving and being lied to by the fleet owners. They're meeting to vote on whether they should go out or not. The whole play, the beauty part of it, Benny, it all takes place before the strike meeting gets under way. The drivers, all these angry tough guys, in this stinking dump on Fourteenth Street, they're waiting for their leader. He's late because he's in an important meeting with the fleet owners down at City Hall. Whatever news he comes back with, that's what will decide the men should they strike or shouldn't they. This strike leader, he's sent these guys a message. Don't do nothing till I show up. I'll bring the dope with me. So the tension is built in. From the minute the curtain goes up, you're sweating it out with these guys, waiting for what the hell kind of news their leader will bring.

"While they're waiting we see a whole series of flash-backs. Maybe ten or twelve. I'm not sure. I only had time to read the goddamn script just once. But these flashbacks, they're the guts of the play. Each one tells the story of one of the hackies pouring into the meeting hall, and what this strike would mean to him. They're ball-breakers, Benny, every one of these stories. They disintegrate you. There's like this young kid, he wants to be a doctor, and he's hack-ing to save enough dough to go to medical school, but he's also stuck on a broad, and the girl wants to get married, but if he goes out on strike that's goodbye Charlie to both medical school and getting married. Then there's, let's see, yeah, there's this guy, his wife is dying. It doesn't exactly say in the script the big C, but you know it's not halitosis either, and he's got to earn the money to keep her in the hospital, and the strike would mean curtains to that. I tell you, Benny, it's terrific stuff. It hits you where you live. I cried, Benny. Can you imagine? Me, Kermit Klinger. I burst into tears. Twice. No, wait. One, two, three. Yeah. Three times, Benny. I cried three times. The tension keeps building and building until you feel—"

"The title of this play," I said. "Would it happen to be *Walda Wexler Wait for Willie Wishingrad: Urgent!?*"

Kermit Klinger looked at me with a frown of annoyance.

I didn't blame him. He had been going good. Building toward his punch line. And I had taken it away from him.

"How did you know that?" Kermit said coldly.

"I was there," I said.

"Where?" Kermit said.

"The Preshinivetz Playhouse," I said. "On West Fourteenth Street. I went to a preview."

"Of *Walda Wexler Wait for Willie Wishingrad: Urgent!*?" Kermit said sharply.

"That's right," I said.

"When?"

"In nineteen thirty-one," I said.

"You really remember it?" Kermit said.

Remember it? I was reliving it. I was no longer sitting in my Madison Avenue office, logging in on my work diary a lucrative visit from a client. I was young again. I was back in 1931. Sitting on a piece of dirty bench in the fourth row, left aisle, of the Preshinivetz Playhouse on West Fourteenth Street. And I was shaking with the impact of this extraordinary theatrical experience. And suddenly Lillian Waldbaum gave me a sharp poke in the ribs.

I gasped. We had come to the climax of the play. Everybody in the audience turned. Down the aisle, striding with majestic decision toward the stage, came the man all the people in the play had been waiting for: the leader of the strike.

"Hey!" Lillian Waldbaum said. "There's one of our former clients!"

I squinted to bring the young man into better focus. He leaped to the stage. He turned to face the audience. He raised his hands above his head. The theater was suddenly hushed. He spoke in a low voice. So low that, like everybody else, I found myself leaning forward to hear it.

"Strike!" Sebastian Roon said.

10

The backstage area in the Preshinivetz Playhouse was not really a backstage area. Just a sort of undefined shallow smudge. Standing in it was the girl who had played the part of Walda Wexler. Standing next to her was Sebastian Roon.

"Benjamin!" he said.

He came across to me, and he did something no other Englishmen I have ever met would have done. Seb threw his arms around my shoulders and held me for a few minutes in a tight hug. He was, after all, a Jewish English man.

"By George," he said, "it's marvelous to see you."

I didn't answer. I couldn't. What had happened the year before, and how I thought I would feel if I ever met him again, was now all mixed up with the way I suddenly did feel. All at once my throat seemed ill-equipped for conversation.

"You two know each other?" said the girl who had played Walda Wexler.

"Know each other?" said Lillian Waldbaum. "These two jokers used to get drunk together in Shane's on Twenty-third Street."

Seb released me. He gave Lillian a sharp, startled, frowning glance. Then his face cleared and he laughed.

"So we did." He held out his hand. "You must know something about the workings of the Maurice Saltzman office, Miss—?"

"Waldbaum," Lillian said.

"I regret to say that the only person I knew in the Maurice Saltzman office was Benjamin," Seb said. "I have a feeling I missed something, Miss Waldbaum."

Lillian gave him the sort of look that would have safely

fastened Martin Luther's thundering assaults on the Pope to the door of the Wittenberg cathedral.

"It's too late to rectify the omission," she said. "I'm loyal." Lillian jerked her thumb toward me. "I'm gunna dance with de guy what brung me."

"What are you two talking about?" said the girl who had played the part of Walda Wexler.

Seb laughed again. "Let's do our talking across some hot food," he said. "I'm famished."

He shoveled us gently out into West Fourteenth Street and then poked us left into the Village. It was an area about which I knew very little. Yet on that night when Sebastian Roon and I met again, it seemed to me that I was rediscovering a once familiar place. I did not realize the reason until much later. Totally unaware of what was happening to him, Benny Kramer was falling in love.

Perhaps that's why Benny still remembers the feel of that walk. In those days the Village was already run down, but in a delicious way. Like Montparnasse. Or Soho. The houses were crumbly at the edges, but they looked soft and inviting. Like good sponge cake that has been cut with a dull knife. You wondered what went on inside those houses.

The Village of 1931 reminded me of the London in which Sherlock Holmes used to leap out of the fog into a hansom cab, bark an order at the desiccated old creep on the box and then, as he sank into the seat, rap out: "And an extra shilling, my good man, if you make Charing Cross before midnight!"

On that night in 1931 we made it to The Family Tricino comfortably under the line. The middle Tricino daughter, Carissima, admitted us at ten minutes to twelve. This was not an unusual hour for diners to show up. Especially diners like Benny Kramer who had not yet learned about dining. All Benny knew about was eating. The Tricinos managed to remain financially afloat by feeding illegally people who ate cheap. The Family Tricino was a speak-easy restaurant. No booze. Just spaghetti. But they served it without a restaurant license.

There was one part of the operation that The Family Tricino seemed to feel was essential to keep the cops off their backs. For a few minutes after customers were seated, one of the Tricino daughters would plump herself down at the table as though she were depositing a dollop of whipped cream on a piece of apple pie. She would utter a few words, always accompanied by giggles, scream with laughter at what she clearly felt was a handful of good jokes, then race out to the kitchen for a coal scuttle full of Mrs. Tricino's pasta.

"It gives the place the camouflage the family feels safe with," Sebastian Roon whispered to me as we were admitted to the brownstone by Mr. Tricino. "If the members of the family sit with the diners, then the diners are not customers but guests. That's seventy cents, old boy."

Seb nodded toward Mr. Tricino's hand, which was outstretched under my nose like a Salvation Army tambourine.

"No, it isn't," Lillian Waldbaum said. "I happen to work in the same office with Benny, so I know how much he earns. This is dutch."

She dropped a quarter and a dime into Mr. Tricino's hand. I fished from my pocket a quarter and two nickels, dropped them into Mr. Tricino's hand, and took a step after Lillian. Sebastian Roon caught my elbow.

"You wouldn't happen to be in possession of another seventy cents, would you?" he said. "I seem to have been caught short."

I did happen to be in possession of another seventy cents. In fact, I happened to be in possession of another two dollars and ten cents, and I didn't have to hunt through my pockets to check. It was a time when I always knew down to the penny exactly how much money I had on my person. It was never much, but it was always enough, and what made it enough was that I had no sense of desperation about it.

The trick in handling money, I learned in 1931, is never to let other people know you are handling it. Seventy cents called for? No need to panic. Since I knew I had two ten on me. If I hadn't kept a careful mental record of every

209

coin concealed on my person, I would have had to start hunting through my pockets.

"Sure," I said to Sebastian Roon.

I reached into my pocket and pulled out the handful of coins, each one of which had left a precise impression of its value on my right thigh by pressure through my pants pocket and underwear. I counted out into Mr. Tricino's outstretched palm two quarters and two dimes. With my free hand poised over the now dangerously diminished hoard, I took a stab at a role that life had thus far denied me: Haroun Al-Rashid in O'Henry's "Baghdad on the Subway."

"If you're strapped," I said to Sebastian, "I can let you have something extra."

Sebastian laughed and winked. "Thanks, Benjamin, that's very good of you, but I'm doing quite well, actually." He winked again. "Elizabeth Ann is wallowing in the stuff."

"Who's that?" I said.

Seb nodded toward the girl who had played the female lead in the play. She was moving across the room with Lillian Waldbaum toward a table near the far wall.

"The people in the cast call her Peggy," Seb said. "But she doesn't like that. She was christened Elizabeth Ann, and that's what she insists on being called. So mind your manners, boy." He took my arm and led me across toward the table.

"If you're both acting in the same play," I said, "why should she be wallowing in the stuff while you have to borrow seventy cents from me?"

"Very simple," Sebastian Roon said. "She is a stage-struck sophomore from Sarah Lawrence College whose father owns most of the real estate on the Philadelphia Main Line, and I am the impecunious nephew of a deceased bankrupt Australian rabbit breeder named I. G. Roon."

We reached the table.

"You sit there," Lillian Waldbaum said to me. She pointed to a chair at the other side of the table. "You," she said to Sebastian Roon. "You sit here." She patted the chair next to her.

"A pleasure," he said.

"We'll see about that," Lillian said. "You didn't even notice me when you visited the Maurice Saltzman office."

"I am willing to make amends," Sebastian said.

"Not for me," Lillian said. "I don't like nuts."

Seb gave her another of those startled looks. If he had spent as much time as I did with Lillian in the offices of Maurice Saltzman & Company, he would have known there was nothing startling about what she had just said. Lillian talked like that all the time.

If George Burns had met Lillian when he was still uncommitted, the vaudeville team of Burns & Allen would have been known as Burns & Waldbaum. No, sorry. Waldbaum and Burns.

"I beg your pardon?" Seb said.

"You're begging the wrong person," Lillian said. "For pardons you call the governor."

The look on Seb's face did not exactly change, but I could see that somewhere inside his head gears were shifting.

"Everybody duck," Lillian said. "Here come the groceries."

They came in the shaky clutches of one of the willowy Tricino daughters. With an expulsion of breath that whistled across my head she set down a bowl of spaghetti as big as a basketball. She did it as though she had brought the bowl on foot, at shoulder height, from Thermopylae: with a thump that shook the table. Some of the red sauce slopped over.

"Ooh!" the Tricino daughter giggled. With a deft swipe of her hand she scooped up the spilled sauce and licked it out of her palm.

"A touch of oregano perhaps?" Lillian said. "Or a pinch of cardamom seed?"

The Tricino daughter giggled. "No," she said. "It's just right."

"You see?" Lillian said to us. "For thirty-five cents you

211

get not only a plate of the best spaghetti this side of the Appian Way, but it's garnished with jokes."

As though she were replacing manhole covers on a construction job, the Tricino daughter set plates in front of the four of us. Mine had clearly been washed in haste. Even more clearly, the spots had been left by the same sauce the Tricino daughter had just licked up from the table. My mother on Tiffany Street would have snatched the plate out from under my nose and rushed it to the sink for a thorough scouring with Fels-Naphtha. My mother had never heard of Louis Pasteur, but she had her own ideas about what brought on rabies.

"Won't you join us?" said the girl who had played Walda Wexler.

It is not one of the more memorable arrangements of syllables in the English language. But somehow she made it sound pleasant. I looked at her more closely. Over her head, on the dirty wall, was pasted a page from the *Daily News*. It was an advertisement for tourist cruises to the Mediterranean. The advertisement was dominated by a head of Botticelli's Venus.

I knew all about Botticelli. Miss Bongiorno, my elocution teacher in J.H.S. 64, had also taught art appreciation. She had been crazy about Botticelli. I had never understood why, but now all at once I did. This girl, whose name I had not caught, and who had just played the part of Walda Wexler, did not resemble even remotely the foolish face of Botticelli's Venus pasted on the wall over her head. But this girl had the same clean look.

"I don't eat," said the Tricino daughter. "I just sit."

She did. Between me and the girl with the clean look. And the Tricino daughter started to ladle spaghetti into our plates. She did it the way W. C. Fields used to mix paint. She spilled some sauce near each plate, but it did not remain on the scarred table top very long. I could see why this girl did not eat but only sat. From the scooping up, and licking from her palm, of tomato sauce she was obviously before long going to have a weight problem.

212

"While we're digging in," Lillian Waldbaum said, "I have a suggestion."

"Now, Lillian," said the other girl. "Don't start that."

"Relax," said Lillian. "I'm not going to say anything that will upset your mother in Wynwood. It's just perfectly obvious to me that these two jokers have not seen each other for a long time? Right?"

"Who, me?" said the Tricino daughter.

"You pipe down," said Lillian. "You just sit."

The Tricino daughter giggled.

"Then you must mean me," Sebastian Roon said.

"You and Benny," Lillian said. "Why don't you get it out of your systems? Both of you?"

"Get what out?" Seb said.

"Like the Dickens," Lillian said. "When this schmo Martin Chuzzlewit comes back from America, and he and this creep Mr. Pecksniff have the And-What-Happened-To-You-In-The-Intervening-Time Scene."

Sebastian Roon and I looked at each other. I knew he knew what I was thinking, and I could tell he knew I knew what he was thinking. His face turned not exactly red but sort of pink. He stabbed his fork into his mound of spaghetti, rolled up a ball, stuck a spoon under it, started to lift both to his mouth, then stopped and put the fork back into the middle of his plate.

"I trust your mother's jazz bow business is prospering," he said.

"Booming along," I said. "She now lets me keep five dollars a week out of my Maurice Saltzman & Company salary."

"Extraordinary woman," Seb said. "Extraordinary."

He tightened the now slack ball of spaghetti around his fork and again started to lift it to his mouth.

"How's Hannah?" I said.

For the second time the spaghetti didn't make it. Seb put the loaded fork back on his plate.

"Very well," he said. "Very well indeed. She sends you every best wish."

213

If that was true he must have told Hannah before he left England that he planned to see me. I did not believe it.

"Thanks," I said.

On the third try he managed to get the ball of spaghetti to its destination. He chewed for a few moments and swallowed. Getting the forkful of spaghetti down seemed to give him confidence.

"It didn't work out, you know" he said. He paused, clearly waiting for me to say something, but I could find no words that seemed eager to step up to the plate. "So she married my brother," he said.

The "so" made it clear that Seb considered his brother a poor second choice. I didn't know what to consider. I was stunned. I didn't know until this moment that Sebastian Roon had a brother. But I was stunned in a totally impersonal way. The way I had been stunned, upon reading *Vanity Fair* for the first time, when Becky Sharp responds to the marriage proposal of Sir Pitt Crawley by revealing she is already married to his son Rawdon. Hannah and the passions of a year ago now seemed remote, as though I was hearing a scrap of personal history about a stranger. What was happening to me at this table, the girl with the clean look, was much more interesting. But I didn't want Sebastian Roon to know I had been stunned, even in a remote way. So I said, "Yes, I know."

Another ball of spaghetti failed to reach its destination. I was pleased to see that I was not the only one who was stunned.

"You do?" Sebastian Roon said.

I was pleased, yes, but it seemed all at once such a tiny victory that I felt ashamed of myself.

"I don't mean I know that it was your brother she married," I said. "I merely know she got married. She wrote me, about a month ago, I think it was, she wrote me and invited me to the wedding."

"Seriously?" Seb said.

It was a tiny victory, but it made him vulnerable, so I felt I could abandon the formality of calling him Sebastian Roon.

214

"It sounded serious enough," I said. "But I'm sure Hannah knew I could not afford to go to Blackpool. Just the same, I thought it was very nice of her."

I wondered if I knew what I was saying. What the hell had been nice about it?

"Yes," Seb said.

The ball of spaghetti resumed its aborted journey and made it. He chewed vigorously.

"That's the point about Hannah," Seb said finally. "She *is* very nice." He thrust the fork back into the mound on his plate and started work on another ball. "She seemed to like my brother more than she liked me."

"Or me," I said.

Seb stopped twirling his fork and scowled at the plate in a troubled way.

"I'm sorry about that," he said quietly.

Perhaps he was.

"Forget it," I said.

I had a feeling he already had.

"I did act badly," he said.

As Jack the Ripper said when he was booked at Bow Street.

"It was a long time ago," I said. "You were very young. Like me."

He gave me a sharp look. As though he suspected I was mocking him. I guess I was.

"That's true," he said finally. "But I did act badly."

He said no more. Perhaps he had more to say but didn't want to say it in front of Lillian and the other girl. I had nothing more to say. Lillian seemed to sense that.

"*Terminé?*" she said to Seb.

"*Terminé,*" he said.

Lillian turned to me. "Your turn," she said.

I had a moment of panic. What could I tell him about the time that had passed? How could I fill in a space in my life that I had obviously lived but about which I could remember almost nothing worth describing? All at once I realized a full year had been added to the count of my life, and I didn't know what had happened in those twelve

215

months. I had a sense of standing still. Of precious time running out. I could see the number of my next birthday like a winking warning light up ahead. My God, I thought, I'm middle-aged!

"Nothing much," I said. "I'm still going to C.C.N.Y. at night. I'm still working for Maurice Saltzman & Company. And—" I paused. I couldn't tell him I was still taking down Ira Bern's vici kids to be shined every morning. For the first time in my life I had a sense of the importance of human indignity. I said, "That's all, I guess."

"Except for one thing," Lillian said.

"What's that?" Seb said.

"In a minute," Lillian said. "First he wants to know what I want to know. How you got involved in this crap at the Preshinivetz Playhouse."

"Now you stop that," said the other girl. "It is not crap. It is a very important and meaningful piece of theater."

I suddenly realized that I agreed with her. I wondered why.

"Florenz Ziegfeld it's not going to put out of business," Lillian Waldbaum said. She reached across the table and tapped the elbow of the Tricino daughter. "You've done your bit here," Lillian said. "Go giggle somewhere else, honey."

The Tricino daughter covered us with a final spray of giggles, rose, and departed. I hoped none of us would spill any tomato sauce. It was pretty peppy stuff. Without somebody to scoop promptly and lick it up, I could see Mrs. Tricino's creation eating its way down through the scarred wooden table top and attacking my Thom McAns.

"It's simple and tedious," Seb said. "After Hannah married Eustace, I counted my money. It wasn't much, but it was enough to get me back to New York."

The other girl said, "Why did you want to come back to New York?"

Sebastian Roon pushed the spaghetti around on his plate and shrugged. "I don't really know," he said.

"Then you'd better learn," Lillian Waldbaum said. "She's told me all about you. As much as you've told her,

216

anyway. And I can tell you why you wanted to come back to New York."

"Why?" Seb said.

"Because in Blackpool you're a Jew boy," Lillian said. "Here in New York you're an Englishman."

"Lillian," said the other girl. "I don't think that's a very nice thing to say."

"Perhaps not," Sebastian Roon said. "But I daresay it's true. I never thought it out very clearly until this moment, thanks to Miss Waldbaum. But I do see now that the point about emigration, any kind of emigration, is that it enables the emigrant to shed his skin." He laughed. "One gets a bit weary of being a Jew boy in Blackpool, you know."

Lillian Waldbaum tapped my elbow. Now it was my ball of spaghetti that splashed back into the plate.

"Benny," she said. "Are you weary of being a Jew boy in New York?"

I gave it the few moments of thought without which any reply would probably be a disaster. It was always wise, I had learned, when answering a Lillian Waldbaum question, to parse the sentences, so to speak, of your reply before uttering it.

"I don't know," I said. "I've never been a Jew boy in any place except New York."

"And you never will be," Lillian said. "Until you stop spending your life getting Ira Bern's shoes shined."

The bottom of my stomach did a small Immelmann turn. I'd thought we were having a small reunion. How had it swung in this direction? Why was Lillian suddenly jumping down my throat?

"Or running hot pastrami sandwiches for Mr. Bern from Lou G. Siegel," she added.

Her remarks were totally unexpected. Maybe that's why they hit so hard. I knew what was wrong. I had been jolted into facing a moment of truth.

In the years since that night I have been forced to face others. But they never hurt as much as they do when you're young. Before the years have built for you the calluses that shield you from the full impact of the blows.

"Lillian," said the other girl. "I think you would send your own mother to the gallows if it meant clearing the way for one of your wisecracks. I do not believe Mr. Kramer is spending his life getting Ira Bern's shoes shined, whoever Ira Bern may be."

"If you knew my mother," Lillian said, "I think you'd be what you have always been, a good friend, and help me truss up the old bitch and carry her to the gallows. As for Ira Bern, naturally you wouldn't know who he is. You're a lifted-pinky WASP from the Philadelphia Main Line, and I'm a hard-working stenographer in an accountant's office on Seventh Avenue. But I don't mind educating the other half that does the real living, so make a note, dear. Ira Bern is my boss, as well as the boss of this good-looking innocent over here who prefers, I'm sure, to be called not Mr. Kramer but Benjamin, so why don't you try?"

At this moment the other girl could have flushed slightly, but I'm not sure. The Family Tricino was not as generous with electric bulbs as it was with tomato sauce.

"Couldn't we just get on with Seb's explanation of why he came back to New York?" said the other girl.

"Don't you know?" said Lillian.

Now there was no question about what happened to the face of the other girl. With more electric bulbs in the vicinity, it might have been accurate to say her cheekbones turned red. In the light provided by The Family Tricino, as I recall, it seemed to me the skin between her nostrils and her ear lobes seemed all at once to change slowly from the color of the plate on which my spaghetti was swimming in tomato sauce to the color of the maraschino cherry on the charlotte russe I used to hand out for a nickel to customers when I worked in Mr. Lebenbaum's candy store on Avenue D.

"Of course I know," said the other girl.

It occurred to me that while her friendship with Lillian Waldbaum was genuine, which was puzzling since they were obviously so different, it was also a source of irritation to her.

"There's nothing much to know," Sebastian Roon said.

218

"You may recall, Benjamin, that about a year ago I spent some time at your home on Tiffany Street."

"In my bed," I said.

"Quite," Seb said. "And while you used to go off to the gallery of Loew's One Hundred and Eightieth Street with my brother's present wife, I remained behind and helped your mother with her 'turning.' "

"Turning?" the other girl said.

"One of the preliminary steps in a cottage industry known as the manufacture of jazz bows," Seb said.

"You mean neckties?" the girl said.

"Well," Seb said, "I suppose they could be worn as sock suspenders, but in most instances they are worn around the neck. At any rate, toward the end of my stay with the Kramer family, Benny's mother had moved beyond mere 'turning' to the manufacture of the completed jazz bow. One evening while I was helping Benjamin's mother with her records, I told her that I would soon be returning to Blackpool. She asked why, and I told her about the demise of my uncle and his complex business ventures, and that it seemed sensible to go home, where I would at least have my own bed to sleep in until I got myself sorted out. Benjamin's mother said going home was a waste of time because I would be back. She said it with so much certainty that I could not help asking how she knew something I did not know myself. Benjamin, do you know what she said?"

I knew it as well as I knew most things my mother had said. She rarely said anything once. I had heard this particular observation many times. But this was Seb's story. And I liked what the inadequate lighting did, as she listened, to the face of the girl across the table from me.

"No," I said. "What did my mother say to you?"

"She said Europe was a rotten worn-out place," Seb said. "A garbage pail was the expression she used. Everybody wants to leave it, she said. That's why she had come here from Hungary, and that's why, when I got another look at the garbage pail, I would come hurrying back to America. When I did, she said, I would always find a bed waiting for me on Tiffany Street."

219

I could see ahead of me a long siege of going back to sleeping on the floor of our front room. Sebastian Roon did not look prosperous. He was wearing the same tveet suit he had worn when I first met him. It looked frayed but, on closer examination, I saw that it was not. What gave the jacket a look of shabbiness was that it had obviously not been pressed for a long time. Perhaps not since it had come off the rack in the store where Seb had bought it. The wrinkles on the sleeves up near the shoulders had a permanent look, as though they could never really be pressed out of the cloth. And of those three buttons that had run so close together down the front like the keys of a cornet, only one remained.

"You mean you just got back from Blackpool today?" I said.

Going to the theater had made it a long day. Taking Lillian Walbaum home would make it longer. Unless Sebastian Roon had called my mother on Tiffany Street to warn her that he was coming up to claim that offered bed, before I got home and hit the sack I would have to make up the sack myself on the living room floor.

"No," said the other girl. "Seb has been here for over a week. I found him the day he arrived."

Seb laughed and said to the other girl, "Look at his face!"

She did, and mine for no apparent reason grew hotter.

"Well, one can hardly blame him," she said. "I did say I found you, which is an odd way to put it."

"You've told me this part," Lillian Waldbaum said. "So I'll just go to the little girls' room." She stood up.

"Do be careful and knock first," Seb said. "At The Family Tricino the little girls' room is also the little boys' room."

"While I'm out," Lillian Waldbaum said, "try to think up a bit of advice that will be new to me. I learned to knock on bathroom doors when I was still in diapers." She walked away.

Seb watched her go. "Interesting girl, that," he said. "Lillian?" The other girl smiled. "She's probably the most wonderful person I know. We met in a sketching class at the Y.W.C.A."

"Lillian?" I said.

The sound of my voice made Seb laugh again. "I know what you mean," he said. "Miss Waldbaum does not look like a sketcher, does she?"

"I don't know what a sketcher should look like," the other girl said. "But Lillian is a darned good one. Now, for how I found our actor friend here. About a week ago, was it?"

"Nine days, actually," Sebastian Roon said. "I came over from England on the cheap. A Norwegian freighter with a few cabins for passengers who don't mind traveling slowly so long as the passage is low, and who have stomachs strong enough to sustain a steady diet of herring. The ship docked at a pier just north of Fourteenth Street, and I went trotting along with my bag down Fourteenth, hunting a phone booth. I wanted to alert your mother that her favorite nonpaying lodger was on his way up to Tiffany Street. Have you ever tried to make a phone call on West Fourteenth Street?"

"No," I said.

"I urge you not to attempt it," Seb said. "The paucity of phone booths in the area is astonishing. In fact, they don't exist. I was becoming a bit irked when I saw one of those round blue and white enamel signs the telephone company nails outside structures that contain public phones. It was nailed to the brick wall of the Preshinivetz Playhouse. I went in and found myself in that small, dismal outer room which you and Miss Waldbaum crossed tonight to get into the theater proper. In one corner was a phone booth. I popped in and called your home. No answer."

"Was it a Monday?" I said.

"Let me think," Seb said. He did. Then: "Yes, I believe it was. Why?"

"On Mondays my mother goes downtown to deliver the jazz bows that were completed the week before," I said. "And my father can't get to the phone because of the wheelchair."

221

"Quite," Seb said. "I thought it was something like that. So I decided I'd wait a bit and try again. When I came out of the phone booth, I heard the damnedest racket from beyond the doors that separate that outer room from the theater proper. Furious voices shouting."

"And screaming," said the girl who had played the part of Walda Wexler.

"Indeed yes," said Seb. "My God, what a brouhaha. I eased one of the doors open an inch or two and peered in. Well, the screams were nothing compared to the sight. A dozen or more people were sprawled on the benches. They were the actors you saw in the play tonight, although I didn't know that at the time. I mean to say, I was unaware that I had stumbled into a theater during a rehearsal. Not that these actors were doing much rehearsing. They were watching and listening to the two people who were going at each other in the aisle. One was an ethereal type with marcelled hair who would have looked more properly dressed in a ball gown. He later proved to be the director. His opponent in the battle of billingsgate was none other than our charming friend here, Elizabeth Ann."

Thank God, Seb had mentioned her name again. I had forgotten it, and I was tired of referring to her in my head as the girl with the clean look. What bothered me was that her name had not registered because I had not really looked at her until I noticed the Botticelli clipping on the wall over her head. Elizabeth Ann. Elizabeth Ann. Okay. I had it. Now back to what she was saying.

"I didn't really want to scream," Elizabeth Ann said. "What I wanted to do was kill that goddamn director because of the way he was butchering my play."

"Oh," I said. "You wrote the play?"

"You mustn't be surprised," Elizabeth Ann said. "Many women have written plays."

That was not what had surprised me. What had surprised me was that just as Lillian Waldbaum did not look like a sketcher type, Elizabeth Ann did not look like a *Walda Wexler Wait for Willie Wishingrad: Urgent!* type.

222

"I'm glad I said I liked it before I found out you wrote it," I said.

"Bravo!" Sebastian Roon said. "We'll make a gallant of you yet, that we shall."

Benny, like Barkis, was willing.

"I don't know what on earth you could have seen on that stage tonight that was worth looking at, much less liking," Elizabeth Ann said. "It certainly is not the play as I conceived it. What I wrote originally has been cut to ribbons and tossed into the wastebasket. That's why I was determined not to give in on this last piece of casting. The savage illiterate had filled all the parts with his dear little epicene friends, not one of whom can act certainly not on a stage. All that was left was the part of Willie, the man they are all waiting for. It's a small role, just one word in the last moments of the play, but it's absolutely crucial. On it the play stands or falls. If Willie isn't absolutely right, the play we have seen up to that climactic moment will be not right. The play will simply vanish. And that day I saw this son of a bitch warming up another one of his simpering friends for the part. Think of it. The part demands a tough, masculine strike leader, and he was going to give it to one of his boys with marcelled hair! Over my dead body, I said, and that's how the battle started."

"It ended with Elizabeth Ann storming up the aisle toward the doors through which I was eavesdropping," Sebastian Roon said. "I ducked backward as fast as I could, but not fast enough." He laughed. "Elizabeth Ann caught me."

She laughed. "No, not caught," Elizabeth Ann said. "I had no idea Seb had been eavesdropping, and it wouldn't have mattered it I had known. I was so damn mad, I couldn't see straight."

"You were actually shaking with fury," Seb said. "A rather frightening sight, I must say. You were trying to get a lighted match up to your cigarette, and missing by at least two inches."

Elizabeth Ann laughed again. "So Seb took the match from me," she said. "And he held it to my cigarette. I filled my lungs with smoke and I blew the smoke in his face. I

223

didn't mean to. It was simply that, in my rage, I hadn't even seen him."

"When she did," Seb said, "she gave me a look that I suppose can only be described as penetrating. Then she walked slowly around me, as though she were a tourist and I was a statue in some public square, and she wanted to remember it when she got home."

"You see," Elizabeth Ann said to me through her laughter, "I thought Seb was an actor who had been sent over by an agent to read for a part in the play."

"She told me it was a very small part," Seb said, "but a very important part." He grinned. "Little did I know how small."

"A good thing you didn't," Elizabeth Ann said. "All I could do was thank my stars. There he was. The actor I had been praying for. Willie!"

"Don't I look the part?" Seb said.

"Well," I said.

Seb beetled his brows into a tough-guy scowl, flexed his muscles, and growled like a bulldog. "Me!" he said. "Tough, masculine strike leader!"

"That's what makes him so perfect," Elizabeth Ann said. "The audience is expecting a crude dese-dem-and-doze oaf. And what do they get? This tall, elegant, blond thing with a British accent you can smear all over Balliol."

"He certainly was effective in the part tonight," I said.

"His best performance, however, was the day he was hired," Elizabeth Ann said. "Before he even stepped on the stage."

"Now, now," Seb said. "We mustn't make too much of that."

"I am making just as much of it as it deserves," Elizabeth Ann said. "Which is a lot." To me: "When I brought him into the theater, and I told the director I'd found my Willie, he said he may be your Willie but he's not mine. My plays, he said, are not cast by amateur virgins from Sarah Lawrence. Whereupon Seb grabbed him by the necktie, lifted him a foot or more off the ground, and said you will apologize to this lady for that, you so-and-so."

224

"Actually," Seb said, "the words I used were 'you mincing bugger.' And I doubt that I had him more than two or three inches off the ground. After all, we can't have swine talking like that to young ladies, can we? Not in this great and glorious country to which your mother and I have fled from the pogroms of Blackpool and the garbage pail of Europe."

"Anyway," Elizabeth Ann said, "I got the apology and Seb got the part."

"And I got a small upstairs bedroom that used to belong to the sexton when the Preshinivetz Playhouse used to be a church," Seb said.

"That means my mother doesn't know you're back in New York," I said.

Seb grinned. "It also means you can continue sleeping in your own bed," he said. "Miss Waldbaum seems to be signaling rather frantically, wouldn't you say?"

Elizabeth Ann and I turned. Lillian was standing in the archway that led from the Family Tricino living room to the hall. She was scowling and waving her hand in a sweeping, impatient gesture toward herself. I stood up and pointed inquiringly to myself. Lillian shook her head irritably and waved me back into my chair.

"That leaves only you," Seb said to Elizabeth Ann. "Miss Waldbaum would hardly be urging me to join her in the little girls' room, would she?"

"Excuse me," Elizabeth Ann said. She stood up and walked toward Lillian. I watched her go.

"Pretty," Seb said. "Isn't she?"

My face grew hot again. I turned back. "Yes," I said. "But it's not that. There's a sort of quality about her. I don't know what it is."

"I do," Sebastian Roon said. "She always looks as though she's just taken a shower."

11

Forty years later, walking up Madison Avenue from my drink with Sebastian Roon at Will's to my apartment at 83rd and Fifth, I was struck again by the funny little feeling in my heart that Seb's remark about Elizabeth Ann had brought me across the spaghetti plates at that table in The Family Tricino.

"Are you in pain, Mr. Kramer?" Sean said.

I came back to 1971.

"Not any more," I said. "Did you win?"

Sean is the day doorman of our apartment house. Noon to 8:00 P.M. It is not a new apartment house. What real-estate brokers identify as "one of those real oldies with huge fireplaces that actually work and those great big high ceilings."

One of the most pleasant things about our apartment house is what Elizabeth Ann calls the staff. Why shouldn't she? She was born and raised in Wynwood on the Philadelphia Main Line. Servants were as normal a part of her existence as toilets in the hall were a part of mine. She knew things I didn't know. It helped when we bought our apartment at 83rd and Fifth.

Elizabeth Ann discovered at once that all our elevator operators, handymen and doormen are Irish. Not Third Avenue Irish. The employees of our apartment house are Irish Irish. Sean O'Casey stuff. They are brought over from Dublin. Or County Galway. Or wherever William Butler Yeats and Lady Gregory rapped the knuckles of John Millington Synge and ordered him to cut the malarkey and go to the Aran Islands where he would learn what life is all about.

For Sean Boyle what life is all about is soccer. What

226

puzzles me about what life is all about for Sean Boyle is where he plays soccer. He tells me he lives on Fox Street. This is where Hot Cakes Rabinowitz used to live. Just around the corner from where Sebastian Roon helped my mother get started in the jazz bow business. Soccer? On Fox Street? Around the corner from Tiffany Street? Preposterous. Peter Stuyvesant and his bunch of Dutch chums playing bowls on Fox Street? Very well, that I will accept. It's a piece of Americana. But Sean Boyle of County Galway playing soccer on Fox Street? Who does he think he's kidding? Obviously, Benny Kramer.

"No, we lost," Sean said.

I detected a note of bitterness. Not good. Bitterness does not sit well on Sean's sunny, open, pleasant and, it distresses me to record, somewhat stupid face. I don't know how other people feel, but when I like someone I like to feel he or she has brains. It hurts to state that Sean, who gives me great pleasure by his mere existence, is a horse's ass.

"They brought in this man from Belfast," he said. "They sprung him on us, Mr. Kramer. It was crooked, of course. The names of the members of the teams had been posted for a week. Every man named properly. And then they brought in this ringer from Belfast."

"That's bad," I said.

It seemed the appropriate comment.

"It was that, Mr. Kramer," Sean said. "Very dispiriting. One expects sportsmen to play fair, and then they bring in a man from Belfast."

"I'm sorry," I said.

"Thank you, Mr. Kramer," Sean said. "But don't you worry, sir. Next Sunday we'll get a bit of our own back." He grinned wickedly. "My cousin Roderick just arrived. He's going on the rear elevator. Midnight to eight A.M. Roderick is from Belfast, too."

"How's the betting?" I said.

"Two to one in favor of Fox Street," Sean said.

"Can I get in for a five-spot?"

"You certainly can, Mr. Kramer. I'll take care of it personally."

I gave him a five-dollar bill.

"If I lose," I said, "don't tell me. If I win, don't tell Mrs. Kramer. She disapproves of gambling."

"Good women always do, sir," Sean Boyle said. "That's what makes them good women."

I was pleased to get this piece of advice from an Irish soccer player thirty years my junior who had thus far reached the altar only for his first communion.

"Your five will get you ten, Mr. Kramer," Sean said. "Don't you worry, sir."

I wished I could stop worrying. But I couldn't. Suddenly, today, the vague fears of months past had surfaced in a clear, unpalatable image. It was part of being punched in the head by a black man in front of Penn Station. Part of being told in a troubled voice by Sebastian Roon over a drink at Will's that after forty years in this country he wanted to go home to die.

At least he had a home to go back to die in. What did Benny Kramer have to go back to? East Fourth Street? The part I remembered, the part where I had been fashioned, had vanished under the asphalt of the East River Drive. Tiffany Street? Like all the rest of the south Bronx it had become an all-black ghetto of junkies. Benny Kramer, a home-loving man, had been jolted into facing an unpleasant fact: he was homeless.

"Is it raining yet?"

I came up out of my thoughts and saw that I had moved from Sean Boyle, our doorman, to Eamon Fleece, the elevator man on our bank. I looked at Eamon. There wasn't much to see. A wisp of a man with frail shoulders. They seemed to sag under the weight of his blue and gold elevator operator's uniform and the tremendous shock of snow-white hair that sat on his head like an enormous snowball.

Eamon had been running the elevator on the A-B bank since 1937. The date had been nailed down in the memory of every employee in the apartment house because Eamon had arrived in America and come to work in our building on the day the *Hindenburg* Zeppelin blew up at Lakehurst. Sean said his older brother, who worked the relief

228

shift on the C-D bank, remembered it vividly. Sean felt this gruesome coincidence had soured Eamon's disposition. Brian Treaner, our building superintendent, disagreed.

Brian once told me he felt what had turned Eamon Fleece into a misanthrope was his marriage. The marvelous thing about the Irish is that you get superintendents of apartment houses who use words like misanthrope. Eamon lived somewhere over in Yorkville with his wife, her spinster sister, and their ancient mother. The wife was maimed, the sister was halt, and the mother was blind.

"A man with a setup like that," Brian had said to me, "he doesn't go dancing among the shamrocks on the banks of the Liffy, now does he, Mr. Kramer?"

I thought at the time it would have been a sensible way to obtain some relief. I remembered Mr. Pflug down on East Fourth Street, a street cleaner whose wife was dying of some unidentified but terrible wasting disease. On the day his only son, who happened to be in my class in P.S. 188, was killed while stealing a hitch on the back of an ice wagon on Avenue C, Mr. Pflug was found dancing on the Fourth Street dock in the middle of the night.

True, they took him away to Bellevue. I don't doubt it was the only course available to the authorities. But I always felt the poor bastard had got some relief out of the strange performance. I will never know, of course. But I'm going to continue believing it. Hope is where you find it.

The trouble with Eamon Fleece, I felt, was that he did not believe there is any to find. So why try? It is, of course, the basic error. Life is hopeless. Everybody dies. What matters is maintaining the pretense that it is not hopeless. The belief that you are indeed going to live forever. So that when death comes you can with a sense of excitement throw up your arms and kick out your legs in a vaudevillian's Four Wings And Scram, and exclaim: "Hey, what a surprise!"

But Eamon Fleece was not equal to the pretense. Inside his dark, brooding, bitter mind he saw only the inevitable horror at the end of the tunnel. And he understood that it could not be avoided. The horror had all the time in the world. It could and of course would outwait him. So he plodded along, day after day, moving closer to the inevitable. This black vision created a curious kind of inverted hope. A sort of gloomy illumination along the tunnel to defeat. So that even bright moments insisted on being turned into mocking shadows.

"No," I said as we rode up in the elevator to the twelfth floor. "It's not raining. The sun is out."

"Never trust the sun," said Eamon Fleece.

I did not answer. Could it be that Eamon Fleece was right? Was it possible that he had touched the root of the trouble? Benny Kramer had always trusted the sun. It had been the only thing on East Fourth Street that was free. I let myself into 12-B with my key.

"Benjamin?" Elizabeth Ann called from the kitchen. "Is that you?"

My heart turned over. No, it soared. By God, there were some things that held. In spite of Mr. Yeats' contention that the center had collapsed. Generalizations are misleading. Everybody has his own center. Part of mine was Elizabeth Ann's attitude toward my given name. She is a WASP. They make the best Jews.

They may be born with restricted vision. But the vision sits solidly on character. If when weary you are ever in doubt about where to place your bottom, take Benny Kramer's advice: eschew the cushions; choose character. It makes for a solid seat.

When George Washington died, Napoleon wept. Not because George was a great general, but because his will was made of granite. Napoleon admired that. So does Benny Kramer.

Once Elizabeth Ann of Wynwood decided to marry Benny Kramer of East Fourth Street, she did the sort of research job on Jews that to Sarah Lawrence girls is what the cadets of St. Cyr do on Clausewitz. Soon Elizabeth Ann was asking me, with a touch of severity in her voice, why we did not fast on Yom Kippur. Was it right for us to be eating Pepperidge Farm Thin Sliced instead of matzos on the First Days of Passover? Wouldn't it be more appropriate, now that Jack was almost six years old, for Daddy to spend his Saturday mornings with the boy at the Park Avenue Synagogue, which was just around the corner from our apartment, rather than trail along behind Sebastian Roon on the Century Club golf course, which was an hour's drive up into Westchester?

As for circumcision. Well! Not that it would ever have occurred to me to object. How could I? After all—oh well, we can skip that part of the argument. Elizabeth Ann saw to it that Jack was circumcised. I stayed out of it. Not for the obvious reason, of course. Circumcision is like adolescence. Once you've gone through it, you don't have to do it again. But Elizabeth Ann got into it up to her armpits.

Before she would allow Rabbi Altshuler, the moël, into the operating room at Doctors Hospital, she had several conferences with Artie Steinberg. Artie is our doctor. He was one of the best reader-jotters we ever had in Troop 244 at the Hannah H. Lichtenstein House on Avenue B and Ninth Street in the days when I was the troop's champion one-flag Morse code signaler. I had the feeling, when it was all over, that Elizabeth Ann had performed the operation herself.

I suppose Freud would say she had. I remember what my mother said when I introduced her and my father to Elizabeth Ann.

First, the moment of shock. Benny marrying a *shiksa?* It can't be! Ah well, like so many other things in life that can't be, it is. The shock waves recede. My mother and father look at Elizabeth Ann. The way my father used to look at the cloth of a suit he was buying for me on Stanton Street. Frowns of doubt. About what? Benny marrying a *shiksa?* So it seemed to Benny. Then, slowly, I learned I'd been wrong.

My mother and father took to this *shiksa.* The way their darling Benny had taken to her. And they had the same reaction. They fell in love with her. And for thirty years they never thought of her as a *shiksa.*

She became to them a nice Jewish girl. The sort of girl it was proper, even inevitable, for their Benny to marry.

231

Whenever the subject of Elizabeth Ann's background came up, if there was some reference to the fact that she was not, as Rabbi Altshuler put it, "of the faith," my mother and father would rock with laughter. Benny and his jokes!

For thirty years Elizabeth Ann was to them the perfect Jewish girl who had been born to marry the perfect Jewish boy. Their son Benny. And after thirty years their son Benny found he shared that belief firmly. Especially when Elizabeth Ann spoke his name.

He might be Benny to his parents. And Ben to his colleagues. But to Elizabeth Ann he was Benjamin. As, oddly enough, he was to Sebastian Roon. Benjamin. What a name. Even leaving aside the glorious idiocy of flying kites in dangerous electrical storms, it was the sort of name that gave a man a sense of dignity. Especially on a day when he'd had his head pummeled in front of Penn Station.

"Yeah," I called down the corridor from the front door to the kitchen. "It's me. You okay?"

"Probably," Elizabeth Ann called back. "But I won't know for another four minutes. I've made you a crème brûlée and I'm tapping the crust in the casserole. Don't you dare come into the kitchen."

"And don't you dare serve if for dinner," I said. "I was up two and a half pounds this morning."

On Tiffany Street I'd never even heard of calories. On 83rd and Fifth they ruled my life the way insulin rules the life of the diabetic.

"You'll be three and a half over in the morning." Elizabeth Ann said. "But it will be in a good cause. If this damn thing comes out. Brown sugar gets stiffer and stiffer. I don't know why. It never seems to happen to Julia Child. Get comfortable. I'll join you in four minutes. No, three and a half. I have something to tell you."

Elizabeth Ann always has something to tell me. She lives the most satisfying life of any person I know. Not because her husband is remarkably noteworthy for being a good provider. Although in that respect Benny Kramer doesn't think he falls too far behind the average. Nor because she is cherished more spectacularly than most women. Although Benny Kramer must confess with as little embarrassment as these statements can be made that on all counts he finds her eminently satisfactory. No. What makes Elizabeth Ann's life good is that she lives it.

Nothing passes her by. I think I should put that more firmly. She *allows* nothing to pass her by. Everything is examined. And squeezed. Like a melon in the supermarket. If it is ripe, Elizabeth Ann is pleased and buys it. If it is not, she leaves it in the bin, but she pushes her cart on with the satisfaction of knowing she's had an experience.

The thought is refreshing. How often do people walk away from a honeydew or a Cranshaw with a feeling Leif the Red had when he first sighted the coast of Labrador? The feeling that his time had not been wasted? The feeling that he had learned something about life worth passing on to his fellow man?

Not often, I'll bet. That's why I admire the effort. Mainly, I suppose, because I have yearned for it and tried for it, but have never achieved it. I have never been able to extract from the day-to-day pulsations of life the satisfaction Elizabeth Ann gets as effortlessly as she gets rich yellow foaming orange juice out of the halved fruit she slaps onto our electric Green Stamps machine. Eleven books. "There's ice in the bucket!" Elizabeth Ann called. "God, this brown sugar is a pain. Make yourself a drink. I'll be another moment. Make one for me, too."

I did, and I sat down in my favorite room. It wasn't anything the directors of the Met would have fought to buy. It was just a nice room, with two big windows that looked out on the Central Park reservoir. A room full of furniture and bric-a-brac Elizabeth Ann had brought back from the various places around the world where we had spent fragments of our thirty years together. But it was not those things that made it my favorite room. I can take furniture or leave it alone. It can please me. It can displease me. But it never sends me. And what pleases me rarely pleases Elizabeth Ann.

I like, for instance, green metal filing cabinets. The kind we had when I was a kid at Maurice Saltzman & Company on West 34th Street. They drive Elizabeth Ann up the wall. No. *Into* the wall. She is always burying my green metal filing cabinets behind expensive cabinetwork. Anyway, what makes me like places is not how they are furnished but what I do in them.

In this room I work. And read *Bleak House*. And take off my shoes. And do something I have not been happy about doing all my life but in this room I somehow manage to do it with less pain than I do it elsewhere. In this room I think.

Which is what the human race hates to do but, as Rabbi Goldfarb used to say over and over again down on East Fourth Street, must do to survive. If there is one thing Benny Kramer wants to do it is survive. I don't know why. There are moments in this room furnished by Elizabeth Ann when I think: What in God's name for?

A nice juicy heart attack? For juicy, read massive. A good clean stroke? For clean, read decisive. That's the way to live, isn't it? Die clean and swift and without pain. What more can a man want? Answer: to live. Why? I don't know. But in this room, which contains all the bits and pieces of the life I've lived for three decades with Elizabeth Ann, in this room I am able to think. And what do I think? I think an unthinkable scream. A cry of irrational outrage.

Not yet! Not yet! Hold that heart attack! Forget that stroke! Put a different address on that embolism. Send that melanoma down to some poor bastard in Chile. River Styx, stay away from this door. The author of these irrational notes is not yet ready to die. The poor slob hasn't even learned how to live.

I made the drink a stiff one. Coming on top of the shot I'd had at Will's with Seb, it did the trick. The trick of making life seem not really impossible. Merely loathsome. When Elizabeth Ann came in from the kitchen, she looked beautiful.

I've said it wrong again. I don't mean Elizabeth Ann looked beautiful because I'd had two stiff drinks. Plus one sock on the medulla oblongata in front of Penn Station by a fellow citizen who, I must remember, meant nothing personal by the outrage. He was merely fighting back against the people who had oppressed his race for two centuries. Elizabeth Ann, as I said, came into the room where I was doing my thinking.

"How was Philadelphia?" Elizabeth Ann said.

"I am not going to answer that," I said. "You know how Philadelphia was. You were born there."

"Yes, of course," she said. "But I keep hoping it will get better. Seb has been trying to get you."

"I know," I said. "I stopped in at the office when I got back. Miss Bienstock told me."

"Anything important?"

I hesitated. Elizabeth Ann loves Seb. So does my son Jack. Seb is the best kind of friend. A family favorite.

"Yes, very," I said.

Elizabeth Ann was reaching for the glass I was holding out to her. Her hand stopped moving.

"Is Seb in trouble?" she said.

I hesitated again. Trouble had not crossed my mind as the way to describe the curious mood of our talk at Will's, yet now it seemed surprisingly accurate.

"Yes, I said. "I think Seb is in very bad trouble."

"Oh, God," Elizabeth Ann said. Her hand moved on, she took the glass I was holding out, and she plumped herself down on the couch facing me. "Some woman, I suppose?"

I thought of Dr. McCarran's wife in Philadelphia. Whom I had not met.

"Yes," I said.

"Anyone we know?"

"Yes," I said.

"What's her name?"

"Britannia," I said.

"What?" Elizabeth Ann said.

I explained as much as I knew. The TV deal Jim Mennen had proposed. The rather surprising financial potential for Seb. Mennen's eagerness to have Seb at any cost. And why the money was important to Seb.

"He wants to retire," I said. "He wants to go home."

I left out why.

"To England?" Elizabeth Ann said.

The surprise in her voice took me by surprise. It occurred to me that to Elizabeth Ann our friend Sebastian Roon had always been an American.

"He seems to have remembered at the age of fifty-eight," I said, "that England is his home."

Elizabeth Ann took a sip from her glass and looked out at the sun coming in fiery red from Central Park West across the green glass roof of the Met.

"Maybe we could go with him," she said.

"I don't think what Seb has in mind is a holiday," I said.

"Neither do I," Elizabeth Ann said.

I sat up straighter in the chair where I do my thinking. I was reminded of a moment during the war in an Edinburgh pub when my C.O., a man of almost terrifying intelligence named Buchanan, shed light for me on a puzzling corner of the complex fabric of the British character.

We had been discussing a project that had brought us up from London, the drafting of surrender leaflets to be dropped by the RAF on Düsseldorf, and suddenly a fight broke out at the other side of the saloon. It was settled in a few minutes, but I did not understand what had happened, and I asked.

"There are three moments in a pub that are crucial," Colonel Buchanan said. "If you and I are having a talk over a glass of bitter, and a third chap starts pushing his way in, you observe in a friendly voice: buzz off, lad. A sensible chap understands you want privacy, takes no offense, and buzzes off. If he's not sensible, perhaps because he's sozzled, and he continues to push his way into the conversation, you put the screws on a bit in your voice and you say: piss off, lad. The chap has to be awfully stupid or awfully drunk not to twig to that. Usually, he does. But if he doesn't, and he persists in being a pest, you come to phase three. Hard, now. Voice tough. You say: Fuck off, buster. That means if you don't, buster, you are in for a fight. That's what just happened over at the other side of the saloon bar a few minutes ago. The chap they just carried out, the poor sod apparently didn't realize those other two chaps had told him they'd reached the fuck off stage."

I had once explained this to Elizabeth Ann. She thought it funny. And every now and then, when a conversation or a discussion would get out of hand, she would say to me: "Let's not reach the fuck off stage." We rarely did.

But now, all at once, without a discussion or even a conversation, certainly without an argument, I sensed that her quickly and quietly spoken words—"Neither do I"—were in the fuck off stage.

I gave myself a moment, then remembered what she had called to me from the kitchen when I came into the apartment.

"You said you have something to tell me," I said.

"Yes," Elizabeth Ann said. "I have something to tell you. Jack called from Bloomington this afternoon."

"Anything wrong?" I said.

"He seems to have suffered an attack of intelligence," Elizabeth Ann said. "Four of his Harvard friends have been killed in the Mekong Delta in the last three weeks. It occurred to Jack to wonder why. They were very close, you know."

I did know. I even knew their names. And I could in my head see their faces. I am a City College boy. Evening session. I am jealous of kids who went to Harvard. Including my son Jack. He made it. Benny Kramer never did. I wished I didn't have enough brains to understand how I felt. More and more, as the years go by, I find myself confronted by the heretical conviction that it is better to be stupid.

"Yes," I said. "I do know."

"And what have you done with your knowledge?" Elizabeth Ann said.

The trouble with being a lawyer is that you detect at once, even in the voices of people who love you, the metallic rasp of the attorney for the prosectuion.

"I went to Philadelphia today," I said. "That's what I've done."

"To help a real-estate crook," Elizabeth Ann said. "For a fat fee."

Among the more distressing horrors of life are the little terminal crevices into which people hurl their way in order to win a minor verbal battle. You have to strike back.

"That fat fee is paying our rent on this apartment in which you and I are now battling while you can enjoy the luxury of trembling about whether or not the crust of your crème brûlée will work."

Elizabeth Ann scowled. The scowl is rarely thought of as an increment to beauty. Next time you get scowled at, by a woman, I mean, pay attention. And count yourself a nice little blessing.

"You did not go to Philadelphia to help that real-estate crook," Elizabeth Ann said. "You had another reason."

No wonder Scotland Yard has had to reorganize from the ground up. The methods of Inspector Lestrade are outmoded. Women have taken over.

"That real-estate crook paid my fare and provided my cover story," I said. "He didn't know it, but I went to Philadelphia to have a secret meeting with a Dr. McCarran."

Elizabeth Ann looked troubled. She sent the look down into her glass. It made her look—well, I'll skip it. I'm too old to take on an imitation of Booth Tarkington describing Gentle Julia. That Hoosier could write.

"And it was about Jack," Elizabeth Ann said. "Wasn't it?"

And that Hoosier could also call the turn. Gentle Julia would have put it exactly the same way.

"Yes," I said. "Jack is obviously going to be summoned any minute now for his physical. And since you are his mother who has known him from the womb out, you know that that kid is going to pass his draft board physical with depressingly flying colors."

"So you went to Philadelphia to organize a way for him to flunk," Elizabeth Ann said. "And you kept it a secret because you knew I would disapprove."

"That," I said, "as my old boss Ira Bern would have put it, that is one hundred and ten percent correct."

238

Elizabeth Ann gave her drink another scowling examination.

"Okay," she said finally. "I guess you better tell me." I did.

"In other words," she said when I finished. "The life of our son depends on his ability to convince a draft board doctor that he wets his bed at night."

Succinct is a word I do not have many opportunities to employ. So I don't. But opportunities do come along. Elizabeth Ann had just provided one.

"You could put it that way," I said.

Elizabeth Ann made a weary gesture with her head.

"You are not the most brilliant man I have ever known," she said. "But you are the most brilliant man I have ever been in love with." She looked across the room toward the windows that faced Central Park. "This is the first time," she said. "In almost thirty years of marriage," she said. "This is the first time I've ever known you to do something almost belligerently un-brilliant."

The phone rang.

"I'll get it," I said.

"No, you won't," Elizabeth Ann said. "It's Jack. I want to talk to him first."

She crossed to the desk.

"Hello?" she said into the phone. "Yes, he just got back from Philadelphia, and it's pretty much what I suspected and told you as a guess. Yes, I know that, and I love you, too, but at the moment I think we'd better hew to the line. I'll put him on, darling." Elizabeth Ann took the phone from her ear and held it out to me. "Tell him all about Dr. McCarran."

I did.

"Well," Jack said when I finished. And so I knew there was trouble. Some people begin conversations by saying "Well." My son does not. Jack begins by saying "Listen, Pops." I missed that. "It was damned nice of you to go to all that effort for me," he said. "I mean going to Philadelphia and all."

"I was paid for that," I said. "By Shloymah Berel Schlisselberger."

"By who?" Jack said.

"Never mind," I said. "He's one of my clients, and he's got more money than he knows what to do with, and I synchronized a job I had to do for him with this visit to Dr. McCarran. I didn't want anybody to know about it."

"But Dr. McCarran knows about it," Jack said.

"And Uncle Seb," I said.

Sebastian Roon was not Jack's uncle. Just his godfather. But it's awkward to say on the long-distance phone that the other person who knows about it is Godfather Seb.

"Now, Pops," Jack said. "Let's not tell any more people about this. It could give me a bad press with some girls I know."

"Of course I won't," I said. "But it seems to me the only way out for you."

Jack laughed and said, "As the leader of the jail break said to the prisoners he was about to lead over the wall."

"Jack," I said. "This is not a kidding matter. In the Mekong Delta, as your grandmother would have said, a person could get hurt."

"Not this grandson," Jack said.

"But if you don't do at your physical what Dr. McCarran suggested," I said, "what else can you do?"

Jack laughed again. "Pops, I've been reading the literature of your youth," he said. "As those John Held, Jr., characters used to say: you just watch my smoke, Pops."

"Jack," I said. "What do you want your mother and me to do now?"

"Stand by for station identification," Jack said. "I'll let you know."

I could feel the rock slide beginning to rumble into movement.

"When?" I said.

"Give me a few days to set some wheels in motion," Jack said.

"Set what wheels in motion?" I said. "We've talked this
240

out long ago. *I didn't raise my boy to be a soldier.* Remember?"

When the draft board had begun breathing down his neck I had told Jack about a Hollywood character named Solly Violinsky. He had insisted that all song titles were too long and all could be reduced to two words. When asked about "I didn't raise my boy to be a soldier," Solly had said: "Don't Go."

"The philosophy of Solly Violinsky is engraved on my heart," Jack said. "Just the same, I do want to set my own wheels in motion."

To a dull steak, Dashiell Hammett once wrote, always comes a sharp knife.

"You betcha," I said. The slang of East Fourth Street. How it clings to the man in the Brooks Brothers suit. "Let me know what you decide."

He said a few other things. None of them the business of third parties.

"Dad," Jack said, "I'll call you."

I hung up. Elizabeth Ann came across the room. She smiled and kissed me.

"Now, what's that for?" I said.

"For your adorable stupidity," she said. "You have no idea what you've done."

12

Perhaps Elizabeth Ann was right. I may not have had any idea of what I had done. But I had a very clear idea of what my rock bottom reaction had been in Will's when Sebastian Roon had told me about his desire to retire to England. Not surprise. Envy.

Seb had a place to retire to. Home. I did not. All I had was a sense of dissatisfaction with my life. The way I was living it. The way I had lived it thus far. And what I was going to do with the rest of it. As the comedians of my youth used to say: Try *that* on your grand piano.

I once did.

A dozen years after Hannah Halpern disappeared with Sebastian Roon from the balcony of Loew's 180th Street while I was buying hot knishes in the Hebrew National next door, I was working in England. The assignment had more or less been arranged by Hitler.

It was a few months after Pearl Harbor. The draft did not appeal to me. I applied for a commission and got it. The U.S. Army seemed to be impressed by degrees. Even degrees from N.Y.U. Law School, Evening Session. Lawyers were definitely in. It was that kind of war.

In the spring of 1942 my C.O., Colonel Buchanan, and I had wound up a series of meetings with our RAF opposites in Edinburgh. The meetings had not been satisfactory. The RAF was not very keen on leaflets. They felt, and told us, that to send a Lancaster over Germany involved the risk of a dozen British lives. When they took that risk, they felt they preferred to drop on the Hun high explosive rather than packets of paper. It was a point of view with which it was difficult to quarrel, although Colonel Buchanan did. With considerable brilliance but no success.

"Look here," he said on our last day at breakfast in our hotel. "I'm not happy with the way this has gone. I think we can do a bit more if we part company and work on two fronts. I'll stay on here in Edinburgh for another day, and I'd like you to go over to Blackpool."

"Blackpool?" I said.

It was like being asked to go on to my father's home town in Austria. Or was it Poland?

"Yes," Colonel Buchanan said. "Do you know Blackpool?"

It did not seem appropriate to say that it was the birthplace of my friend Sebastian Roon.

"Only that it's a resort town for Lancashire mill hands," I said. "Sort of like our Coney Island, I've heard."

"It is that, yes, but at the moment it's become a bit more important," Colonel Buchanan said. "Although the natives are unaware of it. The RAF has a big do just north of the town. It's quite an operation, and classified, of course. Perhaps that's why they've got some intelligent bodies running the show. One of them is Colonel Morpurgo. Good man. We jumped for Jesus together. He beat me by three quarters of an inch against Oxford in the standing broad, and he ran up good marks in the pole vault. I think if you see him, and tell him what we're up to, you might get a more sympathetic response than we've got here in Edinburgh. You take the car. I'll lay on another one to get me back to London tomorrow."

It was that kind of war. You went everywhere in cars. With drivers, of course. Who were not assigned but laid on. I never knew Kay Summersby, but I didn't do too badly. On this day in 1942 I drew Sergeant Gilpin. She was a fat little cherub of a girl, cheerful to the point of occasional nausea. She had joined the Auxiliary Territorial Service as a private at the age of eighteen on the day Hitler invaded Poland. By the time I was assigned to Colonel Buchanan she had risen to what was considered for a girl her age an enviable rank. The best thing about Sergeant Gilpin, for me at any rate, on that day was that she came from Lancashire.

"Blackpool?" she said when I gave her the slip of paper on which Colonel Buchanan had written my destination. "Do I know Blackpool you ask, sir? Why, Major Kramer, I was born in Blackpool. I was."

It was difficult to tell from her voice whether she spoke about her roots with genuine enthusiasm. Sergeant Gilpin was enthusiastic about everything.

"Well," I said, "I have a friend in New York who came from Blackpool."

"I don't suppose I'd know him," Sergeant Gilpin said. "Would I, sir?"

It didn't seem likely. In 1942 I was twenty-nine, and Seb was, of course, my age. Sergeant Gilpin had been promoted sergeant six months ago at the age of twenty-one.

"I don't know," I said. "His name is Sebastian Roon."

"Not the actor, sir?"

"Yes," I said. "The actor."

"Why, sir, we had his latest film in our mess just the other night," Sergeant Gilpin said. *"The Hour Before the Dawn*. Have you seen it, sir?"

"Twice," I said.

Seb had invited me and Elizabeth Ann to a preview. She couldn't go. Her mother was dying again in Wynwood. Mrs. Foster again did not die, but Elizabeth Ann felt she had to see everything Seb did. I refer, of course, to his professional life. So I took Elizabeth Ann to see the movie when it opened at the Paramount. The line at the box office went around the corner deep into 43rd Street. I was not surprised.

The Hour Before the Dawn had been guided through its script and camera phases by the British Ministry of War Information. The film had the good fortune to be released shortly after Pearl Harbor. America, which was suddenly very much in the war, was suddenly very pro-British. We Were In This Together. We were also, Elizabeth Ann and I, in a jam-packed movie palace. I scarcely noticed. The picture got to me. It seemed even better than when I had seen it the first time at the preview.

The Hour Before the Dawn dealt with the life of a Royal

244

Navy destroyer and its crew. Sebastian Roon played the captain. An aristocratic university man commanding a crew that had to be described, of course, as motley. Not unlike the crews that later appeared in our Air Force films. A cross section of the country for the survival of which the crew was fighting.

A Cockney with a passion for growing roses. A black boy from the Punjab who had hoped to find in England what he had been unable to find in India. A curate's son from Harrow who was trying to solve his sexual problem. A Scot who sneered at John Knox but started to pray like mad when the Stukas came over. A radical whose intercourse with his fellows consisted not of human speech but of quotations from the works of Harold J. Laski. A conservative whose family had owned a thousand acres in Lincolnshire since long before the Domesday Book had been composed, and was slowly awakened to the fact that the future of England lay in the hands of all—ALL—the people. A deeply religious Catholic who delivered endless lectures about Father Campion. A sardonic, wisecracking Church of England exlorry driver who did imitations of Gracie Fields. And a Jew straight out of *Potash and Perlmutter,* except that he came from the East End and had cut furs in a shop on Tottenham Court Road instead of taffeta in a dress factory on Seventh Avenue. In our later Air Force films he always came from Brooklyn and he was usually played by John Garfield. Sebastian Roon was superb. When he went down with his ship at Crete the audience sobbed. "My God," Elizabeth Ann whispered. "How can Seb lend himself to such garbage?"

"It's a lovely film, sir, isn't it?" Sergeant Gilpin said.

"Wonderful," I said.

"Imagine you being a friend of Mr. Roon, sir. Wait till I tell the girls in the motor pool."

"I met him a long time ago," I said. "When he first came to America. That's why I asked you if you knew Blackpool. As long as we're going there, I wondered if I could look up his family."

"I don't see why not, sir," Sergeant Gilpin said. "Do you have the address, sir?"

"No," I said. "That's the trouble."

"No trouble at all, sir," Sergeant Gilpin said. "There's always the telephone directory, sir, isn't there?"

Indeed, there proved to be a couple. After I finished my talk with Colonel Morpurgo at the RAF operation, I asked if I could bring in my driver so she could look up a phone number in Blackpool for me.

"Why, Major, we'll be delighted to do it for you," Colonel Morpurgo said. "Bert!" he snapped.

"Sah!" the adjutant snapped back.

"Get the Blackpool telephone directory for Major Kramer," Colonel Morpurgo said.

He pronounced it Krahmer. It reminded me of a dentist I once knew. His name was Blumenstein. But he always corrected me. He wanted his name pronounced Blumensteen. I did not understand why.

"Right, sah."

He brought over a Blackpool telephone directory. I thumbed the pages. I found four Rubins. Colonel Morpurgo may have jumped for Jesus, but I doubt that he had ever met an American until I walked into his office. I think I captured at least a fragment of his interest the way a bird watcher might find his eye drawn to a strange specimen. I could feel him watching me as I thumbed the pages.

"No luck?" he said finally.

"Too much," I said. "There are four Rubins in the area."

"Bert," Colonel Morpurgo said.

"Sah!" The adjutant snapped back, and went to work. Five minutes later he said, "Fourth try, and bull's-eye. The Rubin family on Islington Crescent would be delighted if Major Kramer of New York would stop by for a cup of tea."

When we reached Islington Crescent I understood at once why Sebastian Roon had said on that first night in our Tiffany Street kitchen that it reminded him of Blackpool. Islington Crescent was exactly that: a curved street that cut

246

in from the main road at one point and emerged in a pleasant sweep at another point about two or three New York City blocks down. Along the crescent, on both sides of the street, were small, neat, well-tended houses, some made of stucco, most put together with red brick, all set in cheerful scraps of hysterically fecund garden. It wasn't exactly Tiffany Street, but it had that same quality of a clean bedroom inhabited by people who spent their days earning a living downtown, wherever downtown was in Blackpool.

"I'll wait for you, sir," Sergeant Gilpin said. As she brought the car to a stop in front of a red brick house near the top of the crescent, the sirens went. "On time," Sergeant Gilpin said. "They always try to spoil your tea. Don't let it spoil yours, sir."

I went up the cement walk and rang the bell. The door was opened by Hannah Halpern. It was opened so promptly that I knew she'd been waiting near the knob. There was a small diamond-shaped window at eye level above the bell pull. I could see her peering through it ever since Colonel Morpurgo's adjutant had established contact by phone. It was only a mental image, of course. But it pleased me. It's nice to be expected.

Hannah laughed and threw her arms around my neck and gave me a kiss. Not a peck. A kiss. One of those great big fat wet jobs that were the joys of my 1930 life in the balcony of Loew's 180th Street.

"Hannah," I said. "Is there any place around here where I can buy a couple of Gabilla's knishes?"

"That won't be necessary," she said. "I've laid on a proper tea."

A what? But my thoughts went no further. Hannah had enveloped me in another great big welcoming kiss.

"Hannah," I finally managed to gurgle. "For God's sake!"

"Oops, sorry," she said. "You're right." She pulled me into the house and slammed the door. "That girl in the car saw me do that."

It was my turn to laugh. "So what?" I said.

"You're an officer, by George," Hannah said.

The "by George" jolted me. I no longer ate Gabilla's nickel knishes but I remembered what it had been like in the days when I did. In those days Hannah would have said, "Jesus Christ, Benny, you're an officer!" Now she said about Sergeant Gilpin, "And she's in uniform so she must be one of those ATS's."

"She is," I said, "but don't worry about it. I have a feeling she expected you to kiss me."

Hannah gave me a sly look. "Did you?" she said.

I hadn't thought about it. But I realized now that I would have been hurt if she hadn't.

"Hannah," I said, "I am now a respectable married man."

She giggled. But it was a disappointing giggle. Not the way she used to giggle on the bench near the Small Mammals House in Bronx Park.

"I wish I'd known," she said. "I would have sent you a wedding present. Anyway, do come in and let's tuck into the tea."

Tuck into the tea, eh? Benny, what's happened to your old flame? She sounds like Aunt Peggotty calling David Copperfield to the table.

I dropped my khaki cap on a chair in the tiny hall, hung my coat on a wall rack, and followed her into a small living room. From the window I looked out on another window that had obviously been built onto the adjoining house by the same man who had built Hannah's house. In that other window sat an incredibly ugly creature. It had at least one, possibly two glass eyes, a full beard, no forehead, and the relentless and disapproving inquisitorial gaze of Abraham Lincoln staring out of the center of the five-dollar bill.

"Hannah," I said. "Before we tuck into the tea, don't you think you should pull down the shade?"

I nodded toward the face in the window at the other side of the driveway. Hannah turned to look, then exploded in a laugh. It took me by surprise. I had forgotten the sound. Had I ever really noticed? Well, at least that had not changed. Her laugh was one of the wonders of the western world.

A sound that came at you not through your ears but through your stomach. Not even a sound, actually. A feeling of warmth. A sense of well-being. For God's sake, Hannah's laugh said, stop looking so grouchy and sour. The world isn't all that bad. How about handing over my knish? Major Kramer wished he had one to hand over.

"That's not a Peeping Tom," Hannah said. "That's Mrs. Rampole's gorilla."

"Mrs. Rampole's what?"

"Mrs. Rampole's gorilla," Hannah said. She motioned for me to sit down facing her across the tea tray. "Mrs. Rampole is my neighbor. She won that gorilla in the lottery on the Music Pier. The last lottery they had on the Front before the war. Cream or lemon?"

I brought my glance from the window to the tea tray. "Uh, lemon," I said.

Hannah laughed again. "Naturally," she said. "Nobody ever heard of tea with cream on Tiffany Street or Vyse Avenue. I wish I could serve it to you the way your mother and my mother served it. From a glass. With a lump of sugar that you held in one hand, took a bite, then took a sip of hot tea through the bite of sugar. But we can't get any lump sugar now. There's a war on, you know."

"Yes," I said, "I know." But the war did not seem particularly important at the moment. Aside from the fact that I was aware of my uniform, the war seemed to have receded. A thought crossed my mind. It was silly. I knew that. Yet I could not help saying, "Hannah, would you like some lump sugar?"

"Oh now, come on, Benny," she said with another laugh. "Don't tell me you've got some sort of black market thing going through your officers' PX down in London, and you can get me all the lump sugar I want."

"No," I said. "I don't have any sort of black market thing going, and I could probably get you a couple of cans of grapefruit juice, or a carton or two of lousy cigarettes called Chelsea, but I don't think the PX has any lump sugar. That's not why I asked. I asked because—"

249

Hannah gave me a funny little look. "Because lump sugar is the Bronx?" she said.

I was startled. But even then I had my moments of perception. Hannah had said exactly the right thing.

"Yes," I said. "I was thinking . . ."

My voice drifted away from me. I knew what I had been thinking, but I was not sure I could put it into words. Hannah did it for me.

"You were thinking I'm a girl from the Bronx," she said. "And now I'm not a girl from the Bronx any more."

"That's right," I said. "I was wondering how it happened."

This time, when she laughed, the sounds jolted me into a puzzling thought. Puzzling for me, anyway. I was suddenly wondering if I had missed something. Something important. Something that had been puzzling me ever since I asked Colonel Morpurgo's adjutant to find the Rubin family in the telephone book. I hadn't known until this moment why I had wanted to come here today. What I was wondering was: Isn't this the girl with whom Benny Kramer should have fallen in love?

"I always liked you, Benny," Hannah said.

She handed me a cup. The delicacy of the china surprised me. It was very thin and very white. Small pink roses climbed gently around the handle of the cup and over the rim into the tea. It was so different from Vyse Avenue and Tiffany Street and the balcony of Loew's 180th Street that I took another look at Hannah. She was different, too.

In what way? My mind tracked back through our last few minutes of conversation and I realized she had been dropping her aitches. Hannah Halpern talking like Sam Weller? Why not? I didn't know why not. When in Rome?

Then I looked at what she was wearing. A sort of wraparound tan smock. The sort of thing Sergeant Gilpin and the other girls in the motor pool wore when they were washing their Daimlers. I tried to remember what Hannah used to wear in the balcony of Loew's 180th Street. I couldn't. All I could remember was my difficulties with snaps and fasteners. The zipper had not yet made its crucial entry into America's sex life.

"I think you liked me, too," Hannah said. "Have one of these. I baked them myself."

"Thanks," I said. "Of course I liked you."

She shook her head and took a sip from her cup. I was pleased to notice she did not lift her pinky. What would Sam Weller have said?

"I don't mean that way," Hannah said. She giggled. "That was, oh, you know."

"Yes," I said.

What would you have said? Edging upon thirty? In the middle of a war? Wearing the uniform of your nation's armed forces? In a place called Islington Crescent, within spitting distance of the Front at Blackpool? To a girl you had once been dead stuck on, but not in love with, who was now living in a country invented by Charles Dickens?

"But something was missing?" Hannah said.

"Yes," I said again.

When you get to the point where you can't get words out, and a small bleating sound seems to do the trick, stick with it.

"During the week," Hannah said, "when I was pounding that typewriter for Gold-Mark-Zweig, Inc., on Mosholu Parkway, I used to have dreams about you."

"Me?" I said.

"Well, why not?" Hannah said. "You were a nice boy. Clean-cut. Polite. Good-looking."

"Me?" I said.

"Good-looking enough," Hannah said. "All you talked about was the new bankruptcy cases down at Maurice Saltzman & Company, and how if you could get a raise out of Mr. Bern you were going to N.Y.U. Law School, and I could practically see you in that black robe getting sworn in as Chief Justice of the United States Supreme Court."

I now came up with an attempt at kidding myself, but I knew I was kidding on the square.

"God," I said. "I must have been a stuffy little jerk."

Hannah frowned into her tea cup. I waited tensely for

251

her to deny my self-condemnation. Then she looked up at me, still frowning. As though she were trying to bring a memory into focus.

"I guess some people might put it that way," Hannah said finally. "But me, Benny, I liked that about you."

Women! Jesus, God!

"You liked my being a stuffy little jerk?" I said.

"Sort of, yes," Hannah said. "Girls have to watch out, you know. You go out with a guy, you know what he wants. So you have to decide. If you give it to him, you could lose not only him, but your reputation as well. If you don't give, you don't get invited out again. The best kind of guys, I found in those days, they were the sort of stuffy ones. What they wanted, if you gave it to them, they didn't act as though they'd won a ball game or something and now they had to challenge another team. They were you could sort of say grateful."

She had certainly nailed the hide of Benny Kramer of Tiffany Street to the old barn door.

"They were gentlemen," I said haughtily.

Hannah laughed. "Don't sound so bitter," she said. "It's nice to be with a gentleman. For a girl, anyway."

She leaned across the tea table to pick up another one of the things she had baked herself. En route she brushed my cheek with her lips. It was the second time in my life when I suddenly wanted to burst into tears in front of a girl. Never mind the first time. That's none of your business.

"How did you know I was a gentleman?" I said.

"You know those knishes you used to buy downstairs in the Hebrew National?" Hannah said.

Did Hannibal's elephants know the Alps?

"Sure," I said. "Gabilla's."

"When you brought them up to the balcony," Hannah said, "under mine, that glazed paper, under mine you always had two pieces."

Hey, Walter Raleigh! You know what you can do with your cloak?

"That wasn't chivalry," I said. "That was so I wouldn't burn my hand."

252

"Who cared?" Hannah said. "It made my heart go."
My heart now proceeded to go.

"You mind if I ask you something personal?" I said.

"Benny," Hannah said. "There's nothing I wouldn't allow a gentleman to ask me."

"How do you know I'm still a gentleman?" I said.

"It's like being a Jew," Hannah said. "You're born that way. You can't change it."

"Okay," I said. "Then I'll ask you."

"Have another one of these," Hannah said.

"In a moment," I said. "First tell me this. If you felt that way about me, how come you ran away with Seb?"

Suddenly her voice changed. She sounded like a politician at a convention placing in nomination "a man who."

"Out of the shadow of the silent screen strides John Barrymore!" Hannah intoned. *"In, and as, GENERAL CRACK!"*

I laughed. "That's right," I said. "That was the night. How come you ran away and left me holding four knishes?"

Hannah looked at the thing she had baked herself, then put it back on the tea tray. I didn't blame her. Mr. Gabilla would not have risked bankruptcy by putting it on the market.

"I'll tell you," Hannah said. "If you promise not to laugh at me."

A moment ago it had taken an effort of will to keep from bursting into tears in front of her. Now she wanted me to promise not to laugh at her. Do women really have any grasp of the emotional climate in which men spend their lives? Don't answer. I can't handle another no.

"I promise," I said.

"I just told you how I felt about you back in nineteen thirty in the Bronx," Hannah said. "What I left out is something I didn't understand until that night you introduced me to Seb."

"What was that?" I said.

"I had been waiting," Hannah said.

"For what?" I said.

"For my life to be changed," she said. "All I knew was the Bronx. School. My mother and father. Vyse Avenue. The office of Gold-Mark-Zweig, Inc. The balcony of Loew's One Hundred and Eightieth Street. And you."

"Me?" I said.

"You bet you," Hannah said. "You were my sweepstakes ticket. I knew there was a whole world beyond the Bronx. It said so in the movies, in the books I read, on the radio. I was dying to see it. I knew the only way was through a boy who would fall in love with me and marry me and take me away. Don't be sore. I'm not saying you failed me, because I'm not sure I understood it at the time. I just knew in my heart that you were a boy I liked, you were going places, you were a gentleman, and when the time was right you would take me along."

You know what's worse than wanting to burst into tears in front of a girl? Wanting to die.

"I let you down," I said.

"No," Hannah said. "You brought me Seb."

"That bastard," I said.

Hannah laughed. "You don't mean that," she said.

I laughed. Anyway, I tried. "No, of course I don't," I said. "He's just about the nicest guy I know."

Hannah frowned. "You mean you're still friends?" she said.

What struck me was not her surprise, but the fact that she seemed to disapprove.

"Sure," I said. "Why should you doubt it?"

"Well," Hannah said. "You said I ran away with him. That means usually—you know."

"No," I said, "I don't know."

I've learned this about myself: I can handle pretty much everything that happens to me, so long as I can dot the i's and cross the t's. I don't have a very good mind. But I have a neat one. If the horror is all wrapped up, no loose ends trailing, and it can be tucked away cleanly on the shelf of memory, it won't come toppling off at odd moments in the future to haunt me. It's sort of the way I've learned to run

254

my office. I never worry about my "closed" files. Miss Bienstock does, of course. But that's *her* problem.

"But you want to know," Hannah said through her extraordinary smile. "Don't you?"

"Yes, very much," I said. "You see, I'm jealous."

The squeal of laughter that came pouring out of her across the tea tray might have made Rudolf Bing wince. But one man's wince is another man's music. For me Hannah's squeal could, as Ring Lardner once put it, have been poured on a waffle.

"Oh, Benny," she said. "Benny, Benny, Benny, you nice son of a bitch. Maybe . . ."

Hannah paused. Then she shook her head. The late afternoon light that was making a horror of Mrs. Rampole's gorilla across the narrow driveway suddenly caught Hannah's eyes. For the first time, and to my considerable astonishment, I noticed that they were violet. I had never before seen violet eyes. How could I not have noticed that years ago?

True, it was dark up in the the balcony of Loew's 180th Street, but—

Yes? But? But what, Benny?

You know what, Benny. Stop pretending you don't. Hannah was a girl you liked but were scared to love. Now that she had made her life with somebody else, you wanted to know what your life would have been like if you had made it with her. That's why you had come to Islington Crescent in the middle of a war. Not a bad objective. If you are going to discover at thirty that you were a louse at seventeen, the best place in which to make the discovery is Islington Crescent, in Blackpool, in 1942, while the air-raid sirens are screaming.

"No," Hannah said firmly. "You live, and you move on, and if you have any brains you know that what you lived yesterday is finished. It's today that counts. I like my today, Benny. Do you understand that?"

I looked around the small, neat, compact room. I looked at the picture of a scowling, fiercely determined Winston Churchill over the fireplace. I looked at the embroidered

255

sampler on the wall over Hannah's head that said: KEEP THE POKER ON THE HEARTH! I looked at the photograph cut from *The Daily Sketch* that showed Paddy Finucane in his RAF outfit smiling out gallantly over the message he had radioed a moment after his Spitfire was hit and went down over the Channel: "This is it, chaps!" And then I saw something I had not seen since Miss Bongiorno's Elocution Class in J.H.S. 64: a framed quote from the "a mighty charge" speech in *Henry V: "And on this charge cry God for Harry, England, and St. George!"* Benny Kramer of Tiffany Street turned back to Hannah Halpern from Vyse Avenue, both of the Bronx.

"Yes, I do," I said. "I understand."

Hannah smiled again. "Then I can tell you," she said. "The way I felt about you, all that was fine. I was happy to coast along and wait. You see, I felt sure of you. So someday you would be a chief justice and I would be Hannah Kramer, the Mrs. Chief Justice."

"My God," I said. "I never knew that."

"Of course not," Hannah said. "Men never know anything."

For a stunned moment I wondered if she was right. If that was the answer to the secret of the whole insane mess known as life. But in the battle of the sexes, you do not deliver neatly packaged ammunition to the other side.

"Now, wait a minute," I said.

"Not in the middle of a war," Hannah said. "You don't wait minutes. You live them." She paused and cocked her head toward the window. The sirens were still wailing. "It's all right," she said. "They're coming in across Bootle north of Liverpool. The RAF will stop them before they get anywhere near here."

My gut had started to twitch. The raids scared me.

"You don't seem worried," I said.

Hannah shrugged. "Actually, I am," she said. "I don't like it much. But you'd be surprised how easy it is not to be too scared. You have to learn one thing."

"What's that?" I said.

256

"To learn to survive," Hannah said, "you have to learn to last it out."

A quarter of a century later it still seems to me the sagest piece of off-the-rack philosophy I have ever heard.

"I'm trying," I said.

Hannah smiled. "Don't hunch over the handlebars," she said. "You'll make it. Boys from Tiffany Street are built to last."

"I didn't last with you," I said.

"Because one night you made the mistake of bringing around a boy named Sebastian Roon."

If something requires rubbing in, you can always count on a woman to do the best job.

"I know it was a mistake," I said. "The facts prove that. But what I've never understood is *how* it was a mistake."

"Seb didn't do anything wrong," Hannah said.

"Somebody did," I said.

"Me," Hannah said.

"That's hard for me to believe," I said.

And leave it to a man to make the more fatuous let's-rub-it-out remark.

"I don't mean dirty wrong," Hannah said. "I mean rotten wrong."

Could my old Hannah of Vyse Avenue have become a devotee of the new war movies? She sounded like Rita Hayworth playing Rosie the Riveter.

"I know I sound like Walter Pidgeon in the big scene with Greer Garson," I said, "but I'm going to say it, anyway. Quote. I don't understand you, darling. Unquote."

Hannah laughed. "Funny you should mention Greer Garson," she said. "First time I saw her, in *Goodbye, Mr. Chips* with Robert Donat, I knew who I wanted to be."

"Who?" I said.

"Greer Garson, you idiot," Hannah said.

"I never thought of you as the Greer Garson type," I said.

"That's what went wrong," Hannah said. "Get that look off your face and have another one of these. I know you think they're terrible, and they probably are, but I did bake

257

them myself, and the stuff you get to bake with these days, honestly, it's a miracle the finished product can be pried out of the pan. Take the middle one. The candied cherry on top helps a little. What went wrong, Benny, is that nobody ever thinks of Bronx girls as the Greer Garson type, except Bronx girls themselves. Consider it for a second. If you were a Bronx girl, would you want to continue being a Bronx girl?"

I considered it. Why not? She was an old friend. You could say we had together taken our first groping steps toward finding out what the hell it is all about.

"I don't know," I said. "I've never been a Bronx girl."

"Count your blessings," Hannah said. "Count your blessings, Benny. But you've been a Bronx boy."

It did not seem the sort of statement from which a man could gain much by a denial.

"Of course," I said.

"When you were a Bronx boy," Hannah said, "do you remember what you used to dream about?"

It seemed wrong to say Jean Harlow, which was the truth. So I made an effort and tried to think of the second thing I used to dream about when I was a boy in the Bronx. It didn't require much thinking. Two words surfaced at once.

"Getting ahead," I said.

Hannah nodded and said, "Ahead where?"

"I don't know," I said, although of course I did. On East Fourth Street it meant getting up to the Bronx. On Tiffany Street it meant getting down to the good parts of Manhattan. It's a desire, however, about which not many people like to talk. I mean the people engaged in the process. People like Benny Kramer. We have an uncomfortable feeling that there is something dirty about such an ambition. It's not Christiaan Barnard and heart transplants. It's just real estate. I said to Hannah, "I guess it meant earning more money so you wouldn't have to stay in the Bronx."

She nodded. "Because nobody wants to stay in the Bronx," Hannah said. "So getting out is the trick. For a boy like you, for instance, it means studying, going to law school, that sort of thing, and if you have any brains that sort of thing is bound to work, the way it worked for you. But for a girl, she has to wait for a boy to marry her and take her out of the Bronx. Meantime, while she's waiting, she types letters for Gold-Mark-Zweig, Inc., on Mosholu Parkway and she dreams of being Greer Garson. In my case, me and you, I never had any doubt it would happen. You had that look."

"What look?" I said it with fear in my heart. If she said I'd had the look of eagles, I would have to strangle her, and I didn't want to do that. I liked her.

"Remember Lindbergh?" Hannah said.

"Lindbergh?"

"Way back when everybody was flying the Atlantic," Hannah said. "Harry Richman and that guy with one eye. Wiley Post? In this plane, a three-engined Fokker it was called, with the wings full of ping-pong balls? And Admiral Byrd with that Swede? Or maybe he was a Norwegian? Bernt Balchen? And that little bald-headed guy, Levine, with that blonde in the gold-mesh sweater? I mean real gold? Fourteen-karat? Mabel Boll?"

"Yes," I said. "Sort of vaguely. What about them?"

"Well," Hannah said, "this kid came along. Out of the West. My God, he looked like maybe eleven years old. And all he had was that cockamamey little airplane and that really but from Dixie five-dollar windbreaker jacket, and that look in his eyes. You could see it in the *Daily News*. You knew he was going to make it."

"What's Lindbergh got to do with Benny Kramer?" I said.

"You had the same look," Hannah said. "I knew you were going to make it. And I think I figured as long as I waited patiently, it would happen to me, too, because you'd take me along."

What a thought to be hit with at almost thirty. In the middle of an air raid.

"I might have," I said. "But by the time I was in a position to do anything about it, you'd flown the coop."

Hannah nodded again. "That's what I meant when I said

259

I didn't do anything dirty wrong, but something rotten wrong."

"By taking off with Seb?" I said.

Hannah giggled. I don't understand it. What's a giggle? A stunted laugh? An explosion of hilarity that gets headed off at the pass? Why should it make you feel twenty years younger? Why should it make you feel you're being lifted out of a war, and a major's uniform, and an encircling air raid, and put you back in the balcony of Loew's 180th Street? When nothing had mattered except the moment? And the moment was Botticelli's Venus coming out of that foolish sea shell? And it had not yet occurred to you that you were not going to live forever?

Hannah sighed and said, "Have another cup of tea?"

Moments of truth arrive at odd moments. Without warning.

"Hannah," I said. "I hate tea."

"Of course," she said. "To you tea is that stuff your mother made you drink when you were stopped up on East Fourth Street."

"And Tiffany Street," I said.

"Yes, yich," Hannah said. "My mother made me drink it, too."

"It was pretty bad stuff," I said.

"Awful," Hannah said.

So at least we had that in common. I thought about it. For the first time in my life I wondered how my mother, an immigrant from Hungary, had decided that the cure for her son's constipation was a detestable herb tea that came from Ceylon.

"Worse than awful," I said. "And this stuff you're pouring now is not like that at all. In fact, this tea is delicious. But it's still tea, if you know what I mean."

"Of course I do," Hannah said. "That's what I thought back in nineteen thirty when Seb and I first got here."

"I'm still waiting to hear how that happened," I said.

"When we double-dated that night in nineteen thirty," Hannah said, "I brought along this girl who worked with me at Gold-Mark-Zweig?"

"Grace Krieger," I said.

Hannah giggled again. "That's the one. She obviously made quite an impression on you."

"She was a very nice girl," I said.

Primly, I'm afraid. And with a blush, I suspect. A sense of inadequacy had sneaked up on me. Byron, at thirty, was banging the wife of his landlord in Venice. Burton, at thirty, was field-testing buggery on the spot in Al-Medinah and Mecca. Benny Kramer, almost thirty, was blushing in Blackpool because he had suddenly been reminded of how he once felt about the contours of a girl named Grace Krieger whom he had met exactly once. It is discomfiting to realize that, no matter what other goodies life may have in store for you, it has not cast you in the role of One of the World's Great Lovers.

"I know Grace was a very nice girl," Hannah said. "Which is what surprised me about what happened. You remember how after we bought the tickets you went next door to the Hebrew National to get the knishes, and Seb and I and Grace Krieger went up into the balcony to wait for you?"

"Two of you didn't," I said.

Hannah gave me a quick look. "I detect a note of bitterness," she said.

She said it not, I saw, with displeasure.

"Well," I said, and I hesitated. How did Byron say these things? Or Burton? I suppose it helps if you speak Italian or Arabic. In old-fashioned Tiffany Street English I said, "Hannah, I obviously failed you in some way in nineteen thirty. But I think you must have known that, even if I was a jerk, I was very fond of you."

She smiled and reached across the tea tray. She touched my hand. It was like a gentle electric shock. I tingled. So Benny Kramer was not One of the World's Great Lovers. So what? Goddamn it, though, there were women who liked him. You can always tell. You wait for the tingle. In Blackpool in 1942 I tingled. As I think I have indicated earlier, it was quite a war.

"Of course I knew it," Hannah said. "And it made me

261

proud. Not to mention my mother and father. Boy, were they proud of you!"

"Me?" I said.

"Oh, shut up," Hannah said. "They adored you, and you know it. To them you were the nice Jewish boy to end all nice Jewish boys. And you were going with their darling Hannah! My God, on Saturday nights, when you came to pick me up, it was like Ferdinand and Isabella standing on the dock waiting for the *Nina,* the *Pinta,* and the *Santa Maria* to come into port. That's why I think it's only fair for me to set the record straight. Benny, in nineteen thirty it wasn't you who were the jerk. It was me."

There are times when a man—a woman too, I suppose —simply does not know what to say. I have learned that in such a situation the most sensible course is to keep your trap shut. I did.

"I see I've taken you by surprise," Hannah said.

"Well," I said, "I have never before known a girl to confess that she's a jerk."

Hannah shrugged. "Maybe it's because most of the time they're not," she said. "The thing about being a girl, especially in the Bronx, which is really what you might call my frame of reference, because after all what do I know about being a girl on, let's say, the Main Line of Philadelphia?"

I thought about Elizabeth Ann. Who had been raised in Wynwood. And whom I had just married. The answer to Hannah's question was: You know absolutely nothing about being a girl on the Main Line of Philadelphia. But I did not make that reply. My mother, a peasant from Hungary, had brought with her to the Golden Land not only two feather beds and a blue and white porcelain soup tureen, but also the basic rules of decent behavior. She had taught her son the elementary guidelines of human conduct.

"It's like this," Hannah said. "For a Bronx girl in nineteen thirty, I was sitting pretty. I had this cockamamy job at Gold-Mark-Zweig, Inc., on Mosholu Parkway. A living. I had a steady boyfriend. A delight. I could read the future more clearly than that dame in the *Daily News* with the horoscope. All I had to do was wait. You would graduate from law school. You would get a job with some good solid Rock of Gibraltar firm with one of those names. You know. White & Case. Sullivan & Cromwell. Weil, Gottschal & Manges. You know what I mean. The lads who sail in the summer on Martha's Vineyard and hire boys from East Fourth Street and Tiffany Street to win the cases that pay for the mizzenmasts. The One Twenty Broadway gang. And pretty soon you'd be earning enought to move your father and mother from Tiffany Street in the Bronx to like say Central Park West or West End Avenue. Then you'd get the old *noodge* from your mother: Benny, it's time you should think about a wife. Well, for God's sake, who was there to think about? Who but Hannah Halpern, from the balcony in Loew's One Hundred and Eightieth Street with the Gabilla's knishes? The wedding? Concourse Plaza. What else? Our first home? Walton Avenue, natch. Sure, it's the Bronx. But the classy Bronx. On Saturdays and Sundays you could go up on the roof with the other young lawyers and their wives and eat Eskimo pies while you looked down into the Yankee Stadium for free and watched Babe Ruth and Lou Gehrig belt Waite Hoyt out of the park. This is bad? Think about it, Benny. Think!"

I did. And in 1942, in a neat little semidetached villa on Islington Crescent in Blackpool, in the middle of a war and an increasingly nervous-making air raid, my thoughts were astonishingly simple. The answer to Hannah's question was: No, it is not bad. But the answer was upsetting. If it was not bad, how come Hannah and I had not achieved it?

"I guess something went wrong," I said.

"Yes, and no," Hannah said. "Now, don't get sore. What I mean is it may have gone wrong for you, but it went right for me. Are you with me?"

I listened to the drone of the planes coming in across Bootle in Liverpool, and I tried to remember I was scared, the way I was always scared in London during a raid, but it wasn't quite the same. To my surprise, this time I was not scared. There was something about sitting with Hannah that settled the stomach. She had substance.

"I'm with you in one way," I said. "And I'm not sore. Honest. But I'm confused."

"I don't blame you," Hannah said. "Look at it this way. You had no way of knowing what was going on in my head. My ambitions, you might say. My dream of the future for you and me. Did you, Benny?"

I thought about it, and I could feel my face grow hot. The truth was brutal. All I had ever thought about Hannah Halpern in those days were getting her up into the balcony of Loew's 180th Street with a couple of hot knishes. What a paltry ambition for a major in the U.S. Army to recall. What a crude desire for a member of the New York bar. Here was Churchill saving the world with the sort of rhetoric that would have foundered if he had lacked the wit to insert in his sentences at regular intervals the word *alas!* instead of commas, and all I could think of was that goddamned set of three snaps at the back of Hannah Halpern's brassiere. Major Kramer wondered if he might not best display his patriotism by resigning his commission.

"Hannah," I said, "this is nineteen forty-two and I'm almost thirty years old. I no longer remember what I thought about when I was seventeen in nineteen thirty."

Hannah gave me one of those over-the-glasses looks, although she did not wear glasses.

"I could refresh your recollection," she said. "But the point is all the Bronx girls I knew were like me. They wanted to get out of the Bronx. And most of them had a sort of rough plan. Like me. Then one night you went and loused it all up by introducing me to an English boy named Sebastian Roon. Never mind that it later turned out to be Seymour Rubin. That night he was Sebastian Roon, and boy did he look it. That marvelous profile. That tweed suit with those three jazzy buttons down the front. That beautiful dark brown hair. Those manners. And my God, Benny, that accent! Can you imagine what it's like to a girl from the Bronx who has secret dreams of becoming Greer Garson to meet Leslie Howard in the flesh? On Vyse Avenue yet?"

"No, I can't" I said. "Because my friends in the theater tell me Leslie Howard was also Jewish."

"Who cares?" Hannah said. "If you look like Leslie Howard, and you talk like Leslie Howard, and you have that slinky smile, and you turn it on a girl from the Bronx, you've got her, boy, you've got her. Now add to that something unbelievable. Are you ready?"

"Until those Nazi bombers dump their payloads on Islington Crescent," I said, "yes."

"Relax," Hannah said. "They'll never get this far. Not a chance. There's an RAF base just north of Hidsup."

"I know," I said.

Hannah looked surprised. "You do?" she said.

"That's where I had lunch before I came on here."

Hannah shook her head. "Major Kramer," she said, "you shouldn't have told me that. The operation at Hidsup is classified."

"Hannah," I said, "there are a lot of things I shouldn't have told you. But I did. And I now think I should have told you more. And if I've violated security, to hell with security."

Again her smile was like the sunrise coming in over the East River on East Fourth Street.

"I was your first girl," she said. "Wasn't I?"

Maybe my only one. But I was a married man. I couldn't say that.

"Yes," I said.

Her smile changed slightly.

"You always made me feel good," she said. "I feel good now. So don't worry about the raid. We get them every day at teatime. You're as safe as houses here. Never before has so much been owed by so many to so few."

"You left out the *alas!*" I said.

"What?" Hannah said.

"Churchill always puts in an *alas!*" I said. "Like a pinch of salt in a recipe."

"He's entitled," Hannah said. "But back to the balcony of Loew's Hundred and Eightieth Street on that night in nineteen thirty. You went off to get the knishes. Grace

265

Krieger went off with Sebastian Roon somewhere on the right. I took a seat on the left and kept the one next to me empty for you. A minute or two later, Sebastian Roon came over and sat down in the empty seat next to me. I was surprised but there was no time to say anything because just then there was this noise. From the front of the theater. *'Out of the shadow of the silent screen strides John Barrymore in, and as, GENERAL CRACK!'* Seb leaned over to me and said: 'Are you much taken with this?' Imagine. *Are you much taken with this?* Jesus! Guess what I said."

"Some variation of *huh*?"

Hannah laughed. "Close, Benny, close," she said. "What I actually said was 'Not particularly.' And guess what he said."

"He took your hand and he said let's get out of here."

Hannah registered an astonishment that I don't think she felt. She was playing up to me.

"How did you know?" she said.

I didn't want to hurt her feelings by saying I've been to a lot of movies without her.

"I've known Seb for a dozen years," I said.

"Well," Hannah said, "that's exactly what he did say, and we walked out of Loew's One Hundred and Eightieth Street, and he said is there any place we can sit and talk? So I took him into Bronx Park. You know that bench on the left side of the Small Mammals House?"

Oh, God, she shouldn't have said that!

"Yes," I said with the sort of restraint Dean Acheson used to employ when talking to Khrushchev.

"Well," Hannah said, "we went over there, and we sat down, and he talked. Boy, did he talk. It turned out underneath that Oxford accent he was lonely, and scared, and not sure what the hell to do. You know, he was really Leslie Howard in those scenes by the hollyhocks where he tells the girl he's not an elegant bounder from those clubs in St. James Street but just a frightened little schnook looking for affection. Did he have a load of *tsuris!* After his uncle died Seb said all he had in the world was nine hundred bucks. He showed it to me. Did you ever see nine hundred dollars in the flesh?"

"Yes," I said. "About a month before you saw it, the day his uncle died, Seb showed it to me."

"Well, he didn't show it to you in the shadow of the Small Mammals House," Hannah said. "It makes a difference. There was a sort of, I don't know, a glow about it. And that's why I suppose it happened."

"What happened?" I said.

"What he said," Hannah said. "Seb. He said it's terribly upsetting. I like it here, he said. This country. I want to stay here. But I've got to go back and see my mum. She's not well. And she thinks her brother, that's my uncle, she thinks he's a big bug over here, and I've got to break it to her that he's not a big bug but he's dead and he died broke, and oh, well, it's a mess, and I hate it, but I've got to go. And that's when I said it," Hannah said. "Right there. That minute. By the Small Mammals House in Bronx Park," Hannah said. "That's when I said it."

"Said what?" I said.

"Take me along," Hannah said.

She paused. I took a bite out of one of the things she had baked herself. The candied cherry on top did not help. I was indeed surprised that she had been able to pry it out of the baking pan. But I was glad she had managed it. It gave me something to do. While I did it, I tried not to think, but it is an effort at which I have never succeeded. I don't mean that my thinking is good. Or constructive. Or even worth recording. But it is feverish.

"Why did you say take me along?" I said.

Hannah looked troubled. "It doesn't matter now," she said.

"It matters to me," I said. "Why do you think I came here today? In the middle of a war? And an air raid?"

The troubled look on Hannah's face didn't exactly change. But it moved. As though she had shifted gears.

"Benny," she said, "I think it would be better if I didn't tell you."

Better for whom?

"I want to know," I said.

"No, Benny," Hannah said. "You don't. Really, you don't."

"I think I'm the one who knows the answer to that," I said. "That night near the Small Mammals House, I want to know why you said to Seb take me along."

"Okay," Hannah said. She sounded sad. "I said it because I had two things in my head. I knew I loved Benny Kramer, but I also knew something else."

"What?" I said.

"I knew something about me that maybe Benny Kramer didn't even know himself."

"What was that?" I said.

"I knew Benny Kramer liked me upstairs in the dark," Hannah said. "In the balcony of Loew's One Hundred and Eightieth Street. Where nobody was looking. But downstairs. During the day. Where people could see us. You were ashamed of me."

"Hannah," I said. "Don't say that."

"It's too late," she said. "I have. I told you it was something you wouldn't like. Still, why not? It's the truth. You never asked me for a date on Sunday. When the sun was shining in the park."

"How could I?" I said. "I had to work on Sunday. At Maurice Saltzman & Company it was a seven-day week."

"Maybe that's why I said take me along to Seymour," Hannah said. "Not really because he looked like Leslie Howard, but because he didn't work a seven-day week for Maurice Saltzman & Company. Our first date, right after John Barrymore came striding out of the shadow of the silent screen, Seymour and I we walked around and stayed up until daylight. He liked me, Benny. The way you did, but also he wasn't ashamed of me, Benny. The way you were."

"So when he said he was going home to England?"

"I said take me along," Hannah said.

"And he did," I said.

Hannah nodded. "The next thing I knew we were on the *United States*," she said.

"Was that the only reason you said it?" I said. "Take me along?"

She gave me another of those over-the-glasses looks. "You mean did I say it because I was in love with him?"

Of course that's what I meant. So I said, "No."

"Well," Hannah said, "I wasn't. He was a very attractive boy, and if you go to see his movies, as I do, you know he's grown more attractive, but that wasn't it. The reason I heard myself saying take me along, I mean in addition to how you were ashamed of me, the reason was that all of a sudden I realized I was tired of waiting to get out of the Bronx. Bone-tired. Scared-tired. I suddenly felt, my God, it may never happen! Where the idea came from, I don't know. But all at once the years of waiting for you to go to law school, and move your mother and father downtown, and get a job with Hartman, Sheridan, Tekulsky & Pecora— Jesus, Benny, all of a sudden I was afraid I wouldn't be able to last it out. And here it was. Sitting beside me on the bench near the Small Mammals House. Instant Out! So I went."

I picked at the sliver of candied cherry on top of the thing she had baked herself.

"But it didn't work," I said.

"It didn't work the way I thought it was going to work," she said. "But it worked better than I can see you think it worked."

"Look," I said. "I didn't mean anything."

"Of course not," Hannah said. "You're Major Kramer now, in a snappy uniform with a lot of fancy colored ribbons, and for all I know you're probably winning the war, but to me you're still a nice Jewish boy from Tiffany Street named Benny Kramer. So I'm not going to tell Major Kramer what happened. I'm going to tell Benny."

I laughed and I bit into the candied cherry. A mistake. But no matter. I smacked my lips. It was not for her culinary talents that I had once been dead stuck on this girl. And now? Take it easy, Benny. There's a war on.

"Tell me," I said. "I'm Benny."

"Well, naturally I didn't tell Ma and Pa I was traveling

269

with Seb. I made it sound I was going alone. When they came down to the ship to see me off, I made sure Seb was out of sight. And well, anyway, Seb and I got here."

"Here?" I said.

"Yeah," Hannah said. "This is where his mother and father and brother lived. This is the house Seb was born in. It's nice, isn't it?"

I took another look around. At the cramped but neat little living room. At the tiny fireplace. At the framed picture of Churchill and the sampler that warned you in black and yellow and blue wool to keep the poker on the hearth. At the tiny foyer, just outside the living room, on the wall of which a row of pegs was hung with stained mackintoshes —did you ever see an Englishman in a clean raincoat?— and Major Kramer's dashing trench coat from the Officers' Commissary on Oxford Street. What I saw gave me a funny little feeling in my chest. It *was* nice.

"It's delightful," I said.

Miss Marine? Were you listening? Benny did not say it was great. He did not say it was the cat's pajamas, or the berries. Benny said it was delightful.

"I'm glad you like it, Benny," Hannah said. "We come from the same place, you and I. If you didn't like it, I'd feel rotten."

If I hadn't liked it, how did she think I would feel?

"You don't have to," I said. "I do like it."

I not only liked it. I suddenly realized I was jealous of her for having it. Hannah had achieved something I was still seeking. Sanctuary.

"Seb didn't," she said.

"What?" I said.

Hannah shook her head as though she was trying to shake off a persistently buzzing fly.

"The moment we got here," she said, "I could see he hated it. You know what it was like?"

"What?" I said.

"It was like suppose what I'd told my mother and father was true," Hannah said. "Suppose I'd really come over here from the Bronx on a job for Maurice Saltzman &

270

Company, and then I had to go home and it was Seb, not me, who said take me along, and I did, and we arrived in that crummy apartment we used to live in on Vyse Avenue. Jesus, Benny, think of it."

I did.

"You would have hated it," I said.

"You bet I would," Hannah said. "And that's how it was with Seb. I was coming to a new country. Dickens. Shakespeare. Thackeray. All that stuff they taught us at school. Remember 'Sir Gawain and the Green Knight'?"

"Sure," I said. "And how about *Gammer Gurton's Needle?*"

"And *Patient Griselda?*" Hannah said. "All those things. All of a sudden it wasn't stuff in books that they taught you in school. All of a sudden it was real. It was here. Islington Crescent. I was so excited there were times I couldn't breathe. No kidding. I just couldn't catch my breath, it was so wonderful. But to Seb? Benny, poor Seb, he was coming back to the Bronx. That's what this place meant to him. His Bronx. He felt awful. All he wanted was to get back."

"To our Bronx," I said.

Hannah scowled at the teapot. "Now, isn't that funny?" she said. "I never thought of it that way, but of course that was it. To you and me the Bronx was the Bronx, but to Seb it was, I don't know, like in school, America was to those explorers, John Cabot and that Frenchman La Salle and oh, you know."

I did. I knew. Boy, did Benny Kramer know.

"A new world," I said.

Hannah nodded. "And that's what Blackpool has been to me," she said. "A new world." Then she did something that it still hurts to remember. She put her hand to her heart and said, "I love it, Benny. I love it so much I could die for it."

What I said next was not particularly brilliant, but it took me a couple of moments to get the words arranged in proper sequence.

"You don't have to do that, Hannah," I said.

"Maybe not," she said. "But I'm like Winston. I mean I know what he means. To save this little hunk of Islington Crescent I will fight on the beaches, I will fight on the landing fields, I will never surrender—!"

"Hannah," I said, "take it easy."

"You're right, Benny," she said. "I am making a horse's ass out of myself."

"You couldn't do that," I said, "if you were entered in a contest."

Think of that one. In fact, you may have it. Courtesy of Major Benjamin Kramer, U.S. Army, formerly of Tiffany Street.

"Jesus," Hannah said, and she turned on me the sort of look that you get only from the top of the Washington Monument. "Jesus," Hannah said again. "Why didn't I wait for you?"

"Because Seb came along," I said.

Hannah shook her head. "Not really," she said. "He came along, and he brought me over here, but then he couldn't stand it. And one day he just took off."

"Leaving you here alone?" I said.

Hannah laughed. "Not exactly," she said. "There was his mum and his dad, nice people both. And there was—"

A noise out in the foyer drew her attention. I turned to follow her glance. A key was scraping in the lock of the front door. It opened. Sebastian Roon came in. Except that it was not Sebastian Roon. It was a man who looked exactly like him. Hannah leaped up.

"Eustace!" she said. "We've got a visitor from the Stytes!"

I wondered if my ear was playing tricks. Had Hannah said Stytes?

"Evening, love," said Eustace.

He came limping into the room, and that explained why he was not really Sebastian Roon, even though he looked exactly like Seb. Eustace wore a shoe with a seven-inch heel.

"This is Benny Kramer," Hannah said. "You've heard me talk of him. We were kids in the Bronx together."

It was not until Eustace snapped a salute at me that I realized he was wearing the rough woolen khaki and the broad slashing V-stripe of a corporal in the British Army.

"Glad to meet you, sir," he said. "Hannah has indeed talked a grite deal about you. A pleasure, sir."

We shook hands.

"Eustace, love," Hannah said, "will you ave a cup of tay?"

"That's why oy came ome, love."

He limped to a chair facing me while Hannah fussed with the teapot. His resemblance to Seb was so startling that I could not stop myself from making the obvious remark.

"You look like Seb's twin," I said.

Eustace laughed. The same, easy, engaging laugh that had helped make his brother one of the most famous actors on the English-speaking stage. But there was a hard core at the bottom of the laugh. A sort of grating metallic sound. It surfaced again when Eustace spoke.

"Why not?" he said. "Since that's what oyam? His bloody twin brother oyam. The only difference between us is that oym the one who got the polio."

"Ere, love," Hannah said. He took the teacup. "It's on account of is leg that Eustace is in the typists' pool up at the arsenal. Ee runs the mimeograph machine."

"It eyn't like piloting a Spitfire," Eustace said. "But Oy daresay it's as much against Itler as playing a eero in the cinema."

So that's the way it is, I remember thinking. And that's the last thought I do remember. No. Not quite. I remember that the sound of the planes had taken on a new note. Nothing loud or disturbing. Except that it reminded me of something very odd. The way Mr. Lebenbaum, in whose candy store I used to work after school on East Fourth Street when I was a boy, used to get the trash ready for the garbage wagon.

Most of the stuff was cardboard boxes. Cracker Jack cartons. Tootsie Roll containers. Mary Jane boxes. Dry stuff. Not sloppy, but it took up space. And Abe Lebenbaum was a neat man. So the day before the garbage man came, he would go out into the room back of the candy store and crush these boxes and cartons into manageable shape. He seemed to enjoy the process. I can still see him jumping up and down on a big fat Tootsie Roll carton, reducing it gleefully to a thin pack of cardboard. And I can still hear the curious crunch crunch crunch the cardboard made as Abe Lebenbaum jumped on the boxes.

It was this sound, this curiously satisfying crunch crunch crunch, that I had been hearing, without knowing I was hearing it, all during my brief meeting with Eustace Rubin in the tiny living room of his house in Islington Crescent. I learned later that this is the sound made by sticks of bombs as they are laid down by aircraft. I had never heard this sound during the raids I had lived through in London.

"Now, now, Eustace." Hannah said. "No woman ever had a better husband, and Oym appy to be your wife. The truth is Oy never was appy until Oy met you, and it's—"

She probably said more. I don't remember. I don't even remember which one of us screamed. It could have been me. All I remember is the clarity with which I was hearing the noise Abe Lebenbaum made when he used to jump up and down on those Cracker Jack cartons, and then that stopped, too.

13

It sounded funny, more than a quarter of a century later, to be hearing that crunching sound again. In the thickly carpeted corridors of the ABTV Building on Madison Avenue. On my way to the meeting I had arranged with Jim Mennen's legal department to work out the terms of Sebastian Roon's TV deal.

It seemed funny to hear that sound again, but it was even funnier to realize the meaningless noise was reassuring. I suddenly felt like the hero of one of those old Warner Bros. movies that were supposed to be the biographical accounts of the lives of noted composers. The plot always turned on the composer's endless quest for the true meaning of his work. I had spent half a century, the script said, combing the world desperately for the magic note that would unify my oeuvre. And suddenly I had stumbled into it in the Dry Cereals aisle at the A&P.

Crunch, crunch, crunch: Abe Lebenbaum on Avenue D in 1927 stamping the candy-store empties into manageable shape for the garbage truck. Crunch, crunch, crunch: a Stuka coming in over the North Sea in 1942, laying a stick of bombs to the front door in Blackpool of a girl with whom I had once eaten Gabilla's knishes in the balcony of Loew's 180th Street. Crunch, crunch, crunch: something making the same noise in the corridors of the ABTV Building in 1971 as I made my way to the room in which I planned to work out the financial arrangements that would ensure the end of Sebastian Roon's forty-year exile.

"May I help you, sir?"

"Yes, you may," I said to the girl at the reception desk. "What is the noise I've been hearing ever since I got out of the elevator?"

She cocked her head to one side. This caused her long, yellow, unfastened hair, parted in the middle, to sway all the way over. Like a couple of frayed hawsers whiplashing across the deck of a tug in response to a sudden thrust at the rudder from the wheelhouse. I realized all at once why this hair style was so popular. It had mystery.

Until the girl moved her head she was just a body encased in yellow fringe through which she squinted myopically to see if the traffic light had changed. Then the hair swung aside, and you saw she had breasts, and you saw she was pretty, and you saw . . . Maybe at fifty-eight you shouldn't, but you do.

"Oh, that," the girl said. "That's the Coca-Cola man filling the Coke machine. Out back, behind that door."

She nodded again. Her hair swayed again. She reminded me of Hannah, swinging her head away from the Islington Crescent tea tray in 1942 to listen for the throb of the bombers coming in across Liverpool.

"Why does filling a Coke machine cause that kind of sound?" I said.

"Well, you see, sir," the girl said, "they bring the cans up in cartons, and after they fill the machine they jump up and down on the empty cartons to crush them so they'll take less room in the freight elevator going down. It's only a few minutes, but while it lasts it does sound unpleasant."

Not if you had been introduced to the sound by Abe Lebenbaum in 1927.

"It also sounds as though everybody is going to get their Coke ration today," I said. "My name is Kramer. Benjamin Kramer. I have an eleven o'clock appointment with Mr. Mennen."

It was as though I had announced that this visit was not to be confused with my First Coming. She snapped up her phone, punched a button, and parted her hair to stare out at me. She did it the way I had always been led to believe Keats had stared at the printed page when he first looked into Chapman's *Homer*.

I was flattered but not fooled. I do not look like Lou Telegan. But neither am I a dead ringer for Lon Chaney. I

276

look the way my experience as a trial lawyer has taught me it is advisable for a successful bank robber to look. A face that does not register on those tricky movie cameras that turn on overhead in the bank at the moment when the gun is pointed at the teller. The kind of face, if seen in a passing crowd, nobody will remember. So it was obvious that this pretty girl was staring at me with awe not because of what she was seeing but because of the man I had come to see.

In forty years I have been in and out of enough offices to have encountered almost every degree of employee deference for executives. This was the first time I had ever encountered what looked like reverence. It occurred to me that perhaps I had made a mistake to base my opinion of TV solely on what I saw on my set.

"Mrs. Hawtrey?" the yellow-haired beauty said into her phone. "This is Nell."

Miss Gwyn, no doubt.

"It's a visitor, Mrs. Hawtrey. He says he has an eleven o'clock appointment with Mr. Mennen. A Mr. Kramer? Benjamin Kramer?" She looked at me as though for confirmation. I nodded. "Yes, that's right, Mrs. Hawtrey. Mr. Benjamin Kramer. He—" Pause. A look of perplexity. "Yes, of course, Mrs. Hawtrey." She hung up slowly. "Mrs. Hawtrey is coming right out, sir."

She arrived so quickly that my mind jumped to what Sebastian Roon had said to me when he asked me to represent him with ABTV on the day we were having a drink in Will's an hour after I had been mugged in front of Penn Station: "Jim Mennen says he wants this series desperately."

Except for the speed with which she had come out to fetch me, you would never have known from her face that Mrs. Hawtrey shared this desperation. It was the sort of face that seemed to belong between a bowler and a riding habit on the cover of the London *Illustrated News*. Those faces did not register desperation. Or even age. Mrs. Hawtrey could have been anywhere from thirty to fifty. If you have a thing for ice, you would have liked her.

"Mr. Kramer," she said, and then she astonished me. She put out her hand.

Involuntarily, I took it, and I understood not only what Mrs. Hawtrey was doing at ABTV, but I was reasonably sure I could make a good guess about her salary. There are states in this country that pay their governors less. With the small gesture Mrs. Hawtrey had shifted some of the balance of power. She was not leading me into an executive's office. She was conducting me into her drawing room.

"Won't you come this way, Mr. Kramer?"

This way was the sort of passage through which Henry VIII used to move on his way to inspect a new bride. Paneled walls. Ormolu clocks. A wood-burning fireplace large enough to accommodate a putting green. Impressive English brass. The sort of furniture that both Hepplewhite and Chippendale would have been proud to claim but could no longer afford, including what were obviously several "signed" chairs. Bronze sconces that had once looked down on the signers of treaties that ended things like The War of the Spanish Succession. Tapestries that were bound to cause an international scandal when it was discovered that they had disappeared from the walls at Bayeux. Plum-colored carpeting as thick as a club sandwich. And not a sound.

At the far end of this drawing room Mrs. Hawtrey stopped in front of a door through which Cecil B. DeMille could have, without crowding anybody, marched a Roman general and his entourage on the way to the Palatine for a Triumph. She tapped on the door.

"Yes?" a man's voice called.

Mrs. Hawtrey opened the door.

"Mr. Kramer," she said.

She dropped the three syllables into the semi-darkness beyond the threshold as though they were Christmas tree balls and she wasn't sure whether she was dropping them into a bed of cotton or onto a marble delicatessen store counter.

"Come in, Mr. Kramer," the man's voice said.

I stepped in. Mrs. Hawtrey pulled the door shut behind

me. At first I thought I had stepped into a movie theater. I blinked my eyes, and saw that in a way it was a movie theater. Several TV sets were built into the walls around the room. With my vision still impaired I counted six, but I saw the flickering of other screens in other parts of the room. Then I noticed that no sound came from all those flickering screens except one. At this moment somebody snapped a switch. The sound from that one screen died away. The pictures faded from all the other screens. And the room blazed up with enough electric light, all from fixtures concealed in the walls, to illuminate the Duchy of Luxembourg for a year.

I could see at once that the scene into which Mrs. Hawtrey had so delicately thrust me had been staged by someone with a touch of originality.

The room was big, of course. The presidents of corporations seem to function best in large quarters. So, at one time, did buffaloes. Bernard Baruch was never the president of anything, although he was confidential adviser to half a century's worth of White House incumbents. Mr. Baruch functioned on a bench in Central Park.

At the top of the big room was the conventional gridiron-sized desk. Just walking to it from the door would have qualified any boy scout of my day for the Hiking Merit Badge. But the man who had staged this scene had thought up something unusual. He had placed a simple straightbacked chair in front of the desk. Not behind the desk, where desk chairs usually sit, but in front of it. Way out in front of it. So that the desk was just a distant piece of furniture, far back in the enormous room. The chair faced the room.

It was a pretty scruffy chair. The sort of chair on which, in movies about backstage life, stage doormen sit and study their dope sheets. Then, on both sides, in a V that fanned out from this modest throne, stretching and spreading all the way down the room to the far corners, the stage manager had arranged two long rows of very expensive executive-type chairs. They had plunging spring backs, and heavy leather headrests.

The point was immediately obvious. The inferiors sat on thrones. The king sat on a stool. He stood up and came forward with hand outstretched, wearing a genial smile and about fifteen hundred dollars' worth of Savile Row tailoring.

"Mr. Kramer," he said. "This is a great pleasure for me."

"Likewise." I said.

Why not? The locutions you learn at your mother's knee never leave you. And on occasion can prove useful.

"I'm Jim Mennen," he said. "I've heard a great deal about you, Mr. Kramer. And not all of it from my legal staff. It's good of you to come."

"I had to," I said. "My client ordered me."

Mennen laughed. It was better than the smile. The smile had in it too many rows of beautifully capped teeth.

"I don't imagine you're a man who takes orders from many people," he said. "But I'm glad you took this one. Is this chair okay?"

It was on his right, and it was one of the expensive executive jobs. In my own office I sit with no more elegance than Ira Bern once did. He was my first model. I have my secret loyalties. They help.

"Of course," I said.

I sat down and stared at the two long lines of the V that stretched away from me and Mennen. There must have been a dozen men in that V, six on each side. Somehow they all looked alike. People who live the same way, and do the same things for long periods of time, take on the same protective coloration. The way married couples, if they've been together happily for many years, are frequently taken for brother and sister.

What made all these men in Jim Mennen's office look alike was not their physical appearance. Fat, skinny, tall, short. All the variations were present. But there were also two emotions in that room. Not visible to the untrained eye, perhaps. But Benny Kramer's eye had been trained on Seventh Avenue in 1930. Those two emotions were rolling around in that room like a couple of loose cannonballs on the deck of the *Bonhomme Richard* in action against the *Serapis*. When they taught you history at Thomas Jefferson High, it stuck to your ribs. I could feel those cannonballs in that room.

One, all those men hated being in that room. Two, they were all apprehensive about what was going to happen while they were in it.

"These gentlemen on our left and right," Jim Mennen said, "are members of my staff here at ABTV. It is not necessary for me to introduce them. Later you may want to meet a few members of my legal staff, Mr. Kramer, the men with whom you will be working. As for the others . . ."

Mennen paused and looked down the two long lines of men, giving each glance more moments than it deserved. But the way he did it cleared away a small puzzle: why was it necessary to have a dozen executives in one room to discuss one TV show? From the way Mennen looked at the two long rows of men, I grasped that there would be no discussion. These men had been brought here the way heavy curtains are brought to the walls of a concert hall: to improve the acoustics.

While Mennen looked at his mute audience, I looked at him. His head was long and well-shaped. In profile, however, the long, lean look took a beating as it descended from his scalp. It ended in a slightly but noticeably receding chin. I was willing to bet that before he reached fifty Mr. Mennen, who now seemed to be in his trim mid-forties, would be growing a neatly clipped, jutting Vandyke.

"No," Mennen said, bringing his glance back to me. "I don't think it is necessary for me to introduce those others. I don't want to waste your time, Mr. Kramer."

Ouch!

I could almost hear thirty solar plexuses in that room wince from the impact. If someone ever decides to revive Murder, Inc., and he starts hunting for a president to succeed the late Abe Reles, I suddenly knew where he could find a dandy.

"I'm sure Mr. Roon has told you about the project he

and I discussed at lunch the other day," Mennen said. He smiled. Worse this time. Only three rows of capped teeth surfaced. "Otherwise you would probably not have accepted his order to be here."

I smiled and shrugged. It was his scene. I felt no compulsion to supply any of the dialogue for him.

"In any case," said Mennen, "I feel it would help matters if I said a few words about the provenance of the project."

Thus he told me he was a college man. Origins was for the up-from-the-gutter tycoon. For the right-side-of-the-tracks mover and shaker, it was provenance all the way.

"Mr. Kramer," he said, "have you given any thought to the Bicentennial scheduled for Philadelphia in nineteen seventy-six to celebrate the two hundredth anniversary of the founding of our great republic?"

It could have been a serious question. On the other hand, it could have been a casual probe intended to humiliate and thus soften up the man who has come to negotiate. "He who has once known Esther is free from destruction's reach." And he who has once known Shloymah Berel Schlisselberger is free from the amateurish efforts of James V. Mennen.

"Frankly, no," I said. "I remember the Sesquicentennial in nineteen twenty-six, when I was a boy, but aside from Tunney taking the heavyweight title away from Dempsey, I don't recall what was accomplished."

"Nothing," Mennen said. "Except that a lot of money was spent. Of course, in those days TV had not yet been invented so they lacked truly mass coverage, but even so, I think what went wrong was poor planning. I intend to correct that."

He paused and waited for me to ask how. For a moment I thought, Let him wait. Then I heard one of my most persistent correspondents: an inner voice. Come on, Benny, it said. Stop being a horse's patoot. Seb could make a lot of money out of this. So I asked, "How?"

"By providing the American public with a TV series called *One Nation Indivisible*," Mennen said. "It will be an hour show, in prime time, and would run for a year before the Bicentennial opens. Then our reruns would be aired simultaneously with the Bicentennial."

"And the one man who will be the star of *One Nation Indivisible,*" I said, "that man will be Sebastian Roon."

Mennen smiled again. "I see Seb has briefed you thoroughly," he said.

Seb? He hadn't told me he and Mennen were friends. Or perhaps Seb had not been aware that one lunch at The Huffing Hickey did the trick.

"Except on one point," I said.

"What's that, Mr. Kramer?"

"It never occurred to me before," I said. "But I can't help wondering why you chose Roon for this assignment?"

Mennen chuckled. Apparently he had at his command an inexhaustible arsenal of charming sounds.

He paused and then he did something I have never seen before or since. With a slow turn of his head, and without uttering a word, Mennen managed to spray a stream of contempt on what I guessed surely added up to about $300,000 worth of TV executives on his left, and another stream of contempt on some $300,000 worth of TV executives on his right.

"Yes," he said, "my executives wondered the same thing. After all, they said, the series will tell the story of America during the past half-century. Roughly the years between the Sesquicentennial and the Bicentennial. It's an American story. Why choose an Englishman to be at the center of it? You see, Mr. Kramer, it is because they ask questions of this nature that the gentlemen seated on your left and right are TV executives, but I, James Victor Mennen, am their president."

I have long ago learned to regret what I did next. I decided to strike a blow for TV executives.

"But I asked the same question," I said.

Mennen gave me a bit of the chuckle mixed with a bit of the smile. Shloymah Berel Schlisselberger would not have wasted his time with such an obvious ploy.

"Yes, Mr. Kramer," he said. "But you are merely a lawyer."

That's what does you in. The merelys of life. All at once I saw myself as James V. Mennen saw me. An easily replaceable artisan. A working stiff needed for laying the bricks and hammering into place the beams that support the towers in which the movers and shakers dream their dreams.

"A lawyer representing Sebastian Roon," I said. "I think it makes a difference."

I hoped he would not ask why. I didn't know the answer. Not yet.

"I agree," Mennen said. "That's why I asked you to meet me here in my office, instead of in the office of my legal staff downstairs. I don't believe any man could be as close to Sebastian Roon for as many years as you have, Mr. Kramer, without getting to know the man's special qualities."

I thought about Seb's special qualities. Great charm. Unusual good looks. Lank hair, now gone snow-white. The kind of white that is called premature and is, of course, sexier than Tony Curtis' jet-black curls. Especially if the owner allows it to grow a bit long and curl up over his collar in the back. Seb did. What else? Well, a shrewd and firm grasp of the actor's role, and how to use it skillfully within the limited terrain available to the eyes of an audience. Also, a capacity to convey without overt statement his desire to share with the world at large his inner sense of bubbling mirth. And, oh yes, that accent, of course.

"That seems reasonable," I said.

"Thank you," Mennen said. "I consider that a compliment. I am the most reasonable man I know, but there are some who think otherwise."

The two lines of executives stretching down from us at the top of the V received a dose of glancing venom from Mennen's eyes. Caught for a moment between the left spray and the right, I noted that Mennen's eyes looked like the eyes of a teddy bear. Big brown shiny shoe buttons with glistening black dots in the middle. Hardly menacing,

I thought, until I realized they were not embedded in a brown furry face fixed in a permanent smile. Far from it.

The color of Mennen's face was what house painters call off-white or oyster-white. The skin was not quite smooth, as though it had been delicately scarred by boyhood acne. Mennen looked as though his head had been encased in the material used to cover those cheap cigarette boxes that are sold in the furniture sections of low-price department stores: flock white plastic.

"My reason tells me," Mennen said, "that the eye of an outsider is sharper than the eye of an insider. Every year, when we start creeping up on the Fourth of July, the networks spend fortunes for TV spectaculars that tell the world all about the Revolutionary War and how it led to the Declaration of Independence. They get Gary Cooper, or whoever is still alive, to play John Adams, and then the ratings come in and what do they show? America has flopped again with the American TV audience. Does that stop them? Nothing, Mr. Kramer, stops the executives who run American TV. If you have the sort of intelligence that permits you to learn only one thing at a time, and you do learn one thing, you're naturally not going to abandon it. Not at fifty thousand a year plus stock options. So next year they do it again. Not with Gary Cooper, of course, because he's dead. This time they try let's say Jane Fonda, because that's a new angle, and she looks like Betsy Ross, and it costs the same six hundred thousand dollars of the stockholders' money, and then the ratings come in, and guess what? Correct. Another bomb."

Mennen's voice had been rising. His eyes had grown brighter. His words were coming faster. I noticed his hands. They sat on his thighs. There was no other place to put them. He had the only straight-backed chair in the room. I suddenly wished he hadn't. There was something upsetting about Mennen's hands. He kept clenching and unclenching them. As though he were working an invisible generator that pumped into him the energies that kept him going but at the moment was irritably impatient with the amount of energy the generator was providing.

In my time I have seen only one person who has been certified insane by the courts. A woman in a private asylum. The judge in a trust case had ordered me to visit her in the company of a psychiatrist assigned by the court to see if she could recall any of the circumstances surrounding the signing of a disputed will. It occurred to me now, as I watched Mennen, that I might very well have met my second certifiable case.

"I have determined that the American public has had enough of that crap," he said. "I want every American kid and every American adult to see what has happened in this great country during the past half-century, yes. But I also want every American kid and every American adult to go beyond seeing."

I was impressed. Joseph Conrad, in stating his credo in the famous introduction to *The Nigger of the Narcissus,* had been content with: "Above all, I want you to see!"

"I want them to understand," Mennen said. "And I want them to remember. Gary Cooper and Jane Fonda were not able to do it. I think Sebastian Roon can."

"Why?" I said.

Mennen nodded once more. He did it to the rhythm of his clenching hands. I was reminded of something I had once read about T. S. Eliot. The rhythms of the born poet were so strongly embedded in his nature that even when he carved a roast the knife descended and ascended to the beat of iambic pentameter. Or, if it was a tough piece of meat, terza rima. Was the certifiable lunatic on the same wave length as the dedicated poet?

Steady, Benny. Don't ask any more questions. Keep working on the ones to which you're still scratching for answers.

"You are a persistent man, Mr. Kramer," Mennen said.

Not to mention a confused one.

"I am what you just called merely a lawyer," I said. "Being merely a lawyer may not be enough for me to do a job I was asked to handle only because I happen to be an old friend of the man you want to hire. Before you turn me over to your legal department, I'd like to pick up as much information as I can."

Mennen laughed. Not good. Those hands were still clenching and unclenching.

"What you really mean, Mr. Kramer, is that if you know more about how much I want Roon for this series, you will know more about how much money you can squeeze out of my network for his services."

"Not squeeze out of," I said. "Bludgeon out of."

Why not? He had set up the scene. And I had been raised on Clifford Odets.

"I am glad, Mr. Kramer, that I obeyed my instinct to meet with you in person before I turned you over to my legal beagles," Mennen said. "You are a man of parts, sir."

And he had obviously been raised on Dion Boucicault.

"Without parts," I said, "we all end up on the junk heap back of the used-car lot."

Benny Kramer, attorney at law and gallus-snapping philosopher.

"You won't, Mr. Kramer," Mennen said.

"I'm here to see that Sebastian Roon doesn't," I said.

This time Mennen's laugh was strictly Sydney Greenstreet telling Humphrey Bogart: "By Gad, sir, you are a character, sir, that you are!"

"Mr. Kramer," Mennen said, "I can assure you that if Seb agrees to do this series, none of us will end up on the junk heap." The eyes, the eyes. Oy! "Not even these characters on our left and right," Mennen said. He turned back to me. "The reason I think Sebastian Roon can do the job that Gary Cooper and Jane Fonda couldn't is that he is unique. What you members of the legal fraternity describe as *sui generis,* if I am using the phrase correctly."

If he wasn't, I had a feeling his legal department would before this day was done rush to his desk a discreet memo straightening him out.

"How is Sebastian Roon *sui generis?*" I said.

Mennen must have felt the concealed power generator was finally coming through. He stopped clenching and un-

287

clenching his hands. He raised them from his thighs and started ticking off points on his fingers.

"One, Sebastian Roon has lived in this country for forty years. Ever since he was a boy. He has had an opportunity to observe the American scene as no native American could observe it. With the eye of an outsider. Two, he has demonstrated over and over again as a guest on talk shows that he is an observer with an acute intelligence, fresh insights, and a wit for expressing those insights as sharp as his eye for seeing them. Three, he is a superb popular performer, especially with women. And four, Sebastian Roon for this assignment is precisely the right age."

Then so was Benny Kramer.

"What has age got to do with it?" I said.

"Maturity," Mennen said. "A man of fifty-eight knows the score."

Benny Kramer was fifty-eight, and for months he'd been living with the uneasy conviction that he didn't even know where the ball park was located.

"A sexy juvenile type would be wrong for this," Mennen said. "What it needs is a man who can bring to the screen the feel of the men who created our great country. Washington. Adams. Jefferson. Hamilton. Men who remind us of what Franklin Roosevelt said about Winston Churchill."

He paused. By now, I was well into the scene. I snapped up my cue.

"What was that?" I said.

"Roosevelt said of Churchill that he was half American and all British."

It seemed to me that with Seb it was just the other way around.

"Have I convinced you?" Mennen said.

"Except for one point," I said.

"What's that, Mr. Kramer?"

"I know now why you want Seb for this assignment," I said. "And I agree with you that he is perfect for it. What I don't yet know is to what extent the ABTV legal department will share your enthusiasm."

The eyes whipped right. "Sewell," Mennen snapped.

A man near the end of the right wing of the V stood up. "Jim," he said.

It was the snappiest salute I had seen since Eisenhower toured our staging area in Cornwall a week before D-day.

"That's Sewell Fortescue," Mennen said to me. "He is the ABTV legal department." Mennen sounded like the cicerone on a bus tour, pointing out the sights for the visiting firemen. "The ABTV legal department is my legal department," Mennen said. "They share all my enthusiasms. They do what I tell them to do. Right, Sewell?"

"Yes, Jim," Sewell Fortescue said, or quavered, or perhaps whimpered. The voice had no shape. There was no metal underpinning in the sounds.

No matter. If I didn't know how to describe the sound, I knew something more important: the funds needed to underwrite Seb's declining years in England were in the bag.

"Mr. Kramer," Mennen said, "I turn you over to my legal department."

I suddenly felt like the baton in a relay race.

"May I ask one final question?" I said.

"Anything," Mennen said.

"When Seb told me about his lunch with you," I said, "he repeated that in telling him how much you wanted him for this series you had used a certain word."

"What is that word?" Mennen said.

"Desperately," I said.

"My feelings about Sebastian Roon as a reporter are confirmed," Mennen said. "That is indeed the word I used." He stood up. "Mr. Kramer," Mennen said, "I want desperately to have Sebastian Roon do this series for ABTV."

I stood up. "I will do my best to arrange it," I said.

"So will Sewell," Mennen said. "Won't you, Sewell?"

"I certainly will, Jim," said Sewell.

Mennen made a gesture with his finger. The gesture a waiter deep in a restaurant makes to the headwaiter at the door. The table was ready. Sewell Fortescue came briskly up to the top of the V.

"Sewell," said Mennen, "meet Mr. Kramer."

289

We shook hands. There is no difficulty about describing the sounds with which we accompanied the meaningless clutch. Sewell Fortescue and Benny Kramer murmured.

"Thank you for coming in, Mr. Kramer," Mennen said. "This is an historic moment in the history of ABTV."

I nodded.

"This way, Mr. Kramer," Sewell Fortescue said.

He took my elbow. As we left the room, I noticed that all the men in both wings of the V had risen and were watching. I half expected them to draw swords and cross them over my head as I moved down the line with Sewell Fortescue, the way they did at military weddings in the newsreels. There was, however, something off about the image. All those executives were not watching me and Sewell Fortescue. They were watching Jim Mennen.

He was a tall man. An inch or more over six feet. He stood very straight. Shoulders squared. Head up. I had the feeling that he was a conductor with baton raised. Every eye in the orchestra was riveted on him. Every performer was waiting for the downward sweep of the stick that would signal the crash of instruments into the opening chord of the performance.

"Do you mind if we walk down?" Fortescue said.

We were in the muted drawing room. Fortescue opened a door beside the fireplace and held it for me. We went down a narrow iron staircase. It was clearly private. The arrangement reminded me of secret passages in the castles of Walter Scott novels. I felt like Darnley—or maybe it was Bothwell?—creeping down in the dead of night to the bedchamber of Mary Queen of Scots. What Sewell Fortescue and I emerged into did not resemble even remotely the room in which Mary had knocked the bottom out of English history. Sewell Fortescue's office was just an office. It was comfortable, spacious, and neat. There were no flourishes. It could have been furnished off the rack, so to speak, by the Itkin Brothers.

"Would you like to wash your hands?" Fortescue said.

So there was a flourish after all. The private washroom is, of course, the great symbol of status in American business, and Sewell Fortescue wanted me to know about his.

In these matters of protocol Benny Kramer had learned not to be chintzy. Like so many other things on which he leaned, Benny had learned it from his mother. She had never been inside an office, but she had told Benny before he was inside his own: "To be nice when it doesn't cost anything could save you money later when it starts costing."

"Why, thank you very much," I said.

He gestured toward the door. I went through it. The washroom was like Sewell Fortescue's office. Functional. Better than East Fourth Street. Infinitely superior to Tiffany Street. But Radio City? No.

I did not have to use what Colonel Buchanan used to call the conveniences, but neither did I want to hurt Sewell Fortescue's feelings. So I stared out at Madison Avenue for what seemed the proper interval, then flushed the bowl. It did not make a Lexington Avenue roar. It emitted a discreet Madison Avenue circular purr.

When I came back out into Fortescue's office, it was empty. Before I could do more than realize I was surprised, the front door opened. In came Nell Gwyn.

"Excuse me," she said. She shook the long golden yellow hair away from her face, and once again she was lovely. "Mr. Fortescue has gone upstairs for a few moments to, you know, to get some papers, and he asked me to pop down and, you know, tell you he hasn't run out on you."

"I'm glad he did," I said. "Doesn't he have a secretary?"

"Yes, but she went to get her flu shot," the girl said. "It's, you know, it's flu shot time. I mean for everybody on the staff, so we're all sort of covering for each other."

Benny the hypochondriac was suddenly trying to remember if he'd had *his* flu shot.

"Tell me," I said. "Your name isn't really Nell Gwyn, is it?"

She looked at me as though I had made an improper advance. In my day an improper advance was—well, I see now that it wasn't really very much. But boy, it was . . . Okay, Benny, that will do. Think about your flu shot. I tried, but I couldn't. Besides, it was one of those things that Miss Bienstock thought about for me. What I found myself thinking was what a kid as young and pretty as this one, in what all those *Reader's Digest* articles called Our Age of New Sexual Permissiveness, would consider an improper advance. It was a line of thought, I found almost at once, on which I should not have embarked.

"Nell Gwyn?" she said. "Who dat?"

"A girl who was loved by a king," I said.

Her eyebrows went up. I was lucky enough to see this happen because as she did it she swung the yellow hawsers of hair away from her eyes to look at me more closely.

"Ah, come on," she said with a giggle. "You're putting me on."

At my age?

"No," I said. "It's true. One of those boys in England named Charles. I can never remember his number. Charles the One or Charles the Two. But I've never forgotten what he said just before he died. Or, if it was the boy with the other number, just before they chopped off his head."

"What did he say?"

"Don't let poor Nellie starve."

The yellow hair swung aside again. "Gee," the girl said wistfully. "Kings must have been, you know, they must have been cool in those days."

It was a startling thought. For a boy from Tiffany Street. So I gave it a moment of attention. The result was surprising.

"I guess maybe it's because in those days there were more of them," I said. "They had to compete with one another. They were bucking for public favor, you might say."

The enchanting yellow-haired creature giggled again. All my life I have been annoyed by gigglers. Suddenly they seemed one of the delights of life.

"Now what did I say that's funny?" I said.

Gather ye rosebuds while ye may, Benny. Yes. But don't shovel them in.

"Are you really Benjamin Kramer?" the girl said.

To have answered with swearing-on-the-Bible courtroom

honesty, I probably should have said there were times when I was not sure. But I sensed the girl was circling toward something.

"That's my name," I said. "Yes."

"And you're, you know, you're a lawyer, Mr. Kramer?"

"Well," I said. "I've been a member of the New York bar for thirty-two years."

The yellow hair swung aside. The delightful face exploded in the kind of smile I had not seen since that terrible day in Islington Crescent when Benny Kramer had made it, but Hannah Halpern had not.

"Then you must be the real Benny Kramer!"

I couldn't stand up. Because I was on my feet. But I felt I should have done so.

"You're making this sound like a TV show," I said. "Do we know each other?"

"No," she said. "But I think you knew my grandfather. Ira Bern?"

I took one look at you, that's all I meant to do, and then my heart stood still. If Richard Rodgers and Larry Hart will pardon this sliver of piracy.

"Ira Bern," I said when I recovered. "Of Maurice Saltzman & Company?"

That giggle again. And Benny Kramer's heart went out the window again. Attention, Dr. Paul Dudley White. Up there in Boston. En garde, please. It's only a pop fly. A little Texas leaguer. But do get under it, Doc. It's the only heart Benny Kramer owns.

"Yes," the girl said. "My name is Annabelle Bern, but my friends, you know, I mean everybody, in school and all over, they call me Nell, which is why I guess, you know, why you got me mixed up with that girl and the king."

No, that was not the reason. But all at once I understood why kings get mixed up.

"Let me get this straight," I said. "You are the granddaughter of the man for whom I used to work on Seventh Avenue and Thirty-fourth Street in nineteen thirty?"

"Uh-huh," she said.

"But why would you know that?" I said. "I'm just a cas-

293

ual visitor to an office. You must have hundreds of visitors coming in and out to see your people here. And Kramer is not a very unique name. I mean, how did you connect me, Benjamin Kramer, lawyer, with the Benjamin Kramer who used to work for your grandfather forty years ago?"

She laughed again. And again swung away from her face the hawsers of yellow hair.

"Mr. Kramer," she said. "Do you believe in, you know, in horoscopes?"

If I didn't blush, the blood suddenly pouring through the veins and capillaries of my face was wasting its time. I felt fiery red.

"Don't give me away to the top executives of the Anglo-British Television Corporation," I said. "But I wouldn't dream of leaving my house in the morning without checking myself out in the New York *Daily News.*"

"What are you?" she said.

A middle-aged, confused, somewhat-at-sea lawyer who was paid fat fees for acting unconfused and firmly-at-the-helm by people who should have known better. But that was a secret. I knew what Annabelle Bern meant.

"I'm an Aries," I said.

"That explains it," she said.

"Explains what?" I said.

"How I guessed who you were," Annabelle Bern said. "This morning, when I checked myself out in the *Daily News,* it said, you know, it said keep your eyes open for an unusual meeting today with someone who has played an important role, you know an important role in your past."

"An important role in your past?" I said. "Miss Bern, I have never seen you before."

Laugh. Hair sway. Heart wallop. My God, these kids have more going for them than the Atomic Energy Commission.

"That's true," she said. "But you've been a part of my, you know, part of my life since I was a kid. Grandpa used to tell us stories about you."

"Me?" I said.

"Yes, sir," Annabelle Bern said with the sort of smile we

would be wise to send to the bargaining tables of stalled treaty negotiators. "Grandpa used to tell, you know, he'd tell about what it was like during the Depression. I mean the office, you know, he'd tell about what it was like on Thirty-fourth Street. Grandpa was very funny about it. A lot of the stories dealt with, you know, with this office boy. Benny Kramer. That's you, isn't it?"

I was no longer certain.

"Yes." I said. "That's me."

Or was.

"How you used to, you know, take his shoes down to be shined?"

"Vici kid." I said.

Another giggle. "That's right," Annabelle said. "And he always gave you, you know, Grandpa always gave you a dime for a ruggle and coffee. And how you used to get his hot pastrami sandwiches from, you know, from that place?"

"Lou G. Siegel," I said.

"That's right," she said. "And how Mr. Saltzman, he had this green piece of leather?"

"It was the hide of a stag," I said.

"And how Mr. Saltzman made you, you know, he made you polish it every morning?"

"I brought up the lights," I said.

Not without pride.

"You what?" the girl said.

"Never mind," I said.

"But the thing that used to kill us," Annabelle Bern said, "the thing that really broke us up was a story about, you know, the day Grandpa got mixed up about a phone call, and he sent you with a note to this client, and the client he took you to lunch in a, you know, a fancy place called Shane's on Twenty-third Street and you got smashed."

"That used to kill you, did it?" I said.

The hair swung. Her face surfaced. She looked upset.

"I'm sorry," Annabelle said.

"Why?" I said.

295

"I guess people don't like to be reminded of things like, you know, things like that," she said.

I thought of Dean Swift. When he was very old a friend found a first edition of *Gulliver's Travels* and brought it to the dean as a present. The old man thumbed the pages slowly. Then, in a voice heavy with sadness, he said: "What genius I had then!" Benny Kramer never had genius. But he did have fun. This girl had just made him realize that. I could not believe my luck. So I crowded it.

"Did your grandfather really make it sound funny?"

For a long time the memory of those early years had been troubling me. Getting Mr. Bern's shoes shined. Running for his hot pastrami sandwiches. Bringing up the lights on Mr. Saltzman's green stagskin. For months the memories had bothered me. I had wasted the green years. Now I was going into the brown, and I felt terrified by the memory of the waste. Until this moment. When I saw what those years looked like not to Benny Kramer, who had lived them, but to this child to whom those years were a scrap of history. The lens of her youth had, unexpectedly, done for Benny Kramer what I had once done for Maurice Saltzman's green stagskin. She had brought up the lights. I suddenly saw myself carrying a hot pastrami sandwich from Lou G. Siegel's delicatessen to Mr. Bern's office. But I saw it through the eyes of this girl. She was looking back at a legend. All at once so was I. And what I saw was not demeaning. Or depressing. I saw it as she saw it: a piece of time that had been preserved by her grandfather's recollections. It made me feel young again.

"Please," I said. "Did your grandfather really make it sound funny?"

She hesitated. "Not with like what you'd call, you know, disrespect," she said. "It's just sort of—well, you know, he got a kick out of you. When you were a kid, I mean. Grandpa said you were so—well, you know, so earnest. The way you ran for those hot pastrami sandwiches. The way you polished that piece of green leather. He used to tell these stories about you and, you know, he'd laugh and

296

he'd laugh, and he'd shake his head, and he'd say they don't make kids like that any more."

I hesitated for a few moments. Savoring my luck. Trying on once more the mantle of youth. My mother used to say never make your own medals. She was right, of course. So I knew that what I wanted to say was wrong. But I also knew it was true. And I wanted to say it. So I did.

"They don't," Benny Kramer said.

The yellow hair swung clear. The delightful face was pinched with puzzlement.

"You must have been——" she started to say.

I nodded.

"I think I was," I said. "Anyway, I hope so. It was easy in nineteen thirty. There were lots of things to worry about, but there were even more things you didn't have to worry about. I was lucky. I knew good people when I was a kid."

Her laugh should have been bottled. Even an inept promoter could have cleaned up with it.

"Jeepers," she said. "You're cool. You know?"

Obviously she had not noticed the blood pouring through the capillaries and veins of my face.

"And you're a very lucky girl," I said. "If I were not an old crock of fifty-eight, and happily married, and the father of a son your age, I would ask you to marry me."

"I'm lucky?" she said. "Man, you're the one that's lucky. If you asked me to marry you, you know, I'd accept."

Well, Benny, it's been quite a day. *Jenny kissed me when we met, jumping from the chair she sat in. Jenny kissed me when we met. Time, you thief, put that in.* He won't, of course. But all at once it was fun to remind the old bastard that he should.

"You know why I'd do it?" Annabelle Bern said.

"Why?" I said.

Yellow hair swung all the way to the right. Face in the clear. Big impish grin.

"In memory of, you know, Grandpa," she said.

My gut jumped.

"Memory?" I said.

"He died four years ago," she said.

As always, when I get this pieces of news, I felt stupid. How could I not be prepared? What could be more expected in life than the news of death? How many times have I heard it? And yet—a line from a poem out of my youth, by a girl named Selma Robinson, tunneled through my mind: *I know, and I know, and I keep forgetting.*

"I wish—" I started to say.

And then, golden hair hanging in hawsers, probably one third my age, she demonstrated she was smarter than Benny Kramer.

"Don't wish," she said. "That kind of wishing, you know, you just pile up trouble. He had a good life. Grandpa did. You were, you know, you were part of it. It's okay, Mr. Kramer. Honest. It's okay."

I nodded.

"Yes," I said. "It's okay."

The hell it was. But she was one third my age. She had plenty of time to learn what Benny Kramer now knew. I shut up.

"You know what's the matter with you?" she said.

"What?" I said.

"You think you're like older than you are," she said.

What she did not know was that Benny Kramer had always thought he was older than he was. At my bar mitzvah I remember feeling I was fourteen.

"And that's not a good thing," I said.

"It's terrible," she said. "You ought to, you know, you ought to cut it out."

"Okay," I said. "For you I'll do it."

14

My first attempt was a failure.

I was doing my damnedest to feel younger when I came into our apartment late that afternoon. But the first thing I heard was the water thudding down in Elizabeth Ann's bathroom. At once my mind was hurled back forty years. To the night in the Family Tricino restaurant when I had first met her.

"She always looks as though she's just taken a shower," Sebastian Roon had said in 1931.

I suppose it was appropriate to discover that she was taking another one on this day in 1971 when Ira Bern's granddaughter had, in effect, urged me to forget those intervening forty years.

As I pulled my key from the lock, I paused to listen to the sounds of the shower from Elizabeth Ann's brand-new bathroom. When it had been an old bathroom I could not hear the water thudding down. All I could hear was a running tap, and I could not hear that until I reached the door of Elizabeth Ann's bathroom. The old bathroom had been like the rest of the old apartment house: a sight to inspire confidence in a New Yorker, the way St. Paul's inspires confidence in a Londoner. It had tonnage.

A bathtub the dimensions of which compared favorably with the lake in Central Park. White marble tiling up the walls to the height of a tall man's eyebrows. Every tile as long and as wide as a building brick. Every tile veined by a network of cracks as delicate as a spider's web. Every web caused by the same thing that had brought the once white tile to a soft, glowing ivory: age.

Like many old things, however, Elizabeth Ann's bathroom slowly ground down. The movable parts creaked.

The fixtures rolled slowly. The water came forth in chugging rivulets rather than roaring torrents. For Christmas the year before I had given Elizabeth Ann a new bathroom. I had not realized it was a process not unlike giving the navy a new aircraft carrier.

The entire apartment had been reduced to a pocket shipyard. Including a dry dock in which small, dark men who did not speak English mixed the cement they then tramped vigorously into the hall carpets. After the months of hammering were over, and the scaffolding was cleared away, and a split of Mumm's Cordon Rouge had been smashed across the toilet seat, Elizabeth Ann owned a nest of chromium and glass, with fluorescent lighting and, when the shower was running, a thrumming drumbeat of sound to which the guard at Buckingham Palace could with ease have been changed.

"What did you say?" I yelled as I came into her bedroom.

"I said hurry up and change," Elizabeth Ann shouted. "Lillian and Seb are coming to dinner."

"How did that happen?" I bellowed. "You didn't say anthing about it when I left for the office this morning."

"I didn't know about it when you left for the office this morning," Elizabeth Ann roared. "Lillian called about ten for a chat, mainly about how your negotiations are going for Seb's series. I didn't know, of course, but like any wife Lillian is understandably interested in how much loot her husband will carry away from ABTV for the project they hope to retire on. So I made reassuring noises, but Lillian said she was not interested in that. She just wanted me to know she and Seb were coming to dinner."

Even for a close friend as forthright as Lillian, this seemed a little high-handed.

"Well," I said, "they're always welcome, of course, but what's the big push?"

Through the thudding of her shower, Elizabeth Ann said something that sounded completely improbable.

"What did you say?" I shouted.

Elizabeth Ann roared, "Lillian said she and Seb had heard that Jack was flying in tonight from Indiana."

"He is?" I bellowed.

"He has," Elizabeth Ann yelled back.

"Where is he?"

"In his bedroom. Go in and talk to him."

It seemed an odd bit of instruction. Did Elizabeth Ann think I would *not* talk to him? Or that, on coming into his presence, I would do something else rather than talk to him? Like, for instance, kick him?

Actually, when I did come into his room, Jack was in a position to receive a good swift one. He was bent over, his back to me. He had one foot up on the chair near his bed. He was polishing his boots.

"If you wear shoes instead of boots," I said, "it's less work."

He turned and grinned and said, "Hi, Pops," and I had a moment of surprise.

Since I had seen Jack last, he had grown a full beard. The surprise was the color: a dull auburn, almost red. His hair on top had always been, and still was, as black as Parker's Quink.

"Shoes are really not less work," he said. "You see, with boots you don't have to shine the high parts because they tuck in under your jeans."

He demonstrated.

"Good," I said. "Bring up the lights on them. We have guests for dinner."

"Who?"

"Aunt Lillian and Uncle Seb."

Jack's brush stopped pushing back and forth across his boot.

"Why?" he said. "I mean why were they invited?"

"I don't know," I said. "You mother said they invited themselves."

"They must have given a reason?" Jack said.

"Aunt Lillian said they'd heard you were flying in tonight and they wanted to see you."

A scowl takes on an extra dimension when it is sur-

301

rounded by a full beard. In addition to the puzzlement there was suddenly a touch of worry on Jack's face. Or the parts of it I could see.

"That's funny," he said.

"Not nearly so funny as the fact that Aunt Lillian and Uncle Seb should know you're coming before your mother and I do."

The brush resumed its back-and-forth march across the instep of Jack's boot. More slowly now.

"I have something to tell you," Jack said. "You and Mom. I didn't want any arguments about it on the phone. I wanted to be face to face with you and Mom when I told you." Pause. Scowl. "That's why I kept it a secret that I was coming up."

"Well," I said, "it's no longer a secret. Whatever it is, unless you want to be telling it to four people instead of just me and Mom, maybe you'd better tell me now, before Aunt Lillian and Uncle Seb arrive."

Jack took his foot from the chair and straightened up. Around the beard the touch of puzzlement sank into an unmistakable look of total worry.

"Where's Mom?" he said.

"In the shower," I said.

"Jesus, God," Jack said. "Since you built her that damned Radio City bathroom, she spends more time in it than she used to spend with the rest of the human race."

"Shall I get her?"

"Would you, Pops?"

I went out and down the hall. The thudding of the water in the shower had stopped. Elizabeth Ann was in her terry cloth robe, doing something to her hair with a comb.

"You look worried," she said. "What's wrong?"

"Jack wants to see us before Lillian and Seb arrive," I said. "Shall I bring him in here?"

"No," Elizabeth Ann said. "I think his room would be better. It's his turf."

We went back down the hall. There was something unpleasant about this marching back and forth in our own home. I felt like the accused, being led back and forth under guard between his cell and the courtroom. When we came in, Jack had started on his second boot. He stopped polishing and straightened up.

"It's like this," he said promptly. "The last time we talked, Pops, you had just come back from that Dr. McCarran in Philadelphia. And you remember, of course, what happened."

The way Leonidas probably remembered Thermopylae. Victories become hazily pleasant, boozy recollections. Defeats get burned into the mind and heart in details so sharply etched that they never stop hurting.

"Of course I remember," I said.

Elizabeth Ann gave me a look. I remembered something else. The kiss Elizabeth Ann had given me that night for what she had called my stupidity.

"I'm sorry I couldn't take you up on that," Jack said. "I appreciated the effort, Pops, but you see I'm not a boy from East Fourth Street. I'm something you made me. A boy from Eighty-third and Fifth. I couldn't pee my way out of this situation."

Meaning that Benny Kramer could.

"I understand," I said.

Only too clearly.

"Jack," Elizabeth Ann said quietly. "Whether or not your father would have used Dr. McCarran's list of answers at an army physical to stay out of the draft is beside the point. He never had to be put to that particular test."

"True enough," Jack said. "I'm sorry, Pops."

I'm sure he was. But that did not change what he had said. All my life I had seen the world through the lens of East Fourth Street. This was a fine time to learn from your own son that maybe the lens was distorted.

"It doesn't matter," I said.

One thing you learn on East Fourth Street is how to lie with the best of them. Without taking her eyes off Jack, Elizabeth Ann touched my arm.

"And you told us, Jack," she said, "that you wanted to think it over, and when you came to a decision about your next move you would let us know."

303

"That's why I flew up today," Jack said. "To let you know."

"Okay," I said, "we're listening."

Elizabeth Ann's fingers dug into my arm. I knew the signal. She didn't want me to reach the fuck off stage.

"Two weeks ago," Jack said, "I wrote to the draft board here in New York, asking them to give me a C.O. classification."

My insides jumped. "Conscientious objector?" I said.

"Yes," Jack said. "They wrote back and said I would have to appear before their board for an oral examination, and they gave me a date."

"Tonight?" Elizabeth Ann said.

Jack nodded. "Seven o'clock," he said.

"Oh, God," Elizabeth Ann said. "It's almost five-thirty. I'd better step on it." She gave my arm an extra hard squeeze. "You stay here, Benjamin, and talk to him."

About what? Feelings about my own son that I did not want to examine?

"I assume you've gone beyond just making the decision to ask for C.O. status?" I said. "I assume you've examined the consequences?"

"There's a draft counselor on campus, Pops. There's one on every campus in the country. I had several long sessions with him before I made my decision."

But not even one short one with his father from East Fourth Street.

"And you're satisfied that his advice was sound?" I said.

"Pops, it's his field," Jack said. "He knows all there is to know about it, and he told it all to me."

"Did he tell you that draft boards are very hostile to young men who ask for C.O. status? That they are suspicious of them? And that they grant very few of these requests?"

"At the very first session, Pops. He told me everything."

I wondered about that draft counselor. Could he have told everything to his own son?

"Did he tell you what the odds are that you will not be granted C.O. status?"

304

"He did, Pops."

"Did he tell you that if you don't get C.O. status you are at the end of the line? There is no further recourse? You can't go back and say, oops, sorry, I didn't really mean to ask for C.O. status in the first place? I didn't have to? You see I wet the bed at night?"

"He told me all that, Pops."

"Nevertheless," I said, "you decided to take the risk?"

"I did, Pops."

"Without consulting your mother or me."

The scowl appeared again around the edge of the beard. "What good would that have done?" Jack said. "I'd already made my decision, Pops."

It wouldn't have done him any good. But it might have prevented Benny Kramer from learning at the age of fifty-eight that there were people who did not consider it such a wonderful thing to have been born and raised on East Fourth Street, and among those people was his own son.

"I'm a lawyer," I said. "Many of my friends, many of my colleagues have sons your age. The draft comes in for a lot of discussion around me. I might have been able to tell you something helpful."

Few things are more pompous than the language of a man trying to conceal a resentment he wishes he did not feel.

"I doubt it, Pops," Jack said. "These campus draft counselors know more about it than any real-estate lawyer in the country."

If you take fat fees from people like Shloymah Berel Schlisselberger, you have to be able to take a jolt now and then even from members of your own family.

"Suppose the board does not grant your request for C.O. status?" I said. "Have you thought about your next step?"

"Yes, I have, Pops."

"Is it a secret?"

Another thing that is difficult for a man with a beard is adding to a troubled scowl the perplexed bite of the lower lip.

"Pops," Jack said. "What are you sore about?"

The day my mother died, her doctor, who was an old friend of mine, had sensed I was in a bad way, and he had said to me: "Don't worry, Benny. I'm here. We East Side boys always stick together." Who was sticking by Benny Kramer today?

"I'll tell you why I'm sore," I said, and I laughed.

Laughs are the traditional beards that get hung on lies. I couldn't tell Jack what I was sore about. What I was sore about could only have been understood by another boy from East Fourth Street. Jack was not a boy from East Fourth Street. He was a boy from 83rd and Fifth. He had just made that perfectly clear.

"I'm sore because I don't think you're giving yourself a chance with that draft board tonight," I said. "Is that how you're going to appear before that C.O. committee? In boots and blue jeans?"

"Plus the beard," Jack said, and he laughed.

His laugh made me feel better. It showed that a boy from East Fourth Street could still put one over on a boy from 83rd and Fifth.

"Come on, Pops, relax. I know you think I've got a better chance with these jokers if I wear my Brooks Brothers blue blazer and take a quick, clean shave."

"No," I said, "I don't think that's what I think."

Anyway, that wasn't all of what I was thinking. The rest of what I was thinking was too difficult for me to state on such short notice even to myself, much less to a boy from 83rd and Fifth. Benny Kramer feels deeply, but he thinks slowly. What had happened to Benny Kramer had just happened, in this room, a few minutes ago. It would take me a few days and a couple of sleepless nights to figure it out. When I did, it might prove to be worse than it seemed now, while the wound was still raw, but it wouldn't hurt so much. Benny Kramer can handle anything, so long as he sees where the blow came from, how much damage it has done, and why it sought him out. Then he can tuck it away in one of his mental boxes, seal it, and hide the box on the back shelf in the dead file of his memory. Benny is finished with it. He is ready for the next blow.

306

"Look at it this way, Pops," Jack said. "People in every war wear different clothes when they visit their draft boards. Think of the guys they rounded up to help Caesar divide up Gaul. Think of what those clowns were wearing. Think of the clothes you wore when you visited your draft board in your war. Now, what's funny about that?"

"I wasn't laughing at what you said," I said. "I was laughing at the picture it gave me of the draft boards in my war. In my war it didn't matter what you wore to the draft board. By the time the examination came around you looked like everybody else. Stark naked."

"I know that," I said. "Which is why I thought you might be interested in something Uncle Seb told me recently. This play he's in now, there's a kid in it who has the juvenile lead, and his draft board classified him One-A. So he applied for C.O., and when he went to his hearing he was surprised to find the members of the board were a different kettle of fish from the clerks he'd met who handled the papers. These men were all dignified, respectable, well-to-do members of the community who had volunteered their services and held these meetings at night after their day's work was done. You know," I said. "Doctors, corporation executives, stockbrokers, lawyers, a well-known priest."

"Sure I know," Jack said. "People like you, Pops."

I walked to the triple mirror over his dresser and made an elaborate business of examining my reflection, as though a salesman in a clothing store had just hung a jacket on me. I turned left, then right, cocking my head and squinting judiciously.

"Yes," I said. "People like me."

Quite a few of whom had come from the East Fourth Streets of the world.

"Well, now, Pops, let me hand you a tough one," Jack said. "Suppose you were in there with your buddies tonight as a member of his C.O. board. Now, forget it's me. I'm just a guy named Irving B. Toklas, say."

"Alice B. Toklas."

"I know that, Pops. We had Gertrude Stein in freshman

English at Harvard. I'm just trying to stop you from thinking of this kid as your son. Yes?"

Koyach, Benny, *koyach.*

"I'll try," I said.

"Okay, this kid comes in before you and the board," Jack said. "He's wearing blue jeans and boots and his face is all hung over with a lot of fuzz. Hold that image. Now focus on the next one. The kid comes in wearing a Brooks navy blue blazer, a white button-down Oxford shirt, and a Hasty Pudding tie. Let's throw in a pair of Peal's wing-tip brogans. Now, Pops, you've got the images fixed in your mind?"

I nodded. I knew where this interrogation was taking me. I had heard hundreds like it in a score of courtrooms. I had even conducted dozens like it myself. Years of practice had given me the skill with which to avoid the trap of the inevitable final question. Even as Jack had been talking, I had already worked out the answer that would not be inevitable, the answer that would spring the trap on my honorable opponent, Your Honor, and cause him to fall flat on his prematurely triumphant face. But Benny Kramer knew he would not make that skillfully fabricated and totally unexpected answer. What a boy from East Fourth Street could do for a client, he could not do to a son. Even if the son did come from 83rd and Fifth.

"I have both images fixed in my mind," I said.

"Okay, then, Pops," Jack said. "Would your decision to grant C.O. status to these kids, the same kid but in two different images, would your decision be influenced by what the kids were wearing? Who would be more likely to be looked on favorably by you? The kid with the beard and the blue jeans? Or the kid in the blazer and the Hasty Pudding tie?"

I was grateful for the fact that he had not reminded me sternly to be honest. Maybe it was an oversight. But Benny Kramer had reached the straw-clutching phase of his life. I wanted to believe firmly that Jack had felt it was not necessary, because the reminder would have been superfluous, to remind his father to be honest. So I was.

308

"I would look more favorably," I said, "on the kid wearing the blazer and the Hasty Pudding tie."

Jack laughed again. "I knew you would."

"How did you know it?" I said.

"You're a kid from Fourth Street on the Lower East Side and from Tiffany Street in the Bronx," Jack said. "Blue blazers from Brooks Brothers and Hasty Pudding ties mean a lot to you."

Why not? I had earned them. With years of hard work at C.C.N.Y., N.Y.U. Law School, and carrying hot pastrami sandwiches for Ira Bern. Something a boy from 83rd and Fifth never had to do.

"More than they mean to you?" I said.

"I've got a closet full of them," Jack said. "You bought them for me. Don't think I'm ungrateful. I was glad to get them. Just as I've been glad to get everything you've ever given me. It's been a pleasure to take things from you, Pops. Because you never even hinted I had to say thanks. That's how I learned that no matter what pleasure I got from the things you bought for me, my pleasure was nothing compared with the pleasure you got from knowing you'd earned the money yourself with which to buy them for me."

As my mother used to say: You can say that again, Sonny.

"That's true," I said. "But I wonder if it's important. After all, we've both had pleasure."

Any good lawyer knows how to drop in the concealed jabs that in the end sway the jury.

"It's very important," Jack said. "You see, Pops, when you were my age there were no issues. It was all very simple. When you got out of high school, if you were lucky enough to make it through high school, you didn't lie around in some acid-rock discotheque trying to decide what would be a relevant way to spend your life. There was no time. Thinking about relevance could cause you to die of starvation. What you did was go out and find a job so you could eat. You had to. Nowadays, kids my age, they don't have to worry about eating. Nice guys like you, Pops, you provide the groceries. So we have time to worry about what we should do with our lives that's relevant. Most of my friends don't even worry. They merely discuss it. Endlessly. Most of the time lying around puffing grass.

"Well, Pops, I don't know how good I am as a son, but you must have made a pretty good score as a father. Because I'm not like most of my friends. I know what's relevant. It's a negative thing. It's in my head. I can hear the words. Don't join the murderers. And because it's negative, I've got to do it in a positive way. If I avoid the draft by convincing an army doctor I pee in bed, what have I accomplished? I've saved one skin. My own. Nobody will know. Except you and Mom and Dr. McCarran and me. You and Mom and Dr. McCarran won't talk. For obvious reasons. But I'll talk. To myself. For the rest of my life. I don't want to spend the rest of my life listening to that kind of talk from Jack Kramer. So I've got to avoid joining the murderers in a positive way. Out in the open. Without tricks. Telling them the truth about how Jack Kramer feels. Maybe somebody will listen. If they don't, to hell with them. They can dish out anything they've got. Including prison. I'll keep on talking. Because I know what's relevant, Pops. Just as you did at my age when you were saving pennies to go to law school at night."

When the words would come I said, "Is that why you grew a beard for this meeting tonight? And why you're going in boots and blue jeans?"

Jack nodded and gave me a friendly smile. Not bad, Benny. Boys from East Fourth Street may be willing to pee their way out of the draft, but they're not so dumb. I had asked the right question.

"That's right, Pops," Jack said. "I'm not asking these dignified, respectable, well-to-do stockbrokers and corporation executives to grant me C.O. status because I own a Brooks Brothers blazer and I picked up a Hasty Pudding tie at Harvard. I want them to grant it to me because I believe in what I'm asking for. I want to win this on my own, Pops."

The doorbell rang.

You see, Benny? There are times when it is not necessary to hold out your hand for a few pennies worth of *koyach*. There are times when fate is kind and just tosses it in your lap. How else but by the clanging of a bell that had to be answered could a boy from East Fourth Street have got out of that room without making a fool of himself in front of a boy from 83rd and Fifth?

"Polish the other boot," I said. "That's probably Uncle Seb and Aunt Lillian."

It was, of course.

"How does he look?" Lillian asked as I stowed coats in the hall closet and Elizabeth Ann came hurrying toward us from her bedroom, calling greetings and fumbling with the fastenings of a bracelet.

"Prepare yourself for a shock," I said.

Neither Lillian nor Seb, however, seemed even surprised.

"Turn to the right," Lillian said.

Jack turned to the right. Lillian examined him for a couple of moments in profile.

"I think it looks even better from the side," she said. "Not that you could exactly call it a slouch from the front."

She reached up and ran her fingers through the growth on Jack's face. He giggled and squirmed.

"Hey, Aunt Lillian," he said. "That tickles."

"Quite handsome, actually," Seb said. "Forbes-Robertson wore one exactly like it in his famous *Othello*. That's why he was known as the bearded Moor. Any difficulties, Jack, of a tactical nature?"

"Well," Jack said, "it's safer to lean forward when you're spooning up soup."

"I should have thought peas would be the bugger," Seb said. "They roll about so."

"Not if you crush them down on your plate with the fork and make a paste before you lift them to the old kisser," Jack said. "Now that the fuzz has passed muster, Mom, how about some vitamins? I don't want to rush anybody, but neither do I want to be late for the big clambake."

"All right," Elizabeth Ann said. "I'll go fetch. We're eat-

311

ing on small tables here in the study because it's quicker, if nobody minds."

"I'm leaving at once," Lillian said. "I hate those damned small tables. They remind me of the days when Benny and I used to work for Maurice Saltzman & Company and I used to eat my lunches from one of those chairs with a wide arm like a tray in Thompson's cafeteria."

"Lillian, stop clowning it up," Elizabeth Ann said. "Jack, fix this for me, will you?"

She held out her wrist. He bent over to fasten the catch on her bracelet, and she kissed him on the forehead.

"Hey, Ma," he said. "Not in front of the stiff-necked British."

"Oh, shut up," Elizabeth Ann said. "Benjamin, make drinks. I won't be long."

"Can I help?" Lillian said.

"You can bring in those damned little tables that you adore and the napkins and things. Come on."

They left the room, and I was suddenly aware of something I had noticed before. Men abruptly left alone together are caught in a moment of shocked awareness, as though they did not really know each other except when women were present to act as intermediaries.

"By the way," I said. "How did you know Jack was flying in tonight?"

"I was at Will's late yesterday afternoon, having a drink with I forget who, and somebody at the next table mentioned it."

This, I knew, had to be untrue. Seb may have forgotten who the wife of Dr. McCarran was, because that had obviously happened years ago, but he could not possibly have forgotten with whom he'd had a drink twenty-four hours ago at Will's. So I knew something was wrong. I went to the bar.

"The usual?" I said to Seb.

His usual was Scotch and soda. Except at Will's where he admitted to drinking martinis because he did not want to upset or argue with the white-haired old lady in black bombazine. Sometimes, however when he was playing a part in which the author had written in some other drink for his character, Seb would order it offstage for a few weeks. It helped him, he said, to settle into the role. I could not remember what, these days, he was drinking onstage.

"No, thanks," Seb said. "Nothing for me."

I looked at him in surprise. He once told me he had long ago adopted Mencken's rule for the consumption of alcohol: never accept a drink during the day; never refuse one at night.

"Technically speaking, because we're eating so early," I said, "it's night right now, Seb."

"No, thanks, Benjamin," he said.

It was only the polite refusal of a drink, but somehow the three words seemed to carry some sort of additional weight that I could not figure out.

"Jack?" I said.

"He shook his head. "Not now, Pops," he said. "I may have one after I come back from the rodeo."

"In that case," I said. turning away from the bar.

"Don't be an ass," Seb said. "Go ahead and have one."

"Sure, Pops," Jack said. "Go ahead."

"Not unless the girls want one with me."

The girls did not want one. After Lillian had set out the tables, and Elizabeth Ann had set down the plates, and we were all seated, they did not seem to want the food either.

"I know it's not as good as The Family Tricino," Elizabeth Ann said at last, "but it's not bad spaghetti, really it isn't, and I assure you it has not been poisoned. Look."

She lifted a forkful and put it into her mouth. I could see, however, that she was making an effort to chew and, when she swallowed, it was a real push. It was the last forkful eaten in that room that night.

I tried to think of something to say. I couldn't. Neither could any of the others. I had a feeling that we were all trapped in a boiler that was slowly filling, but, as the encircling waters rose, nobody had the energy to get up and make an effort to save us. Finally, Jack stood up.

313

"I hate to run," he said, "but I don't want to start off with these boys by getting a bad mark for tardiness. Goodbye, Aunt Lillian, Uncle Seb. It was great seeing you. Mom, Pops, don't wait up for me. I don't know how long these things last, and there are probably a few guys ahead of me, so I may be late getting back." He grinned and waved. "Come Donner, come Blitzen," he said, "and to all a good night."

He was out in the hall when it happened. Sebastian Roon jumped up.

"Wait, Jack!" he called as he ran out into the hall. "I'm coming with you."

It was all over, including the slam of the front door, before I began to react.

I had been debating with myself whether or not I should offer to accompany Jack. "Pops," he had said in the bedroom, "I want to win this on my own."

I could feel the stirrings of a jealousy that I knew was unreasonable but was nevertheless intensely real. I looked at the girls. They obviously knew what was going through my mind. Lillian broke the tension with a laugh.

"It's like the day after *Walda Wexler Wait for Willie Wishingrad: Urgent!*" she said.

"What are you talking about?" Elizabeth Ann said.

"That time back in nineteen thrity-one when we all had spaghetti at The Family Tricino and we all decided we were going to get a raise for Benny out of that old skinflint Ira Bern so Benny could go to law school. Don't tell me you've forgotten that."

"Of course not," Elizabeth Ann said. "But what has that got to do with what just happened here?"

"Boy," Lillian said, "you used to be quicker on the uptake when we were in that sketching class at the Y.W.C.A. It has this to do with it. When we had the whole thing worked out, and it came time for Benny to spring it, don't you remember how Seb looked at Benny and then shook his head and said to me and to you Benjamin will never make it on his own?"

Elizabeth Ann's face cleared. "My God, yes, now I remember," she said. "And Seb turned back to Benjamin and said: 'I'm coming with you.'"

I, too, remembered.

15

The day after he said it, Seb met me in the lobby of 224 West 34th Street a few minutes after twelve, when I came down for lunch. We went across the street to Bickford's for a sandwich and a final rehearsal.

"Right," Seb said when we had finished both. "Everything looks tickety-boo. No, remember. Let me do all the talking."

Even then, when I did not know him as well as I do now, I sensed that this was a pretty silly injunction. Sebastian Roon always did all the talking.

"Don't worry about any interference from me," I said. "Today I'm your audience."

"Let's go, then," he said.

We crossed back to 224, and went up to the Maurice Saltzman & Company offices. Miss Bienstock peered out at us with her perplexed little frown as we passed the small window over the switchboard. I was sure she recognized Seb, but he had told me not to pause for anything so I waved to her and led Seb quickly across the reception room, into the corridor, and knocked on Mr. Bern's door.

"Come in," he called.

He sounded a bit choked, but I knew the reason. When I opened the door Ira Bern, behind his desk, was finishing the last piece of pickle that had come with the hot pastrami sandwich I had brought for him from Lou G. Siegel just before I went down for my own lunch.

"Mr. Bern," I said. "Look who I just ran into out in the reception room."

Elizabeth Ann, who had written everything else, had also written this opening line for me. It was also my closing line. Sebastian Roon stepped forward with a smile and an outstretched hand.

"Mr. Bern!" he said. "What a great pleasure it is to see you again."

"Likewise," said Mr. Bern. He put out his hand to meet Seb's, then snatched it back. "No, wait," Mr. Bern said. "I got pickle juice all over me." He snatched up a paper napkin, dried his hand, then thrust it out again. "So, Mr. Roon, how is the world treating you?"

"Superbly," said Seb. "I trust the same is true of you, Mr. Bern."

"I have no complaints," Ira Bern said. "Firms are going bankrupt all day long, and we get our share of the audits, not to mention our list of clients, which is solid."

"Could you make room in your solid list for another one?" Seb said.

Mr. Bern's little mustache twitched. This always happened if he tried to smile or speak too soon after he had finished a pastrami sandwich. He tried to do it without revealing his teeth, which were still stuck full of bits of meat.

"If it's the right person," Mr. Bern said, "I can always make room, and by me, Mr. Roon, for you there is always room, because by me the nephew of my old friend I. G. Roon is always the right person."

"That's very kind of you," Seb said. "You see, since the death of my uncle and the bankruptcy of all his enterprises, I've been hunting about for something else, and on my recent visit to England I found it."

"Oh, so that's where you were," Mr. Bern said. "I wondered what happened to you."

"There are these chaps I'd known at school," Seb said. "Their families are filthy rich, and one in particular staggeringly so. The family owns a chain of theaters throughout England."

"Theaters?" Mr. Bern said.

He didn't seem to be able to say more, and I knew why. Behind his tightly closed lips Mr. Bern was with his tongue working loose the last bits of pastrami from between his teeth.

317

"Quite," Seb said. "I told them I was interested in helping them extend their operations to America, and asked them to provide the financial backing for an exploratory foray."

"A what?" Mr. Bern said.

"A probing expedition," Seb said. "They agreed to put up the money for me to come back here to America and try to find theaters they can add to their chain. I've been working at it for some time, and I've at last found one that looks like a promising start. My reason for coming to you, Mr. Bern, is that I need an accountant to guide me, and of course I thought of you at once."

"Taking that from where it comes," Ira Bern said, "I consider that a big compliment, Mr. Roon."

"Please call me Sebastian," Seb said. "All my friends do, and since this may grow into a rather large account, which could lead to your taking over the work of the British chain as well, I want to think of you as my friend."

"You must, Sebastian, you must," Ira Bern said. "It's a very nice name, and you, you must please call me Ira."

"It will be a privilege," Seb said. "I have always been fiercely partial to Ira."

"I only wish my mother was alive to hear that," Ira Bern said. "My father wanted to call me Irving, but my mother said no. Ira or nothing."

"Your mother was right," Seb said. "Have I intruded on you at a bad moment, Ira?"

"Sebastian," Ira Bern said. "How could a visit from you be an intrusion or even a bad moment?"

"My word, Ira, you are a gracious man," Seb said. "Indeed you are."

"I came from East Fifth Street," Ira Bern said. "The way Benny, here, he comes from East Fourth Street. One thing we East Side boys are, we're gracious. Right, Benny?"

I smirked. Elizabeth Ann had not written in a line for me to cover this.

"My reason, Ira, for asking if I'd popped in at a bad

318

moment for you," Seb said, "I wondered if you could come downtown with me right now to examine this property?"

"Could I come downtown with you right now," Ira Bern repeated slowly. He gave it a moment of thought, and then that look came into his eyes. The look of the firmly decisive executive. He snatched up the phone. Into it he rapped out, "Miss Bienstock, I'm going downtown."

He slammed down the receiver and smiled. When they were not speckled with bits of Lou G. Siegel pastrami, Ira Bern had very nice teeth.

"See?" he said. He came out from behind his desk. "Come, Sebastian, we're going downtown."

"Do you mind, Ira, if Benjamin comes with us?" Seb said.

"Benny!" Ira Bern snapped at me. "You're coming downtown with us!"

He grabbed my arm, took Seb's a bit more gently, and marched us to the door.

"Oh, by the way," Seb said. "I understand, Ira, you have in your employ a girl named Lillian Waldbaum?"

Mr. Bern paused at the door.

"Lillian Waldbaum?" he said. "Sure, Benjamin. She works out there with Miss Bienstock. Why, Sebastian?"

"I met her at a party the other night, Ira," Seb said. "I was telling her about my plans, and when I said I was looking for an accountant she suggested you, Ira. After all, she said, for years and years Mr. Bern was your uncle's accountant. Why shouldn't he be yours, Miss Waldbaum said. You'll never get a better man, she said. I agreed at once, of course, which is why I'm here today, and I thought it would be—how shall I put it, Ira—yes, it would be an augur of good fortune, so to speak, if she accompanied us downtown, don't you think, Ira?"

Mr. Bern dropped our arms, hauled open his office door, and bellowed down the corridor: *"Lillian, get your coat!"*

Out on the sidewalk Seb started down 34th Street toward Seventh Avenue.

"Sebastian," Ira Bern said. "Where are you going?"

"The subway," Seb said. "It stops at the corner of Four-

319

teenth Street and Seventh Avenue, which is half a block from the theater."

"Sebastian," Ira Bern said, "I'm surprised at you."

Then he did something I had not seen, or heard, since I left East Fourth Street. Mr. Bern folded his pinky and middle finger down into his palm and held them flat with his thumb. The remaining two fingers he stuck into his mouth and blew a shrill blast that compared favorably with anything I had ever heard come out of a police whistle. I looked at Mr. Bern with admiration. I had a new feeling of respect for him. He was able to do superbly what I had never been able to do even adequately.

"When a client travels with Ira Bern," he said, "it's not in the subway, Sebastian."

A cab pulled up to the curb. When it stopped in front of the Preshinivetz Playhouse, I had a moment of panic. My first visit to the theater had been at night. I had been aware that the building lacked the ornate, pointless, gargoyles-pasted-on grandeur of the Paramount or the Capitol or even Loew's 180th Street, but the lack had not seemed important. Now, in the bright afternoon sunlight, it occurred to me that it could be crucial. In the bright sunlight the Preshinivetz Playhouse looked like a section from those photographs in my P.S. 188 history book that showed the streets of Verdun after the worst of the German shelling.

I took a quick look at Mr. Bern as we crossed the sidewalk. I could see that in his thinking a sudden gap had appeared between the bright promise of Seb's words on 34th Street and the dismal reality of Fourteenth Street. Mr. Bern's mustache was twitching.

"Let me just see about the lights," Seb said when we came into the theater.

I thought this was a mistake. In the semi-darkness the interior of the Preshinivetz Playhouse looked somewhat better than its exterior. The rows of benches and the high ceiling and the crude stage up front did manage to convey the impression of a theater. Then Seb jumped up on the stage, snapped a switch, and I saw that he knew what he was doing.

What had come on was not the houselights, but the single overhead work light onstage. It gave the place a curiously professional air. Also, bathed in the beams from above, Seb suddenly looked more than handsome. He looked commanding.

"Now, then," he called down to us. "One of the things we want to do this afternoon, Ira, is check the acoustics. So I'm going to ask you all to cooperate, if you will. Ira?"

"Yes?" Mr. Bern called up to the stage.

He sounded the way I remember sounding in school when a teacher called my name unexpectedly from the desk in front of the classroom. A little scared. There was authority in Seb's voice.

"Ira, would you mind coming down front here, and sitting in the center of the first row?"

"My pleasure," Mr. Bern said. He came down to the front of the theater and settled in the middle of the first bench. His forehead was about two feet below Seb's shoes. "Like so, Sebastian?"

"Perfect," Seb said. "Now, Benjamin, please take the last seat in the far left corner at the rear of the theater." I did so. Seb nodded, then said, "And you, Miss Waldbaum, would you be kind enough to take exactly the same position as Benjamin's, but at the far right corner?"

"Okey-doke," said Lillian, and she took her seat.

"There, now," Seb said from the stage. "That's perfect." He turned toward the shallow area at the right of the stage and called, "Is Miss Foster in the house?"

Elizabeth Ann came out on stage, squinting against the harsh glare of the work light. Seb crossed to her and took her hand.

"Ira, this is Miss Elizabeth Ann Foster, the author of the play currently on the boards here in this theater, *Walda Wexler Wait for Willie Wishingrad: Urgent!* Elizabeth Ann, Ira Bern."

"Delighted to meet you, Mr. Bern," she said.

"Likewise, Miss Foster," said Ira Bern.

It sounded like a vaudeville routine by Gallagher and Shean.

321

"Now, Ira," said Seb. "In order to put the acoustics of the theater to a professional test, I have asked Miss Foster to write a short play, just a skit, really, so that we can act it out in front of an audience. You, Ira, are part of that audience, plus Benjamin and Miss Waldbaum. I hope you don't mind, Ira?"

"Mind?" said Mr. Bern. "Listen, Sebastian, how often does a man get invited to a free show?"

"If our plans work out, Ira, and I think they will," Seb said, "I assure you of a steady stream of free invitations to all our shows. Right now, you are our guest at the first one. It is called—Elizabeth Ann, please, what is the title?"

She drew a deep breath and said, *The Reform of Scrooge Without Having To Sit Through All That Nonsense About the Ghost of Christmas Past and the Ghost of Christmas Present and the Ghost of Christmas Future."* She gasped.

Seb laughed. "Good girl," he said.

"Miss Foster sure likes long titles, doesn't she, Sebastian?" Ira Bern said.

"So long as they don't have to go up in lights," Seb said, "I don't mind. Ready, Ira?"

"My ears are flapping, Sebastian," Ira Bern said.

He chuckled. He made very few jokes. It seemed only fair not to frown on his admiration for the few he did make.

"Very well, Elizabeth Ann," Seb said.

He pulled from his breast pocket two batches of white sheets of paper. He handed one to Elizabeth Ann, unfolded the second batch, and scowled down at the top page of his batch.

"Oh, by the way, Ira," he said, "this is a two-character play. It takes place in a business office somewhat like yours, Ira. Do you mind?"

"Mind?" Mr. Bern said. "I'm flattered, Sebastian."

"Good-good." Seb said. "One more thing. One of the characters is an older man, a boss. The other character is a lad of—oh, say eighteen, pushing nineteen. He is the older

322

man's office boy. Just to give the whole thing a bit of veri-similitude."

"How's that again, Sebastian?" Mr. Bern said.

"The ring of truth, Ira," Seb said. "Reality, as it were, if you know what I mean, Ira?"

"I catch," Mr. Bern said.

"To make it seem real," Seb said, "which after all, Ira, as you undoubtedly know, is the only way to check acoustics properly, we have decided to call the boss Ira Bern, and the office boy Benjamin Kramer. Do you mind, Ira?"

"Mind?" Mr. Bern said. "Sebastian, I'm flattered."

"And you, Benjamin?" Seb called out into the dark theater. "Okay with you?"

"Absolutely," I called back.

It wasn't really a line. The script had indicated that I was merely to register approval. So Elizabeth Ann had allowed me to choose my own word.

"And one final point," Seb said. "I will play the part of Ira Bern, and Miss Foster will play the part of Benjamin Kramer. All clear, Ira?"

"Like a bell," said Mr. Bern.

"Very well, then, Ira, we will begin," Seb said. He began to read from the pages he was holding. "Time: the present. Place: the private office of Ira Bern on West Thirty-fourth Street in Manhattan. At rise: Ira Bern is seated at his desk eating a hot pastrami sandwich. Ira Bern is one of the most prominent, successful, and wealthy certified public accountants now practicing in New York City, some say the finest C.P.A. in all of America. This is obvious from the way Mr. Bern eats his hot pastrami sandwich. A moment after the curtain goes up, and he is in the midst of taking a huge bite out of his sandwich, there is a knock on the door.

BERN (Seb)   [*His voice muffled by a mouthful of bread and pastrami*] Woomph!

       [*Door opens. Enter* BENNY (Elizabeth Ann)]
BENNY (Elizabeth Ann)   Excuse me, Mr. Bern.
BERN (Seb)   [*Chewing mightily*] Woomph!
BENNY (Elizabeth Ann)   I beg your pardon?

BERN (Seb)   I said woomph!

BENNY (Elizabeth Ann)   Oh, I'm sorry, Mr. Bern. I thought you said come in.

[BENNY (Elizabeth Ann)   *turns and goes back to door*. BERN (Seb) *manages to swallow his mouthful of hot pastrami sandwich*]

BERN (Seb)   Where you going?

BENNY (Elizabeth Ann)   I'll wait outside, Mr. Bern, until you finish your sandwich.

BERN (Seb)   Benny, why? Don't you like the way I eat a hot pastrami sandwich?

BENNY (Elizabeth Ann)   Mr. Bern! How can you think that? I admire the way you eat a hot pastrami sandwich. I think you eat a hot pastrami sandwich with more style, more class, more élan than any other certified public accountant now practicing in New York City, possibly in all of America.

BERN (Seb)   Benny, what's élan?

[BENNY (Elizabeth Ann) *goes to desk and picks up a slice of pickle*]

BENNY (Elizabeth Ann)   It's like a piece of pickle, Mr. Bern, with a hot pastrami sandwich. It adds fillip.

BERN (Seb)   Next time, Benny, ask Philip he should add a little more mustard.

BENNY (Elizabeth Ann)   Mr. Bern, do you mind if I ask a personal question?

BERN (Seb)   First give me back the pickle.

[BENNY (Elizabeth Ann) *hands back the slice of pickle to* BERN (Seb). *He munches the pickle as* BENNY (Elizabeth Ann) *speaks*]

BENNY (Elizabeth Ann)   Mr. Bern, what do you think of me as a pastrami sandwich bringer from Lou G. Siegel?

BERN (Seb)   Without hesitation or equivocation, with complete candor and beyond peradventure of a doubt, I can say Benny Kramer is the finest the most accomplished hot pastrami sandwich bringer from Lou G. Siegel now functioning in New York City, possibly all of America.

BENNY (Elizabeth Ann)   Thank you, Mr. Bern. That is indeed praise from Sir Hubert.

BERN (Seb)   Who is he?

BENNY (Elizabeth Ann)   I don't know. But Miss Bongiorno, my elocution teacher in J.H.S. Sixty-Four, when you did something good, and she said so, she would always add: "And that, my dear Benjamin, is praise from Sir Hubert!"

BERN (Seb)   Well, you mind we keep him out of it?

BENNY (Elizabeth Ann)   Not at all. Mr. Bern. Whatever you say, Mr. Bern. May I go on, Mr. Bern?

BERN (Seb)   [*Poking about among the paper napkins, the wax paper, and the bag in which his pastrami sandwich had been wrapped*] Benny, next time ask them to put in two pieces of pickle.

BENNY (Elizabeth Ann)   Two pieces of pickle. Correct. I have made a mental note of it, Mr. Bern. Now, then, sir, may I ask what you think of me as a carrier of vici kid shoes to the bootblack in the lobby for shining every morning?

BERN (Seb)   Without hesitation or equivocation, Benny, with complete candor and beyond peradventure of a doubt, I can say Benny Kramer is the finest, the most accomplished carrier of vici kid shoes to the bootblack in the lobby for shining every morning now functioning in New York City, possibly in all America.

BENNY (Elizabeth Ann)   Thank you, Mr. Bern. That is indeed praise from Sir—oops, sorry. He's out, isn't he?

BERN (Seb)   Unless he comes in with another piece of pickle. [*He bursts into laughter*] Pretty funny, huh?

BENNY (Elizabeth Ann)   [*Getting the hint, he also explodes in a roar of laughter*] Funny? Mr. Bern, you could sell that to Jack Benny.

BERN (Seb)   I doubt it. He's gotten along for so many years with the same old jokes, why should he buy new ones?

BENNY (Elizabeth Ann)   Now that I know how you feel about me as a pastrami sandwich bringer and a vici kid carrier, Mr. Bern, may I ask what you think of my character?

BERN (Seb)   I think you are as honest as the day is long. No matter if it's Eastern Standard or Daylight Saving.

BENNY (Elizabeth Ann)   Thank you, Mr. Bern, but I don't mean that.

BERN (Seb)   What do you mean, Benny?

BENNY (Elizabeth Ann)   When you look at me, Mr. Bern, what do you see?

BERN (Seb)   Why, I see a nice, clean-cut, good-looking, one hundred percent Galitzianer American boy, a boy I am proud to have working for me.

BENNY (Elizabeth Ann)   Thank you, Mr. Bern, but is that all you see?

BERN (Seb)   [*Examines him closely*] Well, Benny, I've been meaning to mention it to you, but I think you're growing up faster than you think, and I feel you really should shave more often than twice a week.

BENNY (Elizabeth Ann)   I will, Mr. Bern. I'm making a mental note of it. But all that is on the surface. I'm talking about what's under the surface. The hidden Benny Kramer.

BERN (Seb)   Benny, for God's sake, you got something to hide?

BENNY (Elizabeth Ann)   Yes, Mr. Bern.

BERN (Seb)   Benny, what? What?

BENNY (Elizabeth Ann)   A seething caldron in my heart.

BERN (Seb)   Benny, please talk English.

BENNY (Elizabeth Ann)   Mr. Bern, you are a boy from East Fifth Street. Would you want a son of yours to spend his life carrying hot pastrami sandwiches and taking down vici kid shoes to be shined? Even for a man who is the finest, the most successful, and some say the wealthiest certified public accountant now practicing in New York, and possibly in all of America?

BERN (Seb)   [*Thoughtful*] I can't really answer that, Benny. You see, my son is now in his second year at dental school.

BENNY (Elizabeth Ann)   And where is Benny Kramer?

BERN (Seb)   Why, Benny, you're here, working for me.

BENNY (Elizabeth Ann)   Carrying hot pastrami sandwiches and vici kid shoes. Is that the proper work for a man?

BERN (Seb)   But Benny, you're not a man.

BENNY (Elizabeth Ann)   I'm getting close. Already I have to shave more than twice a week.

BERN (Seb)   [*Incredulous*] Benny, you want to improve yourself?

BENNY (Elizabeth Ann)   Didn't you, Mr. Bern, when you started shaving more than twice a week?

BERN (Seb)   [*Slow*] My God. I forgot.

BENNY (Elizabeth Ann)   I'm still young, Mr. Bern. I haven't lived long enough yet to forget.

BERN (Seb)   [*His voice breaks*] I—I remember when I —when I started shaving more—more than twice— twice a week.

BENNY (Elizabeth Ann)   Before you started eating dollar pastrami sandwiches.

BERN (Seb)   [*A sob*] I ate—I ate ruggles.

BENNY (Elizabeth Ann)   Before you wore vici kid shoes.

BERN (Seb)   [*Choked*] I wore Thom McAn.

BENNY (Elizabeth Ann)   Mr. Bern, that's what I eat now. Ruggles. That's what I wear now. Thom McAn.

BERN (Seb)   [*The tears well up in his eyes*] And you want to eat pastrami? You want to wear vici kid?

BENNY (Elizabeth Ann)   Why not? I'm a nice, clean-cut, one hundred percent Galitzianer American boy.

BERN (Seb)   [*Another sob*] And I've been holding you back.

BENNY (Elizabeth Ann)   Not intentionally, Mr. Bern.

BERN (Seb)   [*Beginning to fall apart*] But I have! I have! What can I do, Benny, what can I do to make you forgive me?

BENNY (Elizabeth Ann)   You can help me achieve my great ambition.

BERN (Seb)   What's that, Benny?

BENNY (Elizabeth Ann)   I want to go to law school.

BERN (Seb)   What's the matter with dental school?

BENNY (Elizabeth Ann)   When I hear a drill I come out in a rash.

BERN (Seb)   All right, then, law school. How can I help, Benny?

BENNY (Elizabeth Ann)   By giving me a raise.

BERN (Seb)   [*Sobbing stops. Voice sharp*] A raise?

BENNY (Elizabeth Ann)   Law school costs money. Mr. Bern, at N.Y.U. it's ten dollars a point. Evening session.

BERN (Seb)   [*Sobbing resumes, but a touch of caution*] How big a raise?

BENNY (Elizabeth Ann)   If I earned five dollars a week more, Mr. Bern, I could swing it.

BERN (Seb)   [*A cry of anguish*] No!

BENNY (Elizabeth Ann)   [*Sags in despair. Voice piteous*] Why not?

BERN (Seb)   [*Through the sobs, a roar of triumph*] Because I'll give you six!

BERN (Seb)   [*Throws his arms around* BENNY (Elizabeth Ann). *They cling together, both sobbing with happiness*]

BERN (Seb)   Curtain!

Silence clapped down on the Preshinivetz Playhouse like the lid on an ashcan. Then, from the first row, Ira Bern rose and turned. The harsh yellow rays from the work light struck the left side of his face. I was surprised, all the way back in the last row, to see that Mr. Bern's face was wet with tears.

"Benny!" he cried. His voice shook with sobs. "Benny, where are you?"

"Here!" I called, standing up.

Mr. Bern stumbled out into the aisle. He came running up to the back of the theater and clasped me in his arms. By now he was weeping desperately.

"Miss Foster is a rotten playwright!" he sobbed. "She got it all wrong! Benny, I'm going to give you seven!"

"Thanks, Mr. Bern," I said. "That's very generous of you. I with there was something I could do to repay you."

"There is, Benny!" he cried. "There is!"

"What?" I said.

In a choked voice Ira Bern said, "Come back to me a chief justice!"

16

I had not made it, of course. And it did not help to tell myself I had never wanted to be a chief justice to begin with. Because if I had made it the way Ira Bern had wanted me to make it, I would not now be sitting in my study at one-thirty in the morning, staring out at the taxi headlights stabbing through the Central Park night, waiting for Jack to come home from his meeting with the draft board.

An Ira Bern-type chief justice would have been able to drop a hint to the right people. An Ira Bern chief justice would have been able to pull what for others were unpullable strings. The son of an Ira Bern chief justice would not have to pee his way out of the Mekong Delta by giving an army medical examiner the answers written for him by a Dr. McCarran in Philadelphia. The failure went beyond a line that never got into *Who's Who*. The failure to achieve Ira Bern's objective posed a tough question: If in half a century you have not piled up enough clout to be able to save your son's life, what good can be said of your life?

A key scraping in the lock saved me from continuing to paw about for an answer to this question. After the scratch of the key came the sound of Jack whistling "I Didn't Raise My Boy To Be a Soldier." I met him at the door. From the look on his face I knew I didn't have to ask the question, so I asked another one.

"Will you have that drink now?"

"I sure will, Pops," he said. "Where's Mom?"

"She's asleep."

"No, I'm not," Elizabeth Ann said, coming into the room. "It worked?"

"It worked," Jack said.

Elizabeth Ann held him for a few moments, then said,

"Don't tell me any more. This is enough pleasure for one night. I'll pick up the details in the morning."

"Are there any details to pick up?" I said after she was gone.

"Thanks, Pops," Jack said, taking the drink. He skimmed off a sip, smacked his lips, and said, "No."

So I knew there were details he didn't want me to know.

"I'm glad I was wrong about the boots and the beard," I said.

Jack looked at his drink as though he expected a message in a bottle to come floating to the surface.

"I don't know that you were wrong," he said finally.

"You got it without your Brooks blazer," I said. "Or your Hasty Pudding tie."

"I got it because a guy on the board said are you the son of Benjamin Kramer the lawyer," Jack said.

"You're kidding the old man," I said.

"No," Jack said, "I'm not. The guy who said it, by the way, was wearing a Brooks blazer."

"Why not?" I said. "It's a sensible garment, sold at a sensible price."

"Not always to men who work for ABTV," Jack said.

It was like the moment in the crossword puzzle when 37 Down locks into 147 Across: "A moment of comprehension in five letters."

Boing!

"Some guy on the draft board C.O. Committee works for the network that's going to do Uncle Seb's TV show?" I said.

"He's in the legal department," Jack said. "He asked me if I was the son of a lawyer named Benjamin Kramer who represented Sebastian Roon in this ABTV negotiation."

"I hope you didn't deny it," I said.

"Only because he didn't make it sound like an accusation," Jack said.

"Did you get his name?" I said.

"No," Jack said, "but I got the impression that he'd been impressed with you. He asked if I planned to become a lawyer, and when I said I didn't know yet, he said well,

330

we can't have such potentially first-rate legal talent killed in places like the Mekong Delta, so he reached for his quill, and he signed his name, and here I am."

Well, it wasn't exactly the same as coming back to my old boss as a chief justice. For the practical purpose of saving his son's life, however, Benny Kramer had come through.

"You mind if I propose a toast?" I said.

"To whom?" Jack said.

"Ira Bern," I said.

"Tonight, Pops, I'll drink to anybody," Jack said. "But why this Ira Bern?"

"He made us both what we are today," I said. "I hope you're as satisfied as I am."

17

"That's good news," Seb said two days later across a drink at Will's. "Not only for Jack's sake, but also for Elizabeth Ann."

"Yes, Jack's okay," I said. "The army is allowing him to work out his two-year C.O. stint doing something constructive rather than destructive. Instead of murdering innocent peasants in the Mekong Delta he'll be jockeying bedpans as an orderly up at Harlem Hospital."

"He'll be mugged a few times," Seb said. "But he'll last it out."

During the war, in Blackpool, Hannah had said it was the only way. She had not known, of course, that all she had left to last out was a quarter of an hour.

"Yes," I said. "He'll last it out."

After all, whether he liked it or not, Jack was the son of a boy from East Fourth Street.

Seb signaled to the white-haired woman in black bombazine behind the small bar. She came across the creaky floor of the dimly lighted room.

"The same, Mr. Roon?" she said.

"Please," Seb said.

"Not the same for me," I said. "May I please have not a martini but some Cutty Sark and water?"

The little old lady gave me a cold look and went back to the bar.

Seb laughed. "You never give up," he said. "Do you?"

"I would if I knew how," I said. "It's one of the courses they left out of the curriculum on East Fourth Street." I leaned across to my brief case and slid the zipper open. "Let's get on with the TV deal," I said. "I've got everything out of Mennen's lawyers that they were able to give, and a few things they didn't even know they had. If this TV series comes off, Seb, you and Lillian will be retiring to your native heath in style."

"It's not coming off," Seb said.

The white-haired woman came to the table. She set down our drinks and left. I did not actually see her. I merely felt the sudden presence of her heavy body, and then the presence was gone. My glance was concentrated on Seb.

"What's not coming off?" I said.

"The TV deal," he said.

"Jim Mennen has changed his mind?" I said. "After all the work I've done with his legal department?"

"No," Seb said. "Jim Mennen's mind has been changed for him. The new Nielsen ratings were made public late last night. Every one of Mennen's shows has nose-dived, and when the market closed this afternoon ABTV common was down eleven points. The jackals went to work at once. Mennen was fired at five o'clock as head of the ABTV network. Every one of his projects was canceled. Mine among them. This will be a big blow to the ambassador."

"What ambassador?" I said.

"My dear Benjamin," Seb said. "To an Englishman there is only one ambassador. Monday night last, Sir Nolan Branch came backstage after the play, introduced himself, and asked if I could take lunch with him next Thursday in Washington. That was yesterday. I flew down, we had lunch at the embassy, and guess what?"

"The Prince of Wales has defected to the Kremlin, and you have been asked to step into the vacant spot."

"Not bad," Seb said. "Sir Nolan, it seems, had heard about the TV series. Through Jim Mennen's P.R. people, no doubt, and it had gone into one of his weekly reports to London. Last week he received a minute from one of the Queen's secretaries saying that when the series was completed I would be placed on Her Majesty's Honors list. None of your evasive Orders of Merit, either. A real honest-to-goodness solid-gold knighthood."

"Sir Sebastian Roon?" I said.

"No less," Seb said.

"That means Lady Lillian," I said.

Seb smiled. "That is most certainly the Benjamin Kramer I first met forty years ago in the office of my uncle," he said. "To think first of what it would mean to Lillian."

"You surely must know by now that my feelings for the Roon family extend to all its members," I said. "But . . ." I paused. A sound he had uttered caught at my mind. Like a bit of sweater catching at a paling as you pass a picket fence too closely. "What it *would* mean to Lillian?" I said. "What does that mean?"

"It means my poor devoted wife is not going to be known as Lady Lillian," Seb said. "Any more than her poor devoted husband is going to be known as Sir Sebastian. Don't look so bloody perplexed. I had to turn it down, Benjamin."

I reached for my drink. It was not, of course, Cutty Sark on the rocks. It was what *she* wanted me to have. All at once the familiarity of the annoyance was comforting. So few things had not changed that even a recurring irritation had the welcome warmth of constancy.

"I'm sure you'll find it in your heart to tell me why," I said.

"Benjamin," Seb said, "why are you so bitter about what is after all a simple piece of social intelligence?"

"Because I'm a boy from East Fourth Street and from the Bronx," I said. "How often does a boy from East Fourth Street or Tiffany Street have a friend who is offered a knighthood by the Queen of England? So what does my friend do? He turns it down."

"Benjamin," Seb said, "you have my assurance that I did not turn down Her Majesty's gracious offer merely to irk you."

"Nevertheless you've succeeded," I said. "Now stop being Douglas Fairbanks, Jr., and just tell me why the hell you turned it down?"

"Because it would have been illegal to accept," Seb said. "I am a naturalized American citizen."

I was too flabbergasted to summon the energy needed to

334

hunt for a less shopworn word. I seized the first one that surfaced. Flabbergasted covered the terrain.

"When did that happen?" I said.

"Right after Pearl Harbor," Seb said.

I gave it a couple of moments, then said, "I think I can understand that."

"Sorry, Benjamin," Seb said. "I don't think you can."

"Why not?" I said. "You had lived in this country for almost a dozen years. You had married an American girl. Now, suddenly, America was at war. You felt the urge to legalize your status in your adopted home. The way we learned in English class Henry James did soon after the First World War broke out. He became a naturalized Englishman."

Seb shook his head and took a sip of his drink. It was, of course, a martini. It occurred to me in another moment of irritated irrelevance that the character he played in his current play was probably a martini drinker.

"Henry James would never have become a naturalized Englishman if he'd been married to Lillian Waldbaum," Sebastian Roon said. "She probably would have flogged poor Henry into coming back to Washington Square and writing propaganda leaflets for the U.S. war effort."

"It was not a question of your loyalty to America?"

"Not a bit," Seb said. "It was a question of Lillian's loyalty to America. She dictated the course of action to me in no uncertain terms. You've had many years of experience with Lillian's terms, uncertain and otherwise, beginning with your days together in the offices of Maurice Saltzman & Company. I'm sure you can imagine the decibels of sound on which these terms issued forth. She told me that while her country was at war she was not going to remain married to a foreigner."

"And you agreed with her?" I said.

"Have you ever tried disagreeing with Lillian?" Seb said.

"No," I said, "but she's never tried to get me to change my citizenship. It makes a difference."

"Not if you love someone," Seb said.

That, I thought, is what comes to trying to argue with an

335

actor. The words mean nothing. The day is carried by the sounds with which they surround the words. Who but an actor could utter a banality so impoverished as the remark Seb had just given to the world, and make it ring in the ears as though you were hearing Jefferson read his first draft of the Declaration of Independence from manuscript?

"That was thirty years ago," I said. "It's a hell of a long time to keep something like that from a friend."

"I'm sorry, Benjamin," Seb said. "Truly I am. But I couldn't tell you."

"Why not?"

"I was ashamed of what I had done," Sebastian Roon said.

I wondered suddenly, if, deep down, Henry James had been ashamed.

"Don't let that get around on the floor of the next D.A.R. convention," I said. "They'll pass a resolution urging American women to find themselves a new British acting idol."

"It was because I became an American citizen that they found me in the first place," Seb said. "I don't have to tell you, Benjamin. You were there. For the first years of my career in this country I was a bust. Lillian had to continue working so we could pay, or rather she could pay, the rent. Then came the war, and British actors working in America went scuttling back to England. I don't believe many of them wanted to go. Certainly not the ones I knew. For British performers the pickings have always been more lush over here in Hollywood and on Broadway than they are in the West End. Most of them felt, however, that their careers would be ruined if they continued on here, living like dukes and tapping the money pots instead of going home to defend King and Country. So they went. Sebastian Roon stayed. I didn't have to defend King and Country. I was an American citizen. And because I stayed, my stock went up. I'm not Beerbohm Tree, you know. But I soon began to look like him and some of those other blokes. It was a case of what Karl Marx is reputed to have said after he dismissed all British economists as incompetents, and some irritated chauvinist said what about John Stuart Mill? Marx replied with a sneer I can reproduce but won't. *The eminence of John Stuart Mill,* old Karl is alleged to have replied, *is due to the flatness of the surrounding terrain."*

Seb laughed. Bitterly? I tried to think not.

"Yes," he said. "Sebastian Roon remained here, and now look." He tapped the briefcase in front of me. "Look at the bundle I almost had thrust into my pocket."

"That's what annoys me about the cancellation of the show," I said. "You've earned the right to this bundle."

"Would I have earned it if I had gone home in nineteen thirty-nine to pilot a Spitfire?" Seb said. "After all, I was only twenty-six years old."

So was Benny Kramer. It didn't seem possible. How had I come from twenty-six, only yesterday, to fifty-eight today?"

"I think there's at least a good chance you might have," I said. "Wars end. Ours did. You would have picked up your career. I wish you would pick up this knighthood."

"I can't," Seb said. "It's conditional on my completing this TV series, and as of this morning there's no longer a TV series."

"That's not your fault," I said. "Besides, there's your long career. Nobody can cancel that. I'm sure with a little prodding Sir Nolan Branch can be induced to recommend that they give you the knighthood for what you've already done rather than for something you were about to do. As your lawyer, I'll be happy to do the prodding."

"It won't work, Benjamin," Seb said. "I've just explained to you why I cannot except Her Majesty's offer."

"Forty years ago you got me into N.Y.U. Law School," I said. "Now I'm going to get you into Burke's *Peerage.* I happen to know something about England that some of her expatriate native sons obviously don't know because they're too damn lazy to find out. Lawyers, however, cannot afford to be lazy. So they pick up the information for a fee that their clients could have picked up with a phone call to any British consulate in the country. Especially if they have clients with numbered bank accounts in Switzerland and the desire to get the hell out of this country and settle somewhere beyond the reach of the Internal Revenue Service."

"Scoundrels," Seb said.

"Not legally," I said. "Quite a few native-born sons of bitches are now living regally in the stately homes of Surrey and Kent because they paid Benny Kramer, formerly of East Fourth Street and Tiffany Street, to look into the British naturalization laws."

"You mean—?"

"Don't give me that damn you-mean-question-mark dialogue out of *The Second Mrs. Tanqueray*," I said. "I know exactly what I mean. The British naturalization laws are childishly simple and they apply to everybody, including former British subjects who for a long time have been subjects of some other country. Sir Nolan Branch could have told you, if you'd had the brains to ask, or if you were really interested in the honor Her Majesty was offering you. I suspect you were not interested, although I can't imagine why. Unless after all these years you've suddenly had a bad attack of stupidity. All you have to do is go back to England, which you told me you've already decided to do anyway, then declare your intention to become a British subject, exactly as though you were in fact a native-born American. Then, in five years, I am sure you won't have much difficulty passing those simple-minded citizenship tests. Even Pakistani busboys in Soho are now passing those tests every day to become loyal and better paid subjects of Her Gracious Majesty. Sir Nolan Branch will be happy to see to it that Her Gracious Majesty keeps your knighthood warming on the back of the stove until you have the legal right to pick it up and convert Lillian into Lady Roon."

Seb looked at me for several moments. I could tell from his small frown that he liked the picture I had sketched but was troubled by the fact that I had left something out. I knew what that something was.

"Are you sure it will work?" he said.

338

"I've made it work for scoundrels," I said. "How can I miss with an incipient knight of the British Empire?"

"There's just one thing," Seb said.

There always was.

"I know," I said.

"You can't possibly know," Seb said.

"After forty years?" I said. "Cut it out. What's missing in the plan, the one thing that troubles you, is that it won't be happening out on a stage."

Seb looked startled, worked up a baleful glare, then laughed.

"You son of a bitch," he said. "You're quite right, Benjamin. I will miss the applause."

"Lillian won't," I said.

"No," Seb said, "I daresay she won't." He laughed again. "What an extraordinary thing. For a Bronx girl, I mean. Lady Roon. Why, it's as though a girl from Blackpool were to become Mrs. President." The laughter drained away. Quietly, Seb said, "Lillian and I have been fortunate in our friendships."

Benny Kramer had always thought the same about himself. But what good was friendship? If the friends went out of your life?

"I think I'd better clear up one point," I said. Benny Kramer had learned another thing from Miss Bongiorno. Never take credit you have not earned. "I'm delighted that Lillian will have this," I said. "But she's not the only one involved."

"Do please clarify that," Seb said.

I hesitated. But not for long. He was more than Benny Kramer's friend. Seb had been part of the beginning.

"You remember Hannah Halpern," I said.

"Couldn't we get through this day without raking up old unpleasantnesses?" Seb said.

"I don't consider Hannah an unpleasantness," I said. "You remember how she died."

"Of course," Seb said irritably. "In my mother's house. On Islington Crescent. With her husband who was my brother. During an air raid. While you were visiting them. Why bring up that gory business now?"

Because I could suddenly hear that terrifying crunch crunch crunch which had not been terrifying when I first heard it in the back room of Abe Lebenbaum's candy store on Avenue D.

"Because I think Hannah would like Lillian to have this," I said finally.

Seb looked down into his glass for a long, long moment.

"Sorry I snapped at you," he said. "Yes. Yes, of course. Lillian will understand that."

"Losing this TV series," I said. "Will it change your plans about going home to England?"

"Not at all," Seb said. "All it will do is speed them up. We can go almost at once. Lillian and I have enough to get us there and settle in. I may not do extraordinarily well at the beginning, but I'll build. I'm not Beerbohm Tree, as I think I just told you, but I'm a good actor." The wintry smile sped across the handsome face. "And, of course," Seb said, "my charm remains unimpaired."

I could not, of course, say the same for Benny Kramer. Even if I could, it would not have helped. All the charm in the world could not have helped.

The series of *Boing!* that had exploded around me during the past few days suddenly felt like the sections of a stockade that had been hammered into place one by one. A sense of entrapment had closed in on me.

Returning from the Philadelphia chore for Shloymah Berel Schlisselberger I had been shocked to find myself asking Benny Kramer: Is this a way for a man to spend his life? Turning away from the unpleasant answer, I had run into the fists of the black man in front of Penn Station. While my head was still throbbing Sebastian Roon, by telling me he wanted to go back to England to die, had forced me to the realization that I had reached the age where it frightened me to lose people. I did not want my friend to go away from me, but they were going.

The death of my barber had made it brutally plain that it did not matter what anybody wanted, or achieved. Even happiness. Things happened without your consent. They were going to continue to happen. I was going to lose more people. Every day from now on. There was no way to stop the erosion of the brightness it had taken half a century of industrious myopia to put together. And Jack, the brightest part of the brightness, had made it plain that only to a boy from East Fourth Street was East Fourth Street an unshakably solid platform on which to build a life.

Time was running out, and Benny Kramer had found in the past few days that there was no turning away from inevitable questions and their unpleasant answers. What had I done with the time I'd had? The time that had seemed endless until the *Boings* of the last few days had driven home the savage truth that time always ran out. There was no way to make it go in the other direction. It never had. It never would. Not for anybody. Not for Benny Kramer.

"Benjamin," Seb said. "Why don't you and Elizabeth Ann come along to England? It will be like old times."

His words brought into focus what I had been trying for days to avoid knowing. It was never going to be like old times. Never again.

"No," I said. "Elizabeth Ann and I couldn't do that."

"I don't understand why not," Seb said. "You're not a poor man, and there's plenty of work for American lawyers with British firms, and Jack is perfectly safe for the next two years." I didn't answer. "Benjamin," Seb said. "When Lillian and I go, you and Elizabeth Ann will be all alone."

At least in one respect Benny Kramer's luck had held. There were men he knew who didn't have someone to be alone with.

"I know," I said. "But we'll have a lot to remember."

"You can remember it with us," Seb said. "In England."

"It won't be the same," I said. "Elizabeth Ann and I can't go. I don't know why, Seb, but we can't."

"I know why," Seb said.

He sounded angry. He turned to look out the window. So did I. Forty-eighth Street was exploding with the senseless noises that had become part of the city. The silhouette of a huge building crane swung slowly past the group at the

341

big round table up front, where Professor Pfeiffer was telling the story of Somerset Maugham and the Internal Revenue Service.

"It's a filthy mess," Seb said. He turned back. I could see from his face that I'd had it wrong. He was not angry. He was bitter. "But to some poor trapped fools it's the same damnable thing that Blackpool is to me," he said. "Home, blast it. Home."

I did not answer. Seb pushed my glass a couple of inches closer to me.

"Go ahead," he said. "Gin is better than nothing."

I took a sip. It tasted the way gin has always tasted to me. The way I felt now.

"Poor Benjamin," Seb said. " 'He fought with none because none was worth his strife. Natures he loved, and after nature, art. He warmed both hands at the fire of life—' "

"And put it out," poor Benjamin said.

"I wouldn't be so hasty about writing him off," Seb said. "You forget something crucial."

"What's that?" I said.

"The lad has *oyach*," Sebastian Roon said.

About the Author

JEROME WEIDMAN, who won the Pulitzer Prize for *Fiorello!*, has long been a distinguished novelist, short-story writer, essayist and playwright. Among Mr. Weidman's seventeen novels are *I Can Get It for You Wholesale*, *The Enemy Camp*, *The Sound of Bow Bells*, *Fourth Street East* and *Last Respects*. His successes in the theater include *Tenderloin* and *I Can Get It for You Wholesale*, which he adapted for the stage from his own novel of the same name. His courtroom drama, *Ivory Tower*, written in collaboration with James Yaffe, was the American Playwrights Theater selection for 1968 and won the National Council of the Arts Award for that year. He has also won the Drama Critics' Circle Award and the Antoinette Perry ("Tony") Award. His short stories—which have appeared in *The New Yorker*, *The Saturday Evening Post*, *Harper's*, *Esquire*, and every other major magazine in this country, England, Canada, Australia, Europe, and Asia—have been collected in seven volumes, including *The Horse That Could Whistle "Dixie," The Captain's Tiger*, and *My Father Sits in the Dark*. His best-known travel books and collections of essays are *Letter of Credit*, *Traveler's Cheque*, and *Back Talk*. His books and plays have been translated into ten languages.

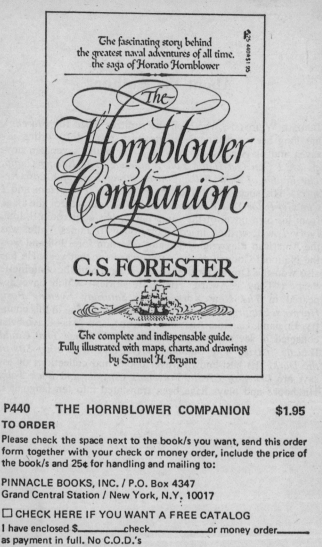

The fascinating story behind
the greatest naval adventures of all time,
the saga of Horatio Hornblower

425 440 $1.95

The Hornblower Companion

C.S. FORESTER

The complete and indispensable guide.
Fully illustrated with maps, charts, and drawings
by Samuel H. Bryant